Patricia Wendorf was  Second World War, h which is where she still BLANCHE is the secon family history. Mrs Wend has two sons and four grandchildren.

Patricia Wendorf

Blanche

Futura

A Futura Book

Copyright © 1986 by Patricia Wendorf

First published in Great Britain in 1986 by
Hamish Hamilton Ltd, London

This edition published in 1987 by
Futura Publications, a Division of
Macdonald & Co (Publishers) Ltd
London & Sydney

ISBN 0 7088 2861 2

Typeset in Bembo by JCL Graphics Ltd., Bristol.
Printed in Great Britain by Hazell Watson and Viney Limited, Member of the
BPCC Group Aylesbury, Bucks.

Futura Publications
A Division of
Macdonald & Co (Publishers) Ltd
Greater London House
Hampstead Road
London NW1 7QX
A BPCC plc Company

Glossary of gypsy words

chavvie	child
chie	gypsy girl or young woman
diddecoi	derogatory term for gypsy. Half-breed gypsy
drom	road
gorgio gorgie	non-gypsy
rai	young man
Rom	gypsy
vardo	caravan

Greypaull Family Tree

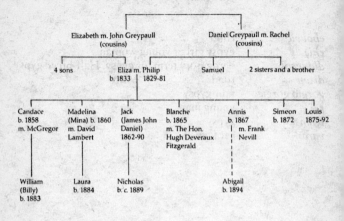

Elizabeth m. John Greypaull
(cousins)

Daniel Greypaull m. Rachel
(cousins)

4 sons   Eliza m. Philip   Samuel   2 sisters and a brother
b. 1833 | 1829-81

Candace
b. 1858
m. McGregor

Madelina
(Mina) b. 1860
m. David
Lambert

Jack
(James John
Daniel)
1862-90

Blanche
b. 1865
m. The Hon.
Hugh Deveraux
Fitzgerald

Annis
b. 1867
m. Frank
Nevill

Simeon
b. 1872

Louis
1875-92

William
(Billy)
b. 1883

Laura
b. 1884

Nicholas
b. c. 1889

Abigail
b. 1894

Carew Family Tree

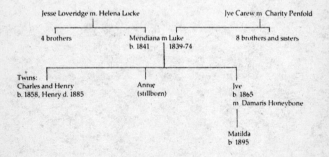

Jesse Loveridge m. Helena Locke

Ive Carew m Charity Penfold

4 brothers   Meridiana m Luke   8 brothers and sisters
b. 1841 | 1839-74

Twins:
Charles and Henry
b. 1858, Henry d. 1885

Annie
(stillborn)

Ive
b 1865
m Damaris Honeybone

Matilda
b 1895

JUST to be aboard the train and bound for London was so exciting that Blanche could hardly bear it. She pulled at the leather strap which secured the window, allowed it to open a hand's breadth, and fluttered her fingers to touch the billowing steam.

'Do close that window,' Candace said sharply, ''tis nothing but smuts and dirt flying from that engine.'

Blanche closed the window. She sat down and studied the compartment; bounced experimentally on the brown plush seat, and stood up again to peer at the pictures of Weymouth sands and Exeter Cathedral that flanked the tiny mirror. She examined her reflected image.

'Do you think I suit black?'

'Suit it or not, you've got to wear it.'

Blanche looked to the corner where Candace sat, bonnet ribbons tied neatly beneath her chin, knees clamped genteely together, her body rigid inside a whalebone corset. She noted with satisfaction how the black cotton dress, voluminous and made-up in haste by their sister, Madelina, sagged and drooped on the skinny figure of Candace, and how ill it contrasted with her sallow skin.

Blanche fingered the cheap black cotton of her own dress. Mama had sewed late into the night, but still the dress was not what Blanche had wanted. She accepted the dreariness of it, the lack of decoration; but why, she had demanded, such a stiff high collar, such a loose and baggy waistline? Why could she not have had just the hint at least of a fashionable bustle? But mourning, Mama had said, was not intended to be stylish. The dress must be simple and hard-wearing since it would be worn for a full year as a token of respect for father.

Blanche had waited so long for Papa to die; sometimes she had despaired, and thought that it would never happen. How he had survived all her spells and incantations, and for so many years, she could not imagine. Desperation had driven her at last to steal candle-ends from unguarded church altars. These lumps of wax, melted down at the midnight hour and fashioned to the figure of a tall man, had then been pierced with Mama's best hat-pin.

Papa, his waxen head run through by the metal pin, had never really stood a chance. A stroke, the doctor had declared! But Blanche knew better.

For as long as she could remember Blanche Greypaull had known that her destiny lay among the rich and famous. The fourth child in a family of seven, she was quite unlike her brothers and sisters. Candace, Madelina and Jack were all small and dark haired. Annis, Simeon and Louis were tall and flaxen. Precisely in the centre of this family group stood Blanche, copper-haired, violet-eyed, a positive changeling.

She turned from her bored contemplation of the Somerset landscape. 'Tell me about London!' she demanded.

Candace shrugged. ''Tis just the same as Taunton, only bigger.'

'It can't be just the same. It's got to be more exciting.'

'You're not going there for excitement. You're going for a skivvy. You'll wear a shabby uniform what fits where it touches. You'll race to answer bells, you'll fill coal buckets, peel potatoes and scrub steps.'

'Well, you've bided there for five years!'

'I had small choice, Blanche. You knows as well as I do what happened to us. Father wagered Larksleve Farm and lost it. We was forced by our Greypaull relations to move down to Taunton. 'Twas Jack and me what had to go away from home to work, and don't you imagine that we found it easy!'

Blanche scowled. 'It was harder for us what stayed behind in Taunton. Hunter's Court is like living in a prison compared with Larksleve. I hate that dark liddle hovel, all they smelly neighbours and their scabby children. At least you got away, Can, out into the wide world.'

Candace pursed her thin pink lips and nodded. ''Tis about the wide world, as you calls it, that I got to warn 'ee. I've heard all about your wild ways from Mama. Berkeley Square is not a bad place, as places go, but no contact is allowed between maids and man-servants.'

Blanche laughed. 'Why, whatever be you talking about, Candace Greypaull? I never wudden dream of soiling my hands on grooms and footmen.' She tilted her head at a provocative angle. 'You've been away from home too long. You don't know anything about me, do you? Let me tell you something.' Blanche leaned forward to gaze into her sister's face. She stretched out her hands and opened and closed her fingers with a grasping motion. 'I just want and want,' she said simply, 'more money than I can ever spend. More gowns than I can ever wear. More diamond rings than I've got fingers.' She smiled at the consternation in her sister's face. 'A rich husband,' she whispered, 'one what I can rule over. One that'll lie at my feet and beg. One that'll crawl like a beaten dog and howl for me to love him.' She sighed. 'I want a man what'll lay his neck underneath my heel, and I mean to get him, Candace!'

'Dear Jesus!' whispered Candace, 'whatever have Mama gone and landed me with? I promised her I'd look after you, keep you on the right path. I knowed you to be a wild and silly maiden, but I never guessed that you was raving mad.' She folded her black-gloved hands together. 'Oh well,' she said, 'there's nothing to be done about it now. But I warn you, Blanche, this job in Berkeley Square means a lot to me. I got friends in London. One wrong move from you, one step away from the straight and narrow, and I'll ditch you right away! Don't come running to me when you burn your fingers.'

'Oh I won't, Can, don't you worry! It might be t'other way round, you never know do you?' Blanche looked smug. 'I won't forget you when I'm rich. You can always turn to me when you be on your uppers. Didden you hear what I said to Mama when we stood on Taunton station? "I'll see you go in silk before this year's out!" That's what I told her, and I always keeps a promise.' She frowned. 'I vowed to finish Pa off, and in the end I done it. You can laugh if you like, but it don't pay to get across me. There's fellers in Taunton what have tried to wrong me, and they won't never live long enough to be any girl's husband. Let me tell you, Candace, I don't never forgive nor forget!'

To leave the enclosed society of the family was never easy. So closely guarded had Blanche been by her Mama that her view of the world was wholly dependent upon the sparse information handed out by her sister Candace.

'What sort of skivvy is you, our Candace?'

'I be first-housemaid. It have took me five years to reach that position. I oversees the cleaning of rooms; I be in sole charge of four other housemaids.'

'Caw!' Blanche assumed an attitude of deep respect. 'That must make you a powerful person?'

Candace bridled. 'I got my pride to consider. I won't have my authority spoiled by the loose behaviour of a younger sister. You must always do exactly as I tell, Blanche. Don't try to take advantage of me because I be your sister!'

Blanche sighed. Commandments, both divine and parental, had ruled her life and she was not naturally submissive. The caustic comment, the witty rejoinder came

4

easily to her. That such talents had not endeared her to her brothers and sisters caused her no concern. But even Blanche had learned early in life that simple affection in her family was never given lightly. Love had to be earned, proof given of devotion. 'If you love me', was the rule, 'then you will keep my commandments.' It was only the gentle, submissive child who earned their Mama's lean and rare approval. Blanche had truly tried to subdue her riotous spirit, to bend her neck low and accept the yoke. But those postures and attitudes of meekness, so easily adopted by the rest of her family, sat incongruously on Blanche. Her head would tilt of its own volition, her chin jut and point in anger. The laughter and scorn would well up inside her and demand a voice.

'Do it help, Can, that you went to school? That you can read and write?'

Candace frowned. 'Now you keep your mouth shut about all that! The gentry don't hold with educated skivvys. I never lets on in London that I be any sort of a scholar. When letters come from Mama I acts all stupid and gets the butler to read 'em to me.' She grinned. 'You won't need to pretend, will you? I offered to show you, but you wudden even learn to write your own name.'

'With looks like mine,' Blanche said simply, 'I don't need to know reading and writing. My face and figure is going to make me my fortune!'

❈

A lady should never remove her bonnet when travelling on the steam-locomotive railway. Neither should she sit with one leg crossed above the other, since this pose would be bound to raise her skirts and reveal her ankles. Mama, who had only once in her life travelled on a train, had warned Blanche not to speak to strangers, or flaunt herself in public places. Modesty, her mother had insisted, was a sure sign of gentility in a young woman. In the dangerous year of 1881, said Eliza Greypaull, in this decade, which was already being referred to as the 'Roaring Eighties', it behoved a young girl to control her mischievous nature, and reveal no more of her person to an evil world than a face of strict and sober virtue, and two helpful, willing hands.

They changed trains in Bristol, and Blanche was impressed by her sister's confident movement from one platform to another. They found a safe compartment in which sat a middle-aged woman and a young man, who must be her son. Blanche, who was several inches taller than Candace, lifted the luggage up onto the rack. A deft wriggle and the upward movement of her arms caused the heavy shawl to slip back from her shoulders. A swift glance sideways confirmed that she had captured the young man's complete attention. Blanche toyed with the leather strap which secured the baggage; she maintained her tantalising pose until Candace said sharply, 'You'd better sit down, Blanche. The train is beginning to move.'

Blanche had thought that just to be aboard the train, and bound for Mayfair, would be excitement enough. But now, she was keenly aware of the young man's presence, and the disapproving face of his Mama. He was a quiet boy, pale and romantic-looking. Blanche began to fidget with the ribbons underneath her chin and, ignoring her sister's scandalised expression, she removed her bonnet. She patted the coils of auburn hair that wound about her head. ''Tis so stuffy in here,' she murmured, 'I do seem to be getting quite a headache.' She began to pull the shawl back from her shoulders.

'Keep it on,' warned Candace, 'you might take a chill.'

'A chill? In June, with all the windows shut fast? I might likely faint away! In fact, I think I –'

'Don't you dare,' whispered Candace. 'If you faint I shall slap your face.'

6

The young man, mindful of his mother's presence, had turned his face towards the window. Blanche wriggled in her seat; she leaned slightly forward and coughed politely. She began to stare at his shiny boots and trousered legs. When his knees twitched beneath her gaze, she was sure of his complete attention. A leisurely inspection of his trouser buttons brought her gaze up towards his jacket and then his starched white collar. Gleefully, she followed the tide of crimson colour that flooded his neck and mounted to his eyebrows. Beads of perspiration sprang up across his forehead, and in the neat centre-parting of his dark hair.

Only then did Blanche relax in her seat. She sighed deeply, so that her remarkable bosom rose and fell. She raised one languid hand to her forehead, and from the concealment of her outstretched fingers, she shot the embarrassed young man a slow and outrageous wink.

❁

Blanche knew that she was beautiful; how could she not know when men admired her, and women were spiteful? At the age of eleven, her Mama had dressed her in loose white pinafores, and bound her developing body to conceal its contours. But still, the vulgar men and boys who lived in Hunter's Court had ogled and whistled.

A volunteer had been required on Sunday evenings to watch over the handicapped Louis; and it had always been Blanche who begged to be left at home, so that Mama and the rest of the family might attend evening service. Hunter's Court was crowded on summer evenings; people sat outside their houses, on chairs and doorsteps. Alone in the house but for Louis, who could tell no tales, Blanche had removed her constricting bonds and, wearing no more than her cotton nightgown, she had leaned from the upstairs window and pulled the nit-comb seductively through her long red hair. The watching men and boys had stamped their feet and

7

whistled. The women had hissed, and called her 'hussy'. Mama, on hearing about the performance, had been very angry. But no punishment could take away the knowledge that it was possible, even easy for Blanche to gain maximum attention, to be the envy of, and target for all eyes.

A few years later, and she had played other games. Last summer had been devoted to the enslavement of three brothers. It had been her duty to fetch water from the standpipe at the top of the Court. She had dallied across the water-buckets, first with one brother, and then with another. What could have been more natural than the unbuttoning of her high-necked blouse and the loosening of her bindings in the August heat? She had grown to be a very tall girl, and had needed to stoop quite low in order to pick up the buckets. The brothers, who seemed to spend all their time leaning up against the wall, looked forward quite obviously to her evening performance; and Blanche had re-entered her mother's cottage, bonds in position, blouse neatly fastened, and Mama had never once become suspicious.

Blanche had pleaded to be allowed to go with Mina, to work in the collar factory. But Mama had said, 'No! You have a tendency to flaunt yourself.' And so she had stayed inside the dark little cottage, and stitched at shirt collars for twelve hours of every day, save Sunday. She had gone to fetch water at that time of the evening when the misty light of October had made Hunter's Court look less ugly, and Mama had dozed beside the fire. The three brothers, separately, and sometimes together, had whispered wicked suggestions in her ear. They would contrive to brush close against her whenever she met them in the narrow alley. Those moments of absolute power beside the standpipe had been the glory of her dreary day. She had leaned close, without actually touching, had teased and enticed them, watched their hot eyes and eager faces, and then she had stooped low, allowed them to glimpse her remarkable cleavage, snatched up the buckets, and strolled demurely away.

The gaslights which illuminated Taunton's main streets had not reached as far as Hunter's Court. Her mother had forbidden her to leave the house once darkness had fallen, but on a December night of hard frost, Blanche had disobeyed. She had pulled on a thick shawl, taken a bucket, and started up towards the standpipe. She had never reached it.

The three brothers, no longer flattering and teasing, had been waiting for her. The bucket snatched and spun away into the darkness. She had smelt gin, had been reminded of her drunken father, and felt revulsion. She had felt their punishing hands upon her body, and she had almost swooned from fear. They had ripped off her shawl and dress, torn her petticoats, found and stripped away her mother's bindings. It was then that she had begun to scream, quite loudly.

The drama had been discovered just in time by Mama and Annis; and Blanche had been revealed in the light of her mother's lamp, spread-eagled up against the wall, wearing only her chemise, and suddenly, and belatedly, weeping. Mama had thrown a coal-hammer at one brother, and used Father's whip on the backs of the others. The brothers had called Blanche 'a bitch'. They had said that she 'had been asking for it'.

She had expected that she might also be whipped, but her mother had not even scolded. 'When you are sixteen,' Mama had said, 'you shall go to London. You shall go into service with your sister, Candace.' Blanche had studied Candace, already five years in service, and still dressed in cotton. She remembered how Madelina had once run away from this same mansion in Mayfair, to return to Taunton and a job in a collar factory. For Blanche there would be no

9

more mistakes; no dallying with drunken youths in shabby alleys; no running back to Taunton and Mama.

She supposed that her sisters could be considered pretty. They were tiny, dark haired girls, who wore high-buttoned blouses, and laced themselves tightly into whalebone corsets. With their pink pursed mouths, unpainted faces, and kiss-curls plastered low across their foreheads they attracted the attentions of Sunday-school teachers and counting-house clerks.

Blanche intended to create her own style in London. Once away from Mama, the detested corset would be burned along with all her other constrictions. In London she would carry herself like a duchess, head and bosom lifted, stomach flat, legs sinuous and gliding beneath her long skirts. The glorious auburn hair would be worn coiled low in her neck; she would paint her lips and cheeks just sufficiently to indicate that she was no prude.

❀

Blanche had expected grandeur, and Berkeley Square did not disappoint her. She halted beneath the plane trees, set down her bag, and looked slowly about her. Her eyes opened wide at the sight of the splendid Georgian mansions with their wrought-iron lampholders and railings; the very air smelled expensive. Even the old man who swept the street-crossing wore a fine red coat with gold-facings.

'You never said it was like this, Can.'

'Like what?'

'Why, so – so fine!' She pointed towards the crossing-sweeper. 'Horse-droppings picked up straightaway, and trees and flowers everywhere.'

'You'll find no trees and flowers in London's back streets.'

'I might see the Prince of Wales. They say he goes about a great deal.'

'Not in the places you're likely to visit. He's not known for coming to the kitchen quarters.'

'You mean he comes here? To this very house?'

'It's been known to happen.'

Blanche followed her sister down the area steps and into a huge and gloomy kitchen. Girls in soiled aprons ran from range to table, fulfilling the shouted orders of a fat man who wore a tall white hat.

'Why does he talk so funny?' whispered Blanche.

'Because he's French. That's M'sieu Armand.'

They walked through a maze of passages and came to a closed brown door upon which Candace tapped, very softly.

'So you're back,' said the housekeeper.

Candace curtsied and nudged Blanche to do likewise. 'Yes, ma'am,' she murmured.

'Did your father die?'

'He did, ma'am.'

Mrs Chumley looked up into the face of Blanche. 'Is this the sister you mentioned?'

'It is, ma'am.'

'She's very tall. How old are you, girl?'

'Just sixteen – ma'am.'

'What's your name?'

'Blanche – Blanche Greypaull.'

'Well, that won't do! We can't have a scullery maid who's got the same Christian name as M'Lady!' The housekeeper turned to Candace. 'Well, Alice, she's your sister, what do you suggest we call her?'

Candace said, 'What about Mary? We haven't got a Mary at the moment.'

'Right you are, then! Mary it shall be. You'll find a double bed in your room, Alice. I thought you'd rather be in together. Get your suppers, and then to bed. I want you up and fit for work in the morning.' She turned back to Blanche. 'I hope you're not going to give me trouble. Your other sister only stayed a fortnight, and then she ran away. Said she was homesick.'

'Oh, I'll never do that, ma'am. I've waited too long already to get to London.'

The staircase was narrow, uncarpeted and badly lit; it rose meanly through the tall house; Blanche tried to hush the clatter of her newly-soled boots on the wooden treads. Already she was disappointed; the area steps, the gloomy kitchen, the frowsty little sitting-room where Mrs Chumley presided, were not at all what she had expected. They came at last to a floor where the staircase ended. 'This is it,' said Candace. 'Top of the house. Us can't rise no higher.' She pushed open a door and Blanche saw an iron bedstead, a clean white bedspread, a wash-hand-stand pushed into a corner on which stood a chipped enamel ewer and bowl.

'This is ours?' she demanded. Candace nodded. 'Why 'tis no better than a good-sized cupboard!'

'What did you expect? A canopied bed, mahogany wardrobes? 'Tis I what should be doing the complaining. There was only a single bed in this room before you come here.'

Blanche hung her few clothes on hooks in a curtained recess. She pushed at the stump of candle in its cheap tin holder. 'Not even a lamp,' she complained.

'By the time you get back to this room each night,' Candice told her, 'all you'll want to do is sleep.'

Blanche sat on the edge of the bed and surveyed her sister. 'Why,' she said softly, 'whatever have happened to you, Candace? You was born a Miss Greypaull of Larksleve. These people have put a harness on you. They have even took away your given name. You didden never dare to tell Mama that, did you?'

Colour rose painfully in the sallow face. Candace said, 'And neither must you, Blanche! 'Tis no consequence what they calls us; not worth making a din about it.'

'I shall make a din about it! If you fancies having a common handle like Alice, that's your look-out. But nobody's ever going to call me Mary, so there! I shan't answer to it! Blanche is my given name and I won't let them change it!'

'But 'tis M'Lady's name. You can't be called the same as her. That wudden be proper.'

'Oh, how right you be, Candace Greypaull! Blanche is a very special name. We can't have two of us bearing it under the one roof.' She paused, picked up the candle-holder and carried it across the room to the scrap of looking-glass above the washstand. She angled and stretched, bent an elbow, dipped a shoulder, and tweaked at the generous folds of the black cotton bodice, so that her tiny waist and full high bosom were more sharply defined.

'What do M'Lady look like?' she murmured.

'Nothing very special. She's a liddle thin woman wi' iron grey hair.'

'Ah,' said Blanche, 'now that do make a difference.' She touched the coils of her copper hair, laid a hand upon her alabaster cheek, opened wide her violet eyes. Satisfaction purred along her words. 'Poor liddle woman, her must need her fancy name much more than I do.' She giggled, 'Tell 'ee what we'll do, Can! Whenever we is talking about M'Lady by our two selves, then us'll call her skivvy-Mary. That'll learn her to try and take my name away!'

❊

A good-looking servant, even if obedient and willing, could still create problems within a household. When the servant was beautiful, and determined to attract male attention, then trouble was assured. Blanche, who was neither obedient nor willing, was watched over closely by Mrs Chumley. Servants, she was told, must wear their uniforms exactly as issued, without pinning and tucking in strategic

13

places. Caps were not to be worn at an angle which revealed the wearer's hair. Humility and respect towards those of higher station were to be reflected in a servant's posture. To carry the head high and the shoulders straightened was not required of a skullery maid. Neither should she presume to stare directly into the faces of her Master and his family.

The work was demeaning. Peeling potatoes, scrubbing steps and saucepans, and carrying coal were the tasks which Blanche had previously sidestepped. But in this house there was no younger sister on whom she might put the unpleasant chores. So much to see in this City, so many wonders waiting to amaze her – and here she was, trapped below stairs, and sent to bed early every night of the week.

'When do they let us out?' she asked Candace.

'We get a half-day off once a month.'

'But that's no good to me! I need to go out and about in the evenings.'

'What for?'

'To meet men, of course! You surely don't think that I intend to stay boxed up much longer in that dreadful kitchen?'

Candace sighed. 'I suppose not.'

'You might as well face it, Can. I'm not like you and Mina.' Blanche stretched out her hands; she opened and closed her fingers with a grasping motion. 'I want,' she said simply, 'I just want and want! 'Tis like a pain inside me. Seeing this house, the way the rich live, have only made it worse. I've got to get out of here, Can, and you had better help me. There'll be trouble for us both if I have to stay here much longer.' She looked around the tiny dormer bedroom, at the iron bedstead and the bare boards of the floor. 'I don't know how you've put up with this attic for the last five years.'

Candace hesitated. 'If I tell you something, will you blab it to Mother when you go home?'

14

'I shan't be going home unless I've got plenty of money. When that day comes — I expect I'll need to ask you to keep your mouth shut.'

'All right, then. Now listen, Blanche! It needn't be so bad here, but you've got to be careful. Don't call so much attention to yourself. Keep your head bent, and your hands busy. Compared to some that I've heard about, you could say that this is an easy-going household.'

'Easy-going? Why, that housekeeper —'

Candace grinned and blew out the candle. 'Get into bed and keep your voice down, and I'll tell you a thing or two about this family. The Master, as you know, is an artist. The Mistress is an invalid, she never goes out; just crawls from her bed to the boudoir-sofa, and back again. I sees quite a bit of what goes on above stairs, being housemaid,' Candace whispered. 'It's my opinion that she drinks, or takes laudenum, or both! Anyway, what with him being an artist, and M'Lady out of Commission, the running of the house is left to Mrs Chumley, and she likes her brandy of an evening.'

'You'd never guess it.'

'She's careful. But I look after her sitting-room and bedroom. Sometimes, she's too fuddled to rinse the glass out. Come ten o'clock of an evening, and Mrs Chumley is sleeping like a well-fed baby!'

'What happens then?'

'There's a door at the back of the house what is never locked. It leads into the Mews where they keeps the carriages and horses. The Mews leads directly into Charles Street. There's an inn at the end of the street called The Running Footman.'

Blanche began to giggle. 'Why, Candace Greypaull! Whoever would have thought it of you?'

'I don't go there for the drink, nor the men.' Candace sounded furtive and appealing, 'I likes to place a bet, every

15

now and again. I've got a friend — he's a racing tipster. I meet him there sometimes of an evening. There's no harm in it, Blanche. I've been to Newmarket with him on my half-day; I've seen the Derby run at Epsom.'

'So that's why you like it here,' Blanche smiled into the darkness. 'I knew there had to be a reason. But what about me, Can? I want some fun too!'

'Promise me that you'll behave yourself in this house; no more flouncing about in the kitchen, and upsetting Mrs Chumley. There's ways and means of getting what you wants in life, Blanche. You've just got to know how best to go about it.'

'Then tell me!'

'You have to know your place. If you're a skivvy, then you must behave like one. But what you do after dark will be your affair. Just remember this, though. I won't be responsible for any trouble you gets into. You won't get out when there's a dinner-party on, or guests stopping in the house. Bide your time! Pick a quiet evening. Watch out for Ma Chumley! Always be careful when you goes through the Mews. The butler, being married, has separate quarters close to the gateway. The grooms and stable-lads live above the stables. Never draw attention to yourself. Always have a good excuse ready in case you gets found in a place where you got no right to be. Do as I tell you, be a good girl, and the next time I go to The Running Footman I'll take you with me.'

❁

They called her Mary in this great mansion, but she never forgot that her name was Blanche. She cleaned the fire-grates in the master-bedrooms and, whenever she found herself unobserved, she touched silks and velvets with a sooty finger. She studied her reflection in gilt-framed mirrors, and discovered that the ill-fitting uniform had not quite concealed the contours of her fine figure. Neither had the skivvy's mob-cap completely hidden the glory of her abundant hair.

I am beautiful, she told herself. I am more beautiful than the hags who visit the Master to have their likeness made in paint. She would hoist her grimy skirts high, and study the length of her shapely legs. She would pose and twirl before the long mirrors until an approaching footfall would send her back to the half-cleaned fire-grate. She would lurk in the stairwell, and in shadowy corners, and observe the men who came calling upon the Master. There was a dark-haired man whose looks intrigued her. She asked Candace about him.

'His name is Solomon I think,' Candace frowned. 'He's an artist, but a poor one. He used to visit regular at one time. He's a Jew. He'd never get further than the doorstep these days if Mrs Chumley had her way.'

'What's a Jew?'

'Don't you remember the Bible? 'Twas the Jews what murdered Jesus.'

'How can you tell he's a Jew?'

'By his long nose and bushy beard.'

'But lots of men have – '

Candace grew impatient. 'What were you doing in the hall, anyway? You know you're supposed to always use the back stairs. I've seen you sneaking off every time there's a ring at the doorbell. Don't you dare get familiar with any man who visits this house. I know I should never have brought you here. You'll get us both sacked.'

Candace droned on, but Blanche had ceased to listen. She was remembering the Jew called Solomon who had spied her that morning in the shadowy stairwell. Her appointed place was in the kitchen, her uniform shabby and unattractive; Blanche was the drab, the drudge in this stylish household. Even those early morning chores, when she swept hearths and carried ash buckets in the main rooms, were usually

17

performed among the comings and goings of less menial servants. It was only in stolen moments when no housemaid or parlourmaid was present, that Blanche would dare to glance about her, to commit to memory the knowledge of quality and good taste that, she was sure, would one day be required of her in her marriage to a rich and cultured man.

The drawing-room carpet was black with sprays of pink roses patterned on it. It showed every dusty footfall, oh, but it was elegant, and anyway, what were servants for? She was intimately acquainted with every inch of that carpet; it was her daily task to clean it by scattering dampened tea-leaves across it, and then crawl about on her hands and knees brushing up the resultant mess! The sofas and chairs were covered in rose brocade to match the draped and tasselled curtains. There were cabinets of shiny black with pictures painted on them; tables of yellow wood, laden down with photographs in silver frames. Little hollows had been scooped out in the walls, and then fitted with narrow shelves. On these stood pieces of rose-coloured glass, and painted china figures. There were crystal chandeliers, a huge piano which had three corners; in an alcove stood an object that looked like an oversized sieve. Candace said it was called a harp, as used by the angels in stained-glass church windows. The wonders of that room were endless, but as she confided to her sister, she hardly dared to breathe, let alone touch, lest some priceless items should shatter and break.

The study was cosy. Blanche loved the rough and friendly feel of its Indian carpet through her thin soled slippers. She liked the darkness of panelled walls, the sporting-prints, the wide jade-leather armchairs, and the impressive desk with its ink-stands of brass, and green-shaded lamps. All the corridors were carpeted in crimson, and lined with portraits of dull and ugly people. She hated the hall, the black and white marbled floor of which she was forced to scrub every Friday morning.

18

Her place of pure delight was M'Lady's bedroom. Done out in shades that ranged from palest sea-green to deepest turquoise, it would have made such a perfect setting for the jewel that was Blanche! The very thought of madam's iron-grey curls on those lacy eau-de-nil pillows was an affront. The rare glimpse of that aristocratic and skinny figure on the velvet chaise-longue was anathema to her.

''Tidden fair,' she moaned to Candice. 'There idden no justice in this world. 'Tis I what should be mistress of a house like this.'

Infuriated by her sister's silence she shouted, 'Well, I got the looks, Can! You got to admit that. What's more, I want it and want it! That do get so bad some days, 'specially when I be forced to scrub they front steps, that I'd do anything at all to get my wish.'

❀

Candace had searched for ways of making Blanche less noticeable, more ordinary looking; but there were none. Even the black mourning-dress, high necked and unadorned, could not subdue the radiance of her; excitement at the proposed walk around Mayfair had already flushed her sister's fine skin and deepened the colour of her violet eyes.

Candace, tiny and unremarkable in her own black dress, paused briefly before the mirror, primped-up the hair which was usually flattened beneath her housemaid's cap, and bit her lips to give them more colour. The time had come to convince Blanche of London's dangers. The second-housemaid, a girl called Ellen, Cockney-born and wise, had advised a walk into Regent Street and Bond Street. 'Leave it to me,' she had promised Candace, 'I'll show the silly little cow what can happen to a gel who don't keep both feet on the straight and narrow!'

They left the house by the area door and mounted the steps that brought them up into the summer heat of

London. They came into Berkeley Square, and Candace and Ellen walked in step, their heads nodding close in conversation. Blanche strolled several paces behind; she dawdled underneath the plane-trees and gazed up at the impressive façades of the mansions which formed the Square. Famous people lived here: lords and generals, artists and musicians, people who wrote books. This was the place where the world turned, she could smell it and feel it. Power and money. She had tried to talk to Candace about it, about the wonder of these houses, but Candace could only complain about the drudgery which must be endured by the servants who worked in such places. The many stairs to be climbed, carrying scuttles of coal. The piles of silver to be cleaned, the vegetables to be peeled, the floors and steps which needed daily scrubbing.

Know your place, Candace had said, you're a skivvy, behave like one. But Blanche did not feel like a skivvy. She was not like her sister. A glass of gin in a common tavern, a sixpenny bet on a horse's nose, these were the vulgar pastimes which had ruined Father and lost them Larksleve. Already she perceived herself to be several notches higher than Candace; and it was not only her looks which made her superior. Blanche had a feeling for fine things. She coveted wealth, and was determined to have it; just as soon as she had discovered how the trick could be worked.

They walked along Bruton Street and into Bond Street. Candace and Ellen paused, waited for Blanche to catch up, and then ranged themselves beside her, one on either arm. 'Don't lag behind again,' sniggered Ellen, 'we don't want to lose you, just yet.' The hansom-cabs came and went. Blanche saw how they drove very slowly, while their male occupants studied the many girls who lingered beside the shop fronts. A gloved finger would beckon from a hansom window, and the chosen one would climb in and be driven smartly away.

'What goes on?' she asked Ellen. The two housemaids giggled.

'Come in here,' said Candace, 'we'll drink a cup of coffee, and put you straight on several matters.'

The coffee-house looked quite clean, but Candace and Ellen dusted the chair seats before sitting down. When the coffee was brought they pulled out clean hankies and rubbed at the rims of the china cups before drinking from them. They instructed Blanche to do the same. 'You never knows what kind o' people uses these places,' warned Ellen.

Blanche had never seen a coffee-house; she stared about her at the little groups of chairs and tables, and the pleasant-looking people who were sipping coffee. 'They looks all right to me.'

'That's because you don't know nuffink,' sneered the second-housemaid, 'you country gels is all the same. Innocent as morning daisies.'

'I bain't that innocent!'

'Yes, you are,' Candace said firmly, 'you must listen, Blanche, to what Ellen has to say.'

Ellen leaned closer. 'Take a good look at that big table in the window. But be careful. Don't stare, or we'll get some trouble. Now tell me what you sees there.'

Blanche was thoughtful. The girls at the window table were a merry crowd. Occasionally, one would leave her friends and return to the street; but her place was soon taken by another. 'I sees six young ladies drinking coffee,' she told Ellen.

Ellen hooted, 'Young ladies? Take another look. What about their clothes and faces?'

Blanche hesitated. The coffee-house was poorly lit, and the taunting Ellen had her flustered. 'Well,' she stammered, 'I s'pose their frocks is cut pretty low in front,' she peered into the gloom, 'and I should say that their faces is probably painted.'

'And what does that show you?'

The violet eyes opened wide. 'Strumpets?' breathed Blanche. 'Real live strumpets?'

'Keep your voice down,' pleaded Candace, 'you'll get our throats cut.'

Blanche became excited. 'Remember Loveday Hayes, Can? She once told me about strumpets, about how they rides in carriages and paints their faces.'

'Did she tell you what else they do?' grinned Ellen.

'Well – I sort o'guessed. Our Papa spent most of his money on the Taunton strumpets.'

'Tarts,' corrected Ellen. 'We calls 'em tarts in London. If you got any thoughts of joining 'em there's something else you ought to know.'

Candace said, 'Why do you think we wiped the chair seats and the cup rims?'

Blanche shrugged. 'You was ever fussy. You and Mama and Mina was forever cleaning and scrubbing.'

'No, Blanche. We was being careful. Tarts often use the coffee houses to find their business, and most tarts is diseased.'

Blanche took another look at the window table; she glanced briefly at Candace and Ellen. 'They looks well enough to me. In fact they looks a good deal healthier than you two!'

Ellen looked angry and shook her head. 'That's the paint and powder. Underneath all that muck, their insides is rotting away. Their arms and legs drop off when they gets older. Their noses crumble and their hair falls out.' Ellen leaned back and drew satisfied breath. 'They goes raving mad in the finish!'

Blanche looked surprised. 'I don't believe a word of it,' she said calmly. 'You two is trying to frighten me. Why should that only happen to tarts and not to other people?'

'It can happen to anybody,' Candace said grimly. ''Tis a

dreadful sickness what gets passed along from men to women. You've got to be warned, Blanche. 'Tis the greatest punishment of the Lord God! He visits it upon the ungodly what indulges in the sins of the flesh. Even unto the fourth and fifth generations! I know what you got in your mind, you silly maiden! You wants gold, and you think that good looks will get it for you. 'Tis a risky game, Blanche, I got to warn you, for Mama's sake.'

Blanche smiled. 'So what about this feller of yours what takes you racing?'

'I be holding out for marriage,' said Candace smugly. 'Anyway, he's a milkman, so he's bound to be clean. 'Tis mostly the gentry what gets diseased.'

They left the coffee shop and walked into Regent Street. Ellen warned them to walk briskly in case their purpose should be misunderstood. 'Nobody's likely to mistake you and me for anything but skivvies,' she told Candace, 'but this damned sister o' yours has already slowed half-a-dozen hansom cabs.'

In Regent Street the older houses were galleried, with balconies which leaned outwards, from them hung trellises across which climbed roses and summer vines.

Blanche stood, entranced, and could not be shifted. Elegant ladies paced on these balconies high above the traffic. At intervals, an elaborately painted face would appear above the trellis, and a white-gloved hand would beckon a passer-by to come up.

'Oh,' breathed Blanche, 'they must be princesses.'

'Tarts,' muttered Ellen, 'high-class whores, I grants you. But tarts all the same.'

'How can they look like that,' Blanche said slowly, 'at this time of day? Who cooks the dinner and makes the fire up, who blackleads their fire-grate? See that one in the red silk – I can't believe she ever did a stroke of hard work in her life.'

'And no more she don't.' Ellen sounded envious. 'Only work she ever does is lying on her back. She'll have servants and a personal maid.'

'Servants?' Blanche's mouth fell open. 'Is you telling me that strumpets got skivvies working for 'em?'

'Only the top-class tarts.' Ellen laughed. 'You don't think they comes down on their knees, and scrubs their own doorsteps, do you? Not looking like that, my gel! Not likely!'

The walk along Regent Street brought them into Piccadilly. Their pace was so rapid that Blanche had no time to stop and stare. With her sister clutching one arm, and Ellen dragging on the other, she arrived in St Martin's Lane, out of breath and puzzled. They halted before a small dark shop, the entrance to which was almost concealed by shabby piled-up furniture and racks of old clothes. These goods were spread right across the pavement and into the gutter, obliging pedestrians either to step into the roadway, or stop and consider a purchase. A small plump woman, seated on a chair in the afternoon sunshine, was dozing beside the door of the empty shop.

'Watchyer, Mam!' screeched Ellen.

The woman twitched, opened one eye, and then the other, and began to smile. 'Where the 'ell 'ave you been, you rotten little bitch? Kettle's been on the boil for the last two hours.' The violent greeting, accompanied by a smacking kiss, alarmed Blanche and amused Candace, who had seen it all before.

'Come on in, then,' ordered Ellen's mother. 'You'll only just have time to drink your tea, before you goes back to feed old Ratface with his dinner.'

'Ratface?' Blanche looked enquiringly at Candace.

'His bleedin' Lordship,' shouted Ellen's mother, 'the h'important h'artist, him wot paints the h'aristocracy, eh gels?' She cackled enormously, and dug Candace in the ribs with a grimy finger. 'You must 'ave been working in Berkeley Square for a good five years now, ain't you, Alice, I bet you could tell a tale – if you was to choose to.'

Candace smiled, and pushed Blanche before her through the gloomy entrance. They passed through the almost empty shop, and into a back room which, although crowded with furniture and knick-knacks, was surprisingly clean. The three girls seated themselves at a circular table that was covered by a starched white cloth, and spread with a half-tea service of delicate bone-china.

'Ooh Mam!' gasped Ellen, 'them's pretty cups and saucers. Where'd you get them, then?'

'Took 'em in last Friday. Lady rolled up in a hansom – veil pulled down across her face – you knows the sort. Could hardly bring herself to set her dainty foot in my shop. Said as 'ow her investments had let her down! Make me laugh, the toffs do. She wanted the money for gin, o' course.' Ellen's mother nodded importantly at Candace. 'You gets to know a lot about 'uman nature in the h'antique business. If I comes across somefink nice, I keeps it for a bit.' She flicked her thumbnail against the valuable teapot and smiled at the resultant ring. 'When times gets bad I has to part wi' things.' This mention of her stock reminded Mrs Gimball of the 'antiques' now left unguarded upon the pavement of St Martin's Lane. A small boy was called in, straight away, from the back yard, and instructed to mount sentry before the shop entrance.

'Full o' thieves, this area.' Ellen's mother lifted the steaming kettle from the fire and made tea. She passed the plate of cakes and filled four tea cups. 'You just came up from the country?' she asked Blanche.

Blanche nodded. 'I be Candace's sister.'

'I thought so.' She turned towards Candace. 'You better watch out for this one, Alice. I ain't never seen looks like that 'cept in actresses and suchlike. And we all know how

25

they ends-up, don't we?'

Ellen spoke through a mouthful of rock-cake. 'Just what we've been doing, Ma! That's why we was late. We took her down to Bond Street, and showed her what goes on there.'

'That's no good. You wants to take 'er to St Giles. Show 'er the crawlers, why don't you? Show 'er what happens in the end to gels who lead a bad life.'

'We'll take her there next time, Ma,' promised Ellen. She pointed at a closed brown door. 'How's the Art business doing these days?' she winked at Candace. 'Seen anyfink of old Solomon just lately?'

Mrs Gimball smoothed her dingy apron. 'Mr Solomon was 'ere this very morning,' she sniffed, 'and I'll thank you, miss, to be more respectful. Mr Solomon is a h'important Artist, wot has never been give 'is rightful dues. Some high-class toffs comes to me these days for Mr Solomon's paintings.'

'I'll bet they do,' giggled Ellen. 'What's he brought you this time, eh Ma?'

'Better pictures than your old Ratface ever turns out.' Mrs Gimball's indignation was genuine and heartfelt. 'Mr Solomon only paints Beauty — he told me so. He don't demean hisself with painting the,' she paused to recall the correct expression, 'with painting the 'orse-faced aristocracy, with their ta-ra-ras on their heads, and their 'aughty faces.'

Ellen's laughter was admiring. 'Why, Ma, I do believe you're getting to be a proper expert.'

Mrs Gimball flushed, and patted her hair. 'Well,' she said, 'I've learned a lot by doin' business with Mr Solomon.'

'You've made a tidy profit, too. Eh, Ma?'

'It's been profitable for both sides, Ellen. Which is as it should be. After all, it's me what takes the risk — he don't.'

'Where's he living these days?'

Ellen's mother looked embarrassed. 'I don't rightly know. He moves about. Never stops very long in the one place.'

Ellen looked knowing. 'He'd have to move on pretty smartish, I reckon. He's not everybody's cup o' tea. Beats me how he gets his models. How about showing us your new selection then, Ma?'

Mrs Gimball seemed uncertain. She glanced questioningly at Blanche and Candace. 'They might talk out o' turn –'

'Not them,' said Ellen, 'they don't know nuffink about Art. Not like you, Ma.'

The flattery drove Mrs Gimball to fetch up a key from her bodice, and unlock the closed brown door. Before entering the room she lit an oil-lamp and handed it to Ellen.

The paintings were large; the figures depicted were both male and female unclothed and set among desolate landscapes. Blanche gasped; even Candace drew breath sharply. There was something unpleasant about the pictures.'Ain't they beauties?' asked Ellen's mother. 'Ain't they better than your old Lordship's po-faced duchesses?'

'I wonder where he finds his models?' repeated Ellen. 'He couldn't never paint like that from memory.'

Mrs Gimball, suddenly nervous, pushed them towards the doorway. She relocked the door, and returned the key to her bosom. She stared fiercely at Blanche and Candace. 'You don't tell nobody about wot I just showed you. Don't you forget, now!'

'Who'd believe 'em, anyway,' grinned Ellen. 'Where would skivvies ever see a whole roomful of dirty pictures?'

'They ain't dirty pictures, our Ellen. That's Art that is! Why you'd never believe in the young gen'lmen what comes 'ere to buy – no names, no pack-drill, o'course; but I sees coronets painted on their carriage doors.' Mrs Gimball, moved by her own rhetoric, wiped a tear from her cheek. 'Mr Solomon is a real nice bloke. He's very quiet and gentle. Them pictures is took from the Bible, and the Greek gods – he talks to me about 'em. He once moved in high circles, but they was jealous of 'im and kicked 'im out. There's nothing sinful in any o' them paintings; and, what's more, they sells like hot cakes.' She looked thoughtfully at Blanche. 'His biggest trouble is getting models. "I need a gel who's got classical beauty" that's what he's always saying.' Mrs Gimball sat down and tapped the teapot, 'More tea, anybody?'

Ellen shook her head. 'No, ta. We'll have to be getting back. We was late in coming. See you in about a month, Ma.'

Candace said politely, 'Thank you for the tea, Mrs Gimball. It was kind of you to have us.'

Blanche said, 'Thank you for showing us they pictures. I thought they was really – well – lovely!'

Mrs Gimball smiled and nodded, 'Now that's what I likes to see – young women what's been proper brought-up to know their manners. Your Ma must be proud o' you two.' She glanced at Blanche, then raised her gaze to a damp patch on the ceiling. 'Artists' models,' she said casually, 'is very well paid. Why, I've 'eard of the top ones pulling-down as much as 'alf a guinea for a single sitting.'

❁

Blanche lay in the double bed she shared with Candace, and the events of that memorable day trooped before her in the darkness. She began to relive the more exciting moments. Blanche in the coffee-house, and the realisation that the pretty painted girls were strumpets. Blanche in Regent Street, looking up towards the balconies on which the expensive ladies of the town displayed their charms. Blanche sipping tea in the dark little shop in St Martin's Lane. The keen eyes of Ellen's mother upon her; Mrs Gimball's comment, 'I ain't never seen looks like that 'cept in actresses and suchlike.'

She recalled the room which held Mr Solomon's paintings; and her own shock at the sight of those life-sized images, their modesty saved only by a wisp of veiling or a floating scarf. Her face grew hot at the memory, and she suddenly recalled that night in Hunter's Court, and the three brothers who had stripped away her own clothing. She remembered the power she had felt at the gasps of admiration which came from the brothers when Blanche had been revealed in the light of Mama's lamp, wearing only her chemise. Ellen had called the pictures dirty, but Mrs Gimball had said that they were Art. Blanche was not quite sure what Art was, but it sounded refined and not a bit disgraceful.

She whispered, 'Be you still awake, Candace?'

Candace tossed and muttered, 'Go to sleep. I'd have thought you'd be tired out too, after all that walking.'

'I bain't a bit sleepy. I been thinking about Mrs Gimball. What she said about artists.'

'Well don't. Tidden no concern of ours, Blanche, what goes on behind that shop.'

'They earns half a guinea for a single sitting.'

'Who do?'

'Artists' models. Wasn't you listening? That's easy money, Can. All they got to do is sit still and take their clothes off.'

'Don't you never believe it!' Candace came wide awake. 'There's more to it than that; why that's a whole month's wages for a skivvy.' She paused. 'You think about it, Blanche. What usually happens to a girl once she's took her drawers off?'

Blanche giggled. 'Ooh Candace! You got quite wicked since you come to London.'

Candace sat up, abruptly. ''Tis a wicked city. I keep trying to warn you. We was mistook, me and Ellen. We shudden never have showed you Bond Street. Now you got wrong ideas. We should have took you down to Holborn, to St Giles's, where the "crawlers" live.'

Blanche said softly, 'Oh, how right you be! That one liddle taste of the city have made me hungrier than ever. Didden you see it too, Candace? The hansom-cabs, the parasols and fine dresses; all they people strolling about in the sunshine.'

Candace grew desperate, 'They wasn't people, Blanche. They was only tarts.'

Blanche reached out a hand and touched her sister's shoulder in the darkness. 'Don't you worry no more about me. I bain't that stupid. I won't never do anything what'll make my nose crumble and my hair fall out. I means to be a lady. But first, I got to get some money. I promised Mama that she should go in silk before this year's out.'

Blanche fell asleep with the thought of Mama heavy on her mind, and her dreams were not of Bond Street, London, but of Larksleve Farm and Buckland St Mary. She stepped back into her childish self, rejected by her brothers and sisters, unloved by her mother, and knew in the certainty of dreaming that all she had wanted, or would ever want, was the undivided love of Mama.

Candace, awakened towards morning by the quiet sobbing, turned to gaze at the sleeping face on the adjacent pillow. The long lashes were wet with tears, the full red lips parted slightly. The firm chin bore that same dimpled hollow which had marked Papa as an idle braggart, and yet, there was more to Blanche than pointless boasting. She had always been one of the persistent kind. It had taken ten years to polish-off Father, but Blanche had achieved it, in the end.

❀

For weeks Blanche had lurked in corners, peeped from the stairwell at wealthy visitors admitted by the butler, earned herself rebukes and punishments from Mrs Chumley and

M'sieu Armand for leaving the kitchen and neglecting her duties. No Prince had come to her rescue; no gentleman had recognised that beneath the shapeless uniform-dress lay a body of exceptional beauty. Even the Master of the house, portrait painter to the rich and titled, had failed to notice the face and form of his exquisite scullery-maid, although she had thrust her cap into her apron pocket and waylaid him whenever opportunity allowed.

Frustration was making Blanche ill-tempered, and Candace, fearing trouble in the kitchen, had promised her a visit to The Running Footman tavern. They went to bed as usual, at nine o'clock, and blew out the candle. At ten they rose, put on their black cotton dresses and, boots-in-hand, they left the mansion by the rear door. A quick scamper through the Mews brought them into Charles Street, and in sight of the inn-sign. They entered the smoky bar room, scuffed their feed through sawdust, and found a quiet seat up against the wall.

'You bide still, now!' ordered Candace, 'don't you even look around you. I got to find Archie before we can have a drink. He've got my winnings from today's race.'

The regular milkman of Berkeley Square looked a less important person without his tall churn and measure, and his horse and cart. Archie Wizard was a little, bow-legged man, with a quiff of black, oiled hair plastered to his forehead, and a broad grin that revealed the many gaps in his teeth. Candace introduced him, and Blanche sat down again, considerately, before shaking him by the hand. A whispered consultation produced one shilling and tuppence from Archie's pocket. He pulled a chair up to the table and seated himself, while Candace fetched the drinks.

'She's a proper wonder, your sister, at picking winners!' Archie whispered. 'There ain't much your Alice don't know about 'orseflesh.' He winked broadly. 'First time in a pub is it, Mary?'

31

'Yes, it is,' snapped Blanche, 'and I'll thank you to use my proper name, Mr Wizard.'

Archie pulled down the corners of his mouth, 'Oh ho! All hoity-toity is yer? And what is modom's proper name, if I might make so bold as ter arsk?'

'My name is Blanche Greypaull,' the words came out stiffly, 'and my sister's name bain't Alice. Her is called Candace, and don't you forget it!'

Archie leaned across the table. 'Let me advise you, young woman, afore you gets a minute older. Before you tells me what I can call your sister, you had better learn to talk proper. Like what I do.' The Cockney whine was laced with venom. 'You got a big opinion of yourself for a skivvy. I 'eard all about you. Now, don't you go giving my Alice any trouble. You come down off your 'igh 'orse, you little bitch. A swede-basher, that's what you are, just up from the country. Why, you shows yourself up every time you opens your ma'rf.'

Blanche clenched both fists. 'If you was big enough to match me,' she threatened, 'I'd come round this table and knock your last few teeth out! Why, you liddle runt, I could gobble you up, and eat you for my brekfus!'

Candace returned with a tray of drinks. She took in Blanche's heightened colour and Archie's wild looks. She sighed. 'Oh dear, I can't take you nowhere, can I?' She pushed a brandy glass at Blanche. 'Here now, drink that and keep quiet, or I'll send you straight home.'

Blanche grew bored. She had expected excitement from The Running Footman and all she had gained so far was an altercation with a bandy milkman. There was no hint of romance in her sister's assignation. Candace and Archie whispered, heads together, about the finer points of horseflesh. They plotted the coming race at Epsom: how they would get there, how much money they would find to wager, and how best to lay-off their bets.

The effect of the brandy was unexpected. Blanche felt frightened. The strange drink had gone straight to her legs; from the waist downwards she had lost all feeling. Her vision had blurred slightly. Alarmed, she interrupted the lovers. 'My legs is gone all numb, Can! I can't see proper, either.'

'And a bloody good job, too,' snarled Archie Wizard. 'I'll fetch you another brandy if it'll keep your silly gob shut.'

Blanche blinked and moved position, and a man at an adjoining table looked up at once and pleaded, 'Please – don't turn your head away. That pose is absolutely perfect.'

She found herself obeying; she maintained her head in its previous position, but her eyes swivelled sideways. The man, head bent to a scrap of paper, was holding a stick of some black stuff in his hand. Blanche felt the heart leap suddenly inside her. Surely this man was the one who had visited her Master in Berkeley Square? The Jew who had fallen on hard times? Head swimming, never daring to move, she waited for the words which would release her. He said at last, 'You can relax now, I've finished.' She glanced fearfully at Candace and Archie, but they were absorbed in one another, and had noticed nothing. Cautiously, Blanche slid along the wooden bench, until she sat facing the stranger. She reached out a hand for the scrap of paper.

'Can I see?'

He passed it over. 'It's only a quick sketch, you know. The light is poor in here, and I'm running short of decent paper. But I couldn't resist the attempt to capture your likeness. I expect you already know that you're a remarkably beautiful young woman.'

Blanche held the sketch first at arm's length; and then much closer. She sounded disappointed. ''Tis such a liddle picture,' she complained, 'you can't tell from this what I

33

really looks like.'

The artist nodded. 'Oh, I do agree. In another place and time I could paint a portrait of you that would make me famous.'

'Is that true, then?' Blanche shook her head to dispel the brandy fumes. She could hear the country drawl in her voice, the slur made more obvious by alcohol, she tried hard not to sound like a swede-basher. 'You can paint me,' she said primly, 'if you wants to. But I be a respectable girl. I don't never take my clothes off.'

'I wouldn't dream of asking you to do so.' The dark eyes glowed in the thin face. 'You have the classical profile, somewhere between the Hebrew concept of beauty, and that of the Greek. You could be an inspiration to me –'

Blanche interrupted, 'I reckon as how you've bin drinking,' she said tartly. 'I didden understand a blinkin' word of all that. Not,' she reassured him, 'not that you don't make it sound quite lovely, whatever it means. You got a way of talking that's what my Mama 'ud call genteel.' She considered his appearance. 'Is you a gentleman? You don't look much like one.'

He smiled wryly. 'If you would sit for me, I would treat you kindly and with respect. I couldn't pay you until the picture was sold. My financial position is somewhat precarious at present.'

'You means that you're flat-broke?'

He nodded. He said with great dignity, 'I reside at present in the St Giles Poorhouse. I'm a resident of some long-duration. They understand me and my ways.' He made it sound, thought Blanche, like the Coburg Hotel or Buckingham Palace.

'Well, I hope you don't expect me to get my picture painted in the Workhouse – I got my pride to consider.'

'But of course. I understand that. Suppose I make my preliminary sketches as I have done this evening – in The

34

Running Footman. Later on we can consider other venues.'

'You mean to draw me here – in this pub?' Blanche shrugged. 'I s'pose so. Yes, all right then.'

'Tomorrow evening?'

She nodded. 'By the way,' she asked, 'what's your name?'

'Solomon,' he said, 'Simeon Solomon.'

❋

Candace was angry. 'I never should have took you there,' she raged, 'I might have guessed you'd get up to something. I only turn my back for one minute –'

''Tis nothing to do with you, Candace. He's a gentleman what wants to paint my picture, that's all. 'Tis my face what takes his fancy – I don't have to take my drawers off.'

Candace said, 'Do you know who he is?'

'He's the fellah who once come calling on the Master. The one you said was a Jew.'

'And what did he tell you his name was?'

'Solomon – I think.'

'And where did you hear that name before, Blanche?'

Blanche tried to think, her head was still aching from last night's brandy.

'Mrs Gimball?' she said. 'Them naked pictures in her back room – ?'

Candace nodded. 'Exactly! Wants to paint your face, does he? Do you still believe that?'

'Well,' said Blanche, 'he can hardly expect me to undress in the middle of a tavern bar room.'

'You're not to go back there. You hear me?'

'I don't hear you, and I shall go!'

'I shall write to Mama and tell her all about it.'

'I shall go home and tell her about Archie Wizard. I shall tell her how you goes racing with him. How you bets on horses. I shall tell her that you made me go in to a tavern, and give me brandy to keep my mouth shut!'

The evening sessions at The Running Footman were to begin the transformation of Blanche. Hope had given her a purpose; her likeness, transferred to paper, and later done in oils, was to make her benefactor famous, and herself a wealthy woman. They sat on a wooden bench in a quiet corner of the taproom, and Mr Solomon sketched her features by the light of a good lamp. His appearance intrigued her. His hair and beard were black and curly, his face pale and sickly-looking. His eyes were a little mad; sometimes, she thought, when he talked about Art, they glinted redly like those of a wild goat. She loved to hear him speak.

'Do sit still,' he pleaded.

'Then talk to me.'

'What shall I talk about?'

'Anything. Every word sounds lovely, the way you says it.'

'Have you got any family?'

'I got that sister what is courting wi' the milkman. You saw me with her the other evening. There's five more of us at home in Taunton. There's Madelina, she's religious. Then there's Jack – he's gone for a jockey. Annis is fourteen; she's delicate; and then we got poor liddle Louis – he's feeble-minded. I got another brother,' Blanche said shyly, 'he got the same name as you, he's called Simeon!'

The artist looked up, he studied her from another angle. 'You're not Jewish, are you?' he asked abruptly. 'No, of course you're not.'

Blanche bridled. 'I should think not, too. I never would have murdered Jesus!'

His head remained bent. 'Who told you that story?' he murmured.

''Tis in the Bible.'

'Do you read your Bible, Blanche?'

36

'Course I do,' she lied, 'every night and every morning.'

'Then you must know that Jesus Christ was also a Jew.'

'No he wasn't. He was English.'

Solomon began to chuckle.

'Don't you laugh at me,' she cried, 'I don't like to be laughed at.'

At once he controlled his features. 'I'm sorry,' he said, 'you obviously know more about Jesus than I do, and so you should, since you are a Christian.'

'What be you then, Mr Solomon? Be you an Unbeliever?'

'I am a Jew, Blanche. I expect your Madelina would rank me among the Ungodly.'

Blanche drew a breath of pure delight. 'Oh,' she whispered, 'I always wanted to meet one of they sort. Do 'ee go in for magic – black magic?'

'What do you know of magic?' His curiosity sounded genuine. Encouraged by his serious attention she said, 'I know more than you think I do. They believes on pixies and fairies where I come from. They goes in a lot for overlooking and ill-wishing.'

'But I thought you were all devoted churchgoers?'

'Oh – that too.' Blanche dismissed the established church with an airy wave. 'The two goes well together. 'Tis all superstition idden it? When you comes down to the truth. I take a bit from one,' she confided, 'and a bit from the other.'

Solomon laid down his stick of chalk. 'How old are you Blanche?'

'I be seventeen,' she lied, 'going on eighteen.'

'I'm forty-one,' he said sadly, 'and in my time I have walked and talked with the wise and famous.' He paused. 'Sagacity at seventeen? Am I to believe this?' He worked in silence for some minutes, and Blanche began to fidget and grow restless. In desperation, he said, 'Tell me something, about your father and mother.'

The change in her was immediate and dramatic.

'Don't look like that,' he cried out, 'I need you serene and untroubled.'

'Then you shudden never have mentioned my father, Mr Solomon. 'Tis a sore subject what I don't care to dwell on.'

'Does he ill-treat you?'

'He's dead.'

'Well, that's all right, then.'

'No tidden all right. He should by rights have been dead these many long years.'

Solomon raised his head, surprised at the bitterness of her tone.

'That wasn't for the want of trying,' she continued, 'why, me and Loveday tried every single spell what we knowed to finish Pa off.'

Solomon became excited. As soon as she spoke of her dead father a change had come over Blanche. The cold and classical beauty had transmogrified to a strange and rampant evil that was almost obscene; the high sweet voice poured out a litany of hate that was purely pagan.

'Who was Loveday?'

'She was our servant. She loved me the best. She showed me all her magic. We tried every mortal thing on Papa: the dead black kitten hidden up the chimney, the pig's heart with father's initials carved on it and stuck around with thorns.' The high childish voice hushed into a whisper. 'We pinched candle-ends from the church when nobody was looking. We melted 'em down to make a likeness of Papa. Loveday said as how church candles would be sure to work – but they never didden.' She sighed. 'That man lived a charmed life. That took a full ten years of magicking before 'un was finished.'

'Why did you hate him so much?' Solomon asked gently.

'He was a gambler. He lost us Larksleve Farm; all that my

38

Mama had worked for.'

'And what else?'

'Nothing else.' As she spoke the malevolence left her features, and her face became calm and beautiful, and closed against him.

'But there must have been something,' he cried desperately.

'Nothing.' The finality in her voice told him that she lied. He looked down at his final sketch and knew it to be unique. He moved cautiously towards her as if fearful of snapping some invisible thread.

'Who are you?' he whispered, 'and what are you?' He reached out a hand and began to stroke her cheek. 'I touch human flesh,' he mused. 'Warm blood flows beneath this exquisite surface. But you are not woman, my Blanche! Tell me,' he repeated, 'what are you?'

Blanche tried to look away but could not. The rise and fall of his beautiful voice, his dark eyes, the disturbing words, evoked a response in her that she could not withhold. 'I don't know,' she cried, 'you shudden never ask me they sort of questions!' She paused. When she spoke again her voice was soft and urgent. 'Don't meddle with what is hidden,' she warned him. 'Some people got the kind of souls what is best stepped across on tiptoe. The Devil was often on the loose up in Buckland St Mary, and I bain't nothing like the rest of the Greypaull family. Loveday said I was a changeling, even my own Mama don't care to lay her hand upon me.' She pulled his fingers down from her face. 'Don't touch me, Mr Solomon. I might bring you ill-luck.'

'No, Blanche,' His voice was so low that she could scarcely hear the words. 'The damned can never hurt the damned – and you and I, my dear, are kindred spirits.' In a stronger tone he said, 'There are words in Solomon's Song that describe you perfectly.' He smiled. ' "Who is she that looketh forth as the morning, fair as the moon, clear as the sun, and terrible as an army with banners?'' Women like you, Blanche, beautiful yet destructive, walked abroad when the earth was young. You are indeed "terrible as an army with banners".'

'No,' she cried, 'I don't like to hear that part. Tell me the first bit again about "fair as the moon", I want to remember that for ever.'

❋

Candace maintained a pursed-lipped silence, until the morning when Blanche, quite worn out with her late night jaunts to The Running Footman, could be roused only with difficulty from her bed.

'No good'll come of this,' raged Candace. 'I bet he's never paid you.'

'He got to sell the drawings first,' Blanche mumbled. 'Oh Can, I be so tired, let me lay a minute longer.'

'Out, miss! On your feet this minute, or you'll get us both sacked. You was late lighting fires every day this week. Don't expect me to do your job as well as my own.'

Blanche stumbled from bed and began to dress; her face was white, her eyes rid-rimmed. Candace said, 'That Solomon got a real bad name. He soaks up the gin like water. He's not giving you drink is he?'

Blanche shook her head. 'I told him I didden want it. That brandy you give me – I didden like it. It made me feel dead.'

Candace snorted. 'Well, you certainly looks dead enough, this morning.' She paused. 'This can't go on, Blanche, you knows that don't you. Late nights don't go well with being a skivvy.'

'I got to let him draw me. 'Tis my first chance in London. He knows the important people. Why, he come to this house one day, to see the Master.'

'Cadging,' said Candace. 'Mrs Chumley don't like him,

she reckons he's a proper chancer.'

'No, he's not.' Blanche was thoroughly awake now. 'He's a sweet man. He got a gentle face and lovely manners. He treats me like I was a titled lady.'

Candace looked curious, 'You're not getting sweet on him, are you?'

'Course I'm not. Have you seen his clothes? He stinks of the St Giles Poorhouse.'

'Well, I'm glad to see you're particular in that respect.' Candace adjusted her housemaid's cap, and marched down the back stairs. Blanche followed reluctantly; just out of earshot, she muttered crossly, 'You're not so particular yourself, dear sister, I wudden be seen dead with that ratty liddle milkman.'

※

Blanche had never owned a sovereign. She fondled it beneath the table, stroked it surreptiously, ashamed to let him see the raw state of her hands.

'Oh, Mr Solomon, I never thought to get so much. Why 'tis one whole month's wages.'

He looked surprised. 'What work do you do, Blanche?'

She flushed. 'I be a scullery-maid,' she confessed, 'I didden want you to know, but I s'pose you'll have to.'

'But why? There's no shame in earning an honest living.'

'Yes there is. 'Tis demeaning, so 'tis! I be so mortified to wear a cap and a baggy frock all streaked wi' coal dust.' She giggled unexpectedly. 'You ought to see me when I been blackleading fire-grates. I looks like one o' they nigger-minstrels.'

He reached for the hand that held the sovereign. He turned it palm downwards and stroked the sore knuckles. 'Poor Blanche. You were meant for better things, weren't you?'

'My Mama always says that you can tell the gentry by the state of their hands.'

She touched Solomon's fingers with one of her own. 'You got fine hands. Just look at how long and white they be. I s'pect that do come from always drawing and painting. You never done no hard work.'

'They made me scrub out the privvies when I first went to the Poorhouse. But I'm a resident of some standing now, I get lighter duties.'

Blanche slipped the sovereign into her bodice. 'Tell me who bought the drawings. How much did he pay you?'

Solomon smiled. 'He paid me two guineas.'

'But that means you give me nearly half the money.'

'You earned it, my dear. I want you to pose for me again, if you will.'

'I shan't take my drawers off. Candace says I mustn't.'

'And neither shall you!' He hesitated. 'There's just one stipulation – '

'What's a stipulation?'

'A condition. When I draw you again, I want you to tell me all about your Papa.'

'Whatever for? I told you – he's dead, God rot him!'

'That's it,' breathed Solomon, 'just that look on your face – demonic; the perfect personification of the female satyr, erotic with a hint of sadism – '

Blanche began to laugh. 'You talks just like a book.' She gazed at him enraptured. 'I don't understand one half of what you say, but I'll let you draw me if you promise to talk to me while you do it.'

❀

Candace had warned that the wages of sin would be, if not death, at least instant dismissal, and Blanche, found sleeping in mid-morning in a linen closet, was in fact ejected most promptly from the house in Berkeley Square. There had been time only for a terrified whisper to Candace before she found herself, bag packed and without a reference, on the area steps.

'Where'll I go, Can? Whatever shall I do?'

'Go to Mrs Gimball, in St Martin's Lane. Stay there until I can get out to see you. Have you got any money?'

Blanche nodded. 'I got a sovereign.'

Candace raised thin eyebrows. 'Have you now? Well, in that case your ladyship had better take a hansom-cab. You'll find one easy enough round in Charles Street. You ought to be safe enough in one of them.'

Nothing had changed in St Martin's Lane. The same rickety chairs and battered tables were piled up on the pavement. Blanche paid off the cabby, and picked her way carefully between the smaller items of Mrs Gimball's treasure. There was a gilded birdcage with two bars missing, a flowered chamberpot with a crack right across the middle. The rack of second-hand clothes held some interesting items. There was a frock of peacock-blue silk, a uniform of scarlet, stiff with gold braid, and some unidentifiable garments made of pink lace.

Mrs Gimball was not at all surprised to see her. Blanche sat down on an elegant button-backed chair of green velvet, which had not been present on her previous visit. The flowered half-tea service of bone china had obviously been sold. Mrs Gimball made tea in an old brown teapot.

'Never tho'rt as 'ow you'd last long in Berkeley Square,' she cackled. 'You got a real naughty look abaht you. What 'appened then, dearie? Was you saucy to that old cow, Chumley? Or did his bleedin' Lordship try to pinch your bottom?'

'He never even looked at me,' Blanche said crossly. 'You'd think a man what does paintings 'ud be able to recognise good looks when he sees 'em.'

'Money,' said Mrs Gimball gravely, 'he gets paid a fat figure for makin' ugly women look pretty.' She winked an eye. 'A little bird tells me that you let my Mr Solomon draw you.'

'How did you know that?'

'I'm what you might call his agent, dearie. I sold them drawings for 'im.' She sent Blanche a sly, sideways look. 'Who did yer think sent 'im round to The Running Footman in the first place.' Mrs Gimball waved a dramatic arm. 'Go! I tells 'im. Take your chalks and your bits of paper, and you'll find a gel the likes of which 'ave not been spied in these parts for many a long day.' She paused. 'Wants to stop with me for a bit, does you?'

Blanche said simply, 'I got nowhere else to go.'

'As it so 'appens, I got a long sofa coming in today.' She gestured towards the closed brown door. 'You can sleep in there. You can mind the shop for me in the daytime. You'll soon be earning, dearie, never you fear! You can pay me back when your ship comes in.'

Late nights spent at The Running Footman, and early mornings in his Lordship's kitchen, had left Blanche feeling so exhausted that the sofa, long and velvet-covered seemed more comfortable than any bed she had ever known. But for the table in Hunter's Court, Blanche had never slept alone, there had always been a baby brother or older sister with whom she had been obliged to share. The little back room in St Martin's Lane, with its cracked brown linoleum and uncurtained window, had a door that locked. She could turn the key and be alone whenever she wished.

To begin with, the paintings and drawings ranged around the walls proved unnerving. Eyes followed her from every canvas, and they were not the cold, haughty eyes of the portraits that hung in the Berkeley Square mansion. These were strange, haunted-looking faces; they made her feel uneasy. She came awake to find them gazing at her in the faint light of early morning, and a pain deep inside her welled up and recognised their pain. The words 'lost souls' came into her mind.

She asked Mrs Gimball who had been the models: 'Could

have been anybody, dearie. He's a rum sort o' fellah. He says,' she laid a finger alongside her nose and looked wise, 'he says that he paints Bible pictures. But if some o' them girls and boys come out of the Bible, then, all I can say is, I'm bloomin' glad not to be religious.'

Blanche could see what Mrs Gimball meant. Many of the pictures were of very young boys, their white, unclothed bodies stretched out on stony ground, underneath the bare branches of black, twisted trees.

Blanche tried to sound casual. 'How often do he come here?' she asked.

Mrs Gimball shrugged. 'All depends on the state of 'is health and pocket. It goes in circles wi' Mr Solomon. First of all he'll be skint and sober. He's quiet then, gentle as a lamb. He'll work like a proper demon; hour after hour he'll sit there, and never a bit o' trouble.' She paused. 'I got to warn you, dearie, he's a devil when he's got money to spend. Gin, that's 'is downfall, among other things. But that won't never need to concern you. Don't you never go down to 'Olborn with 'im.'

'Why not?'

'Never you mind! If he wants to draw you he can do it 'ere. You can watch the shop for me while I does a bit o tottin'.'

Minding the shop perched on a plush-seated chair in the autumn sunshine, was a job which suited both her temperament and inclination. Blanche sold several items. Old gentlemen grew skittish, and made purchases they did not need, so that they might stand close and touch her hand when she handed them their change and parcel. Mrs Gimball was delighted. 'I shall 'ave to go tottin' every morning, at this rate. We're nearly out o' stock. Why! business never been so good before, dearie.' She became persuasive. 'Just sit with your legs crossed, eh? That'll show off your ankles. You got nice ankles. Bring the silly men round here like flies to 'oney, that will.'

In October it began to rain, and the furniture and old clothes could no longer be displayed upon the pavement. Selling from within the shop was slower and less exciting; Mrs Gimball no longer departed every morning with the horse and cart, but gave all her time to the renovation and repair of her existing stock. She employed a handyman called Josh who could, with a few nails, a selective eye, and a pot of glue, transform several broken items of furniture into one sound 'antique'. Blanche was also obliged to do her share of the patching and mending, of the steaming and brushing. Sometimes a stylish hat or gown came in.

''Ave it, ducks,' Mrs Gimball said, 'if it's wot you fancies. Come from a toff's house, that did. You won't need to worry too much about fleas and suchlike.' She grinned. 'My Ellen don't like me to go out tottin'. Reckons I'm too old, but it's in the blood, and wot is in the blood will out! My old dad was a totter; well-known he was around St John's Wood and Kensington. I keeps up 'is beat; toffs never know what their stuff is worth. It's tottin' what brings in the bargains.'

Mrs Gimball never cooked. 'Waste of good time,' she told Blanche. St Martin's Lane contained several cookshops, a pie-shop, a confectionary and bakers, and there were always the street-vendors selling ha'penny ices, muffins, and ginger beer. Food could always be fetched in, piping hot and savoury, or cold and sweet according to your taste and mood.

❈

Mr Solomon came back to St Martin's Lane in November. He was found one morning by the handyman Josh, asleep in a corner of the stable. The state of his clothes and person was pitiable. Blanche was instructed to build up the fire and put a big pan of water on to boil. Mrs Gimball dragged the tin bath from its hook on the yard wall, and set it beside the fire-grate. Between them they stripped the verminous rags from his body and removed the soleless galoshes from his feet. They dumped him, half-conscious into the steaming water.

'I don't know 'ow I puts up wiv' 'im,' moaned Mrs Gimball. 'It's the same old story every time. I sells a few pictures for 'im, does 'im a favour, and the minute he's got a few sovereigns in 'is pocket, this is the result.'

Blanche viewed with horror the bruised and skinny frame of the artist. There was an odd sweetish smell about him; she mentioned it to Mrs Gimball.

'That'll be the laundanum, dearie. He's very partial to that, even when he can't afford it.' She soaped and sponged the matted hair and beard with a gentleness that did not match her voiced irritation. When he was clean they lifted him onto a warmed towel, and dried him. A set of fresh underwear, a pair of striped trousers, and a fisherman's knitted sweater had been set to air across the fire-guard. Mrs Gimball pulled a pair of blue silk socks onto the artist's feet. 'Plays the devil with my stock, he does, every time he goes off on one of 'is binges.' She surveyed with satisfaction the de-loused and strangely attired Solomon. 'There now, ducks! Don't he look lovely?' She fetched her purse. 'Nip across the road and fetch me an ounce of fresh-ground coffee; and mind that you watches while they grind it. I don't want no floor-sweepings mixed in with it.'

They fed him on eel-pie and hot spiced doughcake, and made him drink pints of strong boiling coffee. He slept, wrapped up in a blanket, on the rug by the kitchen fire. After three days and nights of shivering and raving, he awoke one morning, remorseful and in his right mind. He asked about his paintings.

'I sold quite a few,' Mrs Gimball admitted, 'but I ain't givin' you no more of that money. I shall buy paint and

47

chalks with it, and paper and canvas. The rest'll have to go towards your new clothes and keep. Like I've told you before, Mr Solomon, I ain't no bleedin' charity ward for you to keep on comin' back to.'

He smiled. 'I'd have been dead long ago, dear lady, but for your kind ministrations.'

She sniffed. 'That's as may be. But now I want you sober and workin'.' She paused. 'I got Blanche livin' here – temporary like. She got kicked out of Berkeley Square, and 'ad nowhere to go. She minds the shop and helps out with the renovations. You was dead keen to paint 'er at one time. Well – 'ere's your chance!'

He looked thoughtful. 'Do you think that she'll allow it?'

Mrs Gimball screeched, 'Allow it? Why, Lord love yer, she's the biggest little show-off I ever did see. You should just be 'ere when I gets a nice hat or gown in. Prances up and down like a duchess, she does. Oh, she's all-there, is Miss Blanche. Got an eye for the men, too.' She looked meaningfully at him. 'Not that she'll bother you in that way, will she?'

He smiled wryly. 'How well you know me, dear Mrs Gimball, and how tolerant you are. Would that my so-called friends had once been so understanding! You're quite right of course. Your little protégée will be quite safe with me. I'll probably be quite a disappointment to her.'

There was a dress of wine-coloured silk hanging on the rail. It was what Mrs Gimball called dee-collow-tee, which must mean, thought Blanche that there was very little of it between waist and chin.

'He wants you to sit for him this morning. I'll watch the shop, ducks. You go and put that dark red frock on – he wants you to wear it. Then you can sit on your long sofa; he always works in that room. Somethin' about the light from that window, he says.' She fussed around Blanche, doing-up buttons and tying ribbons. 'I'll bring you some tea later on, and a nice hot muffin. Posin' for Mr Solomon can be real hard work.'

The wine-red gown was more dee-collow-tee than Mrs Gimball had expected. But, as she exclaimed as she wrestled to make the dress less indecent, there was more of Blanche to be exposed than with most young ladies.

'You got a lovely figure, dearie,' she said sadly, 'shame is that he won't notice.'

'He's real keen to paint me,' said Blanche.

Mrs Gimball shook her head. 'From what he says it's your face wot fascinates 'im.'

'Then why did he want me to put this frock on?'

'He thought as 'ow it 'ud make you feel happy. He's considerate like that. O' course, he might change 'is mind when he sees you.'

'I already told him once, that I won't never take my drawers off.'

'Did you, now? Well, that might make a difference. But you don't need to worry. Mr Solomon ain't made like other men.'

Blanche remembered the tin bath, and giggled. 'He looked very much the man, as I recalls.'

'That don't always mean wot you thinks it does, dearie. Anyway all artists is a bit funny in the 'ead.'

Blanche draped herself artfully across the sofa, one arm outstretched.

'You'll get cramp in about three minutes,' he warned her. 'Just arrange yourself in a comfortable position, and try to forget me and what I'm doing.'

She began to study him as if she were the artist and he the sitter. How ill he still looked, how fragile. He was such a gentleman too: he stood up when she entered the room, he opened doors for her. He always called her Blanche, and never Mary.

49

'Why do you do it?' she asked suddenly.

He looked up, the chalk poised between his fingers. 'Do what?'

'Get drunk – more than drunk – unconscious. You was disgusting. I tell you something, I wudden never have took you into my house. Not in that state.'

'Mrs Gimball,' he said gently, 'is an exceptional lady. She takes in all kinds of people who find themselves in trouble.' He raised a quizzical eyebrow. 'She collects us. Like lame-dogs. Keeps us and feeds us until we get fit and well.'

Blanche coloured. 'I wasn't drunk when she took me in. I earns my keep in this place.'

'So do I, Blanche; at least, I try to.' He looked grim. 'You don't like drunkards, do you? Even when they sober-up?'

'My Mama says that drinking is a sign of weakness.'

'And she's quite right. But people drink for many reasons, usually to forget how unpleasant life is, or has been. Tell me about your Mama, Blanche. She sounds like a most unusual person.'

'Oh, she is! She's tiny – only comes up to my shoulder. She's got red curly hair, and the greenest eyes you ever did see. She's not frightened of nothing, not a swearing man nor a mad bull, that's what Loveday always said.'

'You were very fond of Loveday?'

Blanche moved uneasily. 'Mama was always having babies. Her had no time for me. I wanted –'

'A mother all to yourself?'

She smiled. 'Yes, that's right. I wonder how you knowed that?'

'You were born on a farm, Blanche?'

She nodded. 'In Somerset, in a village called Buckland St Mary. The farm was called Larksleve. Oh, 'twas such a pretty house, all white with pale blue shutters and a thatched roof. There was a porch before the door what had

50

bench seats in it. I often used to sit there with Loveday and whisper secrets.'

'Secrets, Blanche? What secrets could a little girl have?'

'Loveday told me things, about Papa. Things which she never told the others.'

'And she taught you about witchcraft?'

'Oh – us was never witches,' she began to giggle. 'Us never went about on broomsticks.' She became defensive. 'You think that I'm stupid, don't you, just because I come up from the country. Archie Wizard said I talk like a swede-basher. Liddle runty milkman! We wasn't always poor, you know. Larksleve was a big house. It had four bedrooms and a parlour done out elegant in blue. My Papa and Mama could read and write, and so can the first three children in our family –' Her voice thinned into embarrassed silence; she could not remember if she had told him that she was the fourth in a family of seven.

He began to talk to her in a way that seemed to tempt the very soul out of her body. No one save Loveday had ever spoken to Blanche and then waited, attentively, for her to answer. 'You began to tell me about your father,' he said gently, 'you said that he had been a gambler –'

'Worse than that,' she cried, 'he caused my Ma to be disfigured, and all because of his whisky drinking. Her face got burned. She got no sight in her left eye.' She clapped a hand to her mouth and then lowered it, slowly. 'I never meant to say that. 'Tis something I don't tell to strangers. He pledged our home and farm to cover his friend's debt, and the friend run off to Australia and Papa was left to pay up. He was not just wicked, Mr Solomon, he was a fool! And fools is best got rid of.'

'That's a hard philosophy, Blanche. Most of us are fools in one way or another.'

'Well, I bain't, nor never shall be. I made a promise to my Mama before I left Taunton. I told her that she should go in silk before this year's out. 'Tis already November, and I still got most of that sovereign you give me in The Running Footman.'

'There'll be another sovereign for you when I sell these sketches.' He paused, 'Now about your Papa – Blanche?'

❃

Whenever Eliza Greypaull remembered Larksleve it was always summer: harvest-time, and the line of reapers swinging out in a wide arc to cut the standing corn. The Lord of the Reapers set up a smart pace, and Eliza, in blue dress and stiff white bonnet had followed on with Loveday Hayes, tying up the sheaves and stooking. It was always the same sky, dark blue and cloudless; always the same year with Candace at three years old, walking sturdily among the pointy stubble, Madelina still a baby, and the other five children not yet born. Recollection would never take her beyond that year of 1861; all that followed after had been disastrous and best forgotten.

Eliza was the kind of woman who never recognised a burden until it had been lifted from her. The realisation that her husband, Philip, would never again stumble up the wooden ladder to lie drunk beside her in the canopied bed was to come only slowly. To lie awake, tense and fearful until his return, had become habitual; so that even now, with Annis sleeping tranquilly at her side, she lay wakeful into the morning hours.

The sudden removal, within one week, of those two problems, Blanche and Philip, had left Eliza feeling curiously unbalanced with mind and soul still braced to take the strain. They had gone into places where she could not reach them: Philip to lie beside his beloved mother in the Buckland churchyard, and Blanche? Eliza did not care to guess where Blanche might yet lay her head.

Letters from Candace were uninformative and rare; they

52

always began 'Dear Mother, we are both well' and ended, 'yours truly, Blanche and Candace.' There were never sufficient lines for a mother to read between; Eliza did not wish to know if it had rained in London, or that fish was to be bought very cheap in Camden.

Her fears for Blanche were great, and yet to part with her had been a relief. Like her father, Philip, Blanche had always been an unsettled spirit in the household. Her inability to live quietly, her talent for high drama, together with her astounding looks, had made her the least beloved of Eliza's children. There was no humility in Blanche, no respect for her elders and betters. Just to think about her thinned Eliza's lips and brought a crease of pain between her eyebrows.

Hunter's Court, Taunton, comprised ten cottages, two earth privvies, and a standpipe that provided water. It was entered through a narrow alley, and was paved with cracked and uneven flagstones. An open drain ran down from the standpipe to a wide grating in the alley. In dry weather the drain lay stagnant with an accumulation of refuse; in wet weather it overflowed. When the grating was blocked the stench was so bad that the tenants of the Court were obliged, even in high summer, to keep doors and windows closed. Poverty was not only the shortage of money and food, it was the creeping shame of overcrowded rooms, the lack of privacy. Sometimes Eliza wearied of the endless battle with dirt and damp that seeped through her unsound doors and windows. She abhorred the need for lines of washing strung between the houses, the roughness and profanity of all her neighbours. She could feel no affinity with any of them, only sorrow for these women who seemed never to have known love or kindness. Eliza had become accustomed to the sounds of weeping from abused wives and hungry children. To the sight of men without hope, who had walked barefoot for twenty miles in one day in the vain search for work.

53

Her only comfort lay in ritual, in regular church attendance, and the belief that Cleanliness stood next to Godliness. Pleasure was still to be had on a Monday morning from the laundering of her sheets and aprons, from the evening hiss of the flat-iron across still-damp linen, from a gleaming blackleaded range, a whitened doorstep.

Widowhood was a state for which Eliza had never prepared herself; the years of toil on Larksleve, the frequent bearing of children, had led her to believe that it was she who would be laid early to rest. It was in the grey hours towards morning that certain memories swam up to taunt her. She would lie in the canopied bed, suspended in that curious state between sleeping and waking, and know of a certainty that Philip was close by. He came back to her, and not as she had seen him in his last days, robbed of speech and strangely altered. He stood before her now exactly as he had been in youth, tall and graceful, the flaxen curls thick across his forehead, the droop of dissatisfaction in his full red mouth. She would close her eyes towards him, but his image still danced against the darkness. She would bid him depart, but he remained. 'What,' she implored, 'do you want of me? I thought you safe in Buckland churchyard, beside your mother.' The ghost would laugh and shake his head. Philip in death was to prove more articulate than he had ever been in life; she would find herself arguing with him. 'I tried,' she told him, 'I tried hard to make a man out of a callow boy. I tried to make 'ee accept the yoke what the Lord God was pleased to put upon 'ee. Why, in those first months of our marriage I felt like a Crusader, bringing the Word to the unbeliever, and I nearly succeeded! 'Twas your mother what made all the trouble!'

'My mother?' The ghost grew angry. 'Oh no, Eliza. 'Twas your mother what made the trouble. Remember Liza? Her come every day with apple pies and stern advice. Your mother knowed how a husband should be managed.

54

But did you ever take a look at your poor father? John Greypaull was Churchwarden, and a big man in Taunton market, but under his own rooftree he was a mouse.' The ghost nodded and grinned. 'Now I was never a mouse, Eliza. You'll agree to that?'

'You was never a mouse – but you was never a man, neither.'

'What chance did you ever give me? You treated me like a bad child what needed spanking. You was ever cold to me, Eliza. 'Twas your love I needed. Warm arms about my neck, sweet kisses, a bit of kindness. Where was you Liza when I needed you the most?'

'I'll tell you where I was, Philip Greypaull! I was up in the field doing your job. I was milking cows, making cheeses, keeping my children fed and clothed.'

'Your children?' The ghost looked sad. 'Oh yes, they was ever *your* children. But did you ever consider the harm you did 'em; you and your family? They was forced to watch your brothers' beating of me. They saw me humbled, not once but many times. Did you find that revenge was sweet? Did it pleasure you to see me suffer?'

'No! 'Twas never like that! I only wanted you to be –'

'Obedient? A good boy, buttoned-up and decent? Church on a Sunday, visits from Parson, getting drunk when nobody could see me?' The ghost drooped its soft red lips, 'I cudden do that, Liza. Not without help, not without love.'

'There was Blanche,' she said, and at the sound of that word the ghost of Philip seemed to waver and dim, as if the single syllable of that name possessed a magical power that could dismiss him.

'Blanche!' he asked.

'Where did she come from?' Eliza demanded. 'There was more to the conceiving of Blanche than a simple act between a man and a woman.' Her voice grew hushed with the horror of it. 'What Devil's trick did you play on me, Philip?'

'No trick – '

'Then why did I bear a child that looked like neither of us. I never could feel that Blanche was flesh of my flesh, bone of my bone. Do she favour your fancy-woman, Philip? Surely you can tell me now, after all these years?'

He frowned. 'You was ever full of silly notions.'

'No, Philip. I was in all respects a sensible and long-headed woman, and very well you knows it! Have you forgot that night? How you threw me down and forced me to your will upon the hearthstone? Remember what you said? "A daughter this time. A daughter wi' dark-red hair an' eyes like vi'lets, an' she shall be called Blanche." ' Eliza paused. ''Tis a foreign name. Not one that you ever heard in the family, or around the inns of Taunton. Who was she, Philip, and was the child I bore that woman's changeling?'

The question diminished him. She saw him grow vague and translucent, he melted and thinned into the grey light of morning, and she was never to be sure in the years to come that he had ever been there.

❁

The square blue envelope bore the postmark of Wisconsin, USA. It arrived in Hunter's Court in mid-November, and Eliza placed the letter, unopened, in her apron pocket, so that she might prolong the pleasure of anticipation. It was not until her morning chores were finished, and Louis settled quietly in his corner, that she sat down in her rocking-chair beside the fire to read.

The many sheets of notepaper were covered with her cousin's hasty but distinctive scrawl. Dear Rhoda! It must be all of twenty-four years since she had sailed for New York to marry George Salter, an Englishman whom she had scarcely known. Rhoda and Eliza had corresponded regularly; the letters from America had always contained some loyal words in praise of George Salter, but there had been hints of loneliness too, which had troubled Eliza, and then, Rhoda's husband had died, suddenly, at the age of forty-three. Two years later she had married Lieutenant James Black, a veteran soldier of the Civil War. The couple had settled happily, with Rhoda's three children, on a farm in Suamico, Brown County.

The once-yearly letter was a source of delight to Eliza. The accounts of her cousin's life on a farm in Wisconsin, had all the drama and pathos of a romantic saga. Rhoda's usage of strange words and curious phrasing, her descriptions of extreme weather, and odd-sounding animals and crops, only helped to perpetuate the dream.

Suamico. September 30th, 1881

Dear cousin Eliza,

Your letter come at the end of Haying, what was late this year due to *bad* Storms. Was into harvesting right away, so no chance to write until now, I am v. sorry to say. If I am to be truthful, news of cousin Philip's passing tho' sad, was not unexpected. The *drink is a curse*, Eliza, what takes a Husband away from hearth and home, and altho' George was a good provider and husband to me, he was always *out at business*. I can dare to say *now* that things was not always what they should have been between us. I did not know how *lonely* I had been with George until my marriage to Mr Black, what is a fine helpmate and a *Rock* to lean on. Philip *never tried* to be a good Husband to you, and you will be *better off* without him.

How are you left for Money, Eliza? You say that the Greypaulls buried Philip, what will have at least saved you the *cost of a coffin*. I shed a tear over your letter, Dear Cousin, to see that you pawned your wedding ring to buy

57

black. Hope your Greypaull Annuity still pays up regular. Do your children help you?

Our Haying and Harvest turned out awful bad this year. Shall have to buy-in feed if the root-crops fail. Will send you a five-dollar bill in my next letter, if the hens lay well.

Glad to know that Blanche has gone away into Service. Working as the hired help for an employer might *mend her ways* before it is *too late*. You have enough on your plate with poor Louis, being the way he is, what must be *awful bad* for you. As things look right now, Eliza, you must feel that you can never find the strength to *start over*. But *do not* lose heart. Just ask for the Lord's help and I know He will *come through*. Everything what happens got to have a Reason. We complained about the rain last Spring, what rotted the hay and brought us corn-blight. But I look now out my kitchen window, Eliza, and I see how our fields have all greened-up real fine this Fall, thanks to that *same rain*.

My children keep in good health, save for John who still has a weakness of the lungs. Rosa is twenty-two years old already, and walking out with a *nice* young man. There is talk of a *wedding* next year. My Georgie is twenty-three and very handsome if I do say so. He dont work on the Farm with me and Mr Black, but follows the Salters proffeshun of butcher. He is a v. hard worker and aims to have his own meat market real soon. He is not courting yet.

Well, Eliza, harvest is about done and I am thankful when it is over, for I am all *tired out*. Next comes apple-picking, we have a fine grove of apples. Then the threshing. But we shall be through with the dog-days by that time, and into cooler weather. Dont know how I shall ever manage when my Rosa leaves me to get wed.

Must finish now dear cousin. Will read my one page of the Bible, and then to my bed. Love to you and all your children.

Your loving cousin, Rhoda.

Eliza laid the pages down, and closed her eyes. She had a vision of Suamico, Brown County. It was, she thought, probably a lot like Buckland St Mary, only much bigger and not so green and hilly. She pondered on the strange words used by Rhoda. The 'dog-days' must be the long hot days of summer. The season which Rhoda called 'Fall' must be the autumn.

Eliza thought about the many years of their correspondence. The Suamico letters were lengthy and more informative these days. Ah well, they were no longer young wives and mothers, but ageing and weary women in need of a safe and confidential ear. She opened her eyes, gathered up the pages, folded them inside the envelope and replaced it in her apron pocket. Selected passages were sometimes read aloud to Annis and Madelina, but not often. The letters from Rhoda were her private, indeed her only, pleasure.

❀

Blanche walked into Hunter's Court on Christmas Eve, without any warning and looking so changed that Eliza hardly knew her. She wore a gown of purple velvet with a matching fur-trimmed jacket. Her hat, perched among dark-red curls, was a frothy affair of feather-plumes and lace in palest violet. She wore fashionable ankle-high boots, the toes of which were long and pointed. None of these items looked exactly new, but Eliza recognised good quality when she saw it. She looked her daughter up and down, then said sharply, 'Where's Candace?'

'She was in London, Mama, last time I saw her.'

'What do you mean — last time — ?'

'I don't see much of Can, just lately.' Blanche spoke in a voice that was tight and hurt. 'Well, aren't you going to let me in, then? I thought as how you'd be glad to see me. After all, 'tis six months since I went away.'

Eliza moved and allowed Blanche to enter; she put up a

hand to her sightless eye, and began to rub the scarred flesh of her left cheek with a nervous, familiar gesture. ''Twas a shock, Blanche,' she murmured, 'seeing you sudden like that, when I thought you was in London.' She turned to Annis. 'Put the kettle on, quick now! Your sister's had a long journey.'

Blanche removed her hat and jacket, hung them on the back of a chair, and went to sit close beside the fire. She looked to where Madelina sat sewing in the light of a tall lamp. 'Well, Mina. Don't you even say hello, then? You bain't usually so quiet.'

Madelina glanced at her mother. ''Tis like Mama said, we wasn't expecting to see you. 'Specially on your own and at Christmas.' She hesitated. 'I don't suppose you'll be staying for long, though?' Her tone was hopeful, her meaning not to be mistaken.

Eliza cried, 'Now, Mina! That's no way to welcome your sister.'

Mina coloured, but looked determined. 'But 'tiv got to be said, Mama.' She turned to face Blanche. 'The Poolwall collar factory is on short-time. We've had Simeon and Louis down with fever.' She pointed towards the cupboard-bed where the two boys lay side by side. 'What with the cost of physic for them, and me being on half-wages – why, we just can't afford to feed another mouth.' Mina laid down the blouse she had been mending. 'You was sent away to make Mama's burden lighter. What did you have to come back for? 'Specially at Christmas.'

Blanche stood up. She reached for her jacket and from its pocket she withdrew a tiny purse. Purposely dramatic, she opened the purse very slowly, withdrew three sovereigns, and tossed them onto the kitchen table. She addressed Annis. 'Get your shawl on, maid. Never mind that old tea-kettle. Hurry up, now! The shops is all but closing. Take a big bag. Buy as much food as you can get with the money.

Don't you dare bring me any change back!'

'Oh, Blanche.' Eliza covered her face with both hands, and began to weep.

''Tis all right, Mama. I come by it honest. Tidden what you think it is. You got no leave to worry.'

Annis was back within the hour, laden down with groceries. She had bought a whole pork loin, a rabbit and a pheasant; fresh vegetables and fruit; a whole quarter pound of tea; a blue bag filled with sugar; quantities of flour and butter. So great was the amount of food purchased with three sovereigns, that she had been forced to pay a street urchin tuppence for his help in carrying home the load. That night they ate hot meat pies, and spiced doughcake, thick with sugar icing. Even the pale little boys in the cupboard-bed revived when they smelled the rare odours of good food.

When the table was cleaned and the dishes washed, Eliza said, 'Annis can share a bed with Mina. You, Blanche, can sleep upstairs alongside me.'

Blanche said, 'I'd as soon sleep on the kitchen table and that won't be for the first time, will it?'

'But there's no need now, maid. Us got more room to spare these days. You had a long journey. You needs your rest.'

Blanche laughed, a forced, unlikely sound that made Eliza shiver. 'You don't think, not for one minute, that I could ever sleep in the same bed where that old devil died?'

'Blanche! Don't ever let me hear you speak like that again about your father.'

Blanche looked at the face of her mother, scarred and white with anger. At Madelina, pursed-lipped and disapproving, at the sweet but terrified features of Annis, who was very young for her fourteen years.

'Hypocrites!' she shouted, 'every one of you. You hated him as much as I did, but now he's dead, and gone to Hell, you pretends that 'tis all forgiven. How can you forget,

61

Mama? How can you sleep in the same bed where that devil died? Because he was a devil, and don't you never doubt it.'

'And so be you, Blanche.' The incongruous words came oddly from the innocent-looking lips of Madelina. 'You makes trouble everywhere you goes. I wonder,' she said softly, 'I just wonder what mischief you've been up to in London. You comes in here, dressed up to kill, you leaves off your mourning, though 'tis only six months since Father's passing. You throws money on the table as if we was starving dogs what needed to be fed –'

'And who was the first one to stick her fork into that meat pie?' demanded Blanche. 'Who grabbed the biggest lump of doughcake?' She leapt to her feet, and towered over Madelina. 'And as for Father's "passing" as you calls it, let me tell you this – he was lucky to die decent in that bed, with all his family round him. He should have had his last gasp down in the gutter. 'Tis where he belonged.'

'You wasn't there, at the very end, was you, Blanche?' It was Annis, tremulous but vitriolic, who had joined in the chorus of condemnation. 'I shall never forget, as long as I live, the way you cursed him when he lay dying. We all heard it, through the ceiling. I reckon Papa must of heard it too.'

'I hope he did! I hope he went through the Fiery Gates with my words ringing in his ears. I hope he –'

Eliza said, 'That'll be enough, maids, I can't stand no more of this. We should be down on our knees and praying. 'Tis night of our dear Saviour's birth. We should be giving thanks to God, not quarrelling.'

✸

They ate pork-loin on Christmas Day with cabbage and potatoes, and thick hot gravy. Mina, who, despite a lack of practice had not lost her feather-touch with pastry, produced an apple-pie that was a delight to eat. Prayer and full bellies had mellowed tempers, and the exchange of gifts brought sobs of joy from all three sisters, so easily could they pass from anger to tears. Blanche received a hair-tidy and an embroidered hanky from Annis and Mina. They were entranced by her gift of necklaces of blue glass (courtesy of Mrs Gimball's junk-shop).

Blanche waited until mid-afternoon, when the table was cleared and the fire burning brightly. 'Sit down, Mama, I've got something for you.'

Her mother sat down, the unopened package in her lap.

'Open it then,' urged Blanche, ''tis what I promised back in June.'

Eliza pulled back the wrappings to reveal a bolt of soft grey silk. She lifted it with trembling fingers, and saw the firelight shimmer and dance in its reflection.

'Oh maid,' she breathed, 'you shudden never have done this. It must have cost a small fortune. I only ever wore silk but the once in my whole life. I went clothed in this on the day of my wedding. Your father wore a suit that was just this same colour, dove-grey, with a ruffled shirt of lavender with gloves to match.'

Blanche said, 'I don't want you to be a lifelong widow, not like the old Queen, forever mooning-about and mourning for that Albert. Your first year of black will be up in June, that gives you and Mina a good five months to sew the dress.' She touched her mother's arm. 'I want to see you going fine to church on a Sunday evening. I promised to bring you silk before this year was out, didden I?'

Eliza looked uncomfortable. ''Tis a fine and generous gift, Blanche, I thanks you for it, from the bottom of my heart. But I got to ask you a question, 'tis my duty as your mother –'

Blanche giggled, 'You wants to know where the money come from.' She sent a look that was all hatred to where Annis sat, close to Madelina. 'I know what you two be

63

thinking. 'Tiv been writ plain enough on your faces since the minute I stepped in through the door. You pair have already decided that your wicked Blanche have gone up to London for a strumpet!'

The silence was so complete that snowflakes could be heard as they whispered against the tiny window. Blanche said, 'Well – you be quite wrong, maids. Blanche have got more sense than what you give her credit.'

'Where are you living?' asked Eliza.

'Oh, I left that old job. I was never cut out for scrubbing doorsteps. I knowed it on the first day, Mama. Why! They even took away my name. They called me Mary.'

Eliza said, 'I asked where you were living?'

'Well, 'twas like this,' Blanche switched from nonchalance to a tone that was overly confidential, 'I got to know a better class of people when I got to London. I met this Mrs Gimball what keeps a very posh shop in St Martin's Lane. She sells furniture and pictures –'

Eliza studied the worn purple velvet gown, the ankle-high boots, 'You means she keeps a pawn-shop, don't you?'

'No, Mama! 'Tis mostly carriage-trade at Mrs Gimball's. I went to live there back in the summer.'

'Shop-girls don't earn sovereigns, Blanche.'

'No more they don't, Mama. But I idden no shop-girl.'

'What are you, then?'

'I'm an artist's model.'

Madelina laughed outright, Annis sniggered, and Eliza looked perplexed. 'An artist's what?'

'A model, Mama. For paintings – like what they hangs on the walls – in big houses. There's this famous artist, he's a good friend of Mrs Gimball. He's going to paint a picture of me what'll make us both rich.'

'Where did you get all this money, Blanche?'

'Oh – he've already done several sketches of me. He uses chalks mostly, you know, sometimes pen-and-ink, it

64

depends on the light and how he's feeling at the time.' Her easy use of unfamiliar terms had them thoroughly confused. 'Mrs Gimball sells the sketches. They fetches upwards of two and three guineas. I get thirty per cent of the price.'

'What's thirty per cent mean?' asked Annis.

Blanche flushed. 'Never you mind, miss. 'Tis more gold than you'll ever see in all your life.'

Eliza said, 'I don't know much about such things. But artists – is you sure that this is a respectable occupation?'

'Mr Solomon paints Bible pictures, Ma! You can't be more religious than that, now can you? He paints Ruth and Jezebel, and Salome.'

Annis grinned. 'Salome and Jezebel idden decent.'

'How do you know,' snapped Blanche, 'you can't read a single word.'

'No more can you, Blanche Greypaull, and I know what's in the Bible. I go to church every Sunday, which is more than you do.'

'Do you go to church, Blanche?' Eliza sounded troubled.

'Not regular, Mama. I been busy you see, but things is settling down now.'

'Promise me you'll go in future.'

'I promise.'

'Thank you for the silk, maid. 'Tis a beautiful gift.'

Blanche smiled. 'That's only the beginning. There's plenty more where that came from.' She bent to kiss her mother's cheek. 'You always wanted daughters what behaved like ladies – well, you just watch me Mama! Just you watch me!'

❄

Madelina had not enjoyed Christmas even though the table had been laden, unexpectedly, with good food. Better, she thought, to have eaten a crust of bread in the peace of the Lord than to have dined, extravagantly, in the company of sinners. That Blanche was a sinner Mina had no doubt. One look at that voluptuous figure swathed in purple velvet, one glimpse of the ridiculous confection of lace and feathers perched among the auburn curls, had been enough to confirm what she had long suspected. Blanche was doomed to become a fallen angel. Whether she had already fallen was not quite clear; that tale about a furniture shop (high-class?) and the artist who painted only Bible pictures, had a ring of truth about it. Blanche had always been the one to whom things happened; she invited danger, craved excitement. For her to have worked soberly, as a scullery-maid in London, had never seemed likely to Madelina. She had been glad when her sister announced that she was returning to her new friends. 'Mr Solomon,' Blanche had said grandly, 'can't paint or draw a single picture these days unless he got me in it.'

It had been an uneasy weekend; apart from the bitterness and quarrels which always occurred when Blanche was present, there had been the risk that David might call, and Blanche still in the house. David Lambert was a Sunday-school teacher; he worked as a house-painter with his father in their small journeyman's business. He was a sober young man who rarely smiled, and never laughed. He was tall and slender, with dark curling hair, a pale complexion, and a high noble brow. Madelina was proud to be seen walking with him on the streets of Taunton.

Theirs was a shy and simple courtship. Mina tried to be like Mama in every way: steadfast and truthful, dependable and God-fearing. In one respect only was she determined to be unlike her mother. When it came to the matter of a husband, it would be Madelina who did the choosing, and that choice must be as different from Papa as it was possible for a man to be. So far, the signs had all been in his favour. David was respectful towards her: a slight pressure of the fingers when he took her hand on parting was as far as he had attempted to go. In fact, it was this very rectitude which caused Madelina her greatest problems.

To conceal from David the more outrageous details of her family's history had become Mina's main preoccupation. Secretly, she believed that Papa's death had been a 'happy release' in more than one way. It had become increasingly difficult for her to present a drunken, reprobate father as a noble figure more to be pitied than blamed. She had told the sad tale of Larksleve Farm to David and his family. How Papa, yeoman and freeholder of many acres of fine land, had, in the goodness of his heart, pledged everything he owned in order to save a friend from a Debtor's Prison. That the friend had reneged on the debt, said Madelina, explained the sorry state of her Papa, who had been Driven to Drink by his disappointment.

The departure of Blanche and Papa, both within one week, had lifted the anxiety from Mina's heart. Her remaining family, even though still housed in Hunter's Court, now presented a more acceptable aspect. After all, her Mama was a lady, she knew how to behave in any situation. David had been impressed by the family hymn-singing on a Sunday evening, with Mama seated at the piano, her children gathered around her. Annis and Simeon were not yet old enough to prove disgraceful, and poor Louis had turned out to be a useful source of pity and commiseration. All in all, Mina had thought, the standing of the Greypaull family had never been so high. Until Blanche came back. A meeting between David and her sister had been avoided this time, but some explanation of Blanche would need to be worked out for future visits. Although her face had been washed clean for the sake of Mama, Blanche had actually boasted to Madelina that she regularly used paint and powder when in London.

❀

Her brother Jack had remained at the Bishop's Hull stables

throughout Christmas, so that the married jockeys and grooms might spend time with their children. He came home on the morning of New Year's Day to find a meal of roast pheasant and apple-pie.

'Have you been poaching, young 'un?' he teased Simeon.

Madelina sniffed, and waved at the laden table. 'Courtesy of the lady Blanche,' she informed him, 'what is now in the money, since she set herself up as an artist's model in St Martin's Lane, London.'

Jack looked to his mother. 'Set herself up as a what?'

'A model, Jack. 'Tis quite true. She've bought us enough food to last three weeks. It seems as how this famous artist is making pictures of her.'

Jack grinned. 'Well, she certainly got the looks for it – and the nerve! Do she have to take all her clothes off?'

This was an aspect that had not occurred to Madelina, and most certainly not to Mama. They both blushed fiercely.

'Oh, Jack – you don't really think she – ?'

'Course not. I was only joshing.' He put an arm around his mother's shoulders. 'You know me, Ma! Anything for a laugh!'

Madelina thought that her heart would burst with love for him. How thin he was, how strained his features, although he was only eighteen years old. She longed to take him in her arms, as she had done when they were children on Larksleve, and he had taken a tumble from his pony.

'How be things with you, Jack?' she asked.

'Pretty good. I had three wins last week at Wincanton. There's talk of me being put-up for more important races.'

'They tells me that you is still riding bare-back.'

He laughed. 'You knows well that I could never abide the saddle.'

'But 'tis so dangerous. I worry every time you goes off racing.'

'There's risk in everything, Mina. That liddle bit of

chancyness is all what makes life worth living.'

'Not for me,' she said quietly. 'Never for me and David.'

❊

Annis put on the blue beads, gift of her sister Blanche, and smiled at the reflection in the spotted mirror. The coloured glass was the exact blue of her eyes; her brother Jack had said so. She lifted a strand of the fair hair that spread across her shoulders, and twisted a curl around her finger. The face in the mirror was that of her Papa when young; even Mama had remarked on the likeness. 'You got your father's good looks,' she had said, 'he was fair and blue-eyed, with that same high colour on his cheekbones.' Mama had sighed then. 'But don't you worry, maid. You don't have his wild nature.'

Annis had grown, quite suddenly. She stood head and shoulders higher than Jack, and Mina, and was almost as tall as Blanche. Sometimes, just lately, Annis had felt the wild nature of Papa rise up in her, and she was afraid. There was always Mama, of whom she must be mindful. Mama who had suffered so much, and on whom the burdens still lay heavy. Not to add to her mother's sorrows was all that Annis truly wanted; the rebellion that seized her was a legacy from her evil father, and must be kept down at all costs.

Papa's death had frightened Annis. The fear she had felt at the sight of him, speechless and incapable of movement, had struck into her soul, and she could never lose it. When Blanche had refused to sleep in the canopied bed, Annis had joined with Mina in condemnation of her. But, secretly, she envied Blanche her dash and fire. Mina said that Blanche had been cast from brazen metal; oh, but she had style! Annis had simply ached to try on the velvet gown, to perch the cheeky little feathered hat on her own head, if only for a moment.

'What did you reckon on Blanche?' she asked Simeon.

Simeon, who had not received a gift from his visiting sister, was still smarting from the hurt. 'Stuck-up hussy,' he muttered. 'She's no better than she should be! Us don't want the likes of her in this house. Good job when she went back to London.'

'Ooh Sim! I don't know where you learns words like that. Don't you let Mama hear you.'

''Tis what they be all saying in the Court. 'Tiv had the whole place by the ears ever since she come prancing back yer.'

Simeon had all the toughness and wisdom of the street urchins with whom he spent his days. It was only Annis who was privy to his secrets. She knew that he did odd jobs around the Market. That he sometimes begged on street-corners, and sang for farthings. He was capable of violent rages, which seemed close to seizures, during which his lips would be flecked with foam. Even Mama had learned to be careful in her dealings with Simeon. Already, he looked much more like his dead Papa than did Annis. But so far, no one in the family had dared to say so.

❀

The end of the first day of this new year, 1882; Jack had gone back to the stables in Bishop's Hull, and Blanche, it was to be hoped, was safe again in London. The house was quiet, the children sleeping; Eliza took the bolt of grey silk, secured its wrappings, and laid it away in the dresser drawer. She smiled to see the blue beads, property of Madelina, already thrust into a dusty corner, and never likely to be worn.

Annis had worn her beads. Eliza had watched her, before the mirror, turning this way and that, touching and admiring. How pretty she was! So tall and slender, so fair, and with the sweet expression of an angel. How lucky to

70

have a daughter like Annis, who never gave, nor would ever give, her mother one minute's worry. Madelina, on the other hand, now carried primness to excess. Eliza nudged the discarded necklace; she supposed that David Lambert would not have approved of even this small vanity in Mina.

Eliza sat in her rocking-chair beside the dying fire, and her hand of its own volition sought and found the bareness of her throat. She looked up to see Annis on the stepladder. 'I couldn't sleep, Ma. I don't like to be in that bed by myself.' Annis came down and crouched beside the fire. Eliza could just see the blue glass beads beneath the flannel nightgown.

'You be fond of your necklace?'

'Oh yes, Ma. 'Tis the prettiest thing I ever had.'

'I had a necklace once, maid. 'Twas a heavy thing made of silver flowers, with coral petals. I got it from a gypsy girl. She was my friend.'

'You was friends with a gypsy?'

The shocked tones of Annis made Eliza smile. 'They idden so very different from the rest of us, you know! A bit fiercer perhaps, but then so might you be if you was driven all your life from pillar to post, and got your bit of dinner from the fields and hedges.'

'I think I remember her,' said Annis. 'Didden we meet her on the Taunton road when we was turned-off of Larksleve? She said something to me, but I can't remember what it was. I was frightened of her, Ma. She looked so dark and angry.'

'Meri always looked like that. It didden signify much, it was just her way. We only had high words just the once. She come up to Larksleve and asked me to give back her pendant. I said no, and just for a second I thought she was going to kill me.'

'It must have been pretty special.'

'Oh, it was, maid! That pendant lying on my neck meant

71

six strong children. No matter what else went wrong on Larksleve, I was always delivered safe of healthy babies.'

'What happened to the gypsy?'

'She had twins the first time. Two boys with crooked spines and shoulders. Then she had a daughter what never drew breath. When Meri come to me on Larksleve it was just six months before the birth of Blanche, she was also with child.' Eliza paused. 'I was in a funny state of mind at that time. Like I was possessed of a devil.'

'What happened?'

'Do you remember when we met the gypsy on the Taunton road she had a tall boy with her? That was Jye Carew. He was born with bad hearing. By the time he was eight years old that poor boy had gone stone-deaf.' Eliza paused. 'Oh yes, that pendant was a powerful magic. It worked for me even though I'm not a gypsy. The bailiffs took it away from me just before your brother Louis was born. I shudden never have parted with it.'

Eliza stroked the fair head that nodded against her knee. 'Time we two was in bed, eh maid?' She sighed. 'I wonder what your sister, Blanche, is up to at this minute?'

'I wonder,' said Annis, 'whatever happened to that poor deaf boy, Jye Carew.'

❀

To be sent away from Montacute to work on an important abbey or cathedral was the ambition of every apprentice mason who worked on Ham Hill. Jye had heard the stories told by the old men, about St Paul's and Westminster. He had imagined himself employed on the loving restoration of work done long ago by the medieval masons, dreamed of a lodge or workshop in some distant city where he might demonstrate his skills. But when the time came, and George Mitchell's selective finger had settled upon him, Jye Carew had found several good reasons why he could not leave his home village, and his dependent mother.

To begin with there was the garden. His mother was not like other women. He might show her what needed to be done in the season – but would she remember? He knew, had always known, that strange rhythms ruled his mother's actions. A certain morning sky, the wind coming from a special quarter, a glimpse of painted waggons winding around the Hill, and Meridiana would rise up and leave her cottage. Usually she would be absent for hours, sometimes for several days. Since his father's death in the Ham Hill quarry she had become even less predictable, and he feared for her. Would she remember to feed his tame rabbits, his doves and tumblers; would she care for his roses?

Jye's inheritance from Luke, his father, had been his set of mason's tools and a single damask rose bush. Two bequests that had been equally significant to a boy whose deafness was increasing. The mason's tools had ensured him the status of a craftsman; the roses were his love, his secret sweetness, his passion. On the evening before his departure for London he walked in the wintry garden, he knelt on the frozen earth, touched the bare bushes and imagined the miracle of June when they would be full of leaf, and heavy with scented blossom.

He went back to the cottage and found his mother, seated in her usual position, on a low stool close beside the fire. He watched as she handled the sharp knife with precision, whittled swiftly at the piece of elder wood, until a chrysanthemum head grew between her fingers. A row of the completed flower-heads lay beside her. Later on she would make dyes of red and yellow, and a deep shade of saffron. She would dip each wooden bloom until it had absorbed sufficient colour, and then mount it on a spray of privet. This was her winter occupation, along with the making of clothes-pegs and the distillation of certain herbs.

It was in winter that the skills of Meridiana were most in demand. Jye was proud of, and yet embarrassed by her.

It angered him to see her hook an arm through the hawking-basket, and set off down the road to Odcombe and distant hamlets as if she were some destitute pedlar-woman forced to cadge for pennies. He placed a hand on her shoulder, and she looked up at him with an intensity that made his heart shake. To be the recipient of so much love weighed heavily on him. He half-hoped that even now she might try to persuade him against the trip to London.

'I still bain't sure about all this — ' he began, ''tis a long way off if you should fall ill and need me.'

She turned to face him, so that he might read her lips. ''Tis your one chance to see the world, boy! Why, when I was your age I was well-travelled. You'm never even see'd the ocean, Jye. Never see'd the great rivers and hills. You still thinks that Montacute is the whole world. I want you to go, Jye. I want you to set your foot, just once, on the Queen's Highway.'

'And will you still be here when I gets back?' His secret fear, finally spoken, made her smile. 'I won't never leave this cottage no more. I won't leave your father's grave, nor your two brothers, even though they locks their door against me these days.' She shook her head. 'Don't worry about I. If I fall sick, there's always your father's old mother that I could rely on, miserable old besom that she is!'

Jye made his last visits, first to his father's grave, and then to his grandmother, Charity Carew. She peered at him with eyes made weak from a lifetime of stitching gloves by rushlight. 'So, George Mitchell picked you out to work for him in London?'

'I was busy on a window for Cerne Abbas; I looked up, and saw Mr Mitchell, there he stood watching me. That made I proper nervous, Grandma! I all but dropped my chisel and mallet.'

' "What's your name, boy?" he asked me.

' "Carew, sir," I said. "Jye Carew."

' "Son of Luke, what was killed by a fall of stone in the quarry?"

' "The very same, sir."

' "What's your age, boy?"

' "I be coming seventeen — next week, sir."

' "How would you fancy a spell of work in London, Jye? As you must know, I got the biggest monumental masons' business in the City. I does contract work on St Paul's and the Abbey. There's a big job coming up in Westminster. I could use a strong feller like you."

' "I don't know, sir. I got a widowed mother —"

' "'Twould be experience for 'ee. They tells me that you be a promising boy. Now tell me, Jye. Where do you think the medieval masons got their training and experience? Why, 'twas in the lodges of the great cathedrals and abbeys. That was what turned rough handlers of stone into skilled stone-carvers and masons; it could do the same for you, boy!" '

Charity Carew said, "Tis a great favour from Mr Mitchell. Your father would of bin so proud. I minds the time when Luke was chose to work on that church in Buckland St Mary. Nineteen-year-old, he was, and never set foot beyond this village.' Charity wiped her eyes with the corner of her apron. 'That's where he met up with they gypos, they dirty hedgecrawlers.' She turned on Jye. 'Don't you never let no fancy woman trap you. Don't you never listen to no sweet words.'

He began to edge away towards the door. 'Well — goodbye then, Grandma. I'll see you when I get back.' It was always the same story whenever he visited Wash Lane, the same condemnation of his mother and her gypsy family.

❀

Three Montacute men had been chosen by George Mitchell

75

to work on the Westminster Abbey contract. There was Jye, inexperienced but strong and healthy, and two middle-aged brothers, Adge and Joby. 'I don't like to employ the Cockney masons,' George Mitchell had said. 'They got a tendency to be flighty, late to bed and then weary the next morning. I can trust the fellers from my home village, all good, God-fearing Baptists, not likely to give way to the temptations of the City.' But the Montacute masons would not lack for all of their home comforts; six barrels of rough-cider were travelling in the goods' compartment of the West Country train, and each man carried a round ripe Cheddar cheese in his canvas bag.

'I hopes,' said Joby Stagg, 'that you knows your good fortune in being picked out for this pertickler job?'

Jye, who felt large and awkward in the narrow railway compartment, stared at his corduroy covered knees and mumbled, 'Oh, I knows it, Mr Stagg.'

Joby nodded. 'Us was a bit surprised that Mr Mitchell chose 'ee. You being only seventeen, and not hearing proper. Let's hope the man knows what he's doing.'

'George always knows what he's doing.' Adge Stagg grinned at Jye. 'Don't you take no notice of thik old misery there in the corner! You was chose for your skill, boy. You done a fine job on that window for Cerne Abbas. Twas just your good luck that George Mitchell should come into the lodge and see it.' Adge turned his face away, and began to talk to Joby. For a minute or two Jye watched their lips, shifted his gaze from one face to the other, and then he looked away. Conversations in which he had no direct involvement were tedious to follow.

They arrived in London in mid-afternoon, and were met by George Mitchell who helped them off-load the cider kegs onto his waiting waggon. They were driven to the master-masons' yard in Westminster, and then made the short walk into the narrow street where lodging had already been arranged for them with a Mrs Murphy. Jye, whose knowledge of his surroundings was dependent on sight and touch, was finding the January aspect of London a dull and gritty prospect until he came into the Abbey precincts and had his first sight of the church. It was then that he stopped walking and stood, as if frozen, in the middle of the pavement. Adge took Jye's elbow and swung him around so that they stood facing one another.

''Tis a humbling sight, eh boy?'

Jye nodded.

'There's something about it,' said Adge, 'what do lodge in a man's heart and bide there. There've been a church on that spot for nigh on eight hundred years, Jye! And 'tis fellers like we — masons and stone-carvers — what have made it all come to pass.' Adge wagged a finger towards the Abbey. 'They cudden have done none of it without us, my old acker!' He gave Jye a gentle push. 'Come on now, 'tis getting dimpsey. 'Twill be dark soon, and Mrs Murphy'll think we be all got lost.'

Over the years, Mrs Murphy's house had adapted solely to the requirements of stone-masons. A good fire, was of prime importance, especially in winter, when wet boots and clothing needed almost daily drying. Equally necessary was the thick mutton stew which simmered endlessly on the hob; and the pallets filled with clean straw which lined the three box-beds in the widow's kitchen. Mrs Murphy welcomed the Stagg brothers as old and valued lodgers. At the sight of Jye she gasped and then laughed.

'Holy Mother! Will ye look at the size of this one. What'll I do with him? He'll never fit into the box-bed.'

Jye flushed and looked embarrased. Mrs Murphy, hands on hips, continued to survey him. 'Ah, but he's beautiful, so he is! Oh, I wish I was thirty years younger. What's your name then, my darlin'?'

'He's called Jye,' said Joby Stagg, 'and you'll have to

speak into his face if you wants him to understand you. He's pretty well stone-deaf. Don't even hear church-bells.'

Tears filled the widow's eyes. 'Ah, the poor boy! And him so big and handsome. I bet he drives all the girls wild even if he can't hear.'

Adge said quietly, 'He's shy, Mrs Murphy. He lives with his mother; she's a widow and a bit touched in the head. I never once saw him speak to a girl, not even after chapel. Keeps hisself very much to hisself, Jye does.'

Settling into number 12 Great Smith Street was a simple matter. The Cheddar cheeses were placed on a stone slab in Mrs Murphy's pantry. Their spare shirts and trousers were put in a wooden trunk in a corner of the kitchen. The canvas bags that contained the tools of their mason's craft were put safely away in a walk-in cupboard underneath the stairs. Three large wooden bowls were set out on the kitchen table, and the blackened cauldron, placed on an iron trivet, was dumped between them.

'There you are, my darlin's,' cried Mrs Murphy, 'I used a whole sheep's head in that lot, and the bread was fresh made this very mornin'.' She went away, and Adge Stagg began to ladle stew into Jye's bowl. 'I hopes you like mutton, boy. 'Tis all she ever cooks, summertime and winter. You'll find all sorts in it, she chucks in whatever she's got handy.'

By drawing his knees up underneath his chin, and hunching his shoulders, Jye just fitted into the box-bed. He slept at once, and all his dreams were of those flying buttresses and the soaring tower glimpsed as he had walked from the master mason's yard, that part of the Abbey which Adge had called the South Face.

❈

They rose early, and after a meal of weak tea and the crusts left over from last night's supper, they prepared to leave the house. Adge had warned Jye's mother that her son would be working at times on the Abbey face, and Meridiana had provided woollen underwear, thick flannel shirts, and warm jerseys. Jye put on his mason's apron, picked up the canvas bag that held his tools, and stepped out into the City of Westminster.

His usual route to work took him up a winding hill-path, between hedges, and with rutted earth lying hard or soft beneath his boots, according to the season. Today he walked on pavements, between rows of houses. He could smell water, and knew that there must be a river close by. He felt nervous and uneasy in the stiffness of new shirt and trousers. Adge Stagg gripped his forearm, and turned Jye around to face him. 'Us got a few minutes to spare. Before we starts work I want to show 'ee something.'

They walked through a grassy place that looked like a village green, but which Adge called the Dean's Yard. They began to skirt the Abbey, following a narrow path between the great height of the building. They passed a huddle of wooden huts and piled-up stone, which stood in a sheltered bay between high walls. 'That's our lodge,' said Adge, 'that's where you'll be working.'

They came at last to an entrance called the north porch; Jye followed Adge into Westminster Abbey, and knew at once that of all the days of his life this was to be the one he would always remember. Winter daylight filtered down from painted windows, and his mind could not hold all the mouldings and carvings, the images and figures, the delicate tracery, the columns and arches. He thought about the men who had raised this building, the medieval masons who had laboured lifelong, and never lived to see their handiwork finished. He felt the break of pain deep inside his chest, and tears lay wet and cold on his face. Adge Stagg laid a rough hand on Jye's forearm, but his voice was gentle. ''Tis an awesome sight, eh boy, first time of looking? Us got nothing in Montacute to match this. Come on now, us had best be getting back to the lodge. Our Joby don't much hold with sightseeing.'

There were fourteen masons at work on the Abbey. They formed separate groups, each one accountable to his own master-mason. The Montacute men had been instructed by George Mitchell to begin work on the worn fabric of the north porch. Jye was set to the retooling of stone that had lost its original hue of gold in the grimy air of London.

'Now,' Joby had said, 'now's the time for 'ee to learn how to work with your left hand as well as your right. You'll find that you needs a crafty left hand to work your way into a right-hand corner.'

Silence, for Jye, was a natural condition. He rarely entered into conversations, never volunteered an opinion. To have lived for so long beyond the hearing of others had set him apart. He could work with these men, stand beside them at adjacent bankers, eat and drink with them at the break-hour, sleep in an adjoining box-bed in Mrs Murphy's kitchen, and still not be of their company. When the first break-hour came at noon, he ate quickly, and returned to his post in the north door of the Abbey. It had begun to snow, fine powdery flakes were falling out of a yellow sky, and Jye moved deeper into the porch for shelter. He was on his knees examining a cracked stone in the fabric, when the edge of a purple velvet hem brushed against his hand. He looked up into the angry face of a young woman who, he guessed, had already been speaking to him for some time without gaining any answer.

'What's up with you, then?' the girl was saying, 'be you deaf or something?'

Jye remained on his knees. He put a hand to each earlobe and nodded. 'That's right,' he said quietly, 'I be total deaf, ma'am.'

The girl looked uncertain. 'Don't you josh me, young feller, I don't like to be laughed at.' She became indignant.

'You can't be deaf, not at your age!'

'From my childhood, ma'am. I wudden lie about it, now would I?'

'Didden you never hear proper?'

'I could hear when I was a liddle shaver — I learned to talk, to read and write. That hearing all growed less as I got older; by the time I was ten the world had got to be a very quiet place.'

The girl shivered and drew her cloak about her. 'I live in St Martin's Lane,' she told him. 'I was taking a stroll through Trafalgar Square and I come into Whitehall.' She looked coy. 'I'd heard that there was some handsome fellers down at the Horseguards, but the only ones I see'd was perched high up on their horses. Not so much as a wink did I get from a single one.' She gazed vaguely about her. 'I must of walked quite a long way. I started to think about home, and things what I promised to my Mama. Then I spotted this old church at the end of the road.' She became confidential. 'Between you and me, I bain't really a believer. Truth to tell, I do hate churches. But I promised Mama to say a prayer.' He could see the glint of unshed tears in her eyes. 'I gets a bit lonely sometimes, but I can't never live no more at home. I can't never do nothing right for my Mama. I don't s'pose praying'll make any difference. But a promise is a promise.'

Jye turned away, embarrassed. He picked up his chisel and mallet and prepared to resume work, but the girl put a hand out and grabbed his sleeve.

'Don't turn your face from me,' she ordered. 'You can't understand a word I say when you're not looking at me.' She looked pleadingly at him. 'There's nobody my own age what I can talk to.' Her face grew hard. 'Anyway, you should be glad that I bother with you. There can't be many maidens what'll waste their time on a deaf bloke.'

'I got work to do, ma'am.'

All at once she seemed to change, to become another person, the very hand on his arm had a different feel about it. She smiled and leaned close enough for him to smell her perfume. 'Don't you find me pleasurable to look at, young feller? Most men seem to.'

He could feel the surge of blood in his neck and face. He tugged at the peak of his cap until it touched his eyebrows. He began to chip very steadily at the stone face. When he looked up again the girl had disappeared.

※

Jye knew that most people thought him stupid, but he had decided long ago that if silence was to be his lot then so be it. But sometimes the thoughts packed so tightly inside his head that he almost spoke them. He lingered that evening over mutton-stew and suet-pudding. He looked across the scrubbed boards of the table at Adge and Joby. Supposing he should tell them? Supposing he should say, straight out, 'Today I spoke to a young woman. She wore purple velvet, and a little feathery hat. She had dark-red hair, white skin, and eyes the colour of wet violets.' They would laugh to begin with, pull his leg, torment and tease him. Then Joby would get angry. He might tell Mr Mitchell. Jye could just hear him.

'First day in London, sir, and this ungrateful lump be already wasting of his time, and talking to young hussies!'

Was she a hussy? He tried to remember every detail of her. She had dressed like a lady, and yet, inexperienced as he was, something told Jye that she was not so. A lady would not have grabbed his sleeve to gain his attention. A lady would never have spoken to him in the first place. She had approached him with the familiarity of one artisan towards another, and yet he felt sure that she was not a servant. Perhaps she was a fallen woman? Jye was not quite sure what the term meant, the fallen women of London were

Joby Stagg's favourite topic when he had cider taken. Why had he not questioned her about it? Why was it only now that the words came to jostle and crowd in his mind?

'Be you all right, boy? You looks fair wore out.' Adge looked concerned.

''Tis that mutton-stew,' muttered Joby, 'that'll take some getting used to, even for a young 'un with strong guts.'

'Think I'll get to bed,' said Jye, 'if you two don't mind.'

'You turn-in, boy. Us got some drinking to be got through.' Adge gestured towards the cider keg in a corner of the kitchen. 'How about a glass, then, my old acker? I could heat up the poker and warm it for 'ee. A nice tot of mulled cider 'ud soon settle your stomach.'

Jye shook his head.

'Leave 'un be,' sniggered Joby, 'he'll be homesick, for a few days. He'll be missing his old mother's hedgehog dinners.'

❀

February came in wet, with rain so torrential that it blocked the gutters. The north face of the Abbey had to be abandoned in favour of work in the sheltered lodges. The time had come, said Adge, for Jye to tackle something more interesting. A crocket perhaps, or a finial. He nodded towards the block of limestone which stood on Jye's banker. 'You can do anything, boy, with a lump of Ham stone. You can undercut 'un, and that do mean the easy carving of leaves and flowers. You can work tracery in limestone, carve out gargoyles and devils. Already, you've done windows and lintels, now 'tis time to move on. You mun test yourself against the craft of they old masons what built this place.' Adge spat on his open palms. 'Oh ah, boy! That do take the men of Somerset and Dorset to show these Cockney stone-crackers how the job should be proper done!'

Jye laid out the tools that had once belonged to his father, Luke. He touched the worn handles with the initials L.C. cut deep into their surface and the cruciform cross which had been his banker mark. Jye had used these same tools in Montacute, and without any great emotion, but here, in the shadow of Westminster Abbey, the familiar mallets and chisels held a new significance for him. He remembered the patteran left by gypsy families, that arrangement of twigs and grasses which informed those who followed after of the conditions that prevailed in those parts, and of whom, and how large a tribe, had recently passed that way.

He fell asleep on the thought that his father's patteran had been the mason's tools, and the damask rose-bush. He dreamed about a girl who had dark-red hair, and was dressed from head to toe in purple velvet.

❋

Spring never came to London, and summer missed the city by a long mile. The temperature had swung lately from damp and cold, to hot and muggy, but that was the only seasonal change that Jye could detect. With the onset of fine weather their work had been resumed on the Abbey's north face. Jye also worked at the dressing of stone-blocks. Occasionally he was allowed to tackle something more important, but not too often.

'You be only an apprentice,' Joby reminded him. 'Us can't have you getting above yourself, just because you be in London. You was very lucky to be chose at all.'

Jye was no longer so certain of his good fortune. In these summer nights he dreamed too often of the honeysuckle hedges out towards Odcombe, and the fat buttercup meadows of Drayton's Farm. He had missed the apple-blossom this year, and the cowslips, and whatever was happening to his roses? He walked the short stretch of road which took him from Great Smith Street to Westminster

Abbey; he never noticed the fashionable people, the fine carriages and liveried footmen. Jye only looked upwards, and he found it difficult to believe that this patch of blue, these white clouds, were the same that hung over his mother's garden and above Ham Hill. He was about to ask George Mitchell if he might be sent home, when the red-haired girl came sauntering back into the Abbey precincts.

He was down on his knees replacing a worn step, when the sight of a dress hem made him look upwards. There she stood, elegant from head to toe in palest lilac silk with parasol to match. She looked like a queen in all her frills and ruffles, with the ostrich-plumed hat nodding gently on her head. He watched her lips: 'So you be still here, then?'

'Yes,' he said, and hung his head. He touched the worn hollow of the old step, and then ran his hand along the firm edge of the new one.

'I be putting in a new step.'

'I can see that.'

He looked up at her lips expecting further questions, but they did not move. Afraid that she might walk away, he took in a deep breath and said quickly, 'What's your name, then?'

'Blanche,' she said, 'Blanche Greypaull.'

'That's pretty,' he said, 'I like that.'

'What's your name, then?'

'Jye. Jye Carew.'

'That's a name I never heard before. Where ever did 'ee get that?'

He said, uneasily and because he was truthful, ''Tis a Romany name. You spells it with a jay and a –'

'I don't want to know how you spells it.' He seemed to have made her angry but he couldn't think why. 'Who named you for a gypo then?'

'My mother.' He spoke reluctantly. 'She lives in a house now, but years ago, when she was young, she was a gypsy.'

85

The girl said suddenly, 'Take your cap off Jye Carew!'

He looked puzzled, and before he could stop her she had ripped the peaked cap from his head. He put up a hand to push the long curls from his neck and forehead.

'I needs a haircut,' he muttered, 'I never found a barber since I come six months ago to London.'

'Don't get your hair cut,' she pleaded, 'that 'ud be a shame.' And all at once, there she was down on her knees before him, silk dress dragging in the ancient dust. She took his face in both her hands. 'You're beautiful,' she said, 'and because you're deaf you don't even know what a power that gives you. If I was the loving kind, Jye Carew — why I do believe that I could love you! There now, that's a rare joke, idden it?' He thought there were tears in her eyes but he couldn't be sure.

'Be you lonely, Jye?' she asked him.

He nodded.

'Can I come sometimes and talk to you? I won't stop you working.'

He thought about it. 'If you talks to me, I got to stop working, so that I can watch your lips move. Anyway, the other masons 'ud spot you and then I'd be in trouble.'

She said, 'You must have a rest hour. What do you do then?'

'I sits in the Chantry Chapel,' he said simply, 'I prays to go home, soon.'

'Well, pray no more, Jye Carew! I will come every midday and sit beside you. But not in that gloomy old church. I hate churches! Us'll find a sheltered spot behind the bushes.'

Confused, and frightened now, Jye bent his head and would not face her. When he looked up, again, she had disappeared.

If the girl called Blanche Greypaull had kept her promise to come back every midday, then Jye did not know about it.

Every instinct warned him that she would bring trouble with her. Jye's unstable mother, high-strung and quick to anger, had taught him very early in life to be wary of impulsive women. He continued to spend his break-hour safe inside the Abbey, trusting to the girl's expressed dislike of churches that she would not follow him there. Sometimes, he would stand enraptured for a full half-hour, tracing with his mind's finger the ornate and intricate carvings which surrounded King Henry's Chapel.

But although he evaded the dangerous young woman, Jye was left with his loneliness, his total isolation. He had once thought that perhaps in London things might be different. He had imagined some mythical friend, perhaps a fellow-mason, who, meeting him as a stranger, might show a little patience with him. Jye knew, had always known, that his deafness irritated people. Even his mother, after some brief attempt to communicate through speech, would often turn away, weary with the effort called for. It was the same with Adge and Joby Stagg. A few words, a sentence or two, flung in Jye's direction, and then they would turn back, with relief, to one another.

There had been no problem with the girl called Blanche. He realised this, belatedly, on a mild day in late September, when his longing for Montacute was more acute than usual. He had seemed to hear, if only faintly, an echo of thin sound every time Blanche Greypaull spoke. Taken together with the movements of her firm lips, he had found no difficulty in understanding, right away, what she had to say. There had been none of those awkward pauses, or the embarrassment of asking the speaker to repeat certain words or phrases. They had spoken together as easily as if Jye had been a hearing person.

He had better, he told himself, take advantage of the autumn sunshine in his break-hour. Quite soon now the yellow fog would rise up from that dirty river they called

Thames. Winter would be upon them, and his loneliness grew sharper in the cold days. He ate his bread and cheese seated on the burnt grass in a corner of the Dean's Yard, and then leaned back upon his elbows to look up at the soaring tower of the south face. He could never, he thought, see enough of this Abbey; not in one year, or a thousand. He felt like a parched drinker whose thirst would never be slaked. Some parts of the fabric spoke quietly to him, in other places the very stones would shout out in triumph. A flash of blue silk close beside his left hand warned him that he was no longer alone.

He saw her smart grey-leather boot lift up and come down with such force that a cloud of dust rose up from the dry earth. He pulled his fingers back just in time. He smiled, but did not look up. She was angry with him. Well, let her be. See if he cared!

She kicked him hard on the shin; he felt the pointed toe of her fancy boot through the corduroy thickness of his trousers. He ran a nervous finger around the inside edge of the collar of his flannel shirt. He looked up at her and said mildly, 'What you done that for?'

'Because I can't make you look at me no other way. You don't hear even when I shout and stamp my foot. I don't know why I ever come back again to see you!'

He said, 'You got no business to be here. This is Dean's Yard. You'll be in trouble if they catches you in here.'

She lifted her chin in his direction. 'I shall say that you told me to come here. I shall say that you 'ticed I in here.'

He was on his feet in one swift movement; he laid a hand on her silken forearm and began to push her, ungently, towards the gateway.

'Out!' he said. He thought that he had probably shouted at her. 'Tell lies about me, would you? Don't you know that you could lose me my job? Get me sent home in disgrace, shamed afore the whole village?'

The force of his action had taken them both into Great Smith Street. They stood face to face, and he noticed, for the very first time, her remarkable blue-silk bosom; it rose and fell alarmingly, and he thought she was about to cry. He began to apologise. 'I didden mean to –' it was then he realised that she was laughing at him. He knew that it must be laughter by the merriment in her eyes and her curving features. At one point she leaned up against the wall, quite collapsed and helpless,

'You,' she choked, pointing at him, 'with looks like yours you could do anything you wanted – and here you bides, chipping away at they old stones, and worritin' about what people might say in some mouldy liddle village.' He began to walk away, but she ran after him and clutched at his shirt sleeve, she swung him around so that he faced her.

'I shall come back,' she said slowly, 'at the same time tomorrow. I'll meet you in that same porch where I first saw you.' She paused and winked her eye. 'You better be there Jye Carew, or you know what I'll do, don't you?'

❊

Adge called it St Luke's Little Summer, these misty golden days of mid-October when the Abbey stones dreamed in the sunshine and Jye was so acutely aware of time past. Sometimes he saw ghosts: cardinals in red vestments, the brown-robed lay-brothers who had once chanted through these ancient cloisters, the bent backs and stooped shoulders of masons long-dead.

The girl, Blanche, was no ghost. She came wearing pink silk, and yellow. As the days grew cooler she appeared in wine-red velvet, the toes of her grey boots peeping out from beneath her long skirts, a tiny hat of soft grey feathers perched among her auburn curls. She seemed to know exactly when and where he was to be found alone.

'I can't talk when I'm working,' he said firmly. 'I can't

watch your face and my mallet and chisel, both at the same time.'

'That's all right,' she laughed. He knew that she laughed by the curve of her mouth and the way she tipped her head back. 'You talk to me when you're working,' she said, 'and I can talk to you when you got your break-hour.' And so it was.

At night he would lie awake in his box-bed and recall one particular conversation.

'You knows a lot about me,' he had said, 'you knows that I be an apprentice-mason, that my mother was gypsy, that I comes from a village far from this place. I don't know nuthin' about you.'

'What do you want to know, Jye Carew?'

'You wears fine clothes, you uses perfume. I bain't too sure, but I reckon you paints your mouth.' He had paused then. 'Be you what Joby Stagg calls a "fallen woman"?'

She had not laughed; she had not even smiled. Instead, she had traced a pattern in the dust with the tip of her parasol. 'Now that's a good question,' she had said, 'and one that I can't easy answer. I don't work for my living – at least not with my hands, like you do.'

'I never thought you was a barmaid,' he said, 'nor yet a skivvy.'

'I was a skivvy – last year – when I first come to London.'

'And now – ?'

'I be what folks call an artist's model.'

He looked worried. 'Say again?' he asked her.

'An artist's model.' She mouthed the words, exaggerating each syllable and letter.

'They be strange words to me.' He produced a stub of pencil and a scrap of paper from his pocket. 'Here,' he said, 'write 'em down for me. I understands much better when I can see the words put in writing.'

'No! No I won't write it down.' He was surprised to see her sudden anger. 'I'll tell 'ee what it means — it means that I stand on a thing called a dais and never move a muscle, while half a dozen young gents paints or draws my picture.'

His lips fell open, and he did not utter.

'Surprised? Yes, I thought you might be. Ever heard of the Royal Academy? No, of course you haven't. That's where I go every morning. 'Tis a kind of school, for artists. It pays well, even if 'tis a bit cold in winter.'

He said, 'Most jobs is cold in the winter. Stone idden exactly warm stuff to handle.'

She giggled. 'You can't complain. At least you is able to keep your clothes on.'

'Keep my — you don't tell I that you has to take your clothes off?'

She nodded. 'All of 'em.'

'Even your — ?'

'Even my drawers.'

He was silent for a long time. At last he said, 'I don't believe you.'

She shrugged. 'Makes no odds to me what you believes. Whyfor should I say it if tidden true.' She leaned towards him, suddenly confidential. 'I got some drawings if you wants to see 'em.'

'With no clothes on?' His face had turned a deep shade of crimson. 'No thank you. I don't hold with lewdness.'

'God made the human body,' she told him, 'so there's nothing lewd about it.'

'How old be you, Blanche?'

'Seventeen. Eighteen come next New Year.'

He looked up, relieved. 'So be I. Eighteen come next New Year. We be both the same age, exactly.' The shared birthday had somehow restored his confidence in her.

She said, 'I got something to ask you. I been listening careful to the way you talk — tidden easy to tell, you being deaf an' all — but I reckon that you be a Somerset feller.'

'That's right. I comes from Montacute. Prettiest place in all England.'

'I comes from Taunton.'

'Is that right, then? Well, there's a thing! I was once in Taunton when I was a boy, with my mother.'

She studied him, closely. 'And your mother is a gypsy?'

'Was a gypsy. She lives in a house now.'

'Makes no diff'rence. Is she a tall woman, with black braids wound around her head? Do she have high cheekbones and dark snappin' eyes?'

'You knows my mother?'

Blanche said slowly, 'I know'd your face right away, the minute I first seen you in that church porch I recognised you, but didden know from where! Why, you was the boy what we met on the roadside in Bishop's Hull. The boy with the gypsy-woman, her what cursed my mother.'

Even as she spoke, he remembered the day, and it was a day he had not wished to remember. He recalled the train, the withy-beds of Athelney, and the flood-water coming in at one side of the compartment and swirling out at the other. He remembered Norton Fitzwarren, the gypsy corner of the village churchyard, and his mother tying scarlet ribbons on the bush that was planted above her parents' grave. He had not wished to hear about these vagabonds, these wandering gypsies. He had feared the effects of this pilgrimage upon his mother, who was, with far less provocation, always liable to roam. How desperate he had been to guide her back towards the train that would take them home, and how mortified he had felt at the altercation that had broken out with the red-haired woman and her children.

He turned to Blanche. 'Which one were you? There was a lot of girls sitting on that farmcart. I don't recall their faces, only the hard words what was spoken.'

Blanche said simply, 'I was the beautiful one, with the long red hair. Your mother didden like me. She liked our Annis.'

He said, 'There was some words said about a baby, or a small child.'

'That was poor Louis. He turned out to be feeble-minded. 'Twas all your mother's fault. I reckon she's a witch.'

He sighed. 'She's a bit odd, but she's harmless really. She didden like you much. She called you a bad 'un.'

'I remember, now,' Blanche said softly. ' "The day will come when you will try to get close to me and mine" that's what your mother said. Well, she's right in that case. I been trying to get close to you, Jye Carew, all summer long.'

❋

It had always been a curious relationship, but now they had reached a stage where they were neither enemies nor lovers, but something uncomfortably close to both. All the pursuit was on her side. He found her quite shameless. She came to the Abbey at least three times in every week; she was always careful to approach him at those hours when he worked alone. Once she had trapped him in a narrow passage, she had pressed the whole length of her body quite deliberately against him. She had placed his hand upon the swell of her blue-silk bosom, and mumured, 'There now, Jye, just feel how you do make my heart pound.'

There had been an occasion when a priest had caught them talking together. Oh, but she was quick-witted! 'I was just asking this young man the time of Evening Service,' she had said, 'but there seems to be something the matter with him. He don't seem to understand what I say.'

The priest had studied Jye. 'Ah yes. The young mason. I'm afraid he's quite deaf. Terrible affliction!' The holy man had been quite enchanted by the sweetness of Blanche. They had walked away, chatting happily together. Just before she had passed beyond his sight, Blanche had glanced back across her shoulder and drooped her eyelid in an outrageous wink.

She had laughed about it at their next meeting. He said, 'You didden ought to tell so many lies, Blanche. I never know what to believe about you. You've never really told me where you live.'

'If I tell you, then you'll be none the wiser. I lives in a furniture shop in St Martin's Lane. Since you never sets foot much beyond this old Abbey you wouldn't never have seen the exciting bits of London. I lodges with a Mrs Gimball, she's a good sort. No lady of course — but then neither be I. We suits one another.' She reached out a hand and touched his knee. 'Come to tea next Sunday, Jye. We could go for a walk. I could show you the Strand and Piccadilly. My word, but that'd make your eyes pop! 'Tis a damn sight more lively than this old graveyard.'

He hung his head. The little white hand on his knee was disturbing, he began to experience a warmth in his loins, and was afraid. He had never expected to encounter the sins of the flesh in Westminster Abbey. He pushed her hand away.

'I can't come,' he said thickly.

'And why not?' Her smile was of that special sweetness which warned him to be wary. He searched for a convincing reason, but could only say weakly, 'Adge and Joby wudden like it.'

She looked grave. 'Adge and Joby. Be they your nursemaids then? Do they spank your bottom when you've been naughty? Frightened that they'll tell your mother about me, idden you, Jye? Come on! Tell the truth now.'

'I wudden want to upset her. My mother got a lot to put up with.' The little white hand had begun to stroke his thigh. 'Then there's the Mason's Rules,' he said hoarsely, 'they don't allow no fornication.'

Her firm red lips fell open, 'Who said anything about

fornication? I only asked you to go for a walk. I'm surprised at you. I thought you was as innocent as morning daisies.'

'How innocent be you, Blanche?'

For the first time since he had known her she looked vulnerable and oddly sincere. The mockery slipped from her features, and he saw just how beautiful she really was.

'I do talk a lot,' she admitted, ''tis mos'ly for fun. I don't mean it. To tell the truth, I wonders sometimes at my own folly.' She brought her face close to his. 'I've never done anything wrong, Jye. Not really wrong, so to say.' She giggled. 'I've had a few close calls, mind!'

'I'm not surprised! If you takes off your drawers for gen'lemen to paint you, then you shudden be 'mazed at anything what follows.'

'That,' she said, 'is the whole secret. Keeping 'em in their places, knowing how far to let 'em go. I can look ever so innocent and shocked when I got the mind to. Anyway, I only come to London for one reason.'

'What's that?'

'Money! Bags of it! More frocks than I can ever wear. More diamond rings than I've got fingers.' She opened and closed her fists with a grasping movement. 'I want, Jye! I just want and want, as much as I can get, of everything!'

''Tis a waste of your time hanging round with me, then. I only earns ten bob a week, and five of that goes back to Mother.'

She took his face in both her hands. 'Don't you know,' she asked, 'don't you know why I keeps coming here?'

'Because you be lonely? We be both of us a long way from Somerset, 'tis only natural –'

'If I was the loving kind – which I am not – oh, how I could have loved you, Jye Carew,' and she bent and kissed him full on the lips, right there, in King Henry's Chapel; then she walked quickly away. He sat for a long time after she had gone. Not praying, not even thinking.

95

Jye was coming home at Christmas. Meridiana had held on to that thought throughout the long dry summer, through the lingering warmth of a protracted autumn, and into the short days of November and early December. She had missed him so much more than she had expected. She had not known that to have Jye about the house and garden, to watch him stride off up the lane every morning and return at sunset, was to keep some part of Luke with her still. Each time she passed the churchyard wall, she would pause and mutter to the lettered headstone, 'While I got Jye, I still got his father.'

She knew that people feared her. It amused and gratified some instinct deep within her to be so feared. In all her life, it had only been Eliza Greypaull who refused to be quelled by the fierce eyes, who had stood fast and defied the Rom woman's expressed wishes. People were frightened by what they could not understand, and Eliza had long ago fathomed Meri's weakness.

She had conformed to village ways only when and where it had been politic so to do, or if by some default she might bring harm down on one of her children. How many of her neighbours could boast of owning their own Ham-stone cottage? How many others could have provided a little house and a spot of ground for the crippled sons who had needed independence?

Nobody knew how much money lay in the canvas money bag strapped around her waist. Oh yes, there was nothing like a body-belt of sovereigns to keep a woman snug in a bitter winter. When the time came for Jye to marry, she would be able to — It was always at this point that the blood ran slow within her. How to give him up? How to part with him to another woman? So much more of herself had gone into the making of Jye; he for whom she had so longed, for whom she had made pilgrimage to Glastonbury while he still lay safe underneath her heart.

There had been days just lately when she had wrapped the warm plaid around her shoulders and walked the Hill as she had done all those years ago, with one twin riding on her back and the other on her hip. She searched the October skies for a sign of Jye's safety, but found none. She climbed high, to that outcrop of stone from which she could see the rich fields of Long Load and High Ham turning brown beneath the plough.

She walked downwards from Jack o' Beards to Tinkers' Spring, and caught the soft sheen of the River Parrett, low now between its banks because of the long dry summer. She had watched for the waggons of her people, and suddenly, carried on the mist of autumn, came the smell of ash-smoke in the lanes. She began to run, and there were the painted vardos and the little brown bender-tents, erected in a long line down the length of the hedge. A waggon had been placed end-ways across each lane entrance to prevent the horses straying. The company was a large one, several families travelling together and all strangers; the heart grew sad within her and then she recognised her cousins' faces beside the fire. Lavinia and Taiso Lock had come back, with Petronell their second daughter, and Absolom their son. As Meri slipped through a gap in the hawthorn hedge and came into the tan, Lavinia and Taiso rose stiffly from the fireside and came towards her. They had grown old before their time. 'Seventeen years,' wept Lavinia, 'seventeen long years since us travelled the drom together out towards Sedgemoor and Glastonbury.'

'Aye,' said Meri, 'that was the last time I slept free underneath the stars.' She sat down, faced-to with them around the fire, and accepted a cup of strong sweet tea.

'You sounds regretful, cousin. Be you still mis-contented?'

'My man is dead,' said Meridiana. 'He was killed by a fall of stone. He've been gone from me this many-a-year.' She turned to Taiso Lock and her voice was bitter. 'I do wonder sometimes in my mind, whyfor I still bide yet in this sad village.'

Lavinia said softly, ''Tis thy chavvies what do hold 'ee, idden it, Meri? Us heard as how the youngest one be stone-deaf.'

'Thass quite true. My children was ever my weakness. When Luke died I was sore tempted to buy me a waggon, and go back to the travelling way of life.'

'You had the money,' said Taiso, 'thik stone cottage would have made a good sum.'

'I cudden do it. I looked at my Charles and Henry. Twin-dwarfs and crippled. I could just see how they might end up in some circus peep-show. As for Jye, how could a deaf boy ever chop and deal in the horse-fairs? He be razor sharp in his brain. He can read and write like teacher. But when that do come to talking and hearing then I got to admit he be terrible slow.'

Taiso said, 'Us do sometimes see your Charles and Henry. In fact you might as well know it, cousin, they do find our tents every time we is in this district.'

Meri shook her head. 'Is that the truth, now? Well, they never told me.'

'Perhaps you never listens to 'em. From what us have heard 'tis the one called Jye what do hold your heart-strings. Oh aye, cousin, 'tis Charles and Henry what got your Rom blood. Us have never clapped eyes on your youngest boy. From what his brothers say, he don't much like gypsies.'

Lavinia said, 'That have took you a long time to find us, Meri. We comes this way at least twice every year.'

Meri hung her head. 'Tidden easy – living in this village. They all reckons I be crazy because I still makes wood-flowers and clothespegs. 'Tis a diff'rent tale when they gets sick and can't afford no doctor. Then 'tis a quick rap at the gypsy's door where the physic comes cheaper. Oh, I knows the gorgie now, inside and out. Poor snivellin' house-bred creatures. No guts — affeared of their own shadows — always wanting to know their futures.' She laughed. 'I tells 'em whatever they wants to hear.' She turned upon Lavinia. 'So you wonders why I never found you in seventeen years? Would a hungry rai stand and stare at a tableful of food, if he was not able to touch it? Oh, I always knowed when you was here in the lane, Lavinia! I come stealing past by night, under starshine, when you had doused your fire, and the whole company slept fast behind closed tent-flaps. Ah, but I wept to see the coloured waggons, Vinnie. Thass a pain what'll never leave me.'

Taiso said gently, 'Come with us now, cousin. We be making our way slow towards Taunton. Us'll be down in Norton Fitzwarren in time for the mistletoe gathering.'

Meri shook her head. 'I thanks 'ee kindly, Taiso, but it can't be done. I got my Jye coming home from London in a few weeks.'

'London? Whatever do your Jye want in London?'

'He's a stone-mason like Luke, his father. They tell me he might make a carver of stone, when he gets the training.' There was a fierce pride in her voice when she spoke of Jye. 'He was chose to go to London. He be putting to rights some old church or other.' She held out her hands, 'So you sees don't you, how I mun bide yer a bit longer?'

'Bide too long, Meridiana, and you'll be too old to travel. You is still a fine looking woman. There's many a lonely rai as 'ud take you to wife.'

'I don't want no other man. In my soul I be wed to Luke Carew and always will be. There's no gypsy-rai what could ever match him.'

'Seems that us can't help 'ee then, Meri.' Lavinia sighed. 'You was ever contrary.'

'Next spring, Lavinia — I could come to the Council in Buckland St Mary. 'Tis so many long years since I saw the menfolk gather to talk around the peeled stick.' Meri paused. 'There was a family, name of Greypaull. Big farmers up in they parts. Do 'ee recall them, Vinnie.'

Lavinia thought about it. 'Do 'ee mean that proud man, the one what got sold-up? Him with the red-headed wife and they seven children?'

'The very one.'

'Oh, he be dead and buried. Must be more than a year since us met his funeral going to Buckland churchyard.'

'So Eliza's a widow too,' Meri whispered, 'well, I reckon she got a happy release from that man. There'll have been no tears shed over Philip Greypaull's coffin. Poor Liza, left with all they maidens to look out for, and that youngest boy looked to me like he was feeble-minded.' She stood up, abruptly. She kissed Lavinia and Taiso, and shook Absolom and Petronell by the hand.

'You got beautiful chavvies, Lavinia, both strong and healthy.'

She turned away with a brief nod, slipped between the hawthorn hedges and made her way back towards the village.

�֎

Jye came at Christmas, and they sat together by the wood-fire, he in Luke's old grandfather's-chair, and she on her low stool.

'Tell all, Jye!' she implored him. 'Tell about all the far-off places. 'Tis you now what be the family traveller, these days, and I what do bide at home. Was it wonderful, boy? Did it lift the heart inside you to be on the Queen's Highway?'

'I went on the steam-train, Ma. Don't you remember? Travelling by train is hot in the summer and cold in winter. A sensible feller bides to home, I reckon.'

She studied him. 'You got no Rom in you. You be just

like your father. I can't understand that.'

He tried to explain it to her. 'Places, Ma,' he said slowly, 'certain places do have a meaning for me. They gets a hold on me and won't let go. 'Tis like that with Ham Hill. 'Tis like something holy – I can't explain it proper.' He leaned forward to speak directly in her face, as if she were the deaf one for whom the words must be made clear. 'That Abbey in London, 'tis a place called Westminster. I got that same feeling there; 'tis like the very stones do speak out, and I can hear them.' He leaned back in his chair. 'I can't never make you understand, can I? All that running about, from one place to another. 'Tis a waste of time, Ma! Biding still, safe in your own village, is all what matters!'

She began to probe in another direction. 'Did you eat well in London? Did that lodgings woman treat you proper?'

'I ate well, Ma. 'Twas mutton-stew every day of the year, but 'twas good and filling. The bed was clean, and she dried my clothes when they got wet on the outside workings.'

'And what else come to pass in the big city?'

He put a hand up to cup his ear, and she repeated the question. 'Nothing came to pass! Why should it?'

'Don't lie to me, Jye Carew. Something else happened up in London, so you'd better tell I.'

He grew angry with her, he who had rarely raised his voice or his hands against anybody. 'I don't know what you mean,' he cried, 'I don't know what you be hinting at. Why, I never had so much as a drink of cider; 'twas work all day and sleep all night. I never set my foot more than twenty paces beyond the Abbey!' He beat the arms of his father's chair with his great bunched fists. 'Go and ask Joby Stagg if you don't believe me. He watched me all the time, like a stoat watches a rabbit!'

She knew he was lying. It was in his face and voice, and he could not conceal it from her. Why, she asked herself, why should he, at the age of seventeen, when he had always been truthful, need to lie to her now? The answer had to be a woman.

❊

The regular, end-of-harvest letter, despatched from Wisconsin in October, had arrived in Hunter's Court in mid-December.

Suamico.

My dear cousin Eliza,

Thank you for the letter received in February. Am a bit late writing to you, but *much* has come to pass in this year of 1882. My Rosalind have got *married* to a Mr Thomas Gillingham of Oshkosh. He is a v. nice young man, quiet and devout, and they are v. happy. But I miss her awful bad, Eliza. I guess I never thought it would be so lonely here without her. We was the *only two women* in this farmstead of menfolk, cepting for Mary, the hired girl. My Rosa have gone to live in Oshkosh, what is not too far off, but might as well be a *thousand miles* for all the time I shall ever get to visit with her.

Father Black is such a kind and understanding stepfather to my children. He says *I must visit regular* with Rosa, but I shant never get the Time, Eliza. We are no sooner done with Haying, than we go into Harvest. Then comes root-crops and threshing, and at all these seasons I got 16 to 18 men *with their boots underneath* my table. Hired men eat meat like it was dirt cheap, and I need to watch what goes on in the kitchen. Cant leave nothing to the hired girl, what have turned out be *flirtashus* around the *harvest and threshing gangs.* Should be ate out of house and home if not v. watchful.

Father Black says I must go to Rosa for my 50th birthday, what falls on Christmas Eve. To do that, I must leave the farm over Christmas, and that not v. fair on Father Black. Oh how a mother's heart do get *pulled all ways.* Eliza, when the chicks leave the nest. I think my Georgie is courting but am not sure yet. Letters have come from a place called De Pere, and I swear the handwriting is of a *young woman*. But George not much on confiding in me or anybody else. He is much like his departed father.

You are lucky to have four Daughters. There will always be one to bide home with you, and *keep you company*. Washday and the Friday cleaning go very slow and dull without my Rosa. Sunday is still kept free for Hearth and Heaven, as it ever was in my young days in Old England. Have put down a deal of hog meat this Fall, and started on a new quilt.

What news of Blanche? Has she visited with you since going to work in London? *Please write* and tell all what have come to pass in the last year. Love to all.

Your affectshunate cousin, Rhoda.

❀

Blanche did not come home that Christmas, and the monthly letter from Candace was so brief that, as Mina remarked, it was hardly worth the penny postage. It was not until New Year's Eve that Blanche walked into Hunter's Court. Eliza and Annis, seated close beside the window to catch the last of the daylight, laid down the collars they were stitching, to watch Blanche make her entrance. She swept into the narrow alley placing her smart grey boots very carefully upon the cracked flagstones, she lifted her wine velvet skirts well above the stinking rubbish that blocked the grating, and nodded quite graciously to the astonished women who were on their way up to the standpipe.

'Oh my,' whispered Annis, 'why, her's grander than ever this time. That's a handsome outfit she's wearing, just see how they feathers do nod and wave in her hat.'

'Handsome is as handsome does.' Eliza sounded bitter.

'Don't you get no wrong ideas about Miss Blanche. There's a lot more going on in London than you and me ever hears about. I'd give a lot to know –'

Blanche came in, and with her entrance the cosy little room seemed overcrowded. Her perfume reached into every corner and, all at once, there was a cloak on this chair, a hat on that stool, her bag had taken up the small space before the fire-grate, and she was depositing parcels and packages over every surface. She kissed her mother and patted Annis. She said lightly, 'Couldn't get down here at Christmas. Lots going on in the city – well, you knows how 'tis, Mama!'

'No,' said Eliza, 'I don't know. We lives very quiet here. A letter would have been a comfort, Blanche. Just to let us know that you was safe.'

Tears sprang at once in the violet eyes, and then spilled over. 'Oh Mama! I be that sorry. I never thought you'd notice my not being here. As for a letter, you knows that I can't –' Blanche began to sob.

Eliza busied herself with kettle and teapot, her features were tight, her fingers frantic. ''Tis all right, maid,' she muttered, 'now don't take on so. You know that I can't abide tears. That do only upset me.'

Annis said shyly, 'Oh Blanche, you do smell lovely.'

'Do I?' Blanche wiped her eyes and brightened. ''Tis the latest perfume from Paris. They calls it Attar of Roses. 'Tis said that the Princess of Wales is very fond of it.' Blanche blew her nose into a lacy hanky. 'All the debutantes do use it.'

The door burst open and Simeon and Madelina came in together. Mina held Simeon firmly by the right ear. 'Do you know what I found him doing, Ma? He was begging for ha'pennies outside Jeremiah's pawn-shop.'

''Tis a good spot,' said Simeon. He gazed around at the room's confusion. 'Why look,' he cried, 'just see what the wind blowed in!'

Mina released her little brother, and stared at Blanche. 'Is that rouge on your lips?' she demanded.

'And what if it is? 'Tis my face. I'll do what I want to with it.'

Simeon waved a hand beneath his nose. 'Something stinks in here,' he said. He stared at Blanche. 'Is it you?'

'That's perfume,' Annis informed him. ''Tis called Attar of Roses and the Princess of Wales do use it.'

Simeon began to laugh, a loud extended guffaw that brought up two bright spots of colour in the cheeks of Blanche. 'How would you ever know what was perfume,' she screeched, 'you spends all your days hanging round the Pig Market.'

'And what do you do all day, our Blanche?' Simeon nodded towards the window. 'They be saying up the Court that you idden no better than you should be.'

Blanche turned to her mother. 'Mama! How can you stand there and let him say such – '

Eliza put up a hand to her scarred cheek. 'Do 'ee be quiet,' she pleaded, 'you do make my head ache with your quarrelling.'

Blanche said, 'Where's your wedding ring, Mama?'

Eliza lowered her hand and thrust it into her apron pocket. 'I do seem to have mislaid it. 'Tis probably laying about somewhere. I shall come across it one of these days.'

'I never knowed you to be without it. Never in all my life. You was wearing it the last time I came home.'

'No, she wasn't.' Simeon's desire to outwit his sister had made him reckless of his mother's warning glances. 'Ma been wearing a curtain ring on her finger for ages, so's you wudden notice that she'd pawned her real one.' He glared defiantly at Eliza. 'Ma's wedding ring been in hock to Jeremiah this past eighteen months. So you maidens needn't think as how you knows all what goes on!'

Mina said, 'Is it true, Mama?'

'We all needed black when your father died.' The words came out hard and fast, 'I wudden never have it said in the church that we Greypaulls showed less than respect for him, even though he was a sinner.' Eliza's voice faltered and then grew strong. 'I had to leave off that old curtain ring, 'twas turning my finger a nasty green colour.'

Blanche said, 'Give me the pawn ticket.'

'No, maid. I'll redeem the ring when I've saved up some money. I won't be beholden to you every time you come home.'

'You'll never save that much money. You know you won't. I won't have you go about without your ring on. Tidden decent, no tidden!'

Blanche held out her hand and Eliza upended a vase on the mantelshelf and retrieved the ticket. Blanche held it between her thumb and finger. 'Don't you never go to pawn again, you hear me, Mama! Anything you want, just write a letter to Candace, and I'll see that you get it.'

❀

Jack came home on New Year's Day. He looked Blanche up and down and then said coldly, 'So we got the Duchess back home again?'

Simeon grinned. 'You better be nice to her, Jack. Her got ever so much money. Anyway, 'tis her birthday today, and you ought to see the grub her's bought.' He covered his mouth with his hand and giggled. 'Eighteen today,' he chanted, 'and never been kissed – so she says.'

Mina said, 'Whyn't you shut up, Sim? You got far too much to say for yourself just lately.'

'Thinking about that good dinner what's cooking, be you, Mina?' Simeon refused to be put in his place. 'How you've changed your tune since you see'd all they sovereigns in her handbag. I don't hear you complaining no more about the rouge on her face.'

Jack said, 'That'll be enough from you, boy.' He turned to Blanche. 'How's life then, in the wicked city? Can I ask what you be doing with yourself, these days?'

Blanche laughed. 'You can ask, James John Daniel, but that don't mean that I shall tell 'ee.'

Eliza said, 'I think we'd all like to know, Blanche. 'Tis clear that you be doing very well at it, whatever 'tis.'

'I be still in the same line of business, Mama. Like I told 'ee before, I be an artist's model.'

'You was working in a furniture shop last time I see'd you.' Jack sounded suspicious.

'Oh yes! So I was! Well, I don't do that no more. I still lives with Mrs Gimball in St Martin's Lane, but I got more reg'lar employment these days.'

'Like what?'

Blanche stood up. She rested an arm on the mantelshelf, and inclined her head towards her mother. Aware of the charming picture she presented, she said proudly, 'Oh, I do sit for titled gen'lemen these days.'

'Where?' cried Simeon, 'on their knees.'

Jack reached out and cuffed his brother hard about the ears. 'Get in your bed,' he shouted, 'lest I take my horsewhip to you.'

'Oh,' moaned Eliza, 'how bad us do need a man in this house!'

'Go on then, Blanche,' urged Jack, 'tell us about these toffs what do paint your picture.'

'I goes to the Royal Academy most days. I sits in what they calls the Life School.' She hesitated. 'They don't paint all of me. They only paints bits.'

'Which bits?' Mina sounded anxious.

'Well,' said Blanche, 'supposing the artist is painting some rich lady, and got her a wrinkled old neck and no — well — no bosom. That's where I come in. He uses the good bits of me in her picture, and that makes her look twenty years younger.'

The silence lasted a good sixty seconds. Eliza said at last, 'Well maid, that do sound quite decent, just so long as you don't have to – well – take nothing off.'

'Oh, I don't Ma! Well, you knows that I wudden!'

From the depths of the cupboard-bed Simeon muttered, 'Her was never so fussy when her lived at home.'

Jack said, 'So that do pay well, do it?'

'If 'tis an important artist, and they mostly is in the Life School, I can earn half a guinea for one sitting.'

Mina gasped. 'Do you know how many collars I must sew to make that much?'

'Well, of course you got to have the looks,' Blanche said simply, 'and you just don't have 'em, do you Mina?'

❁

Bad things happened only to wicked people; to be disobedient to your parents was to flout the laws of the Lord God, and He would visit His wrath and His retribution upon you. This had been the belief of Eliza's mother, who had always traced every disaster, every painful experience straight back to its source. Catch a cold in May, and it was bound to be your own fault. Hadn't you cast some clout? Left off your cap or your woolly vest long before your mother said you ought to. If your husband lied and cheated, treated you with less respect than he would his horse, then that could also be laid at your door. It was your own inability to manage him correctly, and hadn't she warned you, often enough? Eliza had never been absolutely sure just where the laws of the Lord God ended and those of Elizabeth Greypaull commenced.

It was this confusion of mind, thought Eliza, that now made her lenient with the unruly Simeon, less demanding than perhaps she should be of those explanations from the glib-tongued Blanche. I don't want, she thought, for them to remember me the way I recalls my own mother, always carping and criticising. But the price of silence was a high one, and she could not always pay it. Too often, she heard herself repeating those old cautions that had ruled her own childhood; and why was it always Blanche whom she so badly mishandled?

Eliza went to church, as she always did on Sunday evenings. She invited Blanche to go with her, but Blanche pleaded a headache. Mina had spent her day teaching in the Wesleyan Chapel, and was taking supper with David Lambert's parents. Simeon was off on some secret business of his own. Annis stayed at home, as was her custom, to watch over her brother Louis. Finding herself alone with Blanche Annis seemed awkward and tongue-tied. Blanche caught her stroking the wine-red cloak, touching the plumes of the feathered hat.

'How would 'ee like to try 'em on?' Blanche asked gently.

'Mamma wudden like it.'

'Mamma bain't here to see.'

Blanche lifted the tresses of golden hair that lay across her sister's shoulders. 'You be nearly sixteen,' she said, ''tis time you put this lot up.' She swept the hair high, twisted and swirled it, and then fastened it with a few pins from her own hair. She placed the hat of soft grey feathers on the new coiffure, and led Annis to the spotted mirror. 'There you are!' she cried. 'Now don't that make a difference?' Blanche began to unbutton the smart grey boots. 'Put 'em on,' she ordered, 'and the cloak. I want to see what you looks like in 'em.'

Annis teetered upon the hearthstone in the unfamiliar heels; she flung the cloak about her with an extravagant gesture. 'Oh Blanche,' she breathed, 'that do feel lovely. I feels so elegant and important.'

'Clothes is important, Annis. Don't you never forget that.'

A sound from the doorway swung them around. Eliza was watching, stiff and decent in her widow's black. Annis felt the heart lurch within her, and her mouth grew dry.

'What's all this, then?'

Blanche laughed. 'We was just seeing if my clothes 'ud fit her. Now admit it, Mama. Don't she look lovely?'

Eliza said, 'Take that silly hat off, Annis, and let your hair down, you bain't sixteen come the middle of October.'

'Oh, Ma!' cried Blanche, 'don't go and spoil it for her. We wasn't doing anything we shudden.'

Eliza's lips thinned into a straight line. 'There's some,' she said, 'as is born to mischief. No matter what you do or what you say, you can't seem to change them. Your father was like that. Fine words and fine feathers! But Annis,' and now the white lips eased as if the very name was precious, 'but Annis never was like that, nor ever shall be while I'm her mother. Annis have always been my liddle maiden.' Eliza looked hard at Blanche. 'Red cloaks and fancy hats might be all right for you, Blanche. You took easy to the city ways, and no mistake. But I'll thank you to remember that the rest of us be still in mourning.'

Blanche said, 'You never did wear the grey silk I brought you. 'Tis still lying in the drawer. That have laid there for a whole year! Why, Mama?'

'I shall wear it, when the right time comes.' Eliza looked long and significantly at Blanche, 'but the right time haven't come yet, and on days like these, then I doubt if it ever will.'

❈

Eliza fetched pen and ink, envelopes and paper; she placed the lamp in the centre of the table and turned the wick as high as it would go. She headed a sheet of notepaper with the place and date, and began to write.

My dear cousin Rhoda,

Your letter to hand just before Christmas. So pleased to hear about dear Rosa's marriage to a *good man*. Hope you are feeling better now, and *not so lonely*. Yes, it must be hard to lose an only daughter, especially in your situation on the farm. I hope you managed to get to Oshkosh for your 50th birthday. I know how hard you must work on the land, dear cousin, but your children *need you too*. I never found time enough for my little brood when they was growing up. Not my fault, but due to *shortcomings* of Philip. But you have Mr Black to support you, and help in the house. A woman *should consider herself* sometimes, Rhoda. Where would they all be without us? That's what I say. Go to see your Rosa as often as you can, Dear Cousin.

Now to my own chicks. All fit and well at time of writing, *most of all Blanche*. She come down from London dressed to kill, and spoilt with fashion. What the neighbours in the Court think about her I dare not imagine. At least the Rev. Jones never saw her, nor Madelina's Affianced. She was not short of money. She redeemed my wedding ring from Jeremiah's, and bought us food and presents. But I am *v. uneasy about it all*, Rhoda. She never was v. truthful, and it do all sound like *tall stories* what she tells us. Candace never come with her, so *could not question her* as to what is going on with Blanche in London.

Only be *thankful* that your Rosalind is *safely wed*. Cannot sleep easy in my bed for worrying about Blanche. Was glad to see her go back to London. Her Influence on Annis is *not good*. Caught Annis trying on *Blanche's clothes* and with her hair up, too. *Spoke my mind* about it, Rhoda, I don't mind telling you. I will not have Annis led away from the Paths of Rightshusness, no Rhoda, *I will not*. She is my youngest daughter, and have always bided close to me. I know that I should never say such a thing, but I could wish that Blanche would keep away from Taunton altogether, and leave us *in peace*. There is always *upset* and *quarrels* wherever she is. Can only pray, and trust in our Saviour that nothing *terrible* will come to pass with Blanche.

This letter full of my Trouble with Blanche. But you did ask, and it is a relief to tell somebody what is also a *mother*, and can understand. Cannot broach such a matter with the *Rev Jones*. Madelina's wedding planned for June. Will write you an account of it when the time comes.

Much love to all.

Your loving cousin, Eliza.

✿

Blanche had come back to London to find the city enveloped in a yellow fog, so dense that hansom-cabs were mistaking their way and careering up onto the pavements. People, so the cabby informed her, were dying in their hundreds from asthma and bronchitis. At three o'clock in the afternoon, St Martin's Lane was so dark that she had difficulty in locating Mrs Gimball's doorway. She came into the little back-parlour to find Candace and Ellen seated by the fire, drinking tea from chipped enamel mugs. Mrs Gimball wheezed alarmingly. She poured a mug of tea for Blanche. 'Sorry, ducks,' she apologised, 'the crockery ain't up to much, but I ain't never got out tottin' for several days now. I been forced to sell off the stock.' She looked anxiously at Blanche, 'I 'ad to sell your long sofa over Christmas. I needed the money. But don't you worry, we can push two chairs together until somethin' turns up.'

Candace grinned. 'Don't you worry too much about her, Mrs Gimball. She has to sleep a-top the kitchen table when she goes home to Taunton. Two armchairs put together'll feel like heaven for our Blanche.'

Mrs Gimball began to laugh, which brought on a spasm

of gasps and wheezes. She said, 'No wonder she walks so proud! Why, I've often said to Mr Solomon, that girl Blanche got a spine wot's as straight as a poker.'

Candace said, 'Well – how was things in Taunton?'

Blanche shrugged. 'Pretty much like always. I hardly saw anything of Mina, her's always across to this feller what plays the harmonium in the Wesleyan Chapel. I got a sight of him one night; he was waiting for her underneath the gaslight at the end of the Court.'

'Do tell,' urged Candace, 'I can't wait to hear what sort of prize our Mina have come up with!'

Blanche said, 'As a matter of fact he's not bad-looking. Tall and dark, with a fine moustache. But proud though. Sort of feller who always looks as if he's just found a bad smell underneath his nose.' She smiled. 'He might have been hand-made for Mina.'

'Talking of religion,' Ellen said, 'I heard as you goes a lot to Westminster Abbey, Blanche.'

'Where did you hear that, then?'

'You was seen by a postman friend of mine. Always popping in and out, you are, according to what he says.'

'It's a pity,' snapped Blanche, 'that some people don't mind their business.' Candace looked enquiringly at her. 'I got a friend who works there,' Blanche burst out.

'Nobody works there,' said Candace.

'Oh yes, they do, Candace Greypaull!' Blanche lifted her chin, and looked haughty. 'My friend is a – a sculptor. He'll probably be famous one day!'

Chandace said, 'What's a sculptor?'

Blanche sighed. 'Oh you country maidens be so ignorant,' she said grandly. 'A sculptor do make figures out of stone. Didden you never see all they likenesses of Prince Albert? The Old Queen do have one made every few weeks. She got 'em stuck up all over London.'

Candace looked impressed. 'Be you walking-out together?'

'Walking-out is for village maidens. My friend do take me to the music-hall. Then we goes on to some quiet little place for supper.'

'Did you tell Mama all about it?'

'No I didden, Can Greypaull! Neither did I open my mouth in Taunton about your backing horses, and swigging brandy with that Archie Wizard.'

❋

The suggestion, made by a fellow artist, that his model, Blanche, might sit to the Royal Academy's Life School, had both pleased Mr Solomon, and yet alarmed him.

His mouth had twisted into that bitter line which was almost habitual with him. 'You'll be sitting to the most respected artists of our time,' he had told her, 'you'll find out the importance of moving in the right company. If you're really lucky, then somebody of stature might take you up. But the nude pose will be required of you.'

'I don't know as how I wants to be "took-up" as you calls it. I promised our Candace that I wudden never take my clothes off. That do only lead to sin and trouble!'

'The Royal Academicians are not in the habit of raping their models. You'll be as safe with them as you are with me. But remember, Blanche, these people have two faces. They will drop you straight away if you don't live according to their rules.' He became excited, and his brown eyes burned redly, like those of a mad goat. 'The amorous proclivities of artists have become a myth. Why, they're so respectable down in Chelsea that they're actually marrying their models. They seem to breed at an inordinate rate. The dull little wives hold afternoon tea-parties and soirées. They spend their evenings playing cards and charades.'

Blanche, confused as usual by his rhetoric, and understanding only one word in ten, had said mildly, 'Well, my Mama don't hold with card-playing, I know, but there's nothing wrong with tea-parties, Mr Solomon.'

The Life School was housed in an impressive building of many long windows and searching draughts. Blanche thought it a cheerless place; it had a curious smell compounded of several odours, unidentifiable by her, but so distinctive that she was always to remember its rooms by their strange aroma. Her sessions in the Life School were like cold penitential islands in the long day. She would, for the rest of her life, recall those years with a marked reluctance to dwell upon details.

She had been directed on that first morning to the cubicles reserved for female models. Her instructions had been to remove every article of clothing and put on the robe which she had brought with her. Her fingers were cold and she fumbled with hooks and eyes, and the many tiny buttons of her dress. The important artist, attended by his semi-circle of waiting students, had not concealed his irritation at her late arrival. He had indicated that she should mount the dais and remove her robe. He had lifted the Greek urn up onto her shoulder, and she noticed how careful he was to avoid any physical contact with her, showing by a mere wave of his fingers the exact positioning he required of her head and limbs. An elderly gentleman had also wandered into the room and appeared to be overseeing these proceedings.

The chill of that January morning had hardly been touched by the sulky coke-burning stove. She clamped her teeth tight together, and willed herself to remain immobile. Her view was a jumble of foreshortened benches and easels, with the occasional peeping eye of a youthful student appearing around the edge of a canvas. No more than ten minutes had passed when Blanche began to suspect that the numbness of her hands and feet was to be the least of her problems. She had whispered, tentatively to begin with, 'Excuse me, but us'll have to stop for a minute. I got to go somewhere.' The master artist had not appeared to hear her. She tried again. 'I got to go out the back for a minute. 'Tis getting a matter of some need.'

Without lifting his gaze from a student's canvas, the master had said, 'We work in sessions of thirty minutes. In fifteen minutes you may retire to the cloakroom.'

From the tone of his voice she had known that he would brook no further interruption, but still she tried. 'This idden no excuse for a rest,' she assured him, 'I really got to go soon. I can't wait for fifteen minutes.' She could hear the tick of the wall clock, the murmur of the master's voice, the scrape of a shoe across the floor as someone changed position. She could bear it no longer. All at once Blanche moved. She flung down the Greek vase and took up a pose that was all her own. Hands on hips, chin lifted, she shouted, 'Now make up your mind, mister! You can either let me go outside for a pee, or have a puddle on your floor!'

The silence had been total. The master moved away from his student's easel and came towards her. 'Young woman,' he said quietly, 'if it were not for the superb pallor of your skin I would make quite sure that you were never again assigned to me.' The elderly gentleman had said nothing but he placed a hand across his moustache, and Blanche was sure that he was smiling.

She had crept away, mortified and silent. Mrs Gimball had laughed until the tears poured down her cheeks. 'Oh ducks,' she wailed, 'I'd of given the world to be a fly on the wall.'

Blanche said, 'I don't know whatever made me say such a thing. But they was all so hoity-toity, and treating me like I was a bit of wood.'

Mr Solomon had first frowned, and then roared with laughter. 'Only you,' he gasped, 'only you would have dared to behave so outrageously in such company.' Later on he spoke seriously to her. 'I want your promise that

116

you'll behave yourself in the future. These are the kind of gentlemen whose wives drape their table legs in case the sight of them should encourage lewd thoughts in their husbands. Nudity is acceptable to them inasmuch as it has to do with Art. Bodily functions are considered to be in bad taste, and never mentioned and it's the wives who set the moral tone these days.' He wagged a reproving finger at her. 'Now remember — decorum and circumspection, at all times.'

She had gone back to the Life School two days later. It had taken courage, but as she told Mrs Gimball, there was small choice for her if she intended to earn what she called 'respectable' money.

Mr Solomon often visited Mrs Gimball's shop in that summer of 1882. He was in one of his more sober and industrious periods when his intake of gin never started before midday. Sometimes he questioned Blanche about the artists for whom she sat, and seemed oddly relieved to discover that they were usually of small importance. 'Who gets into the Life School these days? What names do you hear spoken?' He hesitated. 'I don't suppose you ever hear my name mentioned?'

'I can't say as I do, Mr Solomon. But then I never listens to 'em.' She grew angry. 'I can't make out why you bothers so much about that lot. I've took a look of what some of 'em is painting, and I reckon our liddle Louis could do as well, given half a chance. They idden a patch on you, Mr Solomon, when it comes to knocking-out a decent picture. Why? I wouldn't use their old blotches and smudges to cover up a damp patch on my wall. I can't never recognise myself no matter how hard they tries to paint me.'

Solomon laughed. 'That's because you never see the finished work, Blanche.'

She said, suddenly curious, 'Whatever was it that brought you to this state? Mrs Gimball said as how you

117

was once friends with that old Sir Frederic Whatsit.'

'I moved in high circles, Blanche. When I was a young man every door in this city was open to me. I was a protégé of Rossetti; Algernon Swinburne was my close friend. They said I had a brilliant future, that I was an artist of unlimited potential. I was unfortunate in certain – friendships – there was an unpleasant incident with a young man, and I spent two years in prison.'

Blanche gazed at him with compassion. 'That must of been hard for you, to be put in prison, you being such a gentleman an' all.' To show him that this time she had been truly listening, she added brightly, 'There's an ice-cream vendor what stands in St Martin's Lane. His name's Rossetti. I wonder if he's any relation to your friend?'

Blanche had a curious knack of seizing upon the irrelevancies of life and awarding them her own importance. Some things, she thought, did not bear too close examination, and there were aspects of Blanche which nobody but Loveday Hayes had ever noticed. To be beautiful did not fulfil her every need. She also had her doubts, her longings, her sad misgivings. Life among the artists seemed only to be deepening and widening the chasm that stretched between her and the literate majority. Even Mrs Gimball could read and write.

She had come upon Jye Carew very much as a blind man might stub his toe on an important diamond. To begin with, all her concern had been for herself, for the effect she was obviously having on this simple country yokel. She had watched the widening of his eyes when he first saw her, the shy and nervous sideways glances at her lovely face and arresting figure. But, once convinced of his almost total deafness, a third eye had seemed to open in Blanche. For the first time in her seventeen years she had felt protective towards someone other than her Mama. She had begun to realise that her inability to read and write was a disability about which she also could do nothing. The written word, for Blanche, was a coiled snake, a lurking Devil. The deafness of Jye brought him down onto her own level. She saw herself and Jye Carew as two beautiful but flawed children, standing together, four-square against the world.

It was his Sunday school virtues which had impressed her; religion for Jye was in his bone and sinew. His transition from the Montacute chapel to high church had been easy. There he sat in his mason's apron, head bowed, hands clasped loosely together; he prayed his simple prayers within the grandeur of King Henry's Chapel and saw no incongruity in so doing. She had told him, impetuously, at that first meeting that if only she had been the loving kind, then it was Jye Carew whom she might have loved.

He seemed curiously unimpressed by the honour which had so nearly been bestowed upon him, had displayed a kind of rustic coolness, which had only spurred her on to greater efforts of entrapment. She had never hinted to Jye of her belief in magic, but that statement made to Candace about the sculptor with whom she attended the music-hall, had not been so much a lie as a hopeful look into the future. Blanche was not yet done with Jye Carew.

❊

The yellow fog, which had muffled the first days of this New Year of 1883, had given way to clear and frosty weather. These were joyous, haphazard times for Blanche, in which she flitted between St Martin's Lane and the Life School, sought out Jye Carew in the precincts of Westminster Abbey, and window-shopped down Oxford Street in the company of other artists' models. Sometimes she travelled on the horse-bus; when times were good she hailed a hansom-cab; walking was only for the poor. People stared at the tall and exquisite girl in her fur-trimmed gaberdines and velvets. New clothes of the quality Blanche favoured were as yet beyond her purse, but the forays of Mrs Gimble into the better class areas of Kensington and St John's Wood, usually brought in one or two hardly-worn and fashionable garments. The careful sponging and pressing of these items, the refurbishing of ribbons and buttons gave Blanche a wardrobe that was the envy of other women. She spent her shillings on lace-edged parasols, feather trimmings, muffs and silk-fringed shawls. She scoured the West End emporiums of those exclusive merchants Mr Swann and Mr Edgar, or Mr Derry and Mr Toms, for bargains in petticoats, camisoles and chemises. Her secret ambition was to wear silk and lace next to her skin.

Ellen Gimball still made her monthly visits to her mother in St Martin's Lane, but she came alone these days. 'Things is looking serious,' she told Blanche, 'with your Alice and her fellah.'

Blanche gasped. 'You don't mean that her's thinking of marrying that runty liddle milkman?'

'Oh no. They fell out ages ago. She caught him welshing on one of her bets. Your Alice won't stand for nothing what interferes with her racing. No dearie, 'tis the postman this time. She meets him of an evening down in Charles Street. He's a nice-looking bloke, and she's dead set on marriage, so I reckon as how you could say his number's up!'

Blanche took the horse-bus up to Westminster. She found Jye Carew at work near the north porch, but disinclined for conversation. He continued to work, gaze riveted upon his mallet and chisel. 'You better hop it,' he told her, 'they old masons is getting proper naggy. They keeps hinting on about how funny 'tis that no smart young women do ever come to them to ask for directions to the Poets' Corner.'

'Suit yourself,' she snapped, not knowing or caring if he watched her lips and understood her. 'I got better things to

120

do than stand about in the cold a-listening to you. If you be frightened of that Adge and Joby then you must bide all on your ownsome.'

She looked at his hands; they were large and square, very clean but rough-grained, the fingernails broad and worn down to their quicks by the constant contact with limestone. She remembered last summer and his painful grip on her silk-clad arm when he had put her out of the Dean's Yard. She wanted him to touch her now. Suppose she should faint, dramatically, within the shadows of the north porch? But even as she imagined herself, caught swooning in his strong arms, a priestly black-robed figure came hurrying down the path towards them.

Blanche walked away towards Westminster Bridge, and stood for a long time, looking down upon the thin crust of ice that was slowly creeping inwards along the banks of the Thames. She thought about Taunton, and her Mama, who had allowed the bolt of grey silk to lie untouched for a whole year in the dresser drawer. She remembered Simeon Solomon, and realised that it was at least two months since he had last called in at St Martin's Lane. She decided, on a sudden impulse, that she needed to talk to him, to hear his voice. Blanche waved an arm to halt a passing hansom. 'The Holborn Poorhouse,' she told the astonished cabby, 'and make it as fast as you can. I'm in a hurry!'

She was wearing a particularly impressive outfit of rich green figured-velvet, the gown and its matching cap trimmed with genuine sable, the tiny fur hat perched above one eye. It had come from a little, tree-shrouded house in St John's Wood, where a military gentleman, who wished to wreak revenge upon an errant mistress, had disposed of her entire wardrobe while she slept.

Mrs Gimball had told the tale with some gusto. 'You should just 'ave seen 'im, ducks. Rushing about in 'is nightshirt, 'e was, bundling up all 'er clobber and fair shoving me off the doorstep in case she woke up. Wouldn't take a penny piece for 'em either! Said as 'ow 'e wanted to learn the silly bitch a lesson. "Let her walk home to her husband in nothing but her shimmy," that's what he said.' Mrs Gimball sniffed. 'There's things goes on in St John's Wood lately what would have turned my old dad white-haired overnight.'

The unfaithful one's loss had been Blanche Greypaull's gain. A matching sable muff, bought at Derry and Toms had been all that she had needed to complete the ensemble. Blanche arrived at St Giles-in-the-Fields looking like a duchess.

The steps of the Holborn Poorhouse were crowded with that section of the population which lived, slept and died in the open air of London. Accustomed as she was to the sight of London's poor, the degree of distress shown by these elderly women almost made her climb back into the hansom. The cabby was not inclined to leave her alone and unprotected in such a district. 'I can wait five minutes for yer, miss. But I ain't keen to hang about for too long in these streets.'

"Tis all right,' she told him, 'I got a friend what lives in the Poorhouse.' She spoke absently, unable to look away from the crowded steps where at least a hundred bodies huddled closely together like so many black and starving crows.

'Tell yer what I'll do, miss. I'll drive round for a bit to keep the 'orse warm. I'll be back in a half-hour, how will that suit yer?'

Blanche nodded. She began to walk, very slowly, towards St Giles-in-the-Fields. In order to gain entrance she would have to run the gauntlet of those crouching figures. For the first time in her life Blanche felt privileged and overdressed. Her bulging purse contained several small coins. If it became necessary, she could perhaps clear a pathway into the

Workhouse by scattering largesse among the crowd. She approached them fearfully and on tiptoe, and saw to her surprise that most of the women were dead asleep. She gathered in her skirts, and by stepping carefully between the inert bodies, she gained the Poorhouse door. It took a lengthy inspection through an iron grille, and several pointed questions, before she was admitted.

The Workhouse Master was a large man, stooped in the shoulders, and with hands that were busy with a continual washing motion. Having noted the quality and style of Blanche Greypaull's dress, and on hearing the name of Mr Solomon mentioned, he had ushered her into his office in the manner of a school's headmaster who receives an influential parent. He dusted the seat of a chair with the sleeve of his jacket and invited her to be seated.

'Mr Solomon a relative of yours, is he m'lady?'

The question made Blanche smile. 'My uncle,' she said gravely.

'You shouldn't have never come down here, not on your own.' The man sounded genuinely concerned. 'Does your Mama know about this visit?'

'I shouldn't think so.' The obvious sincerity of this statement had a heartening effect upon the Workhouse Master. 'Ah,' he cried, 'there's not many good women left in this world today, but you m'lady must be one of the best!'

Quick-footed as ever, Blanche moved to follow up her advantage. 'Do you think perhaps, if it's not too much trouble, I might be allowed to see him?'

The man looked uneasily at her. 'You picked a bad time to visit,' he told her. 'Your uncle is not always,' he hesitated, 'he's not always a well man. In fact, there's times m'lady when I despairs of his very life and reason.' He tapped his forehead. 'I expect you knows what I mean?'

'Five minutes?' pleaded Blanche. 'You see, I need his

advice on a problem.'

'Advice?' The astonished man shook his head. He looked doubtfully at her. 'Well, he's your uncle o'course, and I reckon you knows your own business best.' He hesitated. 'He gets very low in spirits, and then he drinks. Nothing we can do except take care of him, and see that he don't harm himself.'

'Harm?'

'He throws hisself about, m'lady. He goes wild and does a lot of damage. In between times he's as gentle as a lamb. But I don't need to tell you that.'

'No,' said Blanche, 'I only know him as a sweet man. He's been good to me.'

The Workhouse Master looked closely at her. 'Ain't you the young lady he's been painting lately?'

Blanche nodded. 'That's right. He's done a lot of pictures of me.'

'If I might say so, m'lady, he ain't quite done you justice in them pictures. But he's not the artist he once was. Don't get me wrong now. We're real proud of Mr Solomon down in Holborn.' The man grinned and looked embarrassed. 'Of course, he's still got his funny little habits; it's them what brought him low in the first place. But he's a gentleman for all that.' A sly note crept into his voice. 'Come far 'ave yer?'

'Berkeley Square,' Blanche lied, 'I have a cabby waiting for me.' She stood up and extended a gracious hand. 'Thank you for your time. Don't mention to Mr Solomon that I called, will you? It might embarrass him.'

'Not a word, m'lady. I can't tell you how long he's likely to be like this. A bad bout can go on for weeks.'

She had intended to leave the Poorhouse, glancing neither left nor right, and seeking only the reassuring sight of the waiting cabby. But the intense cold had driven the women to huddle closer up against the Poorhouse door and Blanche now found it difficult to step between them. She no longer found them frightening, such was their lethargy and state of weakness that a single slight push would have sent the strongest of them toppling backwards. One face turned up towards her and she saw the thin features of a very young girl. Blanche hesitated on the top step, and the child edged away from the green velvet skirts with so much fear that Blanche was shocked into unwilling speech. 'I won't hurt you,' she said sharply, and then more gently, 'What's your name, then?'

The answer came after a long pause, and in a surprised tone. 'They calls me Mollie, ma'am.'

'How long have you been here, Mollie?'

'Dunno. That was hot weather when I first came, now it's freezing.'

'But why do you sit out here in the cold? Why don't you ask to go inside the Poorhouse.'

Mollie did not answer; her head drooped sideways and she seemed to have fallen again into a light doze. Bruises showed plainly through the encrusted grime on the girl's face. Blanche could see the suppurating inroads made by scabies among the bald patches of her scalp; the lobe of her left ear was missing, and the scars of old burns seared her neck. Blanche lifted her foot intending to make a move between the close-packed bodies and the child at once jerked awake.

'They won't let us in there,' she said dully, 'if you tries to get into the Casual Ward more than twice in a month then you lands up in Holloway.'

'But how do you manage?' Blanche cried. 'What do you eat? Do you go up West and beg?'

An unexpected note of pride strengthened the girl's voice. 'Naw,' she said, 'naw, ma'am! I ain't no beggar!' She glanced sideways at her sleeping companions and said with satisfaction, 'I got a job I 'ave! I goes rag-picking down the bone-yard.'

125

'Then what are you sitting here for?' asked Blanche, 'when you should be working?'

'I never woke up in time this morning,' the child said simply. 'You got to get round there well before daylight if you wants a day's work. They only lets in so many pickers, and then they locks the gates. I never had nothing to eat since Tuesday,' she explained, 'the stomach ache kept me awake all night, and I must have dropped-off towards the mornin'.'

'How much do they pay you?'

'Depends on how quick you are, how many sacks you can fill.' Mollie looked contemptuously at her elder companions asleep upon the steps. 'It's better'n begging! It buys enough hot tea and stale bread to keep me goin'.'

'So why haven't you had anything to eat since Tuesday?'

'I 'ad two ha'pennies,' said Mollie, 'but one of these old bitches must've pinched 'em off me while I was asleep. I ain't usually this 'ungry,' she said fiercely, 'it's a good job picking rags. There's perks too.'

'Perks?'

Mollie plucked at the layers of ragged garments that cocooned her body. 'Can't you see 'ow much better I'm dressed than these rotten old scarecrows? If I come across a decent petticoat or frock, or a pair of shoes what still got soles on, then the boss'll sometimes turn a blind eye and let me keep 'em for meself.' She paused, 'I 'as to oblige him first, of course. But he likes 'em young, so that's no problem.'

Blanche felt her stomach turn. 'How old are you, Mollie?' she whispered.

'Dunno. Eleven, twelve maybe. Nobody ever told me exact.'

Blanche pulled out the velvet coin purse, she slipped it quickly between the verminous rags that covered the child's legs. 'Go to the Public Baths right away and scrub yourself

126

clean with soap. Go to a pawnshop and fix yourself up with some decent clothes.' She looked down on the balding scabrous scalp, 'And buy a cap to cover your head! When you're clean and dressed proper, you can try for a job in a hotel kitchen or in a private house.' Blanche did not wait for a reply from the astonished child; she thrust her booted feet between the recumbent bodies, cleared a path for herself down the crowded steps, and ran back towards the waiting hansom-cab.

'You all right, madam? You looks a bit green.'

'The women,' she faltered, 'the poor souls have to live on the Workhouse steps —'

'The "crawlers" you mean? You don't want to feel sorry for them. They only gets what they deserve, that's all!' He lowered his tone to a respectful whisper. 'Ladies of the night that's what they once was, if you'll pardon me using such language in front of you, madam.' The cabby's sanctimonious face assumed a hard expression. 'Vicious criminals, that's what they are. Brought low by disease and old age. Why, even the peelers won't go near 'em for fear of what they might catch!' He raised his whip, and as Blanche climbed into the hansom she heard him shout, 'Just deserts, madam! That's all you've witnessed this day. Just deserts!'

❁

Annis was frightened of her brother, Louis. Although she had never dared to show it, any kind of disability, physical or mental, disgusted and appalled her. She could perhaps have better borne the shame of Louis if he had not, in his looks, been a cruel caricature of Simeon and herself. He had the same fair curls and blue eyes, the same tall and slender body. But in Louis the eyes had a vacant stare, the mouth was slack and damp, and he moved with an unsteady gait, as if he might, at any moment, fall over. It was her very fear of Louis that made her wish to appear solicitous of him.

The plight of those people less fortunate than herself was also a frequent source of hurt to Annis. She would put herself quite deliberately in the way of that pain, by standing outside the Taunton Poorhouse on a Friday evening. She would watch the tramps as they stood in line, the lucky ones to be taken in would chop wood and clean floors in exchange for a week-end's shelter. But the larger number was inevitably turned away.

Whenever she could, Annis withheld her penny from the Sunday morning church collection. All week long she would resist the temptation to spend it on cakes or sweets. She would wait until Friday evening for that moment when the rejected men moved away from the Poorhouse door, then she would make her choice; Annis would select the tramp whom she considered to be the most deserving, and press the penny into his grimy hand.

Lately, she had experienced thoughts that were less than Christian. Annis felt envy for those members of her family who had got away, and yet even to think of escape in relation to Mama had made her feel guilty and ashamed. Letters came only rarely from Candace. Madelina was to marry the upright, irreproachable David. Blanche had flown the coop more spectacularly than any of them; not even Jack, who was making a name for himself in racing circles, could equal the daring and style of Blanche. Simeon was the only one in whom she dared confide.

'Put your hair up if you want to,' he advised her, ''tis your hair idden it?' He urged her to still greater rebellion. 'And if our Blanche ever offers you a gift of her old clothes, then you ought to take 'em. You be both the same height and figure, in fact,' Simeon grinned hugely, 'there's fellers what I know, who is very keen to be introduced to you, our Annis!'

'I don't believe it.'

'Cross my heart, spit in the wind, and wish to die!'

'Don't you ever let-on about they fellers to Mama. Her's very funny on that subject. I s'pose 'tis all the worry what she had with Blanche that do make her so strict on my account.' Annis paused. 'I can't really understand it though, Sim. Mama don't never seem to fret about Mina and Candace.'

Simeon said, 'You must be a bit simple in your head. Don't you never take a good look in the mirror? No wonder Mama won't let you put your hair up. Why, you be ten times better looking that that snotty Blanche!'

'No I idden, Sim. Blanche got style.'

'That only comes from the way she walks and them fancy clothes.'

Annis said sadly, 'Blanche did already look fetching at the age of twelve, when her wore pinafores and still had her hair loose.'

'Well, I don't like her looks,' muttered Simeon, 'and I really hates that red hair!'

❁

The marriage of Madelina Greypaull to David Lambert was solemnized in the Wesleyan chapel on the 7th day of June 1883. It was a simple affair memorable among the Greypaulls only as being the day on which Annis, for the first time in her life, disobeyed her mother, and the occasion on which Eliza at last wore the grey silk that had been the gift of Blanche.

The tiny Mina, in a simple gown of pale blue, had entered the chapel on the arm of her brother, Jack. What she had not been prepared for was the sight of her sister Annis, tall and elegant, her hair taken up, and wearing a gown of yellow silk, that had, quite obviously, once belonged to Blanche. She confided later on to Jack, 'That quite spoiled my day to see Mama all dressed up in our Blanche's grey silk. However was the money earned to buy it? That's what

I ask myself! As for Annis — we was all agreed that her should wear that white frock what her was confirmed in, and keep her hair down. Mama must have been persuaded at the very last minute to let her turn up looking like a — well, you saw for yourself Jack, what our Annis looked like!'

'Annis is growing up, Mina. That can't be denied.'

'Well, all I can say is, that Mama had better watch her. Dressing her up to look like Blanche is a risky thing to do. Why, her even strutted, and swayed her hips as her walked out of chapel. I don't mind telling you, Jack, my heart turned right over.' Mina swallowed hard, and rubbed her eyes. 'I won't cry on my wedding-day. That'll only upset me. But I so wanted it to be my day, Jack. I wanted them all to be looking at me just this one time; after all I was the bride.'

'And so they was, Mina.' Jack put an arm around her shoulders. 'Why you was the prettiest one of all. David never took his eyes off you, no more could I. Our Annis looked proper silly in that yellow frock. I intend to have a word with Mama about that, so don't you worry. There's been enough trouble in this family already; and one Blanche Greypaull is plenty enough for us to bear with.'

Mina sniffed determinedly. 'Oh Jack, I do feel better already.' She smiled, 'Well at least our Blanche never come down for the wedding. Mama wrote to Candace, and they was both invited, but I don't mind telling you, 'twas a real relief to me when they never turned up.' She nodded, furtively, to where her new husband was handing out tea and cakes to his relations. 'You'll never know what trouble I've had making sure that David and his family don't get to know about Blanche.'

'You means to tell me that David Lambert never met our Blanche?'

Mina looked triumphant. ''Twas a close shave at times. I dreaded Christmas when she come back to Taunton. Whatever would he have made of her, Jack? Dressed up like

130

a silly mommet, and all that loose talk about London and artists' models. He's so devout, see! There's such a lot of things what David don't hold with.'

Jack nodded. 'But you'll be safe with him, Mina. I got him all sorted out as soon as I know'd that you was serious about him. Dependable – that's David Lambert. Everybody says so. I wouldn't never have let you marry him, else.'

'Oh, Jack.' This time the tears overflowed. ''Tis so nice to know that you worries about me.' She gripped both his hands until her knuckles whitened. 'I worries about you, too. More than you'll ever know. I can't bear the race days and the thought of you riding bareback. You will be careful, won't you? I couldn't bear it if anything happened –'

'Nothing's going to happen, Mina. Jack Greypaull can look out for hisself, and no mistake! I'll be godfather to your first-born; I even got a name picked out if it should be a girl.'

Mina blushed. 'What name, Jack?'

'Laura! 'Tis a name I once heard down to Wincanton. There's a wealthy owner, a Lord, what got a daughter named Laura.'

❄

Annis knew that she had offended Madelina. The prim little mouth had pursed up at the sight of the yellow gown, and Mina had pointedly ignored her younger sister for the whole of that wedding day. Annis told Simeon all about it.

'You should just have seen 'em, Sim! They Wesleyans is such a stiff lot of people. I thought for a minute that we had walked into a funeral instead of a wedding.'

Simeon, who had volunteered with suspicious alacrity to forgo an attendance at his sister's nuptials, in order to take care of his brother, Louis, began to laugh. 'Do 'ee tell, Annis!'

'Well – there was all these old Lamberts, dressed in black and smelling of mothballs; and you should just of seen their parson. He looked more like a shop floor-walker, no proper vestments, no nothing! Mama was a bit put-out by it all, I can tell 'ee, her being high church and used to things being done proper. O'course, they Lamberts was paying for everything, so 'twas their idea that the wedding must be held in their chapel.' Annis looked significantly at Simeon. 'Like I said to Mama after 'twas all over, it would never surprise me to find out that they chapel weddings is un-legal, and our Mina not proper married after all.'

Simeon guffawed. 'I bet their eyes come out on stalks when they first lamped you!'

Annis simpered. 'I got to confess, Sim, that frock did cause a bit of a stir. Mind you, I didden know that it was going to show my – that the front was so low-cut.'

'What did Mama say?'

'She asked what had happened to the white frock.'

'What did you say?'

'I said what you told me to. That I had accidentally poured a cup of tea right down the front, and since the yellow frock was the only other one what fits me lately – well, o'course I had to wear it.' Annis looked anxious. 'You did remember to put some tea on the white frock didden you, Sim?'

'Soaked it,' he said briefly, 'reckon you'll never be able to wear it again.'

Annis giggled. 'If Mama hadn't gone off early to do the chapel flowers, us'd never have managed it, Sim.'

❁

A letter came from Candace, brief and disturbing, in which she informed her mother that she had married a postman called McGregor, and gone to live with him in Hampstead. A postscript, which said that when last seen, Blanche had been 'in the pink' and 'flush with money', completed the odd little missive. Eliza read and re-read it; everything was changing, and so swiftly that Eliza found it difficult to remember them as her biddable little Greypaulls. Mina conspired with Jack; Simeon with Annis; Candace had removed herself to Hampstead with a postman; and Blanche trod a dangerous path among the artists of London.

She remembered Philip Greypaull's prediction in that final conversation before he had been struck down. 'There is a streak of me in every single one, save Mina', and how accurately he had assessed his own children! Even Annis, whom she had kept so close as befitted the youngest daughter, had appeared in the Wesleyan chapel most unsuitably dressed for a respectable wedding, and with her hair up. As was usual whenever her troubles weighed heavily on Eliza, she found her thoughts turning back to America, to that farm in Suamico, Brown County, where her cousin Rhoda was finding contentment with her patchwork quilting, and the salting down of hog-meat.

2, Hunter's Court,
Taunton, June 1883.

Dear cousin Rhoda,

Not my turn to write I know, but many things on my mind, and nobody to talk to. My Madelina become Mrs David Lambert on June 7th. They have a nice little house, all furnishings paid for by thrift and careful saving. Nice wedding presents from his family was a great help. D. Lambert a *Wesleyan*, but *Chapel* is better than *nothing*. He is a v. sober young man, but hard working.

That wedding did *upset* me, Rhoda. *Not* that I was sad to lose Mina. I knowed that she was going to a good man. No, Rhoda. It was the behavur of Annis what was such a *shock*. She went *behind my back* and disobeyed me, turned up in Chapel wearing one of Blanche's cast-offs, a lewd gown with hardly any *front* to it, and she had put her hair up. I was only too thankful that we was in a *Chapel* and not in our own Church. Oh how lucky you were in marrying Mr Black. My children do so need a Father's guidance, there is times when it all gets too much for me on my own, Rhoda.

I got to be *v.* firm with Annis in the future, or she will go to the *bad*, same as Blanche. The life in Taunton v. dangerus for a young maiden. We got Jellalabad Barracks full of drunken soldjers, and the factorys do make the maidens v. foul mouthed, and *independent*, them having their *own money* of course.

Have kept Annis out of the factory *so far.* We do outwork from the Poolwall Collarmakers, so I always got her *safe beside* me. If only Blanche did not make her restless with tales of London, and giving her such *rude clothes.* I must put my foot down. Life is changed so much from our young days, Rhoda. I mind well the time when you left Buckland St Mary to marry George Salter. You went off to New York, to a strange land and a man what you hardly knowed, and all because your *Father wished it.* Your dowry was paid over, and you done your duty, Dear Cousin, but the young ones of today is not so easy to manage. Look at me. I was told to marry Cousin Philip, so I done it without a murmur, and *made the best of it,* like you had to with your George.

Have read this letter back over and find it full of grumbles, what is not fair because my children *v. good on the whole.* But not Blanche. Think I must be tired, Rhoda. Louis a great strain to look after. Still need to watch him every minit tho nearly nine years old. My worst fear is that neighbours will complain, and that he will be put away in the Asylum. Annis bides with him, for me to go to Church on a Sunday. Church my great pleasure of the week, also your letters, what I keep in a speshul drawer and read over when I am low in spirits.

Hope all is well with you and yours. How is John's health these days? How fares dear Rosa, living in Oshkosh? Do you go to see her? What news of Georgie, is there a Betrothal yet?

Please write when you have time. I start to look out for your letter round about November. Love to all.

Your loving cousin, Eliza.

❋

Jye Carew's absorption with his occupation had almost enabled him to put Blanche Greypaull out of his mind. She had not appeared within the Abbey precincts since that January day when he had told her, quite bluntly, that her presence was becoming an embarrassment to him. But still, the sight of a slender figure dressed in wine or purple would set his heart to thumping in a most alarming way. He tried not to remember the way she had kissed him, full on the mouth, in King Henry's Chapel. 'If I was the loving kind,' she had once said, 'which I am not, oh, how I could have loved you, Jye Carew.'

His suspicion that Blanche was a dangerous woman had been strengthened by every word she uttered, each impulsive gesture. His grandmother had warned him about the folly of ensnarement, and he knew that she had been hinting at that old family story of his mother's crafty catching of his father. 'Don't you never let no fancy woman trap you,' Charity had said. 'Don't you never listen to no sweet words.'

The presence of Blanche within the Abbey walls had always, he now realised, made him feel uneasy. Even on her first appearance when she had run out of a snowstorm and into the north porch, Jye had felt that uneasy pricking of his thumbs, had seemed to sense a frown on the face of the Almighty, which could only occur in the presence of evil. I done right to send her away, he told himself. He tried to work out what it was about Blanche that had so alarmed him, that had made him expect to be struck down by a bolt of righteous lightning every time she walked in at the Abbey door. Her perfume, she once told him, was called Attar of Roses. So why did he catch a whiff of brimstone on the air whenever he was in her company? Only a lewd and sacrilegious woman would have kissed him full on the lips in King Henry's Chapel. This year of 1883 progressed swiftly from summer to autumn. Jye crouched among the stones of London and dreamed of the honeysuckle hedges, the clover-scented meadows of the Somerset heartland. He pictured his mother, hawking basket hooked across her arm, setting out with that long stride peculiar to gypsy women, to sell her wares as far away as Hinton St George, and Cricket St Thomas. Jye stood beneath the cloisters' entrance and watched the shadows lengthen across the pale grass of Dean's Yard, and he knew that very soon now he would ask to be sent home.

George Mitchell came into the masons' lodge at the end of November. He clapped Jye on the shoulder, and then stood with him, face-to-face. He indicated the work which lay on Jye's banker. 'You be much improved since you come to London.' The master-mason smiled. 'You be nineteen years old come next New Year; apprenticeship'll be all over and done with then, eh boy?'

Jye nodded.

George Mitchell said, 'I won't beat about the bush. You're the sort of feller I could do with having in my Monumental business.'

'Gravestones?' Jye asked.

'Aye, boy. Gravestones. The Londoners is very fond of their cemetery furniture. There's a powerful fashion just now in the life-sized marble angel. What do you say?'

Jye shook his head. 'I likes the church work, Mr Mitchell,' he said diffidently. 'Don't think as how I don't appreciate the favour.' He held out his hands, chisel in one, mallet in the other. 'My father always worked on churches and abbeys, see, and that wudden feel right somehow, if I was to bide shut up in your yard, chipping out gravestones.'

George Mitchell considered him. 'You be set firm on that decision?'

'I be, sir.'

'Would you come back to London if I was to find you work on other churches. Our contract have finished on Westminster Abbey. Adge and Joby'll be going home for good, come Christmas.'

Jye still looked unhappy. 'I'd like to come back. 'Tis an experience, a chance to learn what might never come my way again. But I wudden fancy lodging in Great Smith Street without Adge and Joby.' He blushed. 'That Irish woman is a bit too forward for my liking. Her's always trying to hug and kiss me while I eats my dinner.'

Mitchell laughed. 'Fancies you, does she? That's the price you pays, boy, for being tall, dark and handsome! Tell you what – go back home for Christmas. Bide a couple of weeks this time, talk it over with your mother. If you be still of a mind to come back in the New Year, then my missus can find you lodgings close to my house. How'll that suit 'ee?'

'I'd like that very much, sir.'

❋

Montacute looked smaller on his return. It was always the same in those first few days, before his mind had stretched out again to find its true length, until his body had relaxed into the quiet shades of a dun-coloured winter, and his eye had measured the height of the magical Hill, the depth of the valley.

He could almost, in these first days at home, comprehend his mother's urgent need to wander. But Jye's compulsion was never with the new, only with a wish to realign his heart and eye with the familiar and well-loved. He beat the boundaries of his childhood by walking to the crossroads at Five Ashes and standing for some minutes beneath the trees that shadowed Pitt Pond. He walked the narrow roads to Odcombe and Martock and found those two villages unchanged. Last of all, on Christmas Eve, he climbed the slippery cropped turf of Ham Hill; already the heavy rains of December had brought up the floods over Athelney and Sedgemoor. He could see the shimmer of silver water out towards the west. He turned back towards the quarry, and looked down upon the little tin-roofed huts of the many lodges perched among the face. He remembered that day, long ago, when he had brought up his father's nammet, and, not finding him at his banker, had looked down onto the stonebed and seen the tall figure in the bloodstained shirt lying dead from a fall of stone. He remembered his own sore hands and aching muscles when he had wrestled, at the age of twelve, with a surly stone.

The completion of Jye's apprenticeship had been 'kept up' in London. George Mitchell had saved a special firkin for that very purpose, and Jye, for the first time in his life, had drunk deeply of cider. A few Cockney masons had joined in with the celebration, and Jye grinned now, as he recalled how they had staggered and reeled after only one mugful.

'Weak heads,' Joby Stagg had muttered. 'See that, boy, and never forget it! That do take Somerset fellers to drink Somerset cider.'

On Sunday morning Jye attended chapel with his mother. He looked down on her carven face as they walked the short step between Bishopston and South Street. Meridiana, in sober black, shawled and booted, still had that same exotic air of some wild and reckless creature who should not be so confined. It came to him, with a sense of shock, that his mother had only ever looked content when dressed in her

138

old faded plaids, her feet and head bare.

He sat down in the polished pew and looked about him with his new eyes. He measured the altar and its cross of brass, the spindle-railed oaken pulpit, the wall-sconces that held the oil-lamps, the whitewashed walls, clean and without adornment. He closed his eyes and conjured up King Henry's Chapel, Westminster, and he knew that no true comparison could ever be made between the two — that here was here, and there was there, and no path, no matter how straight and even, could ever be beaten between Montacute and London.

Almost one whole year it had taken them to raise this chapel. The foundation stone had been laid in June 1879. On Thursday, May 27th 1880 the new building had been opened. It had cost them all of a thousand pounds, even though the masons and many other workers had volunteered their labour, and stone from the old chapel had gone into the rebuilding of the new. Squire Phelips had given the land, and the Baptist church of Norwood had donated a circular stained-glass window, made under the architect's directions by German workers in Munich.

But it was the laying of the white marble step that formed the main entrance which had given Jye the greatest pleasure. It had been donated by George Mitchell and was made from a worn step which he had recently replaced before the high altar of St Paul's Cathedral. It was on that day Jye first learned about the man called Mitchell. This thin energetic mason, who described himself as 'one from the plough', had been born in Montacute in 1827. He had begun work at the age of seven as a bird-scarer on the Abbey Farm, and at the age of eighteen he had received a weekly wage of four shillings, with no limit set upon the number of hours worked. Now, at fifty-six, he was a wealthy man, a master-mason, but he had never forgotten the Sunday school and chapel of his boyhood, or the people of his home village. His financial help had enabled them to raise a new School House and chapel; he recruited the masons from Ham Hill who were anxious and willing to earn good money in London. The chance to work on the great abbeys and cathedrals did not, thought Jye, come to every mason. He looked up to find the service ended, and his mother waiting for him.

❊

Spend two weeks at home, Mr Mitchell had told him, talk it over with your mother. But already, on New Year's Eve Jye was growing restless.

''Tis a chance to learn more of the stone-carving, a chance what may never come again,' he told Meridiana.

'How long will it be this time?' Her voice was hard, her face tight and shut against him.

'A year,' he said, 'at least a year.'

She fixed him with that penetrating stare which struck dread into the village people. ''Tis a woman, idden it, Jye? You might as well own-up, for I can read you clear enough.'

He joked and smiled. 'You been sneaking a look at my palm when I wasn't looking?' But she was not to be gainsaid.

She said, 'I always knows, direct from my head to your head, what you be thinking. There's no chance for you to tell a lie and make me believe it. There's a girl jammed away in the back of your mind; a girl of the sort that you be shamed of knowing.' She leaned forward. 'How far have it gone, boy? Have you laid down yet with this gorgie?'

He blushed to the very tips of his ears. Only a Rom woman, he thought, would have dared to be so blunt in her speech, so 'immodest'. 'No,' he muttered, 'and I haven't never come close to doing such a thing!'

She considered him, calmly. 'Then p'raps 'tis time you did, boy. Get the harlot out of your blood, for her's doing

140

you no good at all.'

'Her idden no harlot!' The admission, made in a rush of temper, had been involuntary.

His mother smiled. 'You be sore tempted, eh Jye?'

He nodded. 'Aye. But her's the Devil's agent. I be feared of her, Mother.' The need to confide was too strong now to be resisted. 'Cast your mind back,' he told her, 'remember a day when you and me went down to Taunton? Remember that farm-cart laden down with furniture, and the red-haired woman and her seven children?'

'Eliza Greypaull,' Meri whispered, 'and that chie with the proud looks and the knowing eyes. However did that one come to be in London?'

'Her come up to work, same as me, Ma. Only difference is, that her don't like work.'

Meri grinned. 'I can well believe that. Her father was the same. Reckoned hisself quite the gentleman did Philip Greypaull.'

'What'll I do, Ma?'

Meri looked at him, and shook her head. 'The deafness have saved you until now from wicked hussies.' She paused. 'I had hoped that you might take a fancy to Petronell Locke, she's my cousin's second daughter.'

'A gypsy?'

'Aye, boy, a gypsy.' Meri's tone became astringent. 'You be yourself three parts Rom. 'Tis only that old Charity Carew what gives you the one part of gorgie blood.'

Jye moved uneasily in his chair. 'I never reckoned on marrying no diddecoi –'

'Diddecoi!' Meri leapt from her stool and stood over him. She gripped his face in both her hands and rocked his head from side to side. 'Don't you never let me hear that word in your mouth again! You is come from stock what is pure Rom, wi'out taint. The diddecoi is a half-breed –'

'And so be I, Ma. You said it yourself, just a minute ago.'

'That old Charity don't matter.'

'Yes she do, Ma! She's my grandmother. She've always been good to me. I won't let you discount her!'

Meridiana took her hands away from his face. 'So,' she said softly, 'you've learned other things in London besides the stone-chipping. Look in the mirror, boy. 'Tis the Rom blood what have made you handsome. No amount of arguing'll change that.'

'And 'tis gorgie blood what have made me steady, and willing to bide still at my chosen work.' His features worked with a rare emotion. 'I was called diddecoi in school. I bet you never know'd that!'

'I know'd it, Jye. But there was nothing to be done about it. They called your father diddecoi when he was a boy. 'Tis the way of the gorgie to fear what he don't understand. But you idden no half-breed. Never forget that. Pass it on to your children, and their children!' He had never known her to be so upset, so passionate in her denials.

''Tis all right,' he soothed her, 'I got no intentions of marrying for many years yet.'

'And the Greypaull chie? However did 'ee come to meet up with her, Jye?'

''Twas accidental. Her come into the Abbey one day when I was working.'

A strange look came into Meri's face. 'That was no accident. That was meant to happen. Tidden none of your fault, boy. You must never blame yourself for anything what comes to pass with that chie! You be as helpless in this matter as was Luke, your father, when he first spoke to me by the walls of Buckland church.' She stretched out her hand, palm upwards. ''Tis all writ in the lines, Jye.'

He thrust out his hand. 'Then do 'ee tell I,' he laughed, 'do 'ee tell I what is writ there.'

'No,' she said, 'no, I can't never tell for family.'

142

The familiar blue envelope was delivered to Hunter's Court in late November. Eliza laid aside the collar she was stitching and opened the letter. A few pressed flowers lay between the pages. She examined them carefully, but could not identify them.

Suamico. October 1st, 1883.

Dear cousin Eliza,

I pick up the pen once again to write my regular letter. Harvest is all done with and we are again into the cooler weather. The heat was something *fierce* this Summer, and with so many hands to cook for, the kitchen range a *real Torment* to stand close to. This is the best time of the year in Brown County. Our winter wheat is in and already showing the first shoots. It should have come good and green before the snows start. I felt so done-up all summer long, but all my old *vim* and *vigour* have come back again, thank goodness. Am up to my elbows in pickling and canning, so much food to be put down for winter days, and hired men *always so hungry*, and will not work well if not *fed good*. Father Black also weary this year. He is looking awful tired around his eyes. The rest of his face is hid behind a fine black beard and moustaches.

Had a good year, all told. Father Black sold our Hay very well in Green Bay. He come home driving a spanking brown and yellow Buggy, a new one *with springs*. So now our ride into Church of a Sunday is not so bumpy as with our old farmcart. Had to retrim my bonnet to keep up with our new transportashun. You ask about George in your letter. Well, Eliza, my Georgie is at last *betrothed*, he will be twenty-six next January. He have brought his intended home to meet with us. A v. nice girl, eighteen years old, and a cabinet-maker's daughter what lives in De Pere. Her name is Sarah Ann Annas, what trips very sweet off the tongue. She is v. quiet and shy, but George got enough *get up and go* in him for both of them. Father Black and me took to her right away. George have nicknamed her Satie. Why, I don't know. They aim to get wed next September. George talks of buying himself a Meat-Market, what was his departed father's line of business. Money lays in trust for Georgie from his father, to come to him on marriage. Satie is one of a family of eleven, so probably no dowry from them.

So sorry to hear of your worry about Annis. But she is very young, Eliza, and can still be *bent to your will*, I am certain. Like you say, dear cousin, things is very diffrent than in our day. I got a hired girl at this minute, what is very *knowing* and *forward*. She hangs about the threshers gang waiting to be *noticed*. I have to get v. sharp with her at times.

John still very weak from bronchial trouble. I *dread* every Winter for him, our Winters here being very long and hard. Rosa is well, no hint of a grandchild yet, but I am hopeful. Christmas is coming close again, and I hope you will not have too troubled a time with Blanche.

What *exactly* is she *doing in London?* Or don't you *know?* Much love to you all.

From your devoted cousin, Rhoda.

❀

The tradition that Blanche would provide for them all had established itself so firmly among her brothers and sisters that they quite expected her arrival on Christmas Eve, laden down with parcels, her purse yielding sovereigns. The emergence of Blanche from the Hunter's Court alley had become an event for which neighbours waited, and she did not disappoint them. The impressive outfit of rich green figured-velvet, its gown and matching cape trimmed with genuine sable, the tiny fur hat perched above one eye, had been so theatrical that this time even Louis noticed. He had claimed the hat even as Blanche stepped across the threshold,

144

had snatched it from her head and retired to his corner, where he cradled it in his arms, crooned and stroked it as if it were a puppy or kitten. Eliza attempted to retrieve it, but Blanche said, 'No! Let him keep it, Mama. He got so little to make him happy. I can easily get another bonnet.' She studied her brother. 'He's getting tall and broad in the shoulder. Do he give you any trouble?'

Eliza looked worried. 'He only goes out when one of us can take him. That do make him restless sometimes. He bangs his head on the wall, and then he cries.' She paused and touched the puckered skin around her eye. 'He do love a heap of straw to play with. Simeon brings some for him, from the Market. But you don't want to hear about that, maid! Put the kettle on now Annis. Your sister have had a long cold journey.'

Blanche opened her purse and took out three sovereigns. Annis and Simeon no longer needed her instructions, they ran from the house to the Christmas market intent on the catching of bargains. As the door slammed shut behind them Blanche looked around the little room, relaxed and sighed. For once in her life she had Mama all to herself, since Louis hardly counted as a person. She was reminded, unexpectedly, of Larksleve. There was the pegged rug laid across the hearthstone, her mother's rocking-chair set upon it. On the mantelshelf stood the two pretty vases of blue fluted-glass, which had once been hidden by Candace and Madelina before the Bailiffs' visit.

'You looks well, Blanche. The life do seem to suit you in London.' Blanche smiled. Without Madelina's sharp tongue and disapproving glances, Mama seemed less inclined to be critical, her tone less reproachful. 'That was a lot of money you gave Annis for shopping –'

'I can afford it, Mama.' Blanche spoke softly. ''Tis money earned honest and decent in the Academy Life School. No need for you to worry about it.'

145

'You still goes among these artists, then?'

'They only paints my neck and shoulders. Sometimes they sketches my face, but not often.'

'I find that a bit surprising, maid.' Her mother hesitated. 'Your brother, Jack, thinks that you would have to — to take your clothes off to earn all that much money.'

'And what do dear brother Jack know about it, Mother!' Blanche spoke softly, but with venom. 'He never been further than Wincanton in all his life. He do live and breathe among horseflesh.' Blanche began to sob. 'He's always hated me. He always told lies about me when I was little. They all hated me, Mama. Didden you never notice that?'

Eliza busied herself among the teacups. 'Now don't start all that, Blanche! You knows I can't stand it. 'Tis Christmas, and if you tells me that what you do up in London is all nice and decent, then I believe you!' She handed Blanche a cup of tea and patted her arm. 'You won't have to sleep on the kitchen table in future. With Mina gone there's a bed to spare in the back room.'

'What's the matter with our Annis?' Blanche spoke abruptly, and Eliza answered her with anger. 'There's nothing the matter with Annis. Why should there be?'

'Her looks pale and peaky.'

''Tis her age. She's outgrowing her strength. She must have grown six inches in the last two years, and we don't eat meat or cheese very often.'

'Simeon looks well enough.'

'He begs his food round the Market.' Eliza flushed with the shame of it. 'I can't do anything with him, Blanche. He's a law to hisself.'

'Annis needs some fresh air.'

'Oh, we do go for walks on a Sunday. We goes out towards Bishop's Hull —'

'I don't mean like that, Ma! Annis needs to be with girls of her own age, not shut up all week in this room, sewing

146

shirt collars.'

Eliza paled, until every freckle stood out, ugly and liver-coloured across her cheekbones. 'You mind your business, miss,' she told Blanche. 'How you carries on in London is your own affair, but I won't have her mixing with the kind of trash that works in the Taunton factories. Why! if we was still on Larksleve, Annis would be –'

'But we is not still living on Larksleve, Mama. This is Hunter's Court, Taunton, and you needs the money very badly. Annis is old enough to go out and earn. If she's as good as you say she is, then the life in the factory won't harm her, will it?'

'I don't know, Blanche. She's all that I've got in life now that Mina's left me.'

'You never minded parting with me and Candace.'

'That was different.'

'Let her go, Ma! If you truly love her then let her have some freedom. She'll still come back to you every night. You can still walk to Bishop's Hull on a Sunday afternoon.'

Eliza shook her head. 'I don't know. I'll have to pray about it. In the meantime – not a word to Annis, mind you! I'll not have you encouraging her to disobey me!' Eliza faltered. 'I – I suppose you got a lot of friends in London?'

Blanche sighed. 'If you mean men-friends, Mama, then why don't you say so?' Her voice became regretful. 'As it happens I don't know all that many people. These artists is a rum lot and not a bit friendly. Some of the men who come to the Life School seems to pair-off together. Truth to tell, Mama, I only got one regular friend in London, and he's a Montacute feller.'

'Whatever is a Montacute boy doing up in London?'

Blanche looked uneasy. 'I don't know what you'll say when I tell you who he is. His name is Jye Carew. He's the son of that gypsy we once met on the side of the road.'

'Meridiana's son?'

Blanche nodded. 'He's doing-up Westminster Abbey, or something! He do make a great fuss about they old carvings what the monks done, years ago. He's always showing 'em to me.'

'How did you come to meet him, Blanche?'

'I was doing what you told me, Ma.' She looked self-righteous. 'I promised I'd go to church, and so I did! I went to the biggest one I could find in London, and there was this Jye scratching away at some old bit of rock.'

Eliza looked troubled. 'You'd best leave that boy alone, Blanche. He's deaf, as you will have found out, and the apple of his mother's eye. It don't do to cross Meridiana Loveridge. She's a dangerous woman.'

Blanche smiled. 'Oh, but so be I, Mama!' she said softly. 'Oh, but so be I!'

It had been a very quiet season. Madelina had sent a note round on Christmas Day to say that she was indisposed, and that David was fully occupied in chapel. Jack had not even troubled to inform them, but had let his absence speak for itself at the New Year. Avoidance of their sister, Blanche, was the object of the conspiracy, thought Annis. She, on the other hand, had enjoyed the annual visit, Blanche brought life and colour with her. The scent of attar of roses on her clothes and person conjured all the glamour and romance of life in London. With Simeon absent for most of the time, there had just been Mama in her rocking-chair each evening, with Annis at her feet on the low stool, and Blanche seated at the table, close to the lamp. Even Louis had seemed to find some rare contentment this year. Curled up in his corner with a heap of straw and the sable hat, he had not once banged his head or wept.

How beautiful Blanche had looked in the lamplight! Annis yearned for that richness of auburn hair, that whiteness of skin. Blanche was also witty and amusing. Even Mama had laughed outright at some of those stories about London people. Just for a moment Annis had been tempted. She had almost cried out, 'Take me with you when you go!' But then she had looked at Mama, and poor Louis in his corner, and she could not say the words. Mama was quite right of course. The rheumatic fever had weakened her constitution, as her mother so often said, Annis was not strong, nor ever would be. There were the headaches which caused complete prostration. There was her tendency to swoon and faint in the face of trouble or the illness of others. The delicacy of Annis had only increased her value in Mama's eyes. Swooning and headaches were a sign of good breeding and fine feelings.

A young woman, Blanche had said, would need to be strong and fearless if she wished to work in London, and Annis had no doubt that Blanche was among the strongest and most courageous of them all, while Annis feared everything, and everybody.

❋

The indisposition of Madelina, had, in fact, been no idle excuse to avoid her sister, Blanche, it continued well into the New Year and caused great concern to Eliza and David Lambert. On the first of March it was confirmed by a doctor that Mina was expecting a happy event, and in this case the euphemism happened to be true. She and David were filled with a shy delight that compensated Eliza for many of her own hurts and disappointments at such times. Knitting and sewing now became the main preoccupation of Annis and her mother.

'Six of everything,' Eliza said, 'and all in white, mind you! No coloured clothes for the first twelvemonths of the baby's life, now remember that, Mina!'

Eliza insisted that Annis should visit Madelina daily, to

check on her condition, and Annis, who found this contact with pregnancy and sickness most distasteful to her, was now forced to enter the little Grey's Road cottage where her sister lay, nauseous and pale upon her front-room sofa.

Annis could not bear to live in a world where she was unloved. The approval of her mother, her brothers and sisters, was as necessary to her as the air she breathed. Since that day when she had appeared at Madelina's wedding dressed in the startling yellow gown once owned by Blanche, a coolness had existed between the two sisters, and Mina held grudges. Annis feared those hooded and venomous glances from her sister's green eyes, that pursing of the pink mouth, the threatening, almost snakelike inclination of the dark head. She longed to hold out her arms to Mina, to say, amid tears, 'I'm sorry. I never meant to hurt you!' But spontaneous weeping had never been encouraged by Mama, and Annis could feel the apology and the love behind it wither up and die unspoken inside her.

David and Madelina Lambert, by the practice of strict economy, had furnished a parlour that was as nearly a facsimile of that in Larksleve as Madelina could possibly make it. Everything was blue; the painted walls, the lino, the homemade hearth-rug and the curtains, the chenille table-cloth with its fringe of silk bobbles, even the pictures on the wall had been chosen for their predominant shades of blue.

'Oh Mina!' breathed Annis, ''tis so elegant and fashionable. How smart the what-not do look with all your wedding-present china set out upon it.' She came closer and bent over her sister. 'I just love your sofa, and how genteel you do look, lying there all pale and delicate-looking.' The hooded eyes grew wide and softened a little, the prim lips parted.

'Well, yes,' conceded Madelina, 'us had to work very hard to get it, but 'twas worth the satisfaction.'

She raised herself on an elbow. 'Do 'ee really like it, then, Annis?'

'Oh yes. I truly do!' Annis who had discovered, accidentally, that flattery would work miracles with Madelina, was in fact quite sincerely impressed by her sister's achievement, and resolved right away that when her own time came, she also would have a parlour done out exclusively in blue.

'How do 'ee feel then, Mina?'

'Sick,' was the terse reply, 'and sicker with every day that passes. I can't keep nothing down save barley water.' Tears of self-pity filled Madelina's eyes. ''Twill be a poor liddle sample of a baby at this rate. I don't know what I ever done to deserve all this.'

Annis said awkwardly, 'Mama says 'tis only at the beginning that you feels so awful. You'll be better soon, just you wait and see.'

'No, I shan't.' There was no consoling Mina. 'I got to go over to Poolwall and tell Mr Gliddon that I shan't be coming back to work any more. I can hardly stand up at the minute. David says I got to give in my notice.' She sniffed and fought back the tears. 'We could have done with the money for a bit longer. But there 'tis!'

'So they'll be wanting a button-holer at Poolwall?'

Mina's look was sharp and penetrating. 'You wants my job, is that it?'

''Tis only for Mama's sake,' Annis murmured. 'I could earn such a lot more money if only I was in the factory. You've said yourself that I be as good as you on the sewing-machine. If you was to put in a word for me with that Mr Gliddon – ?'

Mina frowned. 'I can't do nothing without first talking it over with Mama.'

'Oh, her'll listen to you Mina,' flattered Annis, 'her got a lot of respect for your opinion and David's. You two being Sunday-school teachers, and all that sort of thing!'

'That might be a good idea, for you to go into the factory,' Mina spoke thoughtfully. 'If Mama or Louis should fall sick 'twould be difficult for Dave and me to give any help, 'specially with a baby coming. You be a first-rate button-holer, Annis. Why, you wouldn't need any training. The extra money would make a lot of difference in Hunter's Court. You wouldn't need to take the charity of our Blanche no more, what, between you and me, is no better than she should be!'

Annis sighed with pleasure, and her eyes shone. 'Do 'ee really think that our Blanche do take all her clothes off?'

'Loose!' snapped Mina, 'that's what our Blanche is. Her was always wild, even at Larksleve. I minds the time when her and Loveday put a pig's heart up the chimney for to make a spell to kill Papa!' Mention of the pig's heart had been a mistake for one in Madelina's condition. She turned a pale shade of yellow and swallowed, but continued bravely, 'There's something evil about Blanche. You'd do well to remember that, Annis! My David do have the gravest doubts about her, but for you he do have a very high regard.'

'Is that true then?'

'Oh, yes! My David have seen you giving alms to the tramps at the Workhouse, and the way you bides at home to mind poor Louis is a lesson to us all, according to Dave.'

'I never know'd that,' said Annis. 'I never thought that David liked me.'

'He's not one to wear his heart on his sleeve.' Madelina nodded. 'But he got a lot of respect for you, Annis. I hopes you never disappoints him.'

'Oh I won't.' To be respected by the likes of David Lambert was more than Annis had ever hoped for. 'Then you'll speak to Mama for me, Mina?'

'I'll talk to Dave about it. Meanwhile, there's certain matters you'd do well to reflect on. The Poolwall factory is a sink of iniquity. 'Tis a hive of temptation, where maidens like yourself is quite easily took-in and done-for. I sees it happening every day. A young girl comes in, all innocent and dew fresh, and before a week is passed, why she's consorting with the men and using foul language. Next thing you know, she's in a certain condition.'

'I won't never do that, Mina.'

'Well, I should hope not. You know what Mama says? We must never forget who and what we are, and the good yeoman stock we sprung from. The Miss Greypaulls of Larksleve, that's what we are, Annis. Never mind about Papa and all what happened. There was Greypaulls at the Court of King Henry the Eighth!'

'I never speaks to any of the neighbours,' said Annis primly, 'there was enough of that with our Blanche. That nearly got her into trouble –'

''Tis the same in the factory. You got to keep yourself to yourself if you wants to bide decent. You can be polite and ladylike, but you don't need to lower your standards. You understands what I be saying?'

'I think so, Mina. Anyway, I won't never do anything to shame you and David.'

Mina smiled conspiratorially. 'You won't never wear any more of that Blanche's clothes, will you, Annis? The cut of her gowns is quite indecent. I shouldn't like David to ever again see you showing yourself off the way Blanche do.'

❋

'So you're one of my outworkers?'

Annis nodded. She stood before the high desk of the factory owner and prayed that she might find favour in his eyes. He looked closely at her.

'I'm told that you've been employed on special orders, you and your mother.' His tone was grave. 'I think you would be very surprised young woman, if you knew how many famous necks are, at this very moment encircled by our collars.' He paused. 'How old are you Miss Greypaull?'

'Seventeen, sir, come October.'

He nodded. 'You'll do well to come into the factory. Our mechanisation has reached a point where we no longer require so many outworkers. In fact, but for a few very special orders, most of our work is now done on the premises. I believe you're a button-holer?'

'Yes, sir.'

'Very well. You can take over your sister's machine in the button-hole department.' He hooked his thumbs into his waistcoat pockets and looked portentous. 'One word before you go, Miss Greypaull. I wish you to remember at all times that collars are important. A gentleman is judged by the collar he wears. It gives an indication of his character and station in life. I like to think that we at Gliddons have made our contribution to the status and high esteem in which this great Empire of ours is held throughout the civilised world! To us has fallen the singular honour of making the "Eton" collar and the "Gladstone", among many others too numerous to mention.'

He paused to draw breath, and Annis murmured, 'Shall I start on Monday then, sir?'

'Monday it is, young woman.' He observed her from head to toe, and chuckled. 'And look out for the boys in the packing department, they're a wild lot!'

The site of Gliddon's collar factory had been well-chosen. It stood beside the Poolwall stream and was within easy distance of the railway station. The fashion in collars and cuffs and detachable shirt-fronts, had enabled Mr Gliddon to modernise his premises, install the gas-engine which drove the machinery, and keep in regular employment a work force of five hundred people.

Annis arrived at the factory gate on Monday morning. She wore a plain dark dress and had her hair up. 'All the girls at

Poolwell have got their hair up,' she had assured Eliza, 'they'll only laugh at me if I don't.' Her mother had relented, 'but no fancy style, you hear me, Annis. You can plait it and coil it neat and tidy at the back of your head. Same as Madelina and me.' The raising of the waist-length hair had made a subtle difference to her appearance, and Annis knew it. She had felt her shoulders straighten of their own volition, her spine stiffen. She had raised her head and pointed her chin at the angle most favoured by her sister, Blanche. The women and girls were watching from beneath lowered eyelids as the forewoman led Annis to the button-holing machine that had lately been worked by Madelina.

'You'll find a difference here,' the forewoman warned her, 'you'll have used a hand machine on the outwork. All our operations are done by gas-power.' She indicated the central shaft which divided the room. 'Just a light touch on the treadle will set your motor working.'

The collars were brought to her in bundles of a dozen. Annis worked until the bell shrilled, pausing only to untie and retie her bundles, her fingers quick and neat, her concentration total. The forewoman praised her. 'Not as how I expected you to be flighty,' she said, 'not with your Mina for a sister.'

They sat on benches in the factory yard to eat their midday bread and cheese, and drink their cold tea. It was pleasant in the April sunshine; Annis sat a little apart from the main group, as was proper in a newcomer and stranger. They talked about her as if she was not present.

'Her's nothing like their Mina,' said a girl called Sally.

'Her looks too proud and haughty to be religious,' said another.

'With a shape like that who needs to be religious?' The question had come from the nearby benches where the men and boys were segregated. Annis could feel the hot blood staining her fair skin, and she raised both hands to

155

cover her cheeks.

'Now look what you've done, Harry Vincent! Her's shy and innocent.' The girl's sly remark roused a shout of derision from both men and women.

'There was nothing shy about their Blanche.' The speaker was a tall young man with a shock of dark-brown hair. Annis recognised him as one of the three brothers who lived in Hunter's Court. 'Game for anything their Blanche was!' He spoke directly to Annis. 'Still got the mark on my back, I have, from that night when your Ma chucked the coal-hammer at me.'

Annis pinned him with an icy stare. 'Serves you right, Tom Bidgood. 'Twas lucky for you that my Mama didden aim a bit higher. Then she might have put your last few brains out.'

There was laughter, and Sally cried, 'Listen to her! She got a "Mama" at home, girls!' She confronted Annis. 'I bet you plays the piano and goes to church of a Sunday?'

'As a matter of fact I don't play piano, but my Mama do.' The girls clutched at one another in an excess of mirth. 'Her don't play piano,' they mocked, 'oh! but her Mama do.'

Annis felt tears prick behind her eyelids, she was about to jump up and run away when the starting bell sounded. As she walked back to her machine a boy in a tweed peaked cap contrived to walk beside her. 'Don't pay 'em no mind,' he muttered. 'They be only jealous because you talks nice and behaves like a lady. If you get any lip from anybody, just you let me know. My name is Frank Nevill, and I work in the packing department.'

❋

George Mitchell had obtained a room for Jye in a respectable house, which stood in the shadow of Westminster Abbey. To have his own proper bed, and a key with which he might lock his door, was confirmation for Jye of his new status as a time-served mason. He was set to work on several London churches, and in May he was taken by George Mitchell to the Mansion House where he saw, for the first time, that impressive building, which had been raised mainly in Portland stone.

The stone from Portland was more durable than the softer Ham stone, which did not weather quite so well in the larger cities. The challenge of working exclusively in this harder and different medium was one that had exhilarated but tired him. After eating the meal prepared for him by the landlady, Jye could do no more than fall into the deep sleep of exhaustion.

He had attended church every Sunday morning since his return to London; he usually worshipped at those same churches in which he had worked for the previous week. The job in the Mansion House promised to be lengthy, and Jye, against his will, now found himself drawn back again to the Chapel of King Henry in Westminster Abbey.

She was there on that Sunday morning, as he had known she would be, waiting for him as he emerged into the July sunshine. She wore an elaborate gown of stiff cream silk with scarlet trimmings; her lips and her parasol were of matching scarlet. She smiled, and he felt the weakness invade every part of his body, a weariness far greater than any he had suffered from the carving of Portland stone. He watched her lips with an intensity of concentration that almost persuaded him that he could hear the high and childish pitch of her voice. 'You've been hiding yourself away from me, haven't you, Jye?' The question had him stumbling and incoherent.

'No – no I haven't. I don't work no more on the Abbey buildings. I works in other places – I –'

She reached out a silk-gloved hand, but he evaded her touch. He began to stride away, decent and tall in his Baptist black and clean white collar. She moved easily beside him, she swung him around to face her. 'No use your trying to get away from me,' she warned him, 'I can walk as fast as you can.' She giggled. 'Shall I tell you a secret? I chucked away my whalebone corsets as soon as I went to live at Mrs Gimball's. I be exactly as nature intended underneath this gown.' She glanced up at him from beneath her parasol. 'You think on that, Jye Carew!'

He was thinking on it; he was also remembering his mother's words. 'How far have it gone, boy? Have you laid down yet with this gorgie?' and he, blushing to the tips of his ears. 'No,' he had said, 'no, and I haven't never come close to doing such a thing.' But he had thought about it. In those nights in the cupboard-bed in Mrs Murphy's kitchen. In those winter days when he had stood in the gloom of Pitts Pond, when he had walked the road to Odcombe, and stood on the slippery turf of Ham Hill. He had thought about himself, lying down with Blanche Greypaull, and the chance was always his; you could even say that she was asking for it.

She halted again as they came up to St Margaret's Church; she looked up into his face. 'What's the matter with you?' she asked urgently. 'Have you already got a girl, or don't you have any manhood?'

'I got no girl,' he muttered, 'I never did have. As for my manhood, 'tis becoming a proper burden to me.'

'I can ease that for you.' She slipped her hand into his and squeezed it. 'Mrs Gimball's gone away for the day. She's off to see her sister in Seven Dials and won't be back till after dark. Come over to St Martin's Lane and see where I live.'

❀

It had taken all of Loveday Hayes' remembered magic to bring this Jye to the place where Blanche would have him be. The more elusive he had proved, the more she desired him. She was tormented by the image of his dark face,

158

his heavy-lidded eyes, and the black curls that tumbled about his ears and forehead. She could not bear the thought of his continued resistance, even though she had no intention of allowing him her 'final favour'. Only foolish girls allowed themselves to be caught in that trap, and Blanche had no wish to end up with the 'crawlers' on the steps of St Giles. Most of the men she met were over-eager to possess her. There were artists in the Life School who regularly offered her inducements of clothes and money, promises of employment that were bound to further her career if she would only do as they required. It was only the stone mason who showed no desire to kiss and hold her. No matter how hard she tried she could never succeed in setting this country boy on fire. It had suddenly become a matter of urgency to Blanche that she should have Jye Carew enslaved and subject to her.

She had filched candle-ends and holy-water from deserted churches, muttered incantations on the edge of midnight, and amazed Mrs Gimball by hammering six iron nails across her shop entrance.

'That won't keep the robbers out, ducks! Nails in the floor ain't no remedy for burglars.'

''Tis to bring somebody in,' Blanche said smugly. ''Tis some magic what I learned in Somerset when I was a child. You got to set six iron nails across your threshold, and then coax the man of your choice to step across them. Once across the nails, and he be yours for ever!'

'Oh Gawd love us!' Mrs Gimball sat down heavily on a wicker chair. 'I don't like the sound of that, Blanche. I never did hold with calling up the Devil. Mr Solomon goes in a lot for that sort of lark, and look 'ow 'e's ended up!'

Blanche laughed. 'There's no harm if you does it proper. Why magic have got me everything I ever wanted, so far.' She clasped her hands together, grinned hugely and looked heavenwards. ''Tis just another way of praying, that's all.'

She had walked, every Sunday morning, up to Westminster Abbey. She had waited, knowing that he would come back to her sooner or later. The need to subjugate Jye had lately become compulsive. To be rejected in her only area of power was something which Blanche would neither tolerate nor permit.

They came into St Martin's Lane. Blanche unlocked Mrs Gimball's shop door, and motioned Jye to walk before her. He stepped across the six iron nails, and she whispered exultantly into his broadclothed shoulders, 'That's done for you, my lover! Now you can never get me out of your heart, no matter how hard you wriggles.'

The back room was dim even at midday. Blanche lit the oil-lamp and invited Jye to sit down at the circular table. Before leaving that morning, she had spread it with a clean cloth, and set out the best bone-china from Mrs Gimball's stock.

Jye said, 'You lives nice here.' He sounded nervous.

'Oh yes,' she said lightly, 'I be most particular about having quality around me. My Mama always been the same, you know.' She was making a great performance of removing her hat, turning this way and that, leaning slightly forwards and raising both arms to remove her hatpins, knowing too well that this was one of her best seductive poses. She removed the hat and began to peel off the scarlet gloves, very slowly, finger by finger. She glanced at his face and saw that he watched her, exactly as a rabbit might watch a stoat. He moved round in his chair, unbuttoned his jacket, and ran a finger around the inside neckband of his stiff Sunday collar. She came up behind him, leaned over his shoulder, and laid her cheek against his. He leaped as if bitten. She came round to face him. 'Well, idden you jumpy! Poor boy, your nerves must be bad, or something?'

'Nothing wrong with my nerves,' he mumbled, 'I don't

like people creeping up behind me. I had a landlady what used to do that when I was eating my dinner. She all but choked me from shock the last time she did it.'

Blanche laughed. 'So the landlady fancied you, did she?'

'Nothing like that. She was just a foolish woman – '

'I fancies you, Jye Carew.' To her ears her words fell heavy and significant into the silence. She saw his walnut-coloured skin grow sallow, and knew that she had finally moved him. She had always assumed, because of his deafness, that words meant less to Jye than actions. 'I always fancied you from the minute we first met in that old church porch. I kissed you once in that liddle chapel, but you never kissed me back. What is it then, Jye? Don't you find me fetching?'

'I finds you fetching. What man wouldn't? But I got my principles, see! I intend to save myself for when I get married.' He spoke slowly and with difficulty. 'I've seen it happen to fellers in my village. It don't never stop at kissing. 'Tis safer to wait until I be married. The Reverend Hardin said so.'

'The Reverend Hardin?' Blanche sounded scornful. 'What do 'ee know?'

'Well, he got eight children,' said Jye, 'so he must know something.'

'But 'tis such a waste. We be only young for such a short time. I saw how 'twas with my Mama. Her never had no happy loving.'

Easy tears filled the violet eyes. Jye swung around in his chair and would not face her, but she had already noted the tenderness in his face. She moved with him. 'Just kiss me the once, Jye,' she pleaded, ''tis all that I be asking. Something to remember for all my life!'

Suddenly Blanche was on her knees before him, her arms encircling his waist, her face raised to his. He bent his head to kiss her and she saw his eyes close, heard his

161

rapid breathing and knew that she had him finally trapped. But when she tried to pull away, his powerful hands fell heavily on her; he gripped and kneaded at her shoulders until she could hardly bear the pain. She twisted her face away from his lips and heard him groan, and all at once he was tearing the neck of her cream silk gown. He ripped and rent apart the dress, and then he fell upon her. As they rolled upon the floor a shower of her tiny cream silk buttons flew across the linoleum with a noise like grape-shot. The sound of buttons popping was not one which Blanche would have expected Jye to hear, and yet it seemed to halt him in his purpose. He looked down at her sprawled half-clad body and moaned. 'What have you done?' he cried. 'What have you made me do?'

She pushed him from her, and he lay inert, spread-eagled across the floor. She stood above him, hands on hips, hair fallen loose about her shoulders, gown gaping open from throat to waist. 'Well that was a nice performance,' she sneered, 'oh, very romantic I must say. Proper stone-mason idden you. I wonder you didden use your mallet and chisel on me!' She stamped her foot in a passion of ill temper. 'Kissing is what I said, Jye Carew, and kissing is all I meant!'

She began to crawl about, picking up hairpins and scattered buttons. Jye raised himself on one elbow to watch her. When she came close enough for him to touch her, he gripped her forearm.

'You silly maiden,' he said quietly, 'don't you know that you can't tempt and entice a man and then expect him to be content with kissing? I idden no London toff, no fancy artist, but even I knows that much.' His eyes opened wide and Blanche flinched before his shamed expression. 'You almost drove me too far,' he said, 'I finds you to be an evil woman. You be full o' tricks and fancies what do smell to me like witchcraft. My Ma said that I should get you

162

out of my blood, and so I will! But I'll do it my own way by earnest prayer, and self-denial.'

'Baptist hypocrite,' she screamed. 'Chapel humbug!' Blanche felt the blood pound in her head and she grew reckless. She stood up, wriggled briefly, and allowed the silk gown to fall about her ankles. She struck a provocative pose and shouted, 'This is how I earns my money! I shows to the whole world what you don't dare to gaze on. Take a good look, Jye, for you'll never see the likes of me again in all your life. There's no maid in Montacute village what have got the body I've got!'

'You're the Devil,' he whispered, 'you're Satan sent to tempt me!' He backed away towards the door.

'Run,' she screeched, 'but don't never think you've got away. I love you, Jye. Do you hear that? I love you.'

'Love,' he cried, 'why you don't know what love is.' He sobbed deep in his throat. 'Love is what my mother felt for my father. 'Tis something beautiful of the spirit. When he died she wanted to die with him.'

The violet eyes narrowed. 'That's all rubbish. When my Papa died 'twas a relief for us all; anyway I made you step across the six iron nails, and that have made you mine for ever!'

❦

Jye made straight for King Henry's Chapel. Sanctuary was what he needed. He dodged among the strolling Sunday crowds of London, between hansom-cabs and broughams, weeping as he ran. The woman had cast a spell upon him, he recalled her malevolent features, the twist of her lips as he had read her parting words. She had spun a web, planned to entrap him in it, and there had been magic in the web.

He should never have gone with her to St Martin's Lane. His grandmother, Charity, had warned him about the sweet talk of women. Jye came into the Abbey, hot and out of breath. He sat down in his accustomed pew in King Henry's Chapel; he gazed at the noble fabric, at the intricate carvings, and a coolness and tranquillity came upon him. He began to murmur, repeatedly, 'Our Father which art in Heaven,' and never knew that he prayed aloud.

❋

Mina knew that she was close to death. A labour of two days and nights, and several unsuccessful attempts at delivery, had still not produced the baby. Too tired to fight, gone beyond fear, and hardly recognising the frightened faces that hung about her, Madelina wanted no one now but her brother Jack. He came at last, smelling comfortingly of saddle-soap and horses. He sat down by the bed and gripped both her hands. He treated her like a terrified mare who was about to foal for the first time.

'Don't give up, girl,' he told her. 'You promised me I could be god-father. Us even picked a name out, do 'ee remember?' He walked to the end of the bed where David Lambert stood, pale and superfluous among the Greypaull women. 'What's the trouble, Dave?'

'Doctor says she's too small for safe delivery. 'Twill be one life or the other. He says he can't save both.'

'What do you say?'

David's thin lips tightened. 'Human life is sacred. 'Tis God-given. The decision cannot be mine. I don't have the right.'

'Well, I bloody well do! Get that doctor back here.' Jack Greypaull pushed his brother-in-law from the room. 'Chapel cant!' he raged, 'don't you know that your wife is dying? You must have been out of your mind to let it go on for this long!'

Laura Lambert was born two hours later, miraculously intact and yelling loudly. That her mother had almost died in the delivery of her was to be the anthem of her life. Eliza, drying the dark damp curls, saw the baby's hair flame slowly red against the white towel. It was not the glamorous auburn of Blanche, but the fierce and angry tint of Eliza's own hair. 'Unlucky,' said Madelina weakly, 'you know what they says, Mama, about red hair, and you should know the truth if anybody does.'

'Superstition,' snapped Eliza. 'The child is alive, what is more than any of us had hoped for.' But out of sight of Madelina, Eliza dipped her finger into a bowl of water and traced the sign of the cross on the tiny forehead. 'God save you from the curse what fell on me,' she prayed. 'God give you a good and happy marriage.'

❀

Madelina was, in many ways, a good wife. David Lambert considered himself fortunate to have found a girl as devout and simple-hearted, one who was ever willing to minister to the sick, and to aid the needy. She was thrifty, a fine needlewoman, a first-rate cook. Those childhood years spent on Larksleve Farm had fitted Madelina for a more demanding life than she now lived. In fact it was her very excess of zeal that made her uncomfortable to be with. Even David, upright and blameless as he was, occasionally found difficulty in living up to Mina. Her concern for her family, her involvement in the slightest of their doings, had at first appeared touching and to be admired. The least hint of indisposition, and it was Madelina who rushed to the sufferer's bedside. The birth of the baby had weakened her, but not for long: in fact, the infant Laura seemed set fair to rank among the foremost of Mina Lambert's obsessions.

Everything must be perfect for Laura. Her food and clothing carefully chosen, her future assured. Insurance policies were taken out in her name for, as Mina pointed out, there would never be a brother or a sister for Laura to turn to; she was, regrettably, to be their one and only. After

165

speaking briefly with the doctor who had delivered his wife, David had learned that another such birth would make a widower of him. Knowing of no other way but total abstention, he had moved himself into the back bedroom, leaving Madelina to rock the cradle and devote herself to good works. A considerate man, was how she would, in future describe him; one who made no unfair demands upon her. If she cried into her pillow in the early hours, then only Madelina knew about it.

The baby became her consolation, the tangle of fiery curls a talisman for all that was precious and wonderful in life. If Mina was ever to doubt her own reason for living, there would always be Laura to refer to: irreplaceable and unique.

❀

Eliza had picked up her pen many times in that year, and then laid it down, the letter left unwritten. To have stated to Rhoda all her fears for Madelina would somehow have been to prejudge the outcome, to make a disaster inevitable. Therefore it was with an increased pleasure that she now assembled pen and ink, envelope and paper. On this occasion the news from Taunton would be joyful.

2 Hunter's Court,
Taunton. November 1884.
My dear cousin Rhoda,
Sorry to be so long in answering your last letter, but my news will explain all. *I am a grandmother.* My Madelina give birth to a daughter on the fourth of October after nine months of sickness and poor health. I can tell you *now*, Rhoda, there was times when I dowted if mother and child would pull through. But the Lord answered my prayers, and a sweet little granddaughter lies in the cradle, while Mina gets her strength back, but v. slowly.

They say the baby favours me. She got my exact same

166

hair, as red as carrots and tight curls. If she will *freckul* is something us wont know until the sun shines. I *wont listen* no more to stories that say red hair is unlucky. Look at *me*, Rhoda. I got my home and my children, and a dear little granddaughter. Was ever a mortal woman *more blessed* than I am? Anyhow, *Blanche* got red hair, and she never once puts a foot wrong. I never saw a girl prosper like that one do. The baby is called Laura, name chose by Jack, he was Godfather. The sad news is that Mina cant never have another child, so you can imagine the value she have set on this *one and only.*

Other news is that Annis have gone to work in the Poolwall collar factory. I did not want her to go, but Mina's job came empty and we need the extra money. You asked about Blanche in your last letter. Well, it seems that she sits on a sofa while titled gentlemen paints her picture, what is a funny way to make a living, but suits her idle nature. This job is called *artists model*. She looks very well on it, I must say, and is never short of *gold*. Do you have such goings on in America?

My big worry is about our Candace. One short note to say that she was married, and since then *nothing*. She was ever *close*, but surely she must think that I will *worry* about her?

Glad to know that your Georgie is courting. What news of Rosa? Are *you* a grandmother yet? Hope you are not so weary as last year, and that Harvest and Haysel went well for Mr Black.

Hope to hear from you any day now. Will answer your next letter *at once*.

Much love to you and all the family.

Your loving cousin, Eliza.

The letter to Rhoda was posted on a Sunday evening, as Eliza walked up to evening service at St Mary's. On

Monday morning a square blue envelope was delivered to Hunter's Court; their letters had crossed.

Suamico. September 4th, 1884.

Dear cousin Eliza,

A busy time here, and I am thankful to sit on the front porch in the evening cool, and pen you this letter. Have *not heard* from you this year, but guess that you are busy. My news is that *George* is *married* to Sarah Ann Annas, or Satie as he calls her.

The Wedding Day was yesterday, Sept. 3rd. and Father Black and me was *awful* worried that we would not be through harvesting in time to go to De Pere. But we got all through with carrying and stacking in good order, and my brother-in-law Mr Vickery come across to take charge for the day while he was away. We come back late last night. Could not stop-over in De Pere for, as you well know, Dear Cousin, a farm *wont* run *itself*.

It was a *lovely* wedding. Satie one of eleven in family, so many bridesmaids. Her father got his own business, so everything done v. nice and tasteful. I only *hope* my George will see what a *Treasure* he got in Satie. A more sweet and homeloving little body I never did see in all my born days. She minds me v. much of myself when I first come to this country. George got a *v. high handed manner* at times, and she seems so shy and timid. But I am sure he loves her. I had strict words with him before the service. He is *twenty-six* and she is only *nineteen*.

My Rosa and her husband come over from Oshkosh for the Wedding. Not much time for private talk but Rosa whispered in my ear that, God willing, I will be a grandma in about six months. I cant tell you how much that news have *pleasured* me, Eliza. I do so long to hold a grandchild in my arms. There is not many joys for us poor women in this *man's world*, but to see the family line go on is the best one of

168

all. Father Black is as tickled by the news as if Rosa was his own flesh-and-blood. What a *good Father* he have proved to be to my three children.

Well, I had better finish now, Eliza. It is getting dark on the porch, but v. pleasant. The whole of Suamico smells of apples at this time of year. Have got my legs *up* on a *stool*. Get trouble with swollen knees just lately, but must expect some aches and pain now I am turned *fifty* and *nearly* a Grandma.

Hoping for a letter from you *real* soon. Hope all is *well* in Taunton.

Love from Father Black, and your loving cousin, Rhoda.

✳

Repairs to the Mansion House had been completed by September, and Jye asked Mr Mitchell if he might now return home. The experience gained in the working of Portland stone had been invaluable to him, but the daily temptation to go down to St Martin's Lane and seek out Blanche Greypaull could be cured only by putting a space of many miles between them.

'And what if a contract should come up for repairs on St Paul's Cathedral?' asked George Mitchell. 'Would you be willing to come back?'

Jye looked doubtful. 'I been away from home a long time, Mr Mitchell. My mother do need a man about the place –'

'I know all about that, boy. But St Paul's is another Portland stone job. You'd enjoy that, wouldn't you?' The master-mason became confidential. ''Tis like this, Jye. I find myself much involved with Joseph Arch and his Union business. You remember Arch, don't you?'

'The man in the billycock hat who spoke on Ham Hill all those years ago.'

'That's the one!' Mitchell looked concerned. 'There's great things about to happen – decisions taken that will

169

change the course of history. The franchise for farm labourers is almost within our grasp. Think on it, boy. A vote for each man! We got Gladstone on our side and Joe Arch to lead us! The Liberal cause is growing stronger all the time.'

'You be very political, sir.'

'And so would you be if you had fought and struggled like me and Joe. They call me "one from the plough" and with good reason. I go away quite a lot on Union business, and I need to employ men that I can trust. Men who can be set to a piece of work and relied on to complete it. You be such a one, Jye.'

''Tis good of you to say so, Mr Mitchell, but truth to tell I be terrible homesick.'

'Go home, then. Go back to work on the Hill for a bit, and when the St Paul's job comes up, I'll get a message to you.'

Jye went home to find orchards deep in grass and bright with cider apples, to dusty, unimportant lanes down which quarry horses pulled their loads of stone, and where lovers walked in the autumn evenings. The late roses sprawled full-blown and reckless upon the stem; the bushes had an untrimmed appearance that did not please him.

'I asked you to look after my roses,' he complained to his mother. But Meridiana laughed at him. 'Why should I? Nobody trims the dog roses in the hedge.'

'But I showed you,' he said, 'before I went away –'

'Such things,' she said, 'is better left to nature. I generally leaves most plants and flowers to go their own way.'

'So I've noticed.' He looked around the overgrown garden. ''Tis high time I come home. Things is going from bad to worse without me.'

'Be easy in your mind, boy,' she advised him, 'too much worritin' and toiling will make you an old man afore your time.'

Later on, when they were sitting beside the fire, she on

her low stool, and he in his father's chair, his mother said, 'I saw Taiso and Lavinia Locke some weeks back. They had Petronell along with 'em. Her's growed up to be a handsome chie, Jye? Us had words on the matter of a marriage, and Petronell is willing to live indoors if you should so wish it.'

'No,' he cried, 'you got no call to go behind my back. I'll find my own wife when the time comes.'

'But 'tiv always been like that, Jye. If we was on the drom, why you —'

'We is not "on the drom" as you calls it; we lives decent in a stone house.' He rounded upon her. 'Who arranged your marriage to father?' She could not meet his stare. 'You managed it all by yourself, didden you, mother? You made your own choice.' His chin drooped upon his chest. 'Let me alone, can't you. Don't try to fix me up with maidens I don't want.'

'What is it Jye?' she asked gently. 'Is it still the London harlot? Is it still Liza Greypaull's red-haired daughter?'

He went back to the Hill on Monday morning, climbed the sloping lane that led up to the quarry, to the little tin-roofed lodge where Luke, his father, had once worked. That sense of urgency, engendered by the busy streets of London, began to leave him now. His muscles relaxed and his step slowed. The image of Blanche Greypaull, down on her knees, hair loose and dress agape, still troubled him sometimes. He recalled her threat.

'I made you step across the six iron nails, and that have made you mine for ever.'

❈

Annis had never been a strong girl. Weakened in childhood by rheumatic fever, and plagued by sick headaches, her delicate prettiness was now enhanced by a degree of pallor that alarmed Eliza.

171

'But 'tis fashionable to have a white complexion, Mama. Why, the girls in the factory have begun to eat the starch-lumps. They say that starch is wonderful for toning down the florid cheeks.'

'But you've never had florid cheeks, maid!'

Annis sighed. 'I want the same alabaster skin as our Blanche.'

'Well, eating starch won't get it for you.'

'But 'tis true, Ma! There's this big wooden box just inside the laundry door where they keep the starch-lumps —'

'I don't want to hear another word about it,' snapped Eliza, 'I never heard such vain and silly nonsense. It'll be a dose of brimstone and treacle on Saturday night, miss, if I see your face getting any paler!'

The collars were washed in the Poolwall factory for six days out of every seven. After soaking in hot soapsuds, the clean linen was plunged into barrels of made-up starch. The next operation was to pass them through the wringing machine, from which they emerged almost dry. Rows of girls, positioned at long laundry tables, were engaged in the sorting and tying of the collars into neat bundles of a dozen. These young women, who were obliged to stand in a fixed position for some eighty hours of every week, were already of an enviable pallor which the sewing machinists had attributed to the laundrymaids' habit of chewing starch. Smuggling and bartering had lately increased between laundress and machinist. The precious lumps, concealed in apron pockets, were exchanged for toffee, a bit of cheese, or some small trinket. The pallor of the button-holers in particular, grew more alarming with every day that passed. Foremen and forewomen from each department were concerned at the increased incidents of vomiting and fainting among their staff. An investigation was finally held in which the inordinate amounts of starch requested recently by the

172

laundry department, was finally linked up to the fashionable pallor now displayed by most of Gliddon's female employees.

Frank Nevill lectured Annis. 'I know you was eating it too, so don't deny it.'

'Not for long,' she giggled, 'I didden like the taste.' Annis often giggled when in the company of Frank. They usually walked home together, since he also lived in East Reach. Frank's father was a maker of boots and shoes. Mr Nevill could be seen on fine days working in the open doorway of his Silver Street shop. Frank was proud of his father; whenever he talked about him, Frank's voice grew hushed and confidential.

'My father is the only man, besides the doctor, what is ever allowed inside the Roman convent.' He told Annis. 'He goes in to measure up the nuns' feet when they need new boots. My Pa don't like going in that convent. They peep at him through a little iron grille before they unlock the door. 'Tis just like a jail, he reckons. Some of they young nuns do go about weeping and wailing. He've seen their faces all bruised and cut. Pa believes that the Mother Superior do whip and thrash 'em. 'Tis said that one young nun once tried to escape, but she fell off the wall and broke her neck.'

'Is that true, Frank?' Annis took his hand and trembled at the thought of the imprisoned nuns.

'Oh, yes, 'tis true. My Pa don't ever lie. He wudden never have no truck with they Roman Catholics, but with eighty-odd nuns all wearing out their boots with so much kneeling, well 'tis the sort of job he can't very well refuse.'

Annis felt safe with Frank. He walked her to the entrance of Hunter's Court and protected her from the brothers Bidgood, who still complained about the damage once done to them by Eliza's coal-hammer and horse-whip. Even Eliza approved of Frank. She took her few boot repairs to Mr

173

Nevill's shop, and reported her findings to Madelina.

'I know they be only walking home together, and he sounds like a steady young man, but 'tis up to me to take a look at his family.'

'And what do 'ee think, Mama,' Madelina, engrossed in the baby Laura, spoke absently and without real interest.

'Well,' said Eliza, 'they got no class. On sunny days Mr Nevill do have his work bench set outside, on the pavement.' She looked troubled. 'They say he gets mixed up with they Roman Catholics, and we've all heard about the screaming and wailing what goes on behind that Convent wall. I asked him point-blank about his professed religion, "Chapel, Mrs Greypaull. Baptist chapel!" that's what he said.'

'Nothing wrong with Chapel,' said Mina coldly. 'You'll never find a better man than my David.' She looked meaningfully at her mother. 'He don't drink nor gamble, neither do he go off every night womanising, like some I can remember! He's very considerate of me in every way.' Mina sighed. 'As for Annis, if Frank Nevill is the best she can get, then she'll have to make the most of it.'

Eliza smiled. 'Her's not yet seventeen until October. I shall get her to bide single for as long as I can. While Annis have got me, there's no need for her to rush and marry.'

❋

The year of 1885 was to see many changes. Eliza's fears about the friendship between Annis and Frank Nevill were soon to prove groundless. The increase of mechanisation in Mr Gliddon's collar factory caused the sacking of fifty hands from various departments. Frank walked many miles each day in the vain search for work.

'I want to join the Navy like my brother, Harold.' He told Annis, 'but father won't put his signature to the enlistment papers. Bad enough, he says, to have our Harry

174

sailing on the high seas, and liable to be drowned at any minute.'

'What'll you do, Frank?'

'I'll go for a soldier, that's what I'll do. I'll go up to Jellalabad gates and tell 'em that I be already eighteen, and don't need no permission from my father.'

'That'll mean you going away, Frank.'

He held her hand very tightly. 'I know, maid. But what else can I do? My Ma still got six young 'uns not old enough to earn. I can't stay and be a burden to my poor father no longer.' He paused and looked longingly at her. 'Tell 'ee what we'll do. We'll make a promise, each to the other. We'll exchange gifts. We'll vow to wait for one another.' He took a bonehandled clasp-knife from his pocket, and handed it to her. ''Tis the only treasure I got. Save it for me!'

She said, 'I got nothing to give you save my blue beads.'

He slipped the necklace into his pocket. 'If I go for a soldier 'tis a ten-year engagement.'

'I'll wait Frank.'

He took both her hands in his. 'When I come back, we'll get married. We'll always be together then. That's a promise.'

Frank took the Queen's Shilling on the second day of August. Six weeks of training on Jellalabad's barrack-square, and he and his fellow-privates were considered able and ready to quell the enemy wherever they might find him. Word ran through the town, as it always did in Taunton, whenever the battalion was about to sail for foreign shores.

Annis stood at the corner of Mount Street on that Sunday morning, and watched as the column of men marched out of the barrack gates. Ragged children danced along beside them, entranced by the music. She saw Frank, tall and splendid in his dark blue trousers and scarlet tunic, his white and gold helmet glinting in the sunshine. She ran with the

175

column as they swung into High Street; out of breath and weeping she stood among the crowds that lined the road to the railway station. She heard a man say, 'Poor liddle devils! That'll be the last their mothers see of them. According to what I heard in the Four Alls last night, this division of the battalion is off to fight the Infidel in Burma!'

❀

They were known as Prince Albert's Own, this Second Battalion of the Somerset Light Infantry. Since the year of 1879 they had become established in stations throughout Lower Burma, while the lands of Upper Burma, and its capital city, Mandalay, were still ruled by a Buddhist king called Theebaw. Recent trouble with this king had made it necessary for a British division to be concentrated in Upper Burma. Frank and his comrades came ashore in late October. The south-west monsoon had just ended, and the country was about to enjoy its pleasantest season of sunny days and cool nights. Four Companies of Prince Albert's Own disembarked at Rangoon, and in those few days before they travelled north, Frank found time to write his first letter to Annis.

Dear Annis,

This is the first chance I have had to put pen to paper. We crossed the water in October and all of us were sick in the Bay of Biscay, where they say that all the waters of the world meet. We come safe into the Bay of Bengal last week, and landed at a place called Rangoon. We are living under canvas, but I at least got a bed all to myself. The dissiplin is awful, and they shaved our heads on bord the ship because of lice. So I am glad that you cant see me. They are sending us to a place called Mandalay what is in the north. Once we have moved there is no telling when I can write again. They keep us busy every minit, cleaning stuff what dont want cleaning.

176

I miss you Annis,

Your friend, Frank

The letter arrived in Hunter's Court in late December.
Annis opened it and handed it to her mother. Eliza
withdrew the single sheet of paper and began to read, and
the words, although spoken in her mother's voice, seemed
to bring Frank Nevill right into the room. Annis heard it
through once and then begged her mother to repeat the
reading. She closed her eyes this time, and could see Frank's
image, head shaved close, living in a tent, cleaning stuff
what didn't want cleaning.

'I wish he'd never gone for a soldier, Mama!'

Eliza folded the letter into the envelope and handed it to
Annis. 'He had small choice. There's so much
unemployment these days. Signing-on for the Army is the
only chance a young man have got to keep himself decent
and out of the gutter.' Her tone softened. 'He'll be all right,
maid, and so will you. 'Twill be a pleasure for me to have
you bide close to home while you wait for Frank. He's a
strong young feller, and after all, 'tis only a very liddle
war.'

'How do you know that?'

'I reads the newspaper reports in the *Courier* window.
They heathens have been skirmishing about for some time
past in Upper Burma.'

Annis gazed admiringly at Eliza. 'Oh Mama, how smart
and informed you be. Why, none of us have got the brain
what you've got.'

'Us don't really know that, Annis. You and Blanche and
Simeon have never had the chance to show what you could
do. For all us knows you might have turned out to be great
scholars. There was always good brains among the
Greypaull family. My great-uncle was a poet and a

177

soothsayer; a very learned man so I heard say. Then there was Walter, son of William Greypaull the carpenter. Now Walter wrote a whole book about Buckland Church. Our uncle Robert is a barrister in London, his father was an architect what built London churches. Every generation have thrown up at least one important person. 'Twas all your father's fault that three of you never had one single day's schooling.' Eliza's voice grew angry. 'When I think that we can trace our line back direct to King Henry the Eighth! Oh that do mortify me, Annis. I can't help wishing sometimes that one of my children at least will rise to greatness. 'Tis in the blood, you know.'

'If any one of us is to make you proud, Mama, then 'twill be Blanche.'

'Blanche? Whatever is you thinking of, Annis? Her can't read nor write her own name.'

'No, Mama, that's true. But Blanche is clever. Didden you never notice the way her talks? Her got a wonderful way of putting words together.' Annis coloured. 'You was sure that Blanche would land up in trouble once she got to London, but she didden, did she? Her's no fool, her knows what is what. 'Tis our Blanche what'll end up making you proud. Just you mark my words!'

❋

The next letter to arrive from Burma had been written at intervals, in a space of several days. It arrived in Hunter's Court at the end of March.

Dear Annis,

Today is Tuesday. They tell us that it is Christmas Day but we dont believe it. But they give us extra rations and a tin of choclat so perhaps its true. We are camped by a river called Irawaddy what is muddy and wide, and smells bad. The life here is awful. We all wish we had never come, but too late now. Billy Bidgood and his brother Joe is out here with me, but they have gone down with fever and is in a bad way. Yours truly gone very skinny but still fit. Our nice red uniforms look awful.

Wednesday.

I could only write a few lines last night because it gets dark very sudden, and candles here in short supply, and needed for the sick tents. We got more sick men than fit ones at the minit. It is very worrying, Annis. I will tell you what have happened to me so far, since landing in Rangoon. We come up river on a steamship, what took two days and nights. Then we was sent into the jungle to fight a battle. The enemy is not proper soldiers like us, but bandits what hide in the trees. They is little brown men and very wild. The officers call them 'dacoits'. Our job is to burn down their villages so that they got no place to go. I dont much like that burning down, but cant say so. I think I must of come 18 years old last Sunday but cant be sure.

Thursday.

This have turned out to be a long letter, Annis, but I feel all the better for riting to you. Cholera is raging. We have captured fifteen bronze and brass guns so far, and lost ten men to the fever. The weather is fine by day, but very cold at night. I keep your blue beads in my top pocket of my tunic, next to my heart. No letters have come yet from England for any of us. The fittest of us are to move out from the Mandalay Base Camp tomorrow morning. We dont know where we are going. Hope your letters catch up with me in the next few days. Please rite as often as you can.

Ever your true friend,

Frank Nevill.

✳

Of the many faiths that flourished beneath Ham Hill, the Baptist persuasion was the most powerful among non-conformists. People still spoke of that Sunday afternoon back in June 1870, when one hundred and fifty friends had partaken of tea in Mr Bool's orchard in a public welcoming of the new Baptist Pastor. In the sixteen years of his ministry among them they had frequently found reason to thank God for his continued presence. Henry Hardin had once trained for the medical profession, but on the eve of his final examinations he had decided to enter the Ministry of Baptists. The village doctor, who lived two miles distant, often sought the Pastor's help, and had never been refused. There had been the outbreak of scarlet fever in which almost every child had been affected; a terrible time in which the Reverend Henry Hardin had gone into every farmhouse, every cottage and hovel, to tend the sick and dying children. From January to March of this year 1886, influenza had raged in Montacute, and it was the Baptist minister who now brought word of Henry Carew's severe illness to his mother and his brother Jye. They had gone at once to the cottage which stood just beyond the village. Jye had taken firewood and food, Meri had carried blankets and a selection of her herbal remedies for fever, but her plea to be allowed to nurse her son had been refused.

Charles Carew had leaned from an upstairs window, 'You put us away from you when we was born,' he shouted. 'Did you think we never know'd that? Go home, Mother! Us have managed wi'out you all our lives, I reckon us can manage to die wi'out your help.'

It was Jye, coming down from the quarry two days later, who had seen the flames leaping high in his brother's garden. He had started to run through the January twilight knowing only too well the significance of such a conflagration. He arrived just in time to recognise the wooden bedstead, the chair, the tiny handmade crutches which Henry had used when his legs were painful. Charred scraps of bedding, the scorched remnants of a flannel shirt, a partially burned jacket, still trembled on the freezing air;

180

Charles Carew, more truly the son of Meridiana than Jye ever was or could be, had handled the passing of his twin in traditional Romany fashion. Somewhere inside that garden a pit would be dug; in it Charles would bury the cutlery and dishes, the knife used by Henry for his carvings and the whittling of clothes-pegs. His brother's body would be given up reluctantly for Christian burial in the Montacute churchyard. If Charles Carew had his way, the body of his twin would be laid to rest secretly, by moonlight, underneath the blackthorns.

Jye raised clenched fists up to his head; he beat both earlobes in a frenzy of emotion. 'Deaf,' he shouted, 'deaf in my heart and soul, as well as in my ears.'

'Aye, brother, you speaks the truth!' Charles Carew, his sad, mis-shapen body lit up by the dying flames of the funeral fire, spoke plainly so that Jye might read his lips. 'Deaf and blind both you and that woman us calls "mother". Put away, we was. Out of sight and out of mind.'

'She did it all for the best, Charles. She wanted you safe provided for, she wanted –'

'Oh, we was safe, right enough! Safe away from her eyes, where she didden have to look upon us, to see the ugliness of us.'

'That's not true, Charles. She loves you, she worries about you. 'Twas always you and Henry what barred your doors against us.'

Charles Carew laughed, and it was perhaps as well that Jye could not hear that dreadful sound. 'Go home, brother,' he sneered, 'go home and ask your mother this one question. Ask her why it was, if she loved us so much, that she never thought to ask Henry and me what sort of life *we* wanted.'

Meri's state of mind at the death of Henry was something Jye could only guess at. She did not weep, at least not in his presence. Meri did what she had always done in times of turmoil. She walked, barefoot and alone through the bitter weather. She became unapproachable and silent until the agony of heart and mind had passed from her. Even when the spring came, and she smiled again, his mother, Jye noticed, was always careful never to walk in the lane which led out to Charles' house.

❋

A new Parson and his family moved into the Vicarage in the early spring. From the hour of their arrival they commanded interest. A genteel family which contained eight children was bound to be a source of business and employment. Servants were engaged, a gardener summoned; supplies of bread and milk were ordered, and purchases made in Miss Sparkes' little shop.

Meri said to Jye, 'Have you seen the new brood across to Rector's house?'

Jye grinned. 'I saw 'em on moving-day. Old Peter Edwardes was giving a hand. He said he'd never had to shift so many gurt books about all his life!'

Meri looked thoughtful. 'I see'd 'em going to church on Easter Sunday. I waited while they crossed the path. I looked into all their faces. The liddle ones was walking in front and the big ones coming on behind. I noticed the oldest one most pertikler. Thass a remarkable rai if ever I see'd one.'

Jye said uneasily, 'You didden frighten him did you, Mother?'

'Me frighten him! 'Twas t'other way about. You should have seen the look he give me! Oh, but that was a beautiful face and head, for all his proud ways. I never see'd gorgio children so handsome as that lot.'

People turned with a sense of relief that spring from their sad experience of the 'flu epidemic, to the fascinating study of the Powys family. Servants talked, and it was said that the three oldest sons were pupils at Sherborne School, which, as everybody knew, was an establishment exclusive to the sons of the wealthy. There were other hints of private income; a level of culture and refinement in this household that had not been apparent in previous incumbents. The Powys children were invited to visit and play with the Squire's children. The new Rector and his lady dined regularly at Squire Phelip's table; on two recent occasions they had actually been seen riding in the Phelips' family carriage. Such hob-nobbing with the gentry by the Rector and his family could mean only one thing, according to those small traders and farmers who knew about such matters. Independent means, was the unanimous conclusion in the Prince of Wales and the Phelips Arms.

Meri, who had always been careful to avoid clergy of all denominations, now found it impossible to escape the Reverend Powys.

'I never know'd such a one for walking,' she complained to Jye. 'He do tramp for miles all by hisself. He's a great hand at talking, too. Never lets I pass by with only a good-morning, like t'other Rector did. Wanted to know if I was one of his flock.'

Jye grinned. 'What did you say?'

' "No," I told 'un, "I was married to a Baptist, and you knows what that do mean, your Reverend!"'

' "Why yes," he said, "that means that you worship in the chapel with the Reverend Hardin. A very good man, so I've been told."'

' "He's right enough," I said, "if you believes in a God what lives behind four walls. For meself, sir, well I'm a Rom woman, born to fields and hedges. I married with the gorgie, and I goes regular to chapel, but –"'

' " – but you don't find the Living God enshrined in stones and mortar."'

183

' "Thass it, sir! You puts it better'n I could, but it means same thing. I wonder in me how you could ever understand that."

' "Perhaps," he said, "perhaps I feel much as you do."

' "Well," I said, all sly-like, "I've yeard 'ee talking to God when you bin walking out Tintinhull Way, and when you've bin looking over towards Dorset."

' "My boys are at school in Sherborne," he said, "I worry about them. I think they get very homesick."

' "I knows all about that, sir," I told 'un, "I got a son what goes away to London. He gets sent up to mend that old Westminster Abbey. He bides away a whole year at a time, and me a widow woman."

' "That's hard for you," he said, "but we have to let our children go away. My wife sheds a private tear each time our boys go back to school." '

Jye said, 'He sounds a sensible feller, that Rector!' He patted his mother's shoulder. 'You don't have to worry about me going away this year. Look at my garden: roses pruned, tiddies planted, hedges trimmed.'

'Aye boy, I sees it. But you is twenty-one years old and not yet wed. Not even a maid in sight what you be fond of, and you the best-looking rai in this whole district.'

✻

A man who has never tasted meat will never hunger for it: the appetite for many things, preached the Reverend Hardin, comes only from men's unwise sampling of them. Jye Carew had never thought much about girls before his meeting with Blanche Greypaull. Sensitivity about his deafness, and the narrowness of chapel dogma, had encouraged his solitary nature, and left him sadly immature. His appetite for Blanche, once roused, but never sated, had spoiled him for other less exotic females, and this was now to be his problem. The memory of Blanche would come to him unbidden and unwanted. She would lean, tantalisingly, just above his banker, when he had reached a critical stage of his work. She would come to taunt him as he tended his roses, when he walked the Hill in the early morning, and when he lay in his bed at night. He knew that she had practised witchcraft on him. 'I made you step across the six iron nails,' she had said, 'and that have made you mine for ever.' He remembered the slow way her cream silk gown had fallen about her ankles, the memory still so sharp that he could almost believe that he had heard the slither of it.

'Take a good look, Jye!' she had commanded, 'for you'll never see the likes of me again in all your life. There's no maiden in Montacute village what have got the body I've got!'

'You're the Devil,' he had whispered, 'you're Satan sent to tempt me.'

'Run,' she had screamed, 'run, but don't never think you've got away.'

The scene had played itself out in his head a thousand times since that Sunday morning. He had sought ways to escape her, given random thought to certain village beauties. There was Dorcas who sat next to him during Sunday night chapel, and whose plump thigh contrived to press up against his whenever the narrow pew became overcrowded. She would glance at him slyly at such moments, gauging his reaction with brown and calculating eyes. There were the girls from the gloving factory, loud-mouthed and made brashly independent by the Friday wages in their apron pockets. He had watched certain lips on a Monday morning, and learned from the young, unmarried masons that such girls were 'easy'. But the fire in his loins had been quickly cooled by the memory that it was those same inviting girls, who had called him dummy and diddecoi not so long ago in the village classroom.

'I'll marry,' he told his mother, 'when I be good

and ready.'

'And what happened with the Greypaull harlot?'

'Nothing happened,' he said shortly, 'and nothing ever will. That's all over and done with, Mother, and I'll thank you to let it rest there.'

❊

Mr Solomon re-appeared in St Martin's Lane, drunk and unrepentant, and offering no explanation of his long absence. Blanche had glimpsed him at intervals in the Strand, and in the side lanes which led into Piccadilly, but there had always been a quality of aloofness about him when walking in the streets that precluded any sign of recognition on her part. Mrs Gimball surveyed him as he lay comotose in her best chair. 'Well, wherever he's been,' she said, 'they've at least kept 'im clean and fed 'im.'

'I thought he lived permanent in the Poorhouse,' said Blanche.

'He don't stop there all the time, ducks. He got friends wot take pity on 'im. I'm not the only dealer he does business with, there's other more 'igh-class than wot I am.' Mrs Gimball laughed. 'He brings me them naughty pictures what he don't dare to show to nobody else. Them college toffs pays a small fortune for 'em, the naughty little tykes!'

'I thought you said as how it was all Art,' Blanche said sharply.

'And so it is, dearie. I don't think you appreciates the quality of Mr Solomon's work. Them so-called painters wot swanks about in your Life School, why, once upon a time they was bound to admit that Mr Solomon had 'em all beat when it came to turning out the goods. O' course,' she said reflectively, 'that was twenty years ago. His poor 'and ain't so steady these days.'

'How old is he, then?'

'Must be in his forties, though he looks a hundred sometimes. Poor devil! He's a victim of circumstances.'

'What do that mean?'

'It means, my gel, that sometimes things 'appen wot is not your fault.' Mrs Gimball sniffed, and wiped her nose absentmindedly upon her apron. 'Like the way you 'ammered them nails across my front doorway to trap that young bloke. It never worked did it? You been mooning about ever since like the cat wot just missed swallowing the canary. As a matter of fact, I should say that it's you wot got caught out with that bit of witchcraft.'

'Witchcraft?' Mr Solomon opened one bloodshot eye and then the other. 'What have you been up to, young Blanche, while my head was turned?'

Blanche giggled. Mrs Gimball said, 'So you're back in the land of the livin', are you, I s'pose you want coffee same as usual.' She bustled away, and Mr Solomon pulled himself upright in the chair.

'Let me look at you,' he demanded. Blanche stood before him, eyes downcast, hands linked together.

'Look at me!' he whispered. She raised her gaze to meet his and heard him sigh with satisfaction. 'That's better. That's the Blanche I know! That's my evil-hearted temptress!'

She pouted. 'You don't have to talk so nasty to me, and you going off like you did after promising to paint me.'

'Why do you think I have returned?'

'Well, tidden because you fancies me, that's for sure! They says in the Life School that you don't care for women.'

Solomon chuckled. 'Oh-ho! So the little birds have been twittering in your ear, have they?'

'I don't listen to 'em,' Blanche said stoutly, 'they be all a funny lot across there. If you ask my opinion they artists is all off their trolleys.' She spoke casually, but a note of pride crept into her tone. 'I done a bit of private work just lately. Gen'leman sent his carriage out from Kensington way. You should have just seen that house, and the size of his studio – ' she began to giggle – 'you'll never believe this, Mr Solomon, but he wudden let me take my drawers off until his wife come in to sit beside us. You should just of seen her! Face like a poker, and legs to match I shudden wonder! "Are you warm enough, young woman?" she asked me. She talked like her mouth was full o'plums. "Ho yes, ma'am," I told her, "I'spect I'm quite a bit warmer than what you are!"'

Solomon laughed until tears glistened in his eyes. Suddenly he sobered. 'You remind me in many ways of my sister. She was also full of life and laughter – '

'I never knowed you had a sister.'

'She's dead.' The finality in his voice warned Blanche to pry no further.

'When are you going to paint me?' she asked brightly.

'Whenever you are prepared to allow me an hour of your valuable time.'

'Don't mock me, I bain't that important.'

'Oh, but you are! I've heard that you're much in demand these days. Who else do you sit to?'

She grimaced. 'There's a funny old chap what lives in a big house near a river. I was frightened to go inside, first time I went there.' She held her nose. 'He got cats. Not just one or two but thousands of 'em. They rules the house. They marches about like a bunch of tigers – ' She paused. 'But he's a nice old buffer. He gives me plates of cold rice pudding and bread and jam. He's quite potty, but he pays up on the nail.'

'Ah-ha! So you're moving in those circles are you?'

'I'll be free all day tomorrow,' she said swiftly. She bent and touched his hand. 'I be so glad to see 'ee back, Mr Solomon! Nobody do ever talk to me as sweet and nice as you do.'

Her bed was still a makeshift affair, a sofa pushed between the stacks of paintings in the locked brown room. She awoke the next morning to find him sketching close beside her. 'I hope you don't object,' he said, 'but I couldn't resist the beauty of your sleeping face.'

'That's all right.' She pushed the thick hair from her shoulders. 'Was my mouth wide open?' she enquired. 'Our Candace always reckons that I snore.'

'I took the liberty of closing it for you,' he said gently. 'We'll continue just as soon as you've eaten. I want you to talk to me, Blanche.'

'But 'tis so much nicer when you talk. You know all about they foreign places. You've mixed with grand people. Tell me about the time when you —' He stood up abruptly and began to move towards the door.

'I am not sure that I can work this morning.' He tore the half completed sketch and threw it to the floor. He held out his hands. 'Look, Blanche! See how they tremble.' He began to weep. 'I try,' he cried, 'oh God, how I try. If I could stay sober long enough to — but then, why should I? I need a drink!'

'Don't go,' she said. 'I got no engagements today. I'll bide with you. You don't have to draw if you don't feel up to it. Let we talk together, Mr Solomon!' Still pleading, she led him back towards the sofa. 'A pot of coffee. Us'll drink a nice pot of coffee. I won't leave 'ee; you can tell me all about they bad dreams what you been having.' She settled him back on her pillows. 'I heard you shouting and screaming in the night,' she said gently. 'I knows myself what 'tis like to have nightmares. I'll ask Mrs Gimball for some breakfast. I'll do all the talking this time; anything what you want to know you just ask me.'

Mrs Gimball brought them coffee; she nodded significantly in the artist's direction, and then went silently away. Blanche held the cup, and he drank from it like an obedient child. Gradually his trembling lessened. 'Talk,' he begged her, 'anything at all, just talk to me, Blanche.' She sat down beside him and took his hand in hers.

'I'll tell about the place where I was born and growed-up.' Even as she spoke the memories of Larksleve reached out to claim her. She was back beneath that great breadth of sky; running down the green sweeps from hill to valley; watching the red earth turning underneath the plough.

'There was campions growing,' she said softly, 'red ones and white ones. They growed on the steep banks above the lane. Loveday always said that if you picked 'em 'twas bad luck either way. If you took white campions, then your Pa 'ud die. If you took the red ones then you'd lose your mother.' Her voice changed, became high-pitched and child-like. 'I always picked the white o' course. I used to drag 'em up in great armfuls and then stamp on 'em.'

'Why did you hate him so much?'

'Do you know what the word rape means, Mr Solomon?'

'I have heard of it.'

She became very still. ''Tis the outcome of rape what you sees sitting here beside you.'

'You mean that your mother was raped –'

'By my father. He was drunk, see, and some Taunton whore had just refused him. Loveday told me all about it. My Ma thinks that I don't know why her have always disliked me. But I have knowed since I was eight years old. I get bad dreams about it. My Ma don't love me like she loves the others. You can't blame her really, can you?'

She sipped at her coffee. 'My Pa was a coward. Our uncles used to come to Larksleve and thrash him somethink wicked! He never did fight back. He'd go limping about for a week, and talking out of fat lips.'

'Perhaps he knew that he deserved to be punished.'

'He deserved to die. Especially when he got us sold-up.'

She sighed. ''Twas such a lovely place, Mr Solomon. A big kitchen, with a fireplace so long and wide that we children could drag the settle in it, and sit by the fire on a winter evening. We had a parlour done out all in blue; feather beds and wash-hand-stands with pretty china jugs and bowls, and little flowered dishes for the soap.' The childish voice faltered. 'I was brought up nice, Mr Solomon. I went to church with my sisters and brother. I once had a velvet cloak and bonnet. My father could read and write. My Mama is a proper scholar, and her can play the piano like any lady. Candace and Mina went to school, so did Jack. I can't even write my name, but that don't matter. As soon as I get rich I can pay other people to do my writing for me.' She was silent for a time, and then she said, 'We had a garden. There was a raised bank where my Mama growed flowers: snowdrops and crocus in the springtime. They told me that the flowers spelled a word, and that word was LARKSLEVE.' She rubbed her eyes with the back of her hand. 'As soon as I get rich,' she said, 'I shall tell my gardener to make a raised bank, and I shall have the name of my house writ in flowers.'

'You make me feel ashamed, Blanche.'

'You got no call to feel shame,' she told him. 'You only damages yourself. I never knowed you to be cruel to women.' She smiled unsteadily at him. 'Why, you be the kindest soul I ever met; for a man that is.' She looked away. 'I got something else to tell, and I got to say it quick or else I'll never say it. I woke up one night, I was only little at the time and easy-frightened. Pa had come home from Taunton. He was drunk like always. I heard his boots on the stairs, heard him fall against the walls. My Mama had been asking him for money. We needed boots, we was almost barefoot. I heard him go into their bedroom. I heard scuffling and crying noises and my mother screaming, "You filth! You evil creature!" I heard him laugh, and then there was

191

a clinking noise across the lino. "Here you are," he shouted, "here's a couple o' sovereigns to buy your children's boots, but I tell 'ee 'tis an overpayment. You idden never worth that much money, Eliza!" He treated her shameful, Mr Solomon. But there was worse to come. She was very ill with her last child. No magic of Loveday's ever seemed to help her. It was more a sickness of the heart and spirit. Pa came home one day, and Loveday started nagging him. She told him that Mama would die if she didden see a doctor. He got out the phaeton, sat my mother on it, and set off for the doctor's house in Whitestaunton. He was drinking whisky straight from the bottle. As they come into that village he whipped up the horses. The phaeton turned over, and Mama was throwed into a strawrick. The candles from the sidelights fell out of their holders and set light to the straw. My Mama's poor face was burned all down one side. Her lost the sight of her left eye. Our Louis was born that night. It turned out later on that he was feeble-minded.'

Blanche raised a hand to her own face. 'I don't think that I could go on living,' she whispered, 'if I was so marked and disfigured as Mama. That do always make me feel guilty, as if 'twer somehow all my fault. I got this feeling, Mr Solomon, that 'tis laid on me to make it up to her, to give her all the things a lady should have. There's something awful about the Greypaulls. I can't explain what I mean. I bain't clever like you. I don't know the right words. But there's something the matter with all of us, every single one. We bain't like other families. I thought I should feel diff'rent in London, free, like a bird. But something do keep a hold of my soul and drag me back there.'

'You spend too much time in this house, Blanche. You should be out and about, enjoying yourself. Meeting eligible young men.'

'I hate all men, saving you, of course, Mr Solomon. But

then, you bain't really like a man to my mind.'

He grimaced. 'You meant that as a compliment, I know, and I shall accept it as such.' He looked closely at her. 'But are you so sure that you hate all men? What about the young mason? He for whom the witchcraft was intended.'

She coloured. 'If I had been the loving kind,' she admitted, 'then things might have been diff'rent. Then I might have loved him.'

'Are you sure that you don't?'

She caught her breath on a sob. 'He's no use to me. He got no money. Oh, but he's beautiful to look at. We do make such a handsome couple.' She pressed her hands together. 'He bain't clever. When he speaks the words do come out slow and honest. I tried to tempt him. I even tore off my frock and flaunted myself!' She looked rueful. 'I forgot one important thing, though. He's a Particular Baptist. His Parson said as how he must save hisself until he gets married.'

Mr Solomon smiled. His hands had stopped shaking, and his features no longer twitched. 'What is it you really want, Blanche?' he asked gently.

'Money,' she said simply. 'A rich husband what I can rule over. One that'll lie at my feet and beg. One that'll crawl like a beaten dog and weep for me to love him.' He heard her white teeth grind together. 'I want a man what'll lay his neck underneath my heel!'

'Then God help him,' said Simeon Solomon. 'God help that man if you ever find him.' He reached out a hand towards her face. He drew a forefinger along the line of her jaw, touched her lips and the little hollow place in the centre of her chin.

'What are you?' he murmured, 'are you Jezebel? Are you mortal or changeling? Womankind or goddess?'

The red fires began to glow behind his dark eyes.

'Kindred spirits, Blanche! Thank you for confiding in me.

I find your presence calming. Fortuitous that you should be here, this morning. But I am a fortunate man in so many of my friendships. I should not be so sad, Blanche. The spring is returning. I will rise now and go about the city in the streets, and in the road ways I will seek him whom my soul loveth: I sought him but I found him not.' He paused and tears filled his eyes. 'I sought him but I found him not.' He repeated. 'The watchmen that go about the city found me: to whom I said. Saw ye him whom my soul loveth?'

Blanche relaxed against her pillows, she closed her eyes and allowed the significant words to fasten, surely and for ever upon her mind.

'I charge you O ye daughters of Jerusalem,' declaimed the artist, 'by the roes and by the hinds of the field that ye stir not up, nor awake my love till he please. The voice of my beloved! Behold he cometh leaping upon the mountains, skipping upon the hills.' Mr Solomon sighed. 'For lo, the winter is past, the rain is over and gone. The flowers appear on the earth, the time of the singing of birds is come, and the voice of the turtle is heard in our land. The fig tree putteth forth her green figs, and the vines with the tender grapes give a good smell. Arise, my love, my fair one, and come away.' His tone lowered to a dramatic whisper. 'Take us the foxes, the little foxes, that spoil the vines; for our vines have tender grapes. My beloved is mine and I am his: he feedeth among the lilies.'

Mr Solomon's voice faltered and broke. 'Until the day break, and the shadows flee away,' he cried.

Blanche opened her eyes. 'Thank you,' she said, 'I shall always remember they words, 'specially that bit about the foxes.' She nodded. 'Oh yes, Mr Solomon, I knows all about the little foxes what spoil the vines.'

❋

Annis Greypaull, eighteen years old and pretty, and the best beloved of her Mama, had settled quite easily into the romantic role of a girl who was waiting for her soldier sweetheart. It soon became known among her colleagues that Annis and Frank were corresponding. That her mother, Eliza, did the actual writing was a detail which Annis had not cared to mention. Waiting for Frank had become her essential occupation; the letters from Burma featured daily in her conversation. Her status was raised to a level which almost equalled that of the married Madelina, or the bold and capricious Blanche. The name of Frank Nevill had also become a weapon, a screen, which could protect her from the risk of a more tangible involvement with those accessible admirers who worked in Gliddon's factory. One glance at her mother's smiling face was sufficient to tell her that a letter had, that day, come from the soldier in Burma. The reading of it had become a ritual with them. Not until supper was eaten and the table cleared, would Eliza reach up to the mantleshelf for the small grey envelope with its official stampings. In early May Frank had written to Annis.

Dear Annis,

Thank you for the letters what take a long time to get here but is very welcom. Your letters very short, but like you say, nothin much ever happens in Taunton. Glad your sisters baby got her teeth at last, all that crying must have been a worry for her. We was in a battle with three thousand dacoits. Thought I would have been afraid but too busy when the time come. Weather gets hotter every day, now 100 in the shade so the officer said. Men still dropping like flies from fever and ague what is terrible to watch. Yours truly still fit at time of writing. Leftenant Peacock hurt in hand-to-hand fighting. It is nearly dark so will go on with this letter on another day.

Sorry not to have finished this letter, Annis, but was in another battle with dacoits and then the monsoon broke.

195

They told us to expect bad storms, but the rains come in very quiet to begin with. That was just a patter on the tent roof, and how it did remind us of England, we not having seen a drop of rain since landing here. The sight of it drove us mad after the long heat. We took all our clothes off and dansed about the compound. Even Sarjeant Bath what is an old sweat and very proper usually. I feel better since the rain come. We see some funny things here. There is girls with lots of brass rings round their necks, and monks in yellow frocks what is very wild when it comes to hand-to-hand fighting. They dont have churches being heathens. They has pagowdas what has pointed roofs and is gold coloured. We find dacoits hiding in these pagowdas so we burns them down, what seems a pity becaus they look pretty. I dont know how long we shall be here. Can you send me a picture of yourself, Annis. Some men got pictures of their sweethearts pinned up by their beds. It would be a comfort to me. We see animals here like in the zoo I heard tell of up in Bristol. There is monkeys by the thousand, tigers, leperds, elefants and rinows. The snakes is poisenus, speshally cowbras. You never seen such pretty birds and butterflies, all colours they are. Spiders as big as a mans hand. Please rite as often as you can, Annis.

Ever your friend, Frank Nevill.

Letters followed on in quick succession, written in the heat of a Burma summer amid the violence and drama of monsoon and battle; they arrived in Taunton to be read by Eliza in the tawny evenings of an English autumn.

'Glad as we was,' wrote Frank, 'to see the rain come down, now we is just about sick of the sight of it. There is leeches bigger than my finger what fastens to your bare skin and takes your blood. Our clothes and boots is wet all the time. The steam comes up off the river and jungel as if there was kettles boiling in them. Everything goes rusty or

196

moldy. We must be forever polishing and cleaning. When we cant sleep we talk about England, and the sort of days when it freezes hard and you cant hardly feel your toes and fingers. I got rite into the pen and ink habit, Annis. I never thowt to rite as many letters as what I do now. I miss you very much. Still waiting every post to get a picture of you. Joe and Billy Bidgood both dead after long months of fever.'

The letters from Burma came in batches of three or four; written on poor grainy paper of an unpleasant grey shade, they were strange little missives, stained and tattered at the edges, as if they too had been involved in battle and monsoon. The photograph, taken in a small shop in East Reach, with Annis looking sad and solemn in a high-necked blouse, was sent to Frank Nevill as a Christmas present, but by mid-December the letters from Burma, until now so prolific, had ceased to arrive. Annis was fretful.

'What could have happened to him, Mama?'

'He could be sick, or the post held up. That monsoon he tells about do sound quite dreadful. Tell 'ee what we'll do, maid. We'll go down to the newspaper office and read the broadsheets in their window. There might be a line or two about the Burma war.'

Simeon was appointed to watch over Louis on that Sunday morning. Eliza and Annis, shawled and booted against the bitter weather, walked briskly towards the *Courier* office in search of news. Eliza scanned the many broadsheets displayed behind plate-glass; she halted finally before the one that was edged in deepest black. She read aloud the caption.

'Fallen on the Field of Honour. The jungle his Final Resting Place after the Turmoil of War.

'We regret to announce the death in Burma of Lieutenant H. T. Shubrick, who fell on June 26th of this year. This brave subaltern, a fine example of Britain's bravest, as exemplified by the Second Battalion of the Somerset Light

Infantry, was obliged to lay down his life for Queen and country while leading a column of his men into battle against the barbarian bandit. The situation, we are reliably informed, was thus on that morning when the gallant Lieutenant made his final stand against the Oriental devils known in military parlance as the "dacoits".

'Word had come in to headquarters Mandalay that the enemy was gathering in THEAGON. On June 24th a decision was taken to deal with the matter. On the morning of June 26th the column moved into, and occupied a tiny hamlet called QUINGYI. A halt was called by the considerate young officer in order that his men might partake of breakfast, and enjoy a brief respite before engaging in further battle. It was while they were thus off-guard that the enemy struck, fighting being very fierce and many fallen among the dacoit. It was Serjeant Bath, a brave son of Somerset, who came upon the young Lieutenant at the precise moment when he expired, held in the arms of a private soldier.

'Serjeant Bath at once took command of the detachment. Two Riflemen had suffered gunshot wounds but were able to march. The officer's body, wrapped in his own cape and blanket, was carried back to base by his sorrowing men. We are informed that there were further skirmishes with bandits throughout that terrible journey. Sergeant Bath distinguished himself at this time as a brave and able leader.

'Lieutenant Shubrick was buried with full military honours, and his jungle grave will for ever mark the place of British occupation, and the determination of our glorious Army, to see order restored among the Infidel in Burma.'

Eliza looked at Annis. ''Twas the officer who died,' she said gently.

'Two Riflemen got injured,' sobbed Annis. 'Frank is a Rifleman. He could be dead of his wounds by now. That news do take such a long time to get to Taunton.'

'If that was the case,' said Eliza, 'then his father would

have been informed, and we should have heard about it.'

Annis gazed at the bulletin and its deep black edging. 'I be glad I can't read, Mama, and I won't never learn how to. I don't never again want to hear the bad news.'

❋

Her annual pilgrimage to Taunton had been made at Christmas, but Blanche had not enjoyed it. Her gowns and hats, her talk of artists, even her generous presents, had seemed insignificant and valueless when set against the sufferings of Frank Nevill in Burma, or the inevitable deaths on the banks of the Irawaddy of her former admirers, Joe and Billy Bidgood: those brothers whom she had once ill-wished all those years ago in Hunter's Court. She had visited Madelina, only to find that David Lambert was absent on chapel business, and Mina preoccupied and frantic on account of her screaming, teething infant daughter. Blanche returned to St Martin's Lane, happy to have said goodbye to the moonstruck Annis, and even to Mama, who had shown even less inclination this time to concern herself with the affairs of Blanche. Her mother's parting gift had been a head and shoulders photograph of Annis. Blanche looked at her sister's likeness, pursed lipped and solemn, the lovely hair scraped tightly back from her face, the high-necked blouse fastened underneath her chin.

'How long will this Frank Nevill be away?' she had asked her mother.

'Ten years,' Eliza had said, 'but she've promised to wait for him. They do correspond very regular.' There had been an excess of satisfaction in her mother's voice.

'She can't wait ten years!' Blanche had cried. 'Oh Mama, that do mean her'll be twenty-seven — that's if he don't die of fever or get blown to bits first!'

Eliza's lips had thinned and whitened; she had touched her scarred cheek, her sightless eye. 'Don't you ever let me hear you say that in your sister's hearing. I believe that you only comes home to cause strife and heartache. Look to your own life, miss! Examine your own conscience! I sees no ring on your third finger, spite all of your fine looks.'

Blanche had also had her photograph taken. She had gone, on her return to London, to a fashionable photographer's in Bond Street. She had worn a low-cut gown that revealed her shoulders and the beautiful column of her slender neck. The man has suggested a pose in profile, one that showed off her coiled and gleaming hair, her perfect Grecian nose, and the delicious pout of her full red lips. She had sent a copy of her likeness to Hunter's Court, Taunton. Mrs Gimball, at Blanche's dictation, had written the accompanying note. 'Taken in Bond Street, London, by the man what photographs the Prince of Wales. Keep this always on the mantelshelf in remembrance of your loving daughter, Blanche.'

Mr Kraus, the photographer, had been very pleasant, which was reassuring since his final bill, Blanche feared, was likely to be heavy. So great had been her delight on seeing the finished prints that she had become rash, and ordered a dozen others. 'With your permission,' Mr Kraus had said, 'I would like to do a life-sized enlargement – at no cost to you, of course, for the purpose of display in my shop window.'

Blanche had often lingered beside that window; never more than three portraits were ever displayed there at any one time. The arrangements were very tasteful, the subjects famous, or exceptional as to looks and bearing. At that moment a full-length study of Mrs Langtry, the 'Jersey Lily', occupied the central position, her exquisite likeness framed in gold and set out among swathes of crimson silk as befitted the former mistress of the Prince of Wales.

'I don't know,' Blanche said, ''tis all getting to sound a bit expensive.'

Mr Kraus smiled. 'Some ladies find it convenient to come

to an arrangement with me. An arrangement, may I say, which is very profitable for both parties.'

Blanche looked suspicious. 'If you be hinting-on at what I think you are – '

The unctuous Mr Kraus held up his hands as if fending off attack. 'My dear young lady, please allow me to explain. Mine is a high-class and reputable business. The arrangement I speak of is regularly taken up by the aristocracy.' He became coy, 'Ladies of quality and breeding whose looks, may I say, are not always up to the standard of your own.' He indicated the framed portraits which lined his walls. 'Take these for example. A reputable artist, Sir Frederic Leighton say, or Mr Millais, would charge a huge sum of money to reproduce those faces in oils on canvas. There is also the time involved; a photograph can be taken in a matter of minutes. I bring possession of these beautiful pictures within the grasp of the ordinary man, something quite unknown before the coming of photography.'

'I don't understand you.'

Mr Kraus became confidential. 'It's not widely known, but I have another business, down in Piccadilly. Copies of these portraits may be purchased there for sixpence a time.'

'How much do I get if I let you sell my likeness?'

'Twelve free copies for yourself,' he said swiftly, 'a life-sized portrait in my Bond Street window, and a penny for every copy that I sell in Piccadilly.'

'A penny-ha'penny each copy,' she demanded.

'But there are expenses to be defrayed,' he protested, 'my photographic plates, materials and labour.'

'A penny-ha'penny or nothing.' Believing that he would refuse her offer, Blanche decided to tease him. She also became confidential. 'I'm an artist's model by profession,' she whispered, 'if you pay me threepence a copy, I'd let you take my picture wi' no drawers on.' As she told Mrs Gimball óver supper that evening, 'You should just have

seen that old goat's face. I thought he'd have thrown a fit!'
"This is a respectable establishment," he shouted, "I think
you have mistaken my purpose. The whole tone of my
photographs is strictly artistic."

' "Oh yes," I said, "Well I've heard that tale before.
There's some very funny business goes on in London by the
name of Art. A penny-ha'penny, Mr Kraus; you can take it
or leave it." ' Blanche giggled. 'Oh, I had him sweating
buckets. You should just of seen him. "You drive a hard
bargain," he said, "let us only hope that your picture sells
well." '

Mrs Gimball had her reservations. 'I don't know what
Mr Solomon'll say. He don't hold with photos.'

'I never meant it to go so far,' said Blanche, 'all I wanted
was a nice picture for my Mama.'

❋

Hugh Deveraux Fitzgerald was in the precarious condition
of a young man jilted. His fiancée, a debutante named
Claire, had helped him to spend, in the previous rapturous
summer, the greater part of his inherited fortune. On
learning that he could not afford to raise sufficient money to
buy her the yacht she craved, the Lady Claire had eloped
with an older, but richer man.

Hugh had consoled himself for a time with the ladies in
the Argyll Rooms in Great Windmill Street. He had visited
Kate Hamilton's Café Royal and discovered that there was
no surer anodyne for an aching heart than good wine,
discreet lighting, and the amorously inclined girls who were
found in the alcoves. Motts in Foley Street was a more select
establishment, with a hall-porter who was trained to
recognise and admit only the nobility and gentry. But the
appeal of the bordello, no matter how regally appointed, had
soon begun to pall. On this day in March he strolled
aimlessly in Bond Street. A small crowd had gathered

around the plate-glass window of the photographer, Kraus. Hugh paused, expecting to see a familiar and notorious face, but the photograph that had drawn the crowd that day was that of an unknown girl. 'Who is it?' he enquired of the old man who stood beside him. 'Gawd knows,' was the answer, 'some bleedin' Gaiety girl, or a bloody duchess!'

Hugh gazed at the photograph; it was not framed in gold or swathed in coloured silk, but set up simply on an artist's easel, as though it were an unframed painting, just completed. The face intrigued him; presented as it was, in profile, many aspects of it remained half concealed. The chin, he thought, might have a dimple in it. The eyes were probably wide-set. The mouth, full and with a delicious pout to the upper lip, must be quite irresistible when seen full-face. The hair, dressed in the fashion of Alexandra, Princess of Wales, curled low across the forehead, and was coiled, thick and shining at the back of the head. There was a choker of fine lace around the slender neck; the ruffled straps of a low-cut ballgown crossed the beautiful shoulders. He guessed at her colouring: brunette he decided, with a creamy skin. She was the personification of the Pre-Raphaelite female. This was the face that had appeared soulful and dolorous, in at least a dozen recent Academy offerings. Hugh considered himself to be a connoisseur of art. He dabbled a little in watercolours. He collected fine porcelain, and played the violin. His desire to possess the photograph was sudden and bizarre; all his instincts warned him against a new involvement at a time when he still grieved about the old. Nevertheless, he entered the photographer's shop, and called upon the proprietor to attend him. Hugh proffered his engraved card, and saw an expectant glow in the eyes of Mr Kraus.

'What,' he asked, 'can I do to oblige you, sir?'

'That picture — the one on the easel. I would like to buy it.'

'I am afraid I only have that one enlargement, sir, and as you can see it is proving a valuable source of advertisement.' Mr Kraus indicated a leather bound album which lay on a side table. 'I have several copies of that particular photo in postcard size. Perhaps you would care to peruse our Book of Beauty, sir. There is an excellent choice: the "Jersey Lily", Vesta Tilley, Sarah Bernhardt and many others, all at sixpence per copy.'

'The enlargement,' demanded Hugh, 'every blasted postcard, and the photographic plates. I'll give you fifty guineas for the lot!'

'But, sir, I can't do that! The young woman is to receive a percentage of all sales made. Whatever shall I tell her?'

'You can safely leave all explanations to me. Just give me the lady's name and address and I will go to see her. I want that picture, Mr Kraus, and I mean to have it.'

'It's all highly irregular, sir. The young woman is quite unknown; not at all the sort of client I normally deal with. But she came in to have her picture taken, and well – you've seen the result for yourself, sir! She's a country girl, not one of your wide-awake city sparrows. I wouldn't like to cause any trouble for her.'

'Trouble!' cried Hugh. 'How can you cause her trouble by effecting me an introduction to her? You are, are you not, proposing to sell her photo to any Tom, Dick and Harry in the city of London?' He tapped Mr Kraus on the chest with his ebony cane. 'Do you know who I am, my man?' Kraus shook his head. 'My brother is Lord Fitzgerald. My cousin is the Govenor of one of the Windward Islands. I dine with the Prince of Wales. I ride to hounds with the Duke of Clarence.'

Mr Kraus blinked. 'Well sir – ' he still sounded doubtful.

'Seventy guineas and that's my last offer.'

'Well all right, sir. Just so long as you go and explain to the young woman.'

'Oh, I will,' said Hugh, 'but it might be as well if you were to tell me a little bit about her. I wouldn't want to upset her, don't you know! Forewarned is forearmed, and all that!'

The photographer allowed himself a smile. 'You may well rue the day you ever stopped at my shop window,' he warned. 'She speaks like a country girl, but she's a strange one and no mistake.' He paused in his wrapping of the large brown paper parcel. 'When you take a picture sir, you naturally spend some considerable time looking at the face. Now, I am not an imaginative man, sir, quite the reverse, in fact. But there was something about this Miss Greypaull that chilled the blood in my veins.'

'She's not disfigured is she?' Hugh asked quickly.

'Oh no, sir. A more perfect example of the female gender you could never wish to see.' He dropped an eyelid, and tapped the parcel. 'What you see here is only head and shoulders. She's tall, carries herself like a queen. As for her figure! Junoesque is the only word that comes to mind, sir.' He lowered his tone. 'It's my belief sir, that she wears no corset. An experienced eye can always detect tight-lacing.' He tied the final knot, and pushed the package across to Hugh. 'But be warned, sir. There's something not quite – well, I don't know how to explain it – not quite –'

'Never mind,' said Hugh, 'you've made a fat profit from her.' He grabbed up his parcel and left the shop. The name and address, printed carefully upon the label, was of a Miss Blanche Greypaull, care of Mrs Gimball, 21 St Martin's Lane, London.

❋

The note was delivered by hand, at midday on Sunday. Blanche returning from the next-door chophouse with a tray which held lamb-chops and mashed potato, set down three plates upon the circular table, and began to serve the meal.

'Letter come for you,' said Mrs Gimball.

'Delivered by hand, said Mr Solomon.

Blanche glanced at the thick cream envelope and helped herself to mint sauce. She dug her fork into a lamb-chop and began to dissect it.

'Nobody writes to me,' she said firmly, 'you must be mistaken.' Through a mouthful of meat and gravy she said crossly, 'Go on now! Eat your dinners, it'll all get cold, and there's nothing worse than a plate of cold mutton.'

'Aren't you even curious?' asked Mr Solomon.

'Letters make me nervous. Anyway, I can see that letter idden come from nobody I know. 'Tis expensive paper.'

Mr Solomon smiled. 'Would you prefer that I read it for you?'

She coloured. 'Please yourself. Eat your dinner first, though. There's no hurry.'

Mr Solomon broke the waxen seal and withdrew the single sheet of vellum. He scanned it briefly. 'You have an admirer, Blanche. A wealthy one too, if his address is any indication.' He began to read. ' "Dear Miss Greypaull, I hope you will forgive my temerity in writing to you. I was given your address by a mutual friend, and since I have in my possession certain articles which belong to you, I deem it advisable that we meet at the earliest date that is convenient. I am residing, temporarily, with my aunt, Mrs Porteous of Russell Square. If you would care to call tomorrow evening, I have property that is rightly yours, and which I wish to return to you.

' "With every hope of meeting you shortly,

' "I am, respectfully yours, Hugh Deveraux Fitzgerald." ' '

Mr Solomon's voice trailed away into silence. They gazed at one another.

Mrs Gimball said, 'What you bin leaving about then, for a gentleman like 'im to pick up?'

206

'Nothing,' cried Blanche. 'I only got a few clothes, and I keep them on my back, save when I'm posing. I never lost my handbag. I don't own no jewellery.'

Mr Solomon advised her to ignore the letter. 'An obvious ploy,' he declared, 'by some young blood who is out to trap you.'

'Russell Square,' mused Mrs Gimball, 'them's grand houses, Mr Solomon; even more 'igh-class than Kensington and St John's Wood.' The extraordinary nature of the letter and its contents, suddenly touched her. 'Sw'elp me Gawd, Blanche!' she whispered. 'Wot the 'ell of you bin up to? Wot sort o' toff have you bin glad-eyeing?'

Blanche giggled. 'I don't know, and that's the truth. You get used to fellers staring at you in the Life School. There's a few mashers what stands gawping outside the Academy's back entrance. They hangs about like stage-door Johnnies, waiting for to see us come out. Not,' she declared, 'that there's many models worth the waiting. There's very few as can match me for looks and bearing.' She became thoughtful; she picked at her teeth with the prong of her fork, a trick she had learned from Mrs Gimball.

'Now, I just wonder which one 'tis. There's a liddle ginger-haired bloke – but no, he do sometimes wear a cloth-cap. There's a tall skinny chap with long black moustaches.' She chuckled. 'There's a couple of officers from the Westminster Barracks. Now, they look likely prospects for a bit of devilment and fun.'

Mrs Gimball tapped the letter. 'This ain't from no back-door masher, nor from some officer wot's looking for a good night out. A gentleman wrote this, my gel! One wot lives in a grand house and knows important people.'

'I know,' cried Blanche, ''tis that very promise of grand things what is so exciting.' She set her tin mug upon the table and pointed at it. 'That's what I be getting tired of. Nothing is ever the same in this house, not two days handrunning. One day we'll be eating off Crown Derby or Chelsea, the next time 'tis tin plates and mugs.' She looked wistfully at them. 'I be grateful for all what you done for me. I never knowed real kindness before I come here. But something got to happen soon. You can see that, can't you? Here I sit, every blessed night, playing cards with your friends, and telling 'em their fortunes. I be already twenty-two years old, and still saving myself for some rich husband.' She chewed reflectively on her little finger. ''Tis springtime again. They be selling primroses and violets down in Covent Garden. I got this awful restless feeling. Just lately, I've been afraid that I might give in, and do something very wild and silly.'

Mr Solomon looked warningly at Mrs Gimball. 'In that case,' he said gently, 'we had better answer the letter.' He picked up the single sheet of vellum. 'But there must be no assignation in Russell Square. We will tell Mr Hugh Deveraux Fitzgerald that Miss Blanche Greypaull will be pleased to meet him on Sunday next in the Garden Room of the Connaught Hotel.'

The response was swift and reassuring. Mr Fitzgerald would send his carriage to collect Miss Greypaull; she might, if she so wished, bring a chaperon with her. He looked forward to meeting her at three o'clock on the steps of the Connaught Hotel, when he would be pleased to return her property to her.

'Don't you stand no funny business from 'im, ducks!' warned Mrs Gimball. 'No going off to 'is private apartments to look at 'is butterfly collection. I've heard all about the h'aristocracy from our Ellen.'

'And don't talk too much,' advised Mr Solomon. 'You have a very pretty voice, but your grammar is quite appalling. Please avoid saying bain't; don't chew at your little finger; and if he offers you food remember that picking your teeth with a fork is simply not done.'

They fussed about her like anxious parents. Her dresses had been reviewed and declared too colourful by the artist. A gown of simple white, with flowing lines, he insisted. A pink rose pinned at the bosom; a leghorn straw hat, banded by a pink silk ribbon; white shoes and stockings. It was not her usual style, and Blanche complained at the sight of herself in the unexciting garments.

'I feel better in red or purple.'

'You want to catch a rich 'usband, don't you?' scolded Mrs Gimball.

Blanche nodded.

'Then you got to look like one of them debutantes, all innocent and morning fresh. The quality is a bad lot when it comes to 'ow they treats a woman, but they is very pertickler about wot they marries. Goods wot even look as if they might've been manhandled ain't got a scrap of value?'

He was waiting for her on the steps of the Connaught Hotel, and he was not the skinny masher with the black moustaches, nor the little ginger-haired man who sometimes wore a cloth cap. He came towards her, hand outstretched, and Blanche felt the heart contract within her. She half-turned and would have run from the place, but he had already taken firm hold of her gloved hand. She looked up at the flaxen curls, the brilliant blue of his eyes, and the high flush of colour that stained his cheekbones. At the touch of his fingers revulsion seized her; she bit hard on her lower lip and willed herself not to faint. It might well, thought Blanche, have been the ghost of her Papa who stood before her.

He relinquished her hand and took a step backwards. 'I – I am sorry,' he stammered, 'but I thought – my name is Fitzgerald – I wrote you a letter –'

''Tis all right,' she murmured, 'my name is Greypaull. I be the one what answered to your letter.' Knowing that she had allowed disgust to show in her face, Blanche said quickly, 'I feel a bit faint – a glass of water –' She felt the pressure of his warm hand underneath her elbow, and recoiled again at the touch. He propelled her gently towards the hotel entrance. 'I've ordered tea,' he said. 'It's frightfully nice here! They serve cucumber sandwiches on Sundays. There's an orchestra playing.' She glanced sideways at him. His frock-coat and trousers were of a soft dove-grey. He wore a shirt of lavender ruffled silk, and his topper gleamed silver underneath his left arm.

They entered the Garden Room of the Connaught Hotel, and as he had promised her, an orchestra was playing. There was a tiny dance-floor, many potted palms, damask-covered tables set with silver and china, which gleamed beneath crystal chandeliers. It was quite the finest scene she had ever witnessed. Blanche sat down on the spindly chair held out for her by an elderly waiter. She accepted and drank from a glass of water; the trembling in her legs and stomach settled down to an uneasy flutter. She agreed that cucumber sandwiches and Victoria sponge-cake sounded rather pleasant; she nodded, rashly, to the suggestion of lemon-tea. Blanche removed her wide straw hat and dangled it, nonchalantly, by its ribbon, from the back of her gilt chair. She patted her coiled hair, tucked in a straying tendril, and examined the chewed nail on her little finger. She gazed around her at the fashionable ladies and their languid-looking escorts; but in the end there was nowhere left for her to look but into the face of Hugh Deveraux Fitzgerald.

'Are you related to the Royal Family?' Her tone was abrupt.

He sat straighter in his chair. 'Why – no! At least – I don't think so.'

'You sound in some doubt about it.'

'No. Not at all.' He laughed. 'It's the sort of detail one's parents would hardly have neglected to mention.' He said, uneasily. 'Why do you ask, Miss Greypaull?'

''Tis no matter.'

The elderly waiter came and went. Blanche poured tea, prised open a sandwich with her index finger and nodded in grudging approval. 'Cucumber's fresh enough. But there's not much of it.' She tasted the lemon-tea, grimaced, and at once took a long drink of water. She began to feel uncomfortable in the face of his persistent stare.

'Well, don't just sit there,' she said crossly, 'you was keen enough to meet me when you wrote that letter. What's up, then? Don't I come up to expectations?'

'Forgive me. It's just — you're so much more beautiful that I had expected. I had decided that you were brunette. Brown eyes, cream skin, brown hair — '

'What do you mean?' she asked ominously. 'More beautiful that you expected? You haven't never seen me before, I might have had a wooden leg and a squint for all what you know'd.'

'I saw your photograph in Bond Street.'

'Did you really!' Briefly, she looked pleased. 'But that don't explain about the — '

'Your hair is Titian,' he interrupted, 'your eyes are violet. Your skin is so fine and white, why it's almost transparent. Your — your — whole person — is so much more — '

'Oh for goodness sake, do 'ee give it a rest! I heard all that years ago. I don't need the likes of you to tell me what I look like.' She leaned across the table. 'Let me tell you something. I don't much like the cut of you. Something sneaky about you, what I don't trust. What for have you brought me here, Mr Hugh Fitzwhatsit. What's your little game, then?' She pointed at the parcel which lay on the carpet beside his chair. 'And what have you got of mine, what has to be wrapped up wi' string and brown paper?'

Hugh looked nervous. 'It's all your photographs,' he confessed, 'the enlargement and all the postcard copies. I —

I took the liberty of also buying-up the photographic plates.' At sight of her contorted features, his voice trailed away into a whisper. 'I couldn't bear the thought of your lovely face on sale to any costermonger who had a sixpence in his pocket. I only wanted to protect you, Miss Greypaull.'

'Protect me? Let me tell you something,' her voice rose to a pitch of shrillness that ensured all eyes were fixed upon them, 'I don't need protecting from costermongers. I bin in London since I was sixteen-year-old, and nobody have ever yet laid a finger on me.' She snatched up the parcel, grabbed her hat, and stood trembling beside him. ''Tis from high-class buggers like you that I need protecting.' She stabbed at his chest with a corner of the awkward package. 'I should have know'd that you was a wrong 'un, the minute I see'd they liddle yellow curls.'

Out on the steps of the Connaught Hotel, Blanche hailed a hansom; she wept all the way back to St Martin's Lane, and pounded the leather seat with both hands when she remembered Jye Carew. Why had the Almighty seen fit to make her only love a stonemason, when a little more forethought on His part could have given her the perfect husband?

He sent her red roses and pink ones, caskets of expensive chocolates, a spray of gardenias, a flacon of French perfume. The accompanying notes declared him desolate, abject in his regret for any pain he might have caused her.

'Cutting off yer nose to spite yer face,' was Mrs Gimball's comment.

'He had no business buying my picture.'

'No ducks, he 'adn't. But can't yer see it? It only goes to show 'ow much he's taken wiv yer. Wants to keep you safe and exclusive. You could travel a lot further, Blanche, and do a lot worse.'

Mr Solomon had made enquiries. 'The young man is of good family. His father was an eminent surgeon; Wimpole

212

Street so I'm told. His mother was French, an aristocrat no less! He inherited a fortune on his twenty-first birthday and he is an Honourable into the bargain. He was educated at Marlborough, and King's College, Cambridge. His aunt has a house in Russell Square, and another in Bath. His cousin is the Governor of some island or other.' Mr Solomon smiled. 'He dines with the Prince of Wales, so I'm told. He's been seen at Epsom with the Duke of Clarence.'

'No!' said Blanche. 'I don't like him!'

'What is it?' asked the artist. 'Surely he is the very man you've been longing to meet? He seems to fit all your exacting requirements. Is he ugly, Blanche? Is there some blemish in him? Is he, perhaps, a heavy drinker?'

'He don't look like a drinker. As a matter of fact,' she burst out, 'if you must know, he's what most women 'ud consider handsome.'

'But you do not?'

'You wudden never believe this, Mr Solomon,' she whispered, 'not unless you'd see'd it with your own eyes. That Hugh is the living breathing image of my Papa. When I first looked upon him I felt my heart turn clean over. I can't abide the sight of him, no I can't!'

'But he is not your Papa, Blanche! Do be reasonable. His looks are surely incidental. You wanted a rich and eligible suitor. You wanted a tame and besotted lover!'

'You be very keen to see me fixed-up, all of a sudden.'

'You're not happy, Blanche. I am afraid that so much discontent will lead you into trouble.' He smiled, wryly. 'Be advised, my dear, by someone who knows too well the dangers inherent in disappointment. Don't dismiss the young man too swiftly. You may find that he improves upon further acquaintance.'

'I don't know about that.' She nibbled on a chocolate, sniffed at the gardenias, and dabbed French perfume liberally upon her throat and wrists. She smiled, 'Anyhow, that won't hurt to leave him on-the-boil for a bit. It don't never pay for a poor maid to look too eager.'

❀

It was in June, when she had almost given up hope of a small grey envelope from Burma, that Annis again had word from Frank Nevill. This time she could not wait for the supper to be eaten and the table cleared.

'Tell me, Mama!' she insisted. 'I got to know right away what have happened to him.'

Eliza sat down and began to read. 'Dear Annis, Very sorry not to have ritten for such a long time, but the situashon been very bad here and yours truly not much in the mood for the pen-and-ink habit. One hundred and sixty-seven men dead of the fever, Major Bradshaw dead, likewise Lt. Shubrick. All spirits very low for some time now.

'This is not the letter, dear Annis, what I had hoped to be sending to you. You would have thowt after all we been thru that they could have sent us back to Taunton for a few months. But, oh no. We are at this very minit sailing down the Irawaddy to Rangoon. I write to you on the deck of the steamship *Shoymyo*. We are to take ship from Rangoon to Madras in India. Then we go by train to a place called Belgaum. England do seem a long way off and only your dear picture and the blue beads to remind me of days past. The next you will hear from me will be from India. Got to get this finished to catch the post in Rangoon.

'I miss you very much.

'Your friend, Frank Nevill.'

Eliza set the letter down and looked at Annis. The brief grey message lay between them, significant and awful.

'He idden coming home, is he, Mama?' Her voice was tremulous, her features appealing. Annis, like Frank, had also hoped that sick and weary soldiers might be sent back to Taunton.

'No maid. Not for a long time I'm afraid.'

'Where's India? Is it further than Burma? What sort of place is it, and why do Frank have to go there?' The tears of Annis, once begun, tended to be wild and uncontrolled. Eliza's tone became astringent, her face stern. 'India lies close to Burma. 'Tis a very hot place, full of dark-skinned heathens. That takes a steam-ship at least six or seven weeks to get out there, so I'll have no crying from you, Annis! Tears won't bring Frank Nevill back no quicker. Just you spare a thought for his poor mother and father, what must be just as upset as you are!' She turned to the fire-grate and busied herself with wood and coal. 'Now stop that crying this instant, Annis. Getting in a state only brings on one of your sick headaches!' She gazed meaningfully at the weeping girl. 'You knows very well that to see you cry do only upset me.'

Annis wiped her eyes, breathed deeply, and clenched her fists to gain control. The bone-handled clasp knife, souvenir of Frank, carried always in the pocket of her dress, rested heavily now against her side. She began to think of it, for the first time, as a possible weapon. Her fragile composure broke.

'I might even kill myself if he don't come back,' she cried, 'there's so many ways that he could die. Just look at what have already happened to some of his comrades! Oh Mama, I don't believe I could go on living without Frank.'

Eliza sighed, and shook her head. She would never fully comprehend these children. How high-strung they all were, how dramatic. She looked across the table to where Annis stood, hand upon her heart, tears upon her face, the high flush on her cheekbones so painfully reminiscent of Philip Greypaull. 'Sit down,' Eliza commanded, 'sit down this instant, and listen to me. There'll be no more talk of killing yourself, miss. I never heard such wickedness! Why, this town is full of mothers and sweethearts all waiting for their soldier-boys to come home. How can you be so selfish? 'Tis no worse for you than for all the others!' Her tone softened. 'Tell 'ee what we'll do now. Us'll sit down together and make plans towards the future. Frank asked you to wait for him, didden he? He talked a lot about marriage?' Annis nodded. 'Very well,' said Eliza, 'so that do call for some action on your part. A few pennies saved every week should amount to a tidy sum by the time Frank gets home. Then there's your bottom drawer. Why, you haven't even begun it yet! When I was your age I already had a trunk full of linen and blankets, embroidered pillow slips and sheets, all with the letter G worked on them.'

'Why the letter G, Mama?' Annis wiped her eyes and looked curiously at her mother.

'The letter G stands for our name. 'Tis the first letter in the word Greypaull.'

'But that could of been all wrong,' cried Annis. 'You might have changed your name on marriage. Most girls do.'

Eliza sat down. She began to pleat the black cotton of her dress between anxious fingers. 'Oh I knew that my name would still be Greypaull, whatever happened. I was told, early on, that I was to marry a cousin.' She glanced swiftly at Annis, and her rare smile puckered the burned skin of her cheek and eyebrow. 'I was never pretty like you, maid. I had this unlucky red hair, and no farmer's son would offer for me. The Greypaulls had always lived on Larksleve, it was important to keep the land in the family. I was my father's only daughter, and Philip was my uncle's oldest son.'

Annis said gently, 'But did you want to marry him, Mama? Did you truly love him?'

Eliza sat upright, her body stiffened. 'Nobody talked about love in my day. Such loose and indecent ways of thinking have only come about since the Prince of Wales have set such low value on his marriage vows. That man do go about far too much, and the poor dear old Queen have grow'd too frail and helpless to control him.'

'But love,' persisted Annis, 'surely it's no new thing? You must have felt it, Mama? The girls in the factory is always talking about it. 'Tis a melting of the heart, a warm feeling when you looks at one another, and he smiles back, all unexpected.' She hesitated. 'I love Frank. I know that tidden genteel to talk about it, and we never didden. But 'tis how I feel, all the same!'

Eliza became very still. 'I think I loved a man; 'twas just the once, mind you! I was standing in church, on my wedding morn, before the altar. I was waiting for your Papa to put the ring on my finger.' She smiled, wryly. 'Don't never ask your mother about love, maid. I went to church with a dowry of sovereigns all tied up in a velvet bag. I was bargained away for a heap of gold to a man what didden want me. I cudden even look at him, Annis. Instead I looked straight past him to where his brother Samuel stood, waiting with the ring that was to change my life.' She paused. 'Sam smiled at me, and, oh maid, that smile did turn my heart clean over. I recalled that time past when Sam and me had danced together at Harvest-Home. The way he had looked at me, all shy and happy. 'Twas in that minute at the altar that I suddenly know'd who it was I really wanted.'

'But why didden you speak up, Mama? They cudden force you – ?'

'Oh, but they could. There's ways and means of making a daughter recognise her duty. I expect your father was persuaded in the same way. There was another reason. Philip had a name in the district. He was known for his wild ways, for being lazy. I saw him as being my Cross, I thought it was my duty to bring him back to the Lord, to guide his footsteps in the paths of goodness.'

'But 'twas all such a waste, Mama! He never altered, you know that he didden! He only got worse. He never repented.'

'Us can't be sure of that, Annis. Just before he died, he smiled at me, just the once. I told him then that all was forgiven. I think he understood me.' Eliza looked uneasy. 'But there's times, just lately, when I seem to hear him talking to me, and I fall to wondering which one of us had the right of it all, and which one the wrong.'

'All those years,' whispered Annis, 'all they seven children born – and quite without love. As I remember Papa, he never even showed you kindness. How could you bear it? You had so many other burdens.'

'The Lord was with me,' said Eliza, simply. 'I never lost faith, never for a minute. Not even when Larksleve was sold-up. I know'd that he was working out His Divine Purpose in me. 'Tis the same with your Frank. Our prayers together have brought him safe from that awful Burma. When he comes home you and Frank shall get married. I made up my mind long ago, that my daughters should choose their own husbands.' She reached out a hand and touched Annis' shoulder. 'Us'll see the waiting through together. Time'll soon pass. Now fetch me the pen and ink and a sheet of paper. Us'll make a start on a letter to Frank. We can send it as soon as we get his new address.'

❉

In November a letter came from Rhoda Greypaull Salter Black, and this time it was the turn of Eliza's cousin to need a confidential ear.

Suamico. July 31st, 1887.

Dear cousin Eliza,

Do not ushally have time to write to you in summer, but v. troubled in my mind about George and Satie. Feel awful bad about not writing to you last year, but no letter comes from you *neither*. Guess we are both getting busier as we get older.

Has some disappointments lately. Rosa had false hopes

218

about a baby, so *no grandchild* after all in Oshkosh. But a daughter born to George and Satie last September 28th in De Pere. They have called her Alma after Satie's sister.

We was almost through Haying last week, when Satie turned-up here, but *without George*. Said she had brought the baby on a visit, but I knowed *different*. Looked like she had cried herself all out, Eliza, and you and me both know how *that* do feel, Cousin. The whole story come out v. gradual. Could *not sit a spell* with her due to having the haying team to feed, but heard *much* about George as we carried our baskets of food to the meadows. Seems like he works all hours in his meat market, and then goes to *places* of *entertainment*, never taking Satie with him. I got the feeling that he *dont* pay no mind *at all* to Satie. She confided in me that she is three months gone with a second baby, and v. happy about it, if only George was *more at home*.

I tell you, Eliza, I was *v. angry* with my Georgie. Good job for him that he was far away in De Pere. Satie stopped over with us till Sunday, and then went on to Oshkosh, since Rosa would never forgive it if she did not visit with her.

We got the last of the hay in yesterday, and I wish you could see it, Dear Cousin. I cant tell you how many loads is in the barn. Its all full and two more loads on the threshing floor. There is stacked outside 12 tons all put up in good shape. Hay sells at 14 dollar the ton in Green Bay, now. I tell you, I am glad its over. I am all tired out. But not *too tired* to write a piece of my mind to young George. This is what I wrote.

George, I told him, you must take good care of Satie and not fret her. Do all you can to make her happy. She makes a lovely Mother and you must be good and kind to her. She has her hands full with Baby this warm weather. We all think Baby has gained so much. She is so *wise* and full of *fun*, and with such a lovely Baby and Mother you ought to be the proudest man living. As soon as business is over spend *all your time* with them. Never go to any place of amusement without you take your Wife. I was left watching and crying in my young days. One side of the house took the good time and I stayed at home and cryed. I never wanted to spend money. I would rather see something for it. I always loved my home and put all I could in it. *So does Satie.* Now George, be good to her and tell her all, and she will be a good helpmate to you. *I* love Satie, and so does *Father Black* and I would like to keep the Baby, she is a dear little thing. Well, thats what I wrote to him, Eliza. Do you think that I was *awful* hard on him? He is a good boy and a hard worker, but we both know how *thowtless men are*, and I just *had* to tell him.

Eliza laid the letter down. She thought about her cousin Rhoda, about those early letters from New York city in which she had always praised her first husband, George Salter. So Rhoda too had been unhappy at times, but had concealed her misery from the Greypaulls in Buckland St Mary. How brave she had been, and how loyal! The Lord had seen fit to reward cousin Rhoda with Mr James Black, and Eliza was glad.

✵

Jye rose at four on summer mornings. He touched a flame to the ready-laid ash-sticks, filled the kettle and set it to boil on the range. The pot of weak tea, made at sunrise and sunset was the single extravagance allowed by Meridiana. Tea was expensive; she called it black gold. The infusing and drinking of it was still a ritual performance, learned in her young days, when she and her people has sipped from coloured cups of thin old china, faced-to around a woodland fire. Jye, who had never slept in a bender tent, or gathered at a breakfast fire, now hunkered down quite naturally by the open door of the kitchen, to drink the first tea of the day, his face turned towards the Hill. He watched the crouched shape of it grow huge in the dawn light, smelled the scents of aromatic herbs borne upon a south wind, felt his blood stir briefly with an alien unease, and never knew from whence that restlessness came. He saw his garden emerge from the shadows, the beans and peas in ruler-straight lines of green, the delicate fronds of the carrot tops, the darker leaves of beet. He would withhold his gaze quite deliberately from the roses, always saving the final exquisite sighting for that moment when the sun swung clear of the horizon. The roses were his weakness; he allowed them to occupy space that was meant for the growing of precious food. But the roses made no demands upon him, he did not need to strain and lean to catch their message. They were his patteran, come from that old damask rosebush, willed to him long ago by Luke, his father.

His foot was the first to tread the Hill path in the early morning. It pleased him to be the first mason at his banker, to come to his work while the mist lay white across the low fields, before he needed to pull on straight away the peaked cap which kept the yellow dust from his thick black hair. On this morning in June, Jye became aware of another presence on the hillside, of eyes that watched him as he climbed. Jye waited for the master-mason, shocked by the changed appearance of the older man. 'Morning to 'ee, Mr Mitchell. You be up and about betimes!'

'I wanted a word, boy. Before the rest of the men gets up yer. 'Tis like this, Jye, I got a few problems lately. Union business mostly. Trouble between Joe Arch and me. 'Tis nothing what needs concern you, but truth to tell I could do with having you alongside me up in London.'

Jye waited, he looked into George Mitchell's face, but the master did not meet his gaze. 'Fact is, boy, that contract on St Paul's Cathedral have been tendered out to me and I could really do with the extra business. So what about it, Jye? Will you come back with me?'

'I reckon there's more to it than that, sir.'

Mitchell looked uneasy. 'Union meetings have got a bit rowdy, Jye. I could do with a strong arm like yours, travelling alongside me.'

Jye shook his head. 'I wudden be no good to 'ee in a rough-house. Ask anybody roundabouts – they'll all vouch that I be a peace-lovin' feller.'

'I know, boy. I don't expect you to fight my battles for me. But don't you see, your very presence at my side – the height and breadth of you – would be just enough to strike terror – ?'

'I'll need to think about it. That'll have to be talked over with Mother.'

'Two days, boy, and then I'll need an answer. I got to be back in London come Sunday.'

❋

They sat beside the open doorway in the cool of the evening. He waited until the supper was eaten and the dishes cleared.

'I spoke wi' George Mitchell, this morning early.'

Meridiana nodded. 'I see'd the man about the village. '

'You never told me!'

'Trouble finds us soon enough.'

He looked at the proud head of her with its crown of dark braids, the cheekbones etched hard and high, the hollowed cheeks, her eyes black and sharp with fear.

'I got to go to London,' he cried, suddenly. 'Can't you understand that?'

'Got to, Jye?'

'Well, I want to,' he said, dully. ''Tis a second chance to work in Portland stone. Like I did that time on the Mansion House. I told 'ee all about it –'

She dismissed his words with a pass of her fingers, turned that gaze upon him which could always lay bare his soul.

''Tis that Greypaull trash what is calling 'ee back there.

Don't you never think that I can't fathom you, Jye.'

Even as he watched, she grew strange and distant. A nimbus seemed to hover about her, a coldness touched the air. Her voice grew shrill and high-pitched, so that even he in his deafness, could make out the broken syllables of sound that came from between her bitter lips.

'That maid have put a spell upon 'ee. But her won't never prosper from it! You and she shall never come together. All her tricks shall lead to sorrow! Death will come to the man she chooses. Sorrow and pain lies in her hands! All her days shall be wormwood, all her nights shall be gall. No peace shall come to her until she lies silent beneath the stone; until she rests with her face towards the sea, the sound of the ocean beating in her dead ears!'

❀

Jye left his garden in the time of roses; his mother's prophecy of Blanche Greypaull still hanging cold and tangible between them. He had packed his spare shirt and trousers, his mason's aprons, his suit of Baptist black, two stiff white collars. He had placed his tools one by one inside the canvas bag, and anchored his thoughts quite deliberately to the new experience of St Paul's Cathedral. Anticipation straightened his shoulders and quickened his step as he marched to the tiny railway station. He was, he reminded himself, twenty-two years old, a time-served craftsman, called upon by a master-mason to do important work in London. He looked back at the Hill, and knew that old tug of feeling, that bite at the soul which always came to him on leaving Montacute. He visualised Westminster Abbey, the grimed and smoke-stained face of it, so many parts of which had been raised long ago from the golden stone, grown here in the very heart of Ham Hill. That the stone grew, and was still growing, he had no doubt. It was not just a tale told by the old men. There were all those cathedrals, all those abbeys and churches; the cottages and barns. No matter how deeply men delved, no matter how many loads were carted, from the hilltop, the supply was inexhaustible, and always would be. The thought gave him comfort, as if he too was a part of the Hill, grown from the stone, unassailable and strong. He came back to a London bright with flowers and street decorations. As they walked out of Paddington station he said to George Mitchell, 'What's happening then, sir? Be they all gone crazy?' Jye halted and stared about him. 'They was planning Jubilee celebrations in Montacute, but nothing like this.'

Mitchell grinned. 'There's to be a procession, and a thanksgiving service in Westminster Abbey. You can come and stand alongside me if you got a mind to. There's a special corner reserved for the masons. Might as well take a look at your monarch while you got the chance. They say that she's getting frail, that she won't last all that much longer.'

❈

The dawn of June 21st 1887 brought proverbial 'Queen's weather'. The sky was an unclouded blue, the sun shone. Since early morning the music of marching bands had mingled with the sounds of cheering and the hammering of nails into the last uncompleted stands along the royal route. Final touches were given to street decorations, London bloomed with potted palms, window boxes filled with flowers, festoons of evergreens, electric light bulbs and paper streams. Banners were hung at strategic points in every street. 'Victoria' they proclaimed 'all Nations salute You.' They came in their thousands on that sunlit morning: peers and peeresses, duchesses and dukes, earls and princes, bishops and archbishops. They came in their ermine, their scarlet and purple, in their diamonds and gold, to pay homage to that seldom-seen figure – the Widow of Windsor.

Ellen Gimball had a friend who lived in Westminster. Mary Higgins rented two attic rooms in a tall and narrow house.

'She's charging half-a-guinea for a view from her window,' Ellen told her mother, 'but it's bound to be worth it. Mary's bedroom looks straight down onto the front door of the Abbey.'

'It ain't worth that much,' Mrs Gimball cackled. 'Why, I wouldn't give yer tuppence to look at that old woman.'

'Well, I would,' Blanche declared, 'after all she is the Queen! She'll be sure to have the crown on; and then there's all them duchesses and princes. 'Twill be just like the music-hall only better. Anyway! According to my Mama we Greypaulls is all descended from Henry the Eighth – so that must make Victoria one of my relations.'

'In that case,' said Mr Solomon drily, 'it will be incumbent upon us to accompany you, to witness the triumph of your noble relation.'

Blanche giggled. 'You thinks you is pulling my leg, don't you? But 'tis all true I tell 'ee! My grandfather had papers wi' writing on 'em what proved it!'

Mrs Gimball finally looked impressed. 'In that case,' she said to Ellen, 'we'll make it a foursome. Tell your friend that her bedroom window is fully booked.'

From the Palace gates up to the Abbey the people gathered. Blanche sat in an attic window with her two protectors and Mary Higgins, and looked down upon the most extraordinary scenes she had ever witnessed. The nobility had started to arrive soon after nine o'clock; carriages and horses paused in front of the great silk awning which had been erected before the west porch. An endless procession of elegant men and women went into the Abbey, and Blanche watched, entranced. All at once she leaned forward. 'There,' she pointed, 'that feller in the grey – the one wi' the fair hair – why, that's him! That's the

225

Honourable Fitz-Whatsit!'

The rest of the party crowded at the window.

'Who's he armin' up the steps!' cried Mrs Gimball.

'That'll be his old aunty from Russell Square.' Blanche sounded disappointed. Mrs Gimball glanced sharply at her. 'There you are,' she said, 'now wot 'ave I been telling yer? Could 'ave bin you trotting in beside 'im if you'd only played yer cards right.' Blanche looked thoughtful. She sat down on the edge of Mary Higgins' bed. The sight of Hugh Fitzgerald moving easily among so much glory had quite ruined her pleasure in the important day. When the Queen of Commonwealth and Empire drove up in her carriage Blanche could only say, 'Why! She's no finer looking than my Mama is. Fancy turning up for a do like this in that old black satin frock and a white lace bonnet. Proper frumpish that is! Where's her crown? That's what I'd like to know. Where's all they jewels she's supposed to have?'

'Probably pawned 'em,' said Mrs Gimball. 'You never knows with the nobility, Blanche. Things ain't always wot they looks.' She grinned. 'That Bertie of hers is always getting hisself in debt. If wot you say is true, and she's one of your relations, then that father of yours must've been a proper chip off the old block!'

❋

Jye stood with George Mitchell among the firebuckets and sand, in the space reserved for Abbey workers close to Poet's Corner. He saw the trumpets lift, and every head turn as the little old lady came into the Abbey. He said, 'But her's only an ordinary-looking body. Sort of sad and lonely.'

Mitchell nodded. 'I heard as how they tried to make her wear the crown, but she wouldn't have it. "I'll stick to my bonnet." That's what she said.'

'I got to remember all this, to tell my mother.'

'Glad you come, boy?'

'Oh yes, sir. 'Tis a sight I shall never forget, not in all my life long.'

❀

On their return to St Martin's Lane, Blanche seemed dimmed and pensive.

''Aving second thoughts is yer, about the Fitzgerald geezer?'

'I never know'd he was that important.'

'I told you,' said Mr Solomon, 'that I had checked up on his credentials.'

'I know,' cried Blanche, 'but seeing him like that – walking into the Abbey with all they high-steppers, well it made him look different, somehow.'

'You could be a high-stepper too, me gel,' Mrs Gimball nodded. 'You got the looks for it, and the bearin'.'

Mr Solomon frowned. 'If you will only allow me to help you with your speech; and of course your table manners are not exactly –'

'And I can't read nor write, neither,' shouted Blanche. 'Well, go on then, tear me to shreds if you want to – see if I care!' She pointed her chin at them. 'I'll show you. I'll catch that Fitzwhosit. I'll have him pleading and begging. I'll have him on his knees, see if I don't. I'll learn how to be a lady even if it kills me.'

❀

The letter arrived in Russell Square on the eve of Hugh's departure for Devonshire. Penned in a large and flowing script, it was both an apology and an invitation. He noted the signature of Miss Blanche Greypaull, and recalled with annoyance that unfortunate scene in the Connaught Hotel. His involvement with the girl had been brief and foolish; the kind of lunatic episode indulged in by a man who had recently suffered, and was still smarting from the shock of female rejection. He sat down by the drawing-room window and began to read.

Miss Blanche Greypaull, it appeared, now regretted any pain she might have caused him by her unreasonable behaviour in the Connaught Hotel. She wished to thank him for his gifts and flowers, acknowledgement of which had been so long delayed due to an unfortunate indisposition from which she was now, happily, quite fully recovered. On reflection, said Miss Greypaull, she had come to the conclusion that his action in purchasing her photographs, and the photographic plates, had been undertaken only with the very purest motives. She would be happy to present him with a tastefully framed enlargement of her likeness, and would at a time and date of his choosing, be pleased to meet him, suitably chaperoned, of course, so that this pleasant task might be accomplished.

Hugh read and then reread the letter. He recalled her ungrammatical speech and strong language; the drawl and burr of the West Country in her voice. He folded the thick white sheet of vellum and placed it in an inside pocket. He smiled. It was surely not possible that she had written such a letter totally unaided, but no matter! He closed his eyes and relived the public shame of that moment in the Connaught Hotel when she had thrust the brown paper parcel hard against his ribs. How magnificent she had looked in anger, and how strongly he had desired her! What was it he had expected of her? A few weeks of idle dalliance? A soothing anodyne to his hurt pride? Blanche Greypaull had shown him that she was not to be used in any casual manner, she had been quite unimpressed by his exalted station. In fact, she seemed positively to have disliked him at first sight!

Hugh opened his eyes, he saw the shadows lengthening underneath the plane trees, and the lamplighter going about his evening business. So why her changed attitude, her apologetic letter? He watched the gaslights bloom all around the Square, and felt the dangerous stir of romance. He pulled out the letter and reread it. Surely there was a hint of intrigue, a promise of love in her closing sentence?

Dawlish would be dull in August, the beach filled with trippers. He pulled at the silken rope which would summon a servant. When the girl arrived he said briefly, 'You can unpack my trunk. I shan't be going away after all.'

He sat down at the escritoire, and began to write a letter to Miss Blanche Greypaull.

❋

Mr Solomon had left them, abruptly, one July morning, and had not returned. This time it was Mrs Gimball who read Hugh's letter. 'It's the H'onourable Fitz,' she announced. 'He wants yer to go to Russell Square. Wants yer to meet his old aunty. Well, fancy that now! Come to tea, he says, next Sunday.'

Blanche looked doubtful. 'I don't know,' she murmured. 'Them's big mansions. Once inside they gurt doors anything might happen.'

But Mrs Gimball, having seen that lady enter Westminster Abbey on Jubilee Day, was quite satisfied now that the Honourable Letitia was no procuress. 'You'll be safe as 'ouses,' she assured Blanche. 'That aunty of his won't countenance no lewd goings-on.'

'So what else do he want me for?' complained Blanche.

Mrs Gimball, usually a patient woman, became exasperated. 'Well, wot the 'ell do yer want?' she demanded. 'If you never intended to see 'im again, why did yer get Mr Solomon to write that letter. Now you listen to me, miss. Your looks is all wot you got to recommend you. You got no book learning, you can't talk proper, and being a h'artist's model ain't no great job, neither. So don't you act 'ard to get when a gentleman like 'im admires you. He's trying to do the decent thing by yer! He's taking a chance

229

you know, by showing you off to his posh old relation. For all wot you knows she might well turn nasty, and kick the pair of yer down her front steps!'

The violet eyes widened. 'So you reckons 'tis more of a risk for him than for me?'

'Course it is. I know you got a 'igh opinion of yourself, but you got to admit, Blanche, you ain't 'ardly in his class, not by a long way. Just you be careful that's all. Keep your wits about you, and remember the crawlers down in Holborn.'

'I can't never forget 'em.' Blanche shuddered. 'I still dreams about 'em.'

'A wedding ring is wot you're after, my gel.' Mrs Gimball nodded. 'Marriage is the thing. There's many a poor gel wot has hooked a Lord, so why shouldn't you land yourself a h'onourable?'

''Tis worth a thought I s'pose. But I never took to 'un, honest I didden. I can't fancy fair-haired men and that's the truth. There's something proper sneaky about 'em.'

'You can handle the likes of 'im, ducks! When it comes to sneakiness, why you can run rings round 'im.'

Recalling Mr Solomon's advice on a previous occasion, Blanche put on the white gown with the pink sash. Lacking tight-lacing and a fashionable bustle, and worn with the Leghorn hat and white shoes and stockings, the outfit lacked style. On any other girl if would have looked innocent and childlike, but nothing, as Mrs Gimball said, could ever conceal the voluptuous charms of Blanche. She stood in her shop doorway and watched the Porteous carriage roll out of St Martin's Lane.

'Gawd's strewth,' she muttered, 'you could dress that gel up in a Lipton's tea sack, and she'd still look naughty. White frock and straw hat might fool Master Fitz, but it's that old aunty of his wot Blanche'll need to look out for.'

✳

230

Mrs Porteous was a stately woman, almost as tall as Blanche, with hair of dull iron-grey, and the parched and yellow complexion of a woman who had lived for too long in the East. Her voice was curt and assertive, pitched just that fraction higher than was usual in order to put Blanche in her place. Her dress, Blanche observed, was elaborate and ugly; an incredible construction of bottle-green grosgrain silk, and black lace. Her bustle was oversized and wobbled slightly as she walked; she extended limp fingers and inclined her upper torso in the visitor's direction, and Blanche, who could hear creaking sounds from the lady's stays, was obliged to bite her lower lip in order to stifle a nervous giggle.

Sunday afternoon tea in Russell Square was an informal affair. Set out upon a wide bench beside an open window, the brew itself was a fragrant Lapsang Souchong, prepared at the table by Mrs Porteous' own hand, and the aid of a silver spirit-kettle. Blanche viewed with distaste the wedge of lemon in her saucer. She was about to demand milk and sugar, but one sip of the tea had convinced her that it was laced with perfume and not fit to drink. The food was equally poor and insubstantial. There were the same little sandwiches that she had seen in the Connaught Hotel, cut in fancy shapes, filled with cucumber, and without crusts. Mrs Porteous had insisted that she sample some sticky brown stuff called parkin. The parkin had stuck in her teeth and Blanche had halted just in time, the questing fork poised halfway to her mouth, to find the astonished gaze of the hostess fixed upon her.

'My nephew tells me that you come from the West Country, Miss Greypaull?'

'Taunton,' enunciated Blanche, careful to give that one word its correct pronunciation.

'Ah,' said Mrs Porteous, 'how very interesting! We are, ourselves, an old Somerset family. Generations of us have been baptised and married in Bath Abbey. We have a small terraced house down there – one of those so beautifully designed by Mr Nash, don't you know!'

Blanche nodded, politely. Mrs Porteous seemed to hover, like a bird of prey anxious for the attack. 'What does your father do, Miss Greypaull?'

'He owned land,' said Blanche, 'but he's dead now. He've been dead these six years.'

'How very sad. So you are quite alone in the world?'

'I got a mother and some sisters.'

'It must be hard for your mother, without a husband.'

'Oh my Mama is well took care of. Her got a private income.'

'Really?' Mrs Porteous blinked and took refuge behind her lorgnette. She studied Blanche closely and at length. 'And you Miss Greypaull? How do you spend your days here in London?'

'Miss Greypaull is involved with Art,' Hugh intervened swiftly. 'She has sat to Sir Frederick Leighton and Mr Marcus Stone.'

'Indeed! You must find that an expensive pastime. Their fees, so I've heard, are quite outrageous.'

'I shudden think so,' Blanche said coolly, 'I be an artist's model. 'Tis them what do have to pay me.' She pointed her chin. 'They paints the best bits of me in their portraits. All what is lacking on them titled ladies.'

'How utterly fascinating!' Mrs Porteous grew suddenly larger, her shelf-like bosom inflated, her features vulpine. 'Do tell us all about it, my dear!' she implored. Her tone was lowered, she became coy, almost playful. 'Tell me,' she whispered, 'are they true, those scandalous stories one hears about artists?'

'You shudden never listen to scandal,' Blanche said reprovingly. 'As for the truth of it, well, the gentlemen I sits to is all very respectable and married. Anyway, my Mr Solomon reckons that the amorous whatsits of artists is all a myth.'

The face of the hostess took on a dazed expression. 'My nephew,' said Mrs Porteous weakly, 'is also something of an artist. He's a keen photographer, he sketches and paints too. But only for his own amusement, you understand. I believe that you also have an interest in photography? Hugh tells me that you met on a photographic expedition?'

Blanche looked at Hugh, and the supplication in his face gave her satisfaction. She allowed the question to hang, dangerously in the air. 'Oh yes,' she said at last, as if the memory caused her effort, 'so we did.'

The moment finally came when Mrs Porteous rose from the table, extended her hand in what was a clear gesture of dismissal, and informed Blanche that the carriage would come round at once to take her home. 'I will leave it to my nephew to bid you goodbye,' she said meaningfully. 'Meeting you has been a unique experience, Miss Greypaull.'

There was just time for Blanche to say, as she stood with Hugh on the front steps, 'I brought my photograph for you, like I promised. 'Tis left on your hall table.'

'I've got to see you again, Miss Greypaull,' he whispered. 'I'll be in Donovan's Chophouse at noon tomorrow.' He handed her into the carriage, and she looked down on his yellow curls, his blue eyes, and the fine flush of colour to his skin.

'Well, I don't know,' she murmured, 'your old besom of an aunty didden take to me, did she?'

'Be there!' he insisted. 'Just be there, Miss Greypaull. I do implore you!'

❋

Letitia Porteous twitched aside a fold of the heavy lace curtain; she saw the carriage waiting at the kerbside, the exultant face of Blanche, and Hugh, his fair head bent imploringly towards her. The sense of déjà vu was very strong. But for the lapse of years, that couple on the pavement might well have been the pleading James Fitzgerald, and his faithless wife, Marianne.

Hugh had never been told the truth about his parents. At first he was very young, later on she had found it too painful and embarrassing to speak of. He had been a shy and sensitive child, acutely aware of the feelings and evasions of those around him. By the age of twelve he had no longer asked questions. The explanation that they had both died, in an epidemic abroad, seemed to satisfy him.

Mrs Porteous allowed the folds of lace to fall back across the window. Hugh had never known how much she loved him, how great was her need to protect and guide him. There was the sound of the front door closing, and a click of heels across the marbled hall.

'Hugh,' she called, 'Hugh, I wish to speak to you!'

He came into the shadowy room, his young face animated; she could hardly bear to see the brightness of his eyes, that smile which had been for the girl called Blanche still lighting his features. 'Sit down,' she said, and he seated himself in the facing wing chair. He was looking in her direction, but she knew that all his thoughts were elsewhere.

'Hugh!' she said sharply, 'I think the time has come for us to talk about your mother.'

'My mother?' Awareness returned to his unfocused eyes. 'Why should we talk about her?'

'Has Julien ever broached the subject?'

'No,' said Hugh, 'my brother was always as reluctant as you, whenever I tried to ask questions about our parents.' He made to rise from the chair. 'Since I never knew them, there seems very little point in resurrecting them now. To be absolutely truthful, Aunt, I've always considered that it was jolly careless of them to go off to foreign climes and expire, when I was only two years old.'

'You were not two years old,' said Mrs Porteous. 'You had been but ten days in this cruel world when you were abandoned.'

'Abandoned? But you always said that my –'

'I know, dear,' she interrupted, 'I have told you a number of untruths. But the time has now come for me to inform you on certain matters.'

'I don't wish to know! I decided a long time ago that something frightful had really happened to them. I used to lie awake imagining them eaten up by cannibals, or decapitated by head-hunters.' Hugh's level gaze made her feel ashamed. 'I always knew that you were lying; children do, you know.' He stood up. 'Let's leave matters as they are, Aunt. The past has no relevance for me, all my concern is for the future.'

'No, Hugh, But for your unwise involvement with this Miss Greypaull, I too would have been content to let sleeping dogs lie. As it is, I am bound to insist that you hear me out.'

The vehemence of her reply shocked him back into the wing chair.

'You must listen to me! The past has a direct effect upon the future. Old mistakes give rise to further errors. I should have told you when you first became involved with Claire. I watched you commit all those same stupid blunders your father had made, all those years ago. I saw you indulge every slightest whim of that scheming little minx, and I lacked the courage to give you warning.'

'Warning?' Hugh became agitated. 'I don't understand your choice of words. Abandoned – warning – for Heaven's sake, Aunt, what are you trying to say?'

'Hugh,' she said quietly, 'your parents didn't die of fever. Your mother is alive and lives in New York.'

'And my father?'

She pointed to the far window, the one which looked out

235

onto Russell Square. 'He died out there,' she said dully, 'on the pavement. He had jumped from the attic window.'

'Suicide?' Hugh whispered.

She nodded. 'He had been drinking whisky for three days. He would never have done such a thing in his right mind.'

'Where were you, Aunt, when all this happened?'

'In Bath. My poor husband had just died. I arrived in London to discover my brother dead, and you, a helpless infant, abandoned in your cradle. The housekeeper had sent word that I should come at once. There was,' she said simply, 'no one else.'

Hugh said, 'You repeatedly use that word abandoned.'

Mrs Porteous sighed. 'There is no way of telling this gently, Hugh. Your mother had just been confined with you. On the tenth day of her lying-in she arose from childbed and eloped with her lover: your father's business partner.'

'Oh, my God! But that's — that's disgusting! What sort of woman — ?'

'Exactly, my dear boy. What sort of woman, indeed?' Mrs Porteous clasped her fingers tightly together. 'I arrived to find your father dead; the whole house was in an uproar. The housekeeper had managed to find a wet-nurse — a footman's wife who had recently been —'

'No more!' Hugh shouted. 'I don't want to hear this! It's all too sordid and shameful. Oh, why did you have to tell me now?'

'Because,' she said, 'because you are turning out to be exactly like your father. My poor brother was just such a fool, led into folly by a woman's beauty, cuckolded, scorned, and deceived. Oh Hugh! Your father was such a sweet man. He never suspected that she was anything but chaste and faithful.'

'Then who am I, Aunt Letitia? Am I my father's son, or

236

the bastard of my mother's lover?'

'You are a Fitzgerald.' She breathed deeply. 'Do you think I didn't wonder about that? But there can be no doubt about your lineage. The family likeness is very striking. You've seen the portraits − father, grandfather, great-grandfather − you are their living image!'

'Very well. So I am at least my father's son. That brings us to the question of my mother. This woman who now lives in New York. I want to know everything about her.'

'You won't contact her, Hugh! You won't feel constrained to pay her a visit!'

'Never,' he said firmly. 'Any creature who would leave a ten-day old baby in the charge of servants; who drove her husband to take his own life −'

Mrs Porteous sighed her satisfaction. 'That is what I hoped you'd say.' She paused. 'You remember the portrait, the one that hangs in my house in Bath, the woman in the black gown, with a corsage of gardenias?'

Hugh nodded. 'You told me once that she was a distant cousin.'

'That is your mother, Hugh. That is Marianne Eugénie Deveraux, harlot, liar, and thoroughly evil woman!'

❊

'Well, wot 'appened then, ducks?' demanded Mrs Gimball. 'You bin that quiet and mopey since you got back from Russell Square.'

Blanche, divested of the white frock and stockings, her Leghorn hat and shoes tossed moodily into a corner, had pulled on a shabby satin peignoir and seated herself at the round table. 'I be starving hungry,' she complained. 'I never ate no dinner, did I, so that I could do proper justice to my tea? I thought as how they'd be sure to have a decent blow-out. But oh no! Just they liddle sandwich things with cucumber in 'em, and the crusts chopped off, and some sticky

237

brown cake what got jammed in my teeth.'

Mrs Gimball grinned. 'I got some mousetrap if yer wants it, and there's plenty of fresh bread-puddin'. I'll make us a nice cup of cocoa, and you shall tell me all about it.'

But, faced with food, Blanche no longer seemed hungry. She pushed her plate away and plucked nervously at the balding swansdown on her second-hand peignoir. 'I shudden never have gone there, Ma. Oh 'twas very proper and all that. But I was so dreadful nervous. That Porteous woman do behave as if she be God's wife. She made me feel like I was the skivvy and her the mistress.'

'Wot was the 'ouse like, Blanche?'

'If it's totting what you got in mind – then don't do it! She'd chuck you down the front steps – her and the butler! Truth to tell, I never noticed. I was too busy watching my p's and q's, what fork and spoon to use, and trying hard not to spill their stinking tea or drop crumbs. I shan't get asked back there. I done it all wrong.' She looked pensive. 'I could hear myself saying all that bad grammar.'

'Wot about 'im, Blanche?'

'Him!' Blanche retrieved her plate and fork and began to stab at the bread pudding. Her derisory laughter was long and shrill. 'He bain't nuthin' but a mouse. He's scared witless of that old woman. He barely opened his mouth all afternoon.' She grinned. 'I reckon he must have asked me there in a fit of madness. He damn soon regretted it, I can tell you.' She hesitated. 'He wants me to meet him again, tomorrow, in Donovan's Chophouse.'

'And shall you?'

'I might. Oh 'tis wonderful sport, Ma! You should just see the way he do plead and beg.'

❀

Donovan's was cheap. It stood on a corner in St Martin's Lane, close to William IV Street. It was used by comedians

238

and actors, costermongers, and the fruit and vegetable porters who worked in nearby Covent Garden. The smells of frying fat and beer hung heavy above the scrubbed-top tables. Blanche kicked a path through the scattered sawdust and seated herself at a window-placing, where Hugh Fitzgerald was already waiting.

'Well, this is a fine spot for an assignation,' she said tartly. 'Don't look so surprised. You're not the only one as can use big words.'

Hugh, who had half-risen at her entrance, sat down. 'If you'd rather go elsewhere − ?' he said stiffly. 'It was just that I wanted to ensure your safety. I don't care to think of you walking unescorted in this vicinity.'

Blanche laughed. 'I'm safe enough,' she assured him, 'they all knows me round about here. They respects the length and the stabbing power of my hat-pin. There's more than one Fancy-Dan what have felt the cold steel of it in his backside!'

Hugh coloured. 'Glad to hear that you can defend yourself,' he muttered.

'Don't take it to heart,' said Blanche. 'I was only sixteen when I first come to London. You either learns very fast to look-out for number one, or else −' She drew a significant finger across her throat. 'Anyway − I s'pose after all they dreadful things I said to your aunty, you don't reckon I deserves anything too posh.'

Hugh grinned. 'When you mentioned Simeon Solomon I almost fainted. But fortunately she seemed never to have heard of him. How well,' he enquired, 'do you know him, Blanche?'

'Mr Solomon,' she said loftily, 'is a very dear and good friend to me and Mrs Gimball, and that's all what I intend to say on that subject.'

'I stand reproved, madam.' Hugh turned to the waiter and then to Blanche.

'What will you have?' he asked her.

Deliberately vulgar, she placed both hands across her stomach. 'Just coffee,' she moaned. 'I was left so hungry after having tea at your house, that I made a proper pig of myself last night on cocoa and breadpudden'.' She smirked, and pitched her tone several octaves higher. 'So I r'ahly couldn't eat a single morsel today, don't you know!'

The coffee was brought, and Hugh watched, astounded, as Blanche pulled out a clean white handkerchief and proceeded to scrub at the rim of her cup. He glanced around, fearful that she was being observed. 'Whatever do you think you're doing?'

'Let me tell you something,' she confided, 'we common girls got our own sort of table-manners; and if you know what's good for you, then you'll do exactly what I do.' She leaned towards him. 'You never knows who have drunk from these cups, and the washer-up idden none too careful.' She pushed her handkerchief across the table. 'Now give it a good hard wipe,' she commanded, 'I shudden like you to catch nothing nasty!'

He rubbed, half-heartedly, at the rim of his cup. She sipped her coffee.

'Now,' she said, 'tell me what you got to say, and be damn quick about it. I idden one of your idle rich. My time is money.'

While handing back her handkerchief he contrived to touch her fingers. Brief as the contact was, a spasm of distaste gripped her features. Almost without hope he murmured, 'I would like it very much if we could be friends.'

'Why for?'

'Because — well because — you're a damned interesting woman! You say exactly what is in your mind. I'm not used to females who never use pretence. You intrigue me.'

She regarded him thoughtfully. 'And that's all? 'Tis only

my interesting mind what you fancies?'

He looked away; he began to tap, nervously with a bent spoon on the saucer. 'You're extremely beautiful, of course. But I tried to say all that when we met in the Connaught Hotel. You didn't want to hear it then.'

'I've changed my mind. I wants to hear you say it, now.'

'I can't get you out of my thoughts,' he confessed. 'At first I was angry with you. Annoyed, don't you know! I decided to go down to Devon. I've got friends in Dawlish. I like to go sailing. Then your letter came, and I told the maid to unpack my bags. Why did you write to me?' His curiosity became suddenly intense. 'I thought you actively disliked me? You actually said as much –'

'I might have been wrong,' she interrupted. 'I was upset about you having my photos. You got to admit that you was pretty high-handed. I got my feelings you know, same as you do. I don't really know anything about you.'

He leaned impulsively towards her. 'Of course you have feelings! As for not knowing much about me – that's easily rectified. Let me take you out to dinner. You shall have my entire life story between soup and dessert.'

'Where would you take me?'

'There's the Carlton, or the Café Royal. There's Romano's in the Strand.'

She considered. 'You wudden expect me to wear that daft white frock would you?'

He grinned. 'Have you anything less virginal in your wardrobe?'

Blanche clasped her hands together. 'Oh yes, I have! Just you wait and see. I got a gown saved-up what'll knock your eye out!'

❀

Dinner at Romano's! She repeated the beautiful phrase, savouring the romance of it. All her sacrifices, her rebuffs of less aristocratic suitors, those deadly evenings spent in playing poker with Mrs Gimball's cronies, the dedicated saving of her matchless body, had, after all, been worthwhile. This was to be her second step upon the ladder. Employment as an artists' model had given her a certain standing; it had certainly prevented her from joining that throng of harpies who paraded night and day down Regent Street and in Piccadilly. But she would be twenty-three next New Year's day, and even looks like hers were not guaranteed to last for ever. If only she did not have this sick feeling in her stomach, this pang of dread in her heart every time Hugh Fitzgerald came near her. Just to sit across a table from him, to make conversation, had required all her wit and concentration. He did not, she told herself, really look at all like her Papa. Her father had been clean shaven; Hugh sported delicate moustaches. He was taller than Philip Greypaull, broader in the shoulder, his voice was firm and deep, his manner assured. But already she sensed the hidden weakness in him, had probed and partially uncovered his inability to withstand the wiles of a determined woman. That he was hers for the asking, she had no doubt. Whether she wanted him would be a matter for the future; for the moment she was content to scheme and plan.

The hip-bath, not usually used in mid-week, had been taken down from its hook on the yard wall, and placed before the kitchen fire. Blanche had made sure that no sitting engagements would interfere with her preparations to take dinner with Hugh on that Wednesday evening. She had washed her hair in the early morning, and Mrs Gimball had brushed it to a state of burnished copper. An application of lemon juice and oatmeal had been applied to the skin of her face and neck in order to enhance its pallor. She had paid special attention to her hands, soaked them in almond oil, pushed back the cuticles, and buffed the nails to a high pink polish. The stick of red colour to be used on her lips lay

242

ready on the kitchen table. The gown, made by Paquin, and brought from Paris by a temporarily embarrassed customer of Mrs Gimball, had cost Blanche the fantastic sum of five pounds and seven shillings, most of which was still owed. It was all black, made of Spanish lace and trimmed with satin ribbons, the bustle was just sufficiently pronounced to enhance the waistline, the decolletage dipped just below the line which English decency permitted. A cloak of rather shabby black velvet, pawned by a music-hall conjuror fallen on hard times, was to complete the ensemble. A fan of pink silk and ostrich feathers, bought that day from Liberty's in Regent Street, lay brand-new and tantalising in its wrappings of tissue paper.

❈

Romano's was like the Connaught Hotel, Blanche decided, only grander. The walls were of panelled wood, the carpets thick, the chandeliers were lit by electric light bulbs, the tables covered with snow-white damask against which gleamed the ranked silver cutlery, and various shaped wine glasses. An orchestra was playing and several couples were dancing. A waiter led them to a secluded table; Hugh remained standing until Blanche was seated; he enquired about her comfort. Was she too warm? Was the music too loud? It was this solicitous attention to her well-being that now began to endear him to her. He had brought her a corsage of gardenias, had offered to pin them on for her in the seclusion of the carriage; but she had convinced him that this was an operation best performed single-handed by a lady herself. How nice he was! There was nothing lewd or suggestive about him. Blanche surveyed Hugh across the narrow table, approved the sheen of his hair, the elegance of his dinner jacket, the whiteness of his bow tie. Charmed by the music, confirmed in the knowledge of her own good looks by the admiring glances from adjacent tables, not even the arrival of hand-written menus was sufficient to alarm her. She averted her gaze from the threat of the large white card. 'I'll have whatever you have,' she told him, sweetly. Covertly she watched him; picked up the required knife and fork just that fraction of a second after Hugh had grasped his; followed his every move among condiments and sauces, noted the way he held his wine glass, and how he dabbed at his lips with the table-napkin. Course succeeded course, the wine waiter came and went, but Blanche drank only water. She needed to keep her wits about her; as she told him, 'I never drink nothing alcoholic, that do always send my body dead from the waist down.' She looked at her corsage and saw that it was wilting; she unpinned the gardenias and placed them in the little silver bowl of water, so thoughtfully provided by the management for that purpose. Hugh seemed embarrassed by this action, she saw him glance swiftly from side to side, as if it mattered whether anyone had noticed. It was not until the fish course was cleared and he used the water bowl to rinse his fingers, that Blanche recognised her one and only gaffe of that evening.

'You promised to tell me the story of your life, Mr Fitzgerald.'

He smiled. 'Are you sure that you want to hear it?'

'If you tell me yours – then I'll tell you mine.'

'It's not a very happy story.'

'You just wait until you hear mine – I'll have you cryin' in your table-napkin.'

He lifted his glass and drank deeply from it. 'My parents had two sons,' he told her. 'I was the younger. When I was ten days old, my mother eloped with my father's business partner, and my father, who was drunk at the time, climbed to the top of the house, and threw himself out of an attic window.' Hugh picked up his glass and drank again. 'I'll bet you can't match that, Miss Greypaull!'

Blanche looked impressed; she leaned forward, face

flushed and bosom heaving. 'Go on, then!' she breathed. 'Tell me more about it. I do love they sort of racy stories.'

'It's no naughty tale,' he assured her. 'I was left, virtually orphaned at the age of ten days —'

'Never mind that! Tell me about your Ma! She must have bin a proper lively spark to have run off like that with your Pa's best friend. I bet she was a looker. Have you got any pictures of her?'

'There's a portrait of her, in my aunt's house in Bath. As a matter of fact you bear a marked resemblance to her. I never realised it until tonight — seeing you in that black dress —'

Blanche said, hurriedly, 'Well, of course, her running off like that and leaving you a helpless baby, now that was a wicked thing for her to do. As for your Pa going and chucking himself out of a bedroom window — now that was plain silly!'

'He was crazy with grief.'

'And with whisky too, from what you said.' Blanche indicated her glass of water. 'I don't hold wi' drink. That's the ruination of a body. What happened to your Ma? Did she ever come back? Didden she never want to see you?'

'Apparently not. Oh, she had plenty of money. Her father was a Duke, she had a private fortune.'

Blanche said, curiously, 'Is that how you come to be an Honourable?'

He smiled. 'Not exactly. My father was a Lord.' He began to crumble a bread roll between his fingers. 'Anyway,' he said, 'my Aunt Letitia — the one you met in Russell Square — well she came rushing up from Bath to fetch me. She's my father's sister. There was a lot of legal business to be sorted out. She engaged a nanny to take care of me, and I was taken back to Bath, to live in her house.'

'What happened to your brother?'

'He was at Eton.'

'What's Eton?'

'It's a school. I only saw him in the holidays. We hardly know one another.'

'What was your Ma's name?'

'Marianne. She was French, I believe.'

'I got a French name too. Mr Solomon said so.'

'I know, and the name suits you perfectly. It seems to say everything about you.'

They gazed, helplessly, at one another. The strangeness of his look prompted her to say, 'You don't really like me, do you, Mr Fitzgerald?'

He flushed. 'You fascinate me,' he said reluctantly, 'I can't stop thinking about you. It's got nothing to do with if I like you –'

'I'm not a bit like your mother,' she interrupted.

He grinned. 'I know you're not.' He threw down the bread roll, and began to rise from his chair. 'Let's dance,' he said abruptly, 'they're playing my favourite waltz. I love "The Blue Danube".'

Blanche remained seated. 'I can't dance,' she murmured, 'my Mama was very strict, so I never learned how to.'

'Never mind. You can follow me, it's aw'fly easy!'

'No!' she cried, 'I can't do that. You'll have to excuse me.' By thinking hard about the plight of Mama, Blanche contrived to bring tears to her eyes. Just the thought of his arm about her waist had her rooted to the chair. At sight of her tears, Hugh was all contrition.

'Sorry,' he muttered, 'didn't mean to bully you. Most girls love to dance, don't you know.'

'Well, I don't.' Blanche snatched up the corsage of gardenias from the finger bowl and stuffed them dripping wet, into her cleavage. 'I'd like to go home now, if you don't mind. I got to be up early for work tomorrow morning.'

He asked a waiter to call the carriage round, and they rode

246

with a space of several inches between them, until a sudden tilting movement as they negotiated a sharp turn, caused Hugh to slide, imperceptibly towards her. He searched for her hands in the darkness, and held them in both of his. It was then that Blanche knew, without any doubt, that she simply could not bear it when he touched her.

'How did you like Romano's, Blanche?'

'I loved it. But I never saw anybody important. I was told that the Prince of Wales often dines there.'

'Not in the public rooms. He has his supper parties in private, usually in the Japanese Room.'

'Have you ever been invited?'

'Several times.'

Blanche willed herself to allow her hands to remain in his grasp. 'Do you ever take a partner with you?'

'It's obligatory when you dine with the Prince. He demands the presence of pretty women. But he doesn't care for single girls. He prefers young married ladies. It's safer, of course, for a man in his position.'

They arrived in St Martin's Lane. The light from the shop spilled across the pavement, Mrs Gimball had waited up for her. 'Don't get out of the carriage, Mr Fitzgerald. Thank you for a lovely evening.' She withdrew her fingers from his, anxious to be gone. As she ran from the carriage to the shop door she heard him shout, 'See you in Donovan's. Midday tomorrow!'

❁

Two letters had arrived in Hunter's Court on that Monday morning. One bore the stamp of India and was postmarked BELGAUM. The other was in the handwriting of Rhoda Salter Black, and the envelope which contained it was black-edged. Eliza sat down in her rocking chair and began to read. 'After many years of suffering and ill-health,' wrote her cousin, 'our dear John James passed away, safe in the

Lord. He was twenty-one years old.'

How terrible, thought Eliza, to lose a child, and after rearing him to the safe age of twenty-one. Many mothers still lost ailing infants, but that was only to be expected. Her thoughts turned, involuntarily, to Jack, who was determined to defy death by riding bareback. She looked to where Louis sat, restless and moaning softly, his fingers busy with the heap of straws. The chain of her family, save for Philip, was still unbroken. Eliza counted herself fortunate. How her heart ached for poor Rhoda, who, having suffered the loss of her stepson Eddie, must now suffer the anguish of losing her last-born. She folded the single sheet of paper into its black-edged envelope, and hid it inside her sewing-basket. Let Annis first have the joy of her letter from Frank; the sad news from Suamico, Brown County, could be saved for another day.

Three months had passed since Frank Nevill's last letter. Annis had left the collar factory in Poolwall to work for Mr Cook in Mount Street. She had busied herself with bits of sewing; she bought lengths of cambric when she could afford them, sewed pillow-slips and embroidered them, hopefully, with a letter N. She watched other girls stroll out for an afternoon of Sunday courting beneath the willow trees in Vivary Park. She heard their giggles and whispered confessions in the shirt factory on a Monday morning, blushed at their revelations, and knew herself to be inconsolably lonely. Annis worked late in the evening whenever a special job required it of her. Simeon would always wait at the factory gate on such occasions for, as Mama often said, with Cook's factory standing next door to Jellalabad Barracks, it was not safe for Annis to walk home alone. It was Simeon who now told her about the arrival of a letter from Belgaum.

''Tis a shame that our Mina's come round,' he said sourly, 'with that David and her howling baby. With any luck they'll soon push off home.'

'Oh no, Sim! I wants them to stay. They can hear how nicely Mama do tell Frank's letters.'

To have Mina present at a reading would be sure to increase the standing of Annis in her sister's estimation; not to mention the worthy David. Annis walked into the cottage with all the drama of a leading lady who makes a long awaited entrance. She paused upon the threshold, nodded amiably to her relatives, and then said in an artificial tone, 'I hears as how a letter have come from Frank, in India?'

Annis greeted the small grey envelope with cries of genuine joy. She clutched it, dramatically, to her black cotton bodice, and declared that she had secretly, in all these longs weeks of his silence, doubted if Frank Nevill still lived. She told Mina and David about the many dangers, always faced with courage and fortitude, by the absent soldier. 'And to think,' she cried, 'that 'twas his dear fingers what last touched this paper!'

Simeon, who was growing increasingly jealous of Frank, said drily, 'So what about all they blackmen what carries the letters to the ship — not to mention old Harry Sweet, the Taunton postman?'

Annis held out the many pages to her mother, but Eliza hesitated. 'Perhaps,' she said, 'you'd rather have Mina read it to you. He've wrote you a long letter this time, and my eyesight is not so good by evening-time.'

Courting by letter was the kind of safe and disembodied romance that Madelina could approve, especially for one who was as high-strung and delicate as Annis. She handed the sleeping bundle that was Laura to Eliza, smoothed her skirts, cleared her throat genteely, and began to read.

'Dear Annis, Sorry not to have rote to you for such a long time but the sickness have caught up with me at last. I went down with a fever just as soon as we got to Belgaum. I been in the military hospital for 6 weeks but is much better now, if still weak on my pins. My neck swelled up something awful, Annis. Could not move my head nor shoulders. They say it is a gland infecshun what comes from drinking dirty water. I bet I got it from that Irawaddy river in Burma what always had a lot of dead things flowting in it. The neck is almost gone down now but I feel just like a baby what cant walk. Never felt so silly in all my born days, cant move unless the orderly helps me. If only you was out here with me, dear Annis, to help pass the long hours and days –'

Mina blinked furiously at this point, and ignoring the quiet sobs of Annis, she continued reading.

'I got some good mates in the hospital. We play drafts and snakes-and-ladders and talk about home. I told them all about you, Annis, and how you is waiting for me. I got your picture pinned up by my bed, in the corner, where I can easy see it. They all says you looks very nice and a lady. I never hardly had time to look at this camp before I took sick, but they say it is the Military Headquarters for Prince Albert's Own. I can see from the window that we got proper brick bilt barracks like in Taunton. It is very hot here just like Burma. We got punka wallahs. That is black boys what sit behind our beds and waves leaves about to keep us cool. The black boys have got to wash us and shave us. I never liked that to begin with but I dont mind it anymore. The food is better than Burma but still a lot of rice. I hope you are well, dear Annis, also your family. How is your sisters baby, have she got her teeth yet?'

It was this final reference to Laura which brought on Mina's total breakdown. 'Oh the poor liddle chap,' she sobbed, 'in spite of his swollen neck he got time to think about my baby. He do sound so lovely, Annis. So very good and Christian!'

Eliza surveyed her weeping daughters. She thought about the black-edged letter hidden in her sewing basket. 'You got no cause for tears,' she told Annis sharply. 'Your Frank is alive and well enough to write a letter. There's others what is not so lucky.'

Later on that night, when her children were sleeping, Eliza retrieved her cousin's letter. She turned up the lamp-wick to its fullest height and began to pen an answer to the sad news from Suamico, Brown County.

❋

The dramas of this year, 1887, were not yet ended. The pomp and ceremony of the Queen's Golden Jubilee, the lavish spending on public celebration, the display of great wealth by a favoured few of Victoria's subjects, had angered many hungry English people. Unemployment was so severe, the sufferings of the poor and homeless so shameful, that pamphlets and tracts, even whole books, were now being published on that thorny subject.

In the countryside, farm labourers had obtained their franchise; since December 1884 they had been recognised as free men. Joseph Arch had become a Member of Parliament. George Mitchell had sought nomination as a Liberal candidate, but had been rejected by his Party. There were hints and rumours of corruption in high places.

In August, Mr Mitchell had publicly charged Mr Arch with squandering the Sickness Benefit Fund: money which had been subscribed by the Union members. Mitchell demanded an investigation into the matter, which Arch refused. Jye Carew had returned to London at a time of change and wild excitement. His solitary evenings were passed in the study of newspaper reports that told of the struggle between these two giants. But Jye found the monumental mason greatly changed. Those rare days when Arch and Mitchell had stood together on Ham Hill, when the Montacute Fife and Drum Band had played them up onto the platform, were all forgotten now. George Mitchell had lost his fire, his old enthusiasm for the Cause.

'Keep out of politics,' he advised Jye. 'Look at me. I have spent my life and fortune in the cause of the Liberal Party, but they have treated me shamefully. Business is falling off, boy. Men who don't like my politics are refusing to patronise me. This cathedral contract might well be the last I shall ever get.'

Disillusion in such a man, on so great a scale, was hard to witness. Jye could only say, 'Perhaps you should go home, sir. Bide quiet for a bit in Montacute. 'Tis a peaceful spot. Sometimes I have to wonder at myself for leaving it to come to London.'

Mitchell patted his arm. ''Tis a nice thought, Jye, but it is too late for me to go back now. Stay away for too long from any place, and you won't ever find your way home. Montacute is only for quiet fellers, like you. I envy you boy. Your only ambition is to do a good job.'

❀

Meridiana watched the trees change; she saw the crowns of the elm trees grow yellow, and felt the shock of a stand of beech trees turned to sudden flame by a crimson sunset. The Hill took on her necklace colours: green changed to yellow, and then to amber. She knew that Jye would not return until springtime; this was to be another sad and lonely winter. She looked for waggons in the lane, sought smoke along the hedgerows, but found none. She turned her gaze upon the village maidens, passed solitary evenings by selecting and rejecting a possible bride for her absent son. She consulted Luke upon the matter, and people who saw her, muttering by the churchyard wall, concluded not for the first time, that the gypsy woman had lost her mind. Perhaps it was as well that Meri knew nothing of the battles taking place in London. An inability to read and write could be a valuable protection against unwelcome knowledge.

❀

Coming back to London had been a painful business, and yet it had been a move that Jye could not resist. There were many lures to tempt him. There was the offer of work on St Paul's Cathedral, and what young mason, he asked himself, could possibly refuse that? Just to be considered able was a matter for pride. To put his skills to the test had always been a happy challenge. There was also his mother. She wanted him tied down in marriage, and to a maiden of her own choosing. He found it increasingly hard to make a stand against her; there were times when the force of her will worked so powerfully upon him that to absent himself from Montacute was his sole defence. The second, more insidious lure, was of course Blanche Greypaull. Just to know that he breathed the same smoky air, that he trod the same stained and cracked city pavements, was enough to make his blood run quicker. There was always that chance that he might see her. Sunday afternoon was his time for walking. The streets of London no longer frightened him. In this city of undersized men, Jye's extraordinary height, his breadth of chest and shoulder, his dark and misleading looks of menace were, he now realised, protection enough. He would walk from St Paul's to Westminster Abbey, and from Westminster Abbey to St Martin's Lane. He would sit at a window table in some coffee house down the Strand or in Piccadilly. He would watch the painted smiles of girls, who were little more than children, as they offered themselves, quite shamelessly, to passing men. To run the gauntlet of these poor creatures had been embarrasing to begin with, but his height and deafness had been a sure defence against their detaining hands and pleading voices. He wandered aimlessly through St Martin's Lane, gazed briefly into Mrs Gimball's shop window, stepped over and around the bric-à-brac which spilled across her stretch of pavement. He never, in any of his wanderings, saw Blanche Greypaull.

✳

The space around Nelson's Column in Trafalgar Square had been taken up since the middle of October by a number of unemployed men. They lived and slept there, wrapped up in old newspapers and sacking. Their purpose, so they said, was to establish their right to hold public meetings. Their continued presence in the Square was attracting the notice of sightseers and the rowdier elements of the criminal population. They used Radical and inflammatory language. Their sworn intention to hold a Meeting of Protest beneath Nelson's Column on Sunday, November 13th had been expressly forbidden by the head of the police force, but the Socialist and Radical Clubs from all parts of London had declared their intention of marching that day on Trafalgar Square. Jye, wandering aimlessly down Parliament Street on that Sunday afternoon, found himself caught up and surrounded by men who brandished iron bars, youths who carried long sticks and had pockets filled with stones. His superior height enabled him to see the contingent of policemen who had assembled at the end of Northumberland Avenue, batons at the ready.

Jye halted. He clung to some iron-railings; but almost at once he found himself dragged forward towards the heart of the struggle. He was carried along to Trafalgar Square, an undeserving target both for flying stones and baton blows. The fighting continued for a long time. He saw shop windows broken and their contents looted. Carriages, caught on their way through the Square, were overturned, their occupants ejected, the horses turned loose, and the vehicles set on fire. He elbowed his way towards the National Gallery, where there seemed to be a brief lull in the battle. Jye saw the open mouths of cheering spectators, as a troop of Horse Guards rode up and began to pace slowly and threateningly, all around the Square. A division of Foot Guards was brought up, and the sight of so many uniforms and bayonets had a sobering effect. The mob began to disperse into the many lanes and side-streets leading to Piccadilly, leaving behind their dead and the most severely wounded.

Jye felt blood, warm and sticky above his temple. He was down on his knees, caught between the Gallery wall and the side of a badly damaged carriage. He pulled off his cap, wiped his eyes clear of blood and looked upwards, straight into the white and terrified face of Blanche Greypaull. He closed his eyes briefly, and then opened them. She was still there. She sat, her body half-turned towards the broken carriage window, her head inclined towards Jye. The arm of an injured young man was tight about her. He wore pin-striped trousers, and a pale grey morning-coat, the shoulders of which were dark with blood. The man's lips moved vaguely behind his luxuriant blond moustaches. Jye thought he made a plea for help, but could not be sure. A coachman, dressed in a dark blue livery which matched the carriage, came running towards them. He began to wrench and pull at the jammed carriage door, and indicated that Jye should do the same. In all this time no word had come from Blance Greypaull. She sat motionless, the young man's manicured hand at her waist, an expression of triumph on her features. She smiled, just once, and it was a victorious smile. Jye noted the opulence of the carriage, the air of ownership displayed by the young man towards Blanche. He pulled himself upright, and began to walk away unsteadily, but with determination, out of the Square and back towards St Paul's Cathedral.

He had looked into the violet eyes and remembered his mother's prediction for this girl. 'All her tricks shall lead to sorrow. Death will come to the man she chooses . . . No peace shall come to her until she lies silent beneath the stone; until she rests with her face turned towards the sea, the sound of the ocean beating in her dead ears.' He had never understood the games Blanche played, had never suspected that in love there would have to be winners and losers. He thought about the injured young blood with his polished fingernails and yellow curls. Whatever her intention had been towards him, Jye did not feel beaten.

❋

Blanche watched as Jye Carew edged away from the carriage, saw him walk, head bent and shoulders bowed as if he carried some invisible burden. When he came to St Martin's-in-the-Fields she saw his head lift and his shoulders straighten. He strode on, and she still strained to see until the tall figure, dressed in Baptist black, had disappeared from view. Her anger at Jye's indifference to their plight was vented now upon the coachman. She kicked at the jammed carriage door.

'Fetch me one o' they iron crowbars, you gurt pudden! God knows there's enough of 'em lying about.' Her sudden movement had dislodged Hugh Fitzgerald; he half fell across her, and she could see the blood that seeped from his head and neck.

The damage had been done by a wooden stave, wielded by a shoeless, out-of-work man who bore an especial grudge against those who rode. 'Get out of there, you lazy sods,' he had shouted. 'Walk until your boot-soles fall off. See what it's like to go barefoot!' It had been the jamming of the carriage door that had saved them from instant ejection and possible death. The terrified horses had snapped their traces and bolted, but slivers of glass from the broken window were embedded in Hugh's neck and shoulders; his need for medical aid was acute. Blanche came to a decision. When the carriage door finally burst open she told the coachman, 'Help me to get him across the road. We'll try to patch him up in my house!'

They carried Hugh, faint from loss of blood, into the back room of the pawnshop. They lowered him into a kneeling position in front of an armchair.

'Hang on there, ducks!' cried Mrs Gimball, 'while I tries to get your coat and shirt off! Blanche – you fetch 'ot water and towels, and the iodine bottle. Better bring my smelling-salts too, while you're about it. His 'ighness is gawn a funny colour!' They worked for an hour removing the glass, bathing the wounds with hot water and pouring iodine into them. They revived the patient many times, at first with smelling-salts, and then with brandy. Finally, his head and neck bandaged, and three-parts drunk, Hugh Fitzgerald was allowed to lie back in a chair and sleep. Mrs Gimball had washed the blood from his matted hair, and combed up his luxuriant moustaches. She surveyed him with a good deal of satisfaction.

'Well, ain't he lovely!' she whispered. 'He got skin like a new-born babe. As for 'is hair! There's many a girl who'd envy 'im curls like that. One thing is certain, he'll have to spend the night 'ere. He's in no fit state to be moved, and the streets ain't safe to walk in.' She made up the fire, placed a pillow behind Hugh Fitzgerald's head, and tucked a blanket around his legs. 'He'll 'ave to see a doctor in the morning, I ain't sure if we got all that glass out.'

Blanche lay awake for a long time that night; the presence of Hugh in the adjoining room was so unlikely, the events of that day so strange and terrifying, that she could not bring herself to blow out the candle. She began to think about Jye. The expression of surprise on his face when he had seen her inside the carriage, had pleased and gratified her. Conscious that Hugh's arm was placed protectively around her, she had watched Jye's look of amazement turn to disgust as he had also realised it. She had known what he must be thinking, but there had been no time or chance for explanations; and so she had put on a face of triumph, outstared him. Dared him to think badly of her.

The candle flickered, shadows leapt across the stacked

canvasses left behind by Simeon Solomon. She could hear the sounds of marching boots and men's voices towards Trafalgar Square, and was reassured. The military, anticipating further trouble, had come back to stand guard through the night. Blanche recalled her first weeks in this room, how nervous she had been, how unsure. Six years on and she was still here. The appearance of the room had changed a little, she had acquired a wardrobe for her many outfits, a dressing-table for her hairbrushes and trinkets. But she still slept on a horsehair sofa, and then there was always the bitter-sweet dream of Jye that came back nightly to torment her.

She considered the aristocrat in the next room, and smiled at the thought of him, blanketed and pillowed in Mrs Gimball's wicker armchair. She imagined him, awaking in the morning to find himself surrounded by the magpie collection of bric-à-brac collected by that lady, knowing that he had slept in the back room of a pawnshop in St Martin's Lane.

Blanche slept late on that Monday morning. She awoke still bemused by the nervous exhaustion of the previous day. Quite forgetting the presence of Hugh Fitzgerald in the next room, she blinked her way towards the breakfast table, the flush of sleep still on her face, the hair loose about her shoulders. At the look of admiration in his eyes, she pulled the shabby peignoir tight about her. Hugh was still sitting in the wicker chair. He looked pale but alert. He bid her good morning and she mumbled a reply.

'No use talking to her, sir, before she's 'ad 'er coffee. Half-dead our Blanche is first thing in the morning.'

He began, very gingerly, to move his head and shoulders. When he declared the lessening of all pains Mrs Gimball sighed her relief. 'I was afraid we might have left some of that glass in. You'll no doubt be stiff for a bit, sir.'

'You did a wonderful job,' he assured her, 'and I owe

Blanche my life. When that ruffian smashed the carriage window she leaned across me, pulled out her hatpin and attacked him. Went straight for his eyes, by Jove! I've never seen anything so brave in all my life!'

Blanche was embarrassed. 'Told you that I could look after myself,' she muttered.

'Well, things is quieted down this morning,' Mrs Gimball assured them. 'The streets is packed with the militia. Them roughs won't dare to start any more trouble.' She began to move away from the breakfast table. She turned to Blanche and said significantly, 'I got a lot of sorting-out to do in the front shop. I'll leave you to take care of your friend.' To Hugh she said, 'Now you stop 'ere for as long as you wants to, sir. Don't you dare move until you feels stronger.'

'You're very kind,' he told her. 'No doubt my coachman will come looking for me shortly – that's if he managed to locate and catch the horses. But I'll be glad to rest for a time, if you don't mind.'

Mrs Gimball closed the door quietly behind her, and Hugh turned to Blanche. 'It was good of you to let me stay.'

'Nothing to do with me,' she said sharply, ''tis Mrs Gimball's house. I be only a lodger.'

He gazed around him. 'I like it here. It's nice and cosy.'

'Don't lie. I've seen the sort of place you live in. I bet you never slept before in a wicker armchair, nor drunk your coffee out of a tin mug.'

'I've been shown kindness here, Blanche, and that's a rare thing in my world. My experience of women has taught me that most of their smiles come pretty expensive!'

'You've had a lot of experience with women?' She asked the question in a bored offhanded fashion.

His reply lit a glimmer of interest in her. 'Only one that was really important to me. She broke off our engagement earlier in the year.'

Blanche sat straighter in her chair, refilled her coffee mug, and prepared to listen. 'Why did she chuck you over, then? Or didden your aunty like her?'

'We got engaged on my twenty-first birthday. I'd inherited some money, from my father. I was in my last year at Cambridge.' He paused. 'Her mother had brought her over from Ireland – for the Season you know – I was invited to her coming-out Ball.'

'One o' they debutantes?' Blanche asked.

He nodded. 'She was the prettiest girl I had ever seen. Delicate and slender, with a cloud of dark hair, and a rosebud complexion. I proposed to her almost straight away, and was accepted. I could hardly believe my luck; for months I walked around in a daze – '

'And then you woke up and found she'd pinched all your money.'

'Something like that. She was very keen on sailing, so am I. We entered for the Henley Regatta, and the Prince had invited us down for Cowes Week. He's not usually keen on the company of unmarried girls, but Claire had the knack of amusing him when he got bored. He gets bored very easily.'

'So what happened?'

'We had rented a boat, or at least, I had. Claire had no money of her own. She began to find fault with it, said that we should buy our own craft. Well – I had to tell her that I couldn't afford it.'

'But you said that you inherited on your twenty-first birthday?'

'And so I did. But I had been spending at a furious rate. Furs and jewellery for Claire, gowns from Worth, lingerie from Paris, St Moritz in the winter, Italy in the spring – '

' – and Henley in the summer.' Blanche sipped her coffee and looked thoughtful. 'Took you for a proper Charlie, didden she? Engaged again, is she?'

'Married, as a matter of fact, last spring, to an earl.'

'About the time you first met me was it?'

'If you think that I was on the rebound –' he said swiftly.

''Course you was! You can't expect me to believe no different. Matter of fact,' she said deliberately, 'I was in much the same predicament myself.'

'I can't belive that any man would jilt you.'

'No more he didden. 'Twas me what chucked him over. He's something very high up in Westminster Abbey. He got bitten by the religion – well, you would wudden you, being shut up all day in a church?'

Hugh looked embarrassed. 'So you're fancy-free?' he said softly.

'As free as what you are.' She stood up. 'I got to get dressed now. I got an appointment in the Life School for eleven o'clock.'

He held out a hand but she pretended not to see it. 'My aunt is closing up the London house,' he told her, 'we shall be going down to Bath for Christmas and the New Year. I would like it very much if you would come with us. We could become so much better acquainted –'

'No,' she interrupted, 'thank you for the offer, but I do usually spend Christmas in Taunton with my mother and family. They'd be heart-broke if I never come. Anyway, your aunty don't like me. There'd be ructions between us.'

'Yes,' he said, 'I suppose there would be. It's just that I can't bear to be parted from you.' He looked anxious. 'But you'll dine with me again, quite soon? I haven't thanked you yet for saving my life.'

'You'd be better to see a doctor,' she advised him. 'They cuts do want looking at as soon as possible.'

'Tomorrow night,' he pleaded, 'you can't refuse a wounded man!'

'All right then. But only if you're fit and well.'

'Oh I will be!' he assured her. 'I'll send the carriage to pick you up at eight.'

✴

People tended to confide in Madelina. There was a quality in her voice, an innocence to her prim unpainted mouth, a mesmeric power in her green eyes that drew forth unintended revelations. She was always gratified to find herself the recipient of secrets: to hold a confidence was to gain power. When her brother Jack arrived in Grey's Road on that Friday evening, Mina sensed at once the atmosphere of mystery that came in with him. He enquired for the baby Laura, and was told that she slept. David, said Madelina, was across at the chapel; the Young Men's Bible Class was held every Friday evening, and he would not be back until nine, but still Jack seemed restless and not inclined to sit down, so she showed him the Christmas tree in the little blue parlour, and Jack said how much it all reminded him of Larksleve. They returned to the kitchen fire, and Mina made cocoa. She persuaded him to sit down, and an unnatural silence fell between them. At last she murmured, 'What is it then, Jackie? Did you ride over for some special purpose?'

The use of his old childhood name unmanned Jack; minutes passed before he was able to speak. 'Can I tell you something?' he asked her. 'Something very private?'

She crossed at once to where he sat, and knelt down before him. She took his hands in both of hers, and looked up into his face. ''Course you can, boy. Didden you always tell me your secrets when we was children?'

'This is something different, Mina. This is something that I couldn't take direct to Mother.'

'Oh – Jack, whatever is it?'

'I got married a year ago – there's a baby – a boy, he's a month old.' He sighed. 'She's a servant-girl in my master's house. I didden quite know how Mother would take it, her having always seen me as the heir to Larksleve.'

She stared at him, quite unable to speak, released her hold on his hands, and sat back on her heels.

'Don't look at me like that! You was the only one I had to turn to –'

''Tis all right, boy,' she said absently, 'you done right to tell me.' Mina shook her head as if to clear her mind. 'After all,' she mused, ''tis done now. You married the girl, without Mother's permission, so that's settled.'

She leaned forward and repossessed Jack's hands. Her voice took on a deeper tone, her hooded eyes gazed deeply and sincerely into those of her brother. 'You done quite right to come to me, Jack. This is not a matter for the family. As for telling Mother,' she dismissed Eliza with a wave of her fingers, 'you be guided by me. There's no telling just how she might take it. Let we keep this matter strictly between us two, eh?'

Jack looked troubled. 'But I wanted Mother to meet Milly. I wanted to show her the baby. I thought if you could sort of pave the way – prepare her a bit –'

'No Jack! Mama got more than enough to bear with at the moment. Later on, p'raps, when times get better, then I'll break it to her. 'Twill be a risky thing to do, mind! Mama do look very frail just lately. You can come and talk to me any time you want to.'

'You won't go telling David Lambert?'

Madelina smiled. 'No,' she said, 'I won't be telling David, you can rest easy on that score.' She gazed up into her brother's anxious face. ''Twill be just like the old times, Jackie, when we was growing up on Larksleve. There's no call for anybody else to know about your liddle secret.'

❀

Blanche would not be coming home for Christmas. A note, penned by Mrs Gimball, informed Eliza that owing to pressure of work, her daughter could not get away from London until the New Year.

❀

Her decision to remain in London over Christmas had been made, Blanche confessed to Mrs Gimball, partly from necessity, but mainly to indulge her rare mood of introspection.

'I've got some thinking to do,' she told that astonished lady. 'There's certain matters what have to be decided. I can't go on, year after year, waiting for something wonderful to happen. That's what my Papa did, and look how he ended up.' A line of worry appeared between the violet eyes. 'I bain't too keen no more on this modelling for artists. The money comes in too slowly, there's nothing regular about it.'

Mrs Gimball laid down the opera hat she was brushing, and gave her full attention to Blanche. 'I've never 'eard you complain before, ducks. Is it that Fitzgerald fellah what is making you discontented? You was 'appy enough when you was chasin' the young mason.' Her voice grew eager and persuasive. 'You ain't thinking of leaving me, is you? Why, I don't know wot I'd do without you. I've never asked a penny-piece of you. The selling and renovating wot you do 'ere more than pays for your bed and board. The money you earns down the Academy is all loose change in your pocket.' She looked pleadingly at Blanche. 'We 'as nice times together, don't we, ducks? Music-hall of a Saturday night, a good long chin-wag of a Sunday morning. A good Sunday dinner from the chophouse, and there's always the chance I might take in a nice gown or hat wot'll take your fancy!'

Blanche sighed. 'I know all that, Ma. Don't think that I'm not grateful to you. God only knows where I might have landed-up without you. You've been like a mother to me.' She frowned again, and quickly smoothed the crease away with her fingertips. 'But it can't go on. I be coming twenty-three this New Year, and all I've done so far is to talk big. I done a lot of boasting in Taunton. Time is running out, Ma!'

'But wot else can yer do, love?'

Blanche smiled. 'Funny you should say that, 'cause I just been offered a job where I'd have to keep all my clothes on. Regular work too, and good money.'

'And where might that be?'

'Liberty's in Regent Street.'

'You ain't never cut out to be a shop-girl!'

'Nor should I be!' She lowered her eyelids. ''Twas Mr Liberty hisself what offered the job. He come visiting down in Chelsea, and saw me posing. I took coffee and biscuits with Mr Liberty in his office this forenoon, we had a long chat together.'

'So wot can you do at Liberty's wot won't call for reading and writing?'

'I can still be a model – but decent! 'Tis the clothes what I shall be showing-off not my –'

Mrs Gimball's laughter covered the final word, 'Well, s'w'elp me Gawd! There's a turn-up. You always falls straight on your feet, don't yer?'

Blanche looked earnest. 'It's to be a new venture.' She spoke carefully, enunciating every word in an obvious parody of Mr Arthur Lasenby Liberty. 'The bustle and the bonnet are on their way out, as is the whalebone corset, rigid stays, buttoned boots and high-boned collars. It is time for women to look more natural.' In her own voice Blanche added, 'I agreed with every word he said. Like I told 'un, I never cudden abide that dratted whalebone.'

Mrs Gimball looked doubtful. 'So wot's this new fashion going to be, then?'

'Japanese! He've purchased a whole lot of gowns from Japan. Oh, you should just see 'em! They be made of pure silk and such lovely colours. Tea-gowns he called 'em. They be all loose and floating. I had to model one for him – he wanted to see how I walk and carry myself. Emerald green it was, with liddle silk slippers to match and a sort of muff thing.' She paused. 'That was such a special feeling, to wear something brand-new.'

'You loves clothes, don't yer?'

'More than anything, Ma!'

'So you'll be taking this new job?'

'I already took it. 'Tis more money than I could ever earn in the Life School, and reg'lar too. There'll be perks as well. I can buy certain goods at discount prices – that means cheaper. I might even get engagements to model clothes in private houses.'

Suspicion hardened Mrs Gimball's features. 'Now you want to be careful about going to private 'ouses. There's a deal of white-slavery going on –'

'Not by the likes of the Princess of Wales or Mrs Lily Langtry,' interrupted Blanche. 'The gentry do have private showings of gowns in their own drawing-rooms, so Mr Liberty told me. 'Tis all done very proper. I should ride in the Liberty's carriage, and have a dresser to go with me.'

'And wot says Master Hugh to all this?'

Blanche spoke slowly. 'I got a feeling he might have took a hand in getting me this job. Funny how that Mr Liberty should ask to see me, when all I ever bought in his shop is a fan and a few ribbons.'

'Things is going well then, with you and the H'onourable? Got past the hand-holding and the kissing 'ave yer?'

Blanche coloured. 'I can't do with maulers,' she said coldly. 'I been fighting 'em off in the Life School for the past six years and more. Just because he buys me a fish-dinner in Romano's, that don't entitle him to any favours!'

'I should have thought you'd at least got to the cuddling stage,' hinted Mrs Gimball. 'You been alone with 'im enough times in his carriage. But I wouldn't have put 'im down as a mauler. I never would of thought that of 'im.'

266

'Well – no. That's to say – not exactly.' Blanche sounded irritable, and unsure of the fine distinction between gentleman and groper. 'He do maul with his eyes,' she burst out, 'you must know what I mean.'

'Can't say as I do, ducks. Mr Gimball was a very direct sort of fellah. Knowed exactly wot he was after and went straight for it. The result,' she said drily, 'was our Ellen.'

'There you are,' said Blanche, 'but you was lucky. He married you, didden he? But Hugh Fitzgerald wudden marry me if I was in the fam'ly way. He'd be off like a shot. He'd swear on a stack of Bibles that he never touched me.'

'You could be right. In fact I 'spect you are.' Mrs Gimball retrieved the opera hat and began to brush it with slow even strokes. 'Trouble is,' she said, 'he'll be a man of the world, already. Now with me and Gimball it was different, we was both sort of innocent. Now your Master Fitz have been to Cambridge. He hob-nobs with the Prince of Wales and the Duke of Clarence.' She laid a finger alongside her nose. 'Mr Solomon have told me what goes on at their little parties. You'll need to be careful, Blanche. If you refuses 'im too much and too often then you could lose 'im altogether.'

'I don't really like all that hand-holding and kissing.' Blanche had grown tense, she began to pace the tiny room. 'That do make me very nervous.'

'You can't lead men on and then refuse 'em, Blanche. That sort of game can see you in an alley with your throat cut!' She set the hat down upon the table. 'Trouble is,' she said softly, 'you don't even mean to lead 'em on. Just the way you looks and walks and holds yourself is enough to drive 'em mad. I've seen the way he watches you, like a 'ungry dog wot wants its dinner.'

Blanche smiled her gratification. 'That's how I want him to feel. 'Tis only a starving dog what comes to heel!'

Mrs Gimball frowned. 'There's something lacking in

you, Blanche. Mr Solomon reckons that you're a cold woman, that you don't really fancy any man.'

'And how would he know?' flared Blanche, 'I've heard proof enough that he don't fancy any women.' She faced Mrs Gimball. 'I'm just being careful, Ma. God knows, you've give me plenty of warning on the subject!'

'I know. Perhaps that's your trouble, perhaps we've killed all your natural feelings.' She gazed at Blanche. 'I'm afraid you're going to land in a lot of trouble when you does get married.' She grinned. 'Better find yourself some old Duke or Earl wot ain't got enough strength left to climb the stairs.'

❋

Hugh Fitzgerald was in love. Removal from London had sharpened his perception; as the days of Christmas shuffled into New Year, the ache for a sight of Blanche Greypaull grew huge inside him. He began to walk the icy streets of Bath, sometimes for whole days, returning to his aunt's house only when he was exhausted. He gazed into shop windows without recognising their contents. He ate in chophouses and cafés but could never have told what it was he had consumed. It had been a season of doubts and questions; a time of upset and conflicting emotions. He had asked his aunt why she continued to display his mother's portrait in such a prominent position. Hung as it was, in a curve of the main staircase, it was impossible to descend from the first floor, without coming face to face with those lovely features, the soft brown eyes. Her intention, his aunt had said, was that the portrait should serve as a constant reminder of the treachery of beautiful women. 'If I am ever tempted to relax my vigilance on your behalf, dear boy, then I look at the face of Marianne Deveraux and remember that it was she who caused my brother's death.' The bitterness in her voice had finally convinced him of her unalterable hostility towards Blanche.

There had been a night when Hugh could not sleep. He had gone onto the staircase, lifted down the heavy portrait, and carried it up to his bedroom. He had leaned the picture against a wall, set a chair before it, and sat in contemplation of this woman who had been his mother. The knowledge that she was alive and living in New York forced him to look closely at her now; he thought about her abandonment of him, all the intrigue and planning necessary for a genteel woman to rise up from childbed and run away to join her lover.

Hugh left his chair, returned to the staircase, and unhooked the matching portrait of his father. He placed the two pictures close together, and resumed his study. He noted his father's fair, waving hair, the blue eyes, the high colour on the cheekbones. He examined the face, feature by feature, and was satisfied that he was indeed his father's son. His thoughts slid away into dangerous areas of supposition. Since he was his father's child, and his mother had a lover, then what about his own conception? He looked closely into his mother's painted eyes, caught a hint of suffering in them, and was seized with a conviction that she had been forced to bear an unwanted child. He tried to escape from the terrible thought, but could not. It explained so many things: her ability to leave him unfed, in the care of servants, and dependent on a wet-nurse. How she must have hated the infant Hugh, the fair-haired, blue-eyed baby, who so exactly resembled the Fitzgeralds! He wondered if she ever thought about him? If, over the years, she had ever written or tried to make contact with him? He knew, without any doubt, that his aunt would have concealed and rebuffed all such efforts. He allowed himself, just for a moment, to imagine his mother's arms about him, the touch of her lips, her perfume, the soft voice begging his forgiveness. Tears came into his eyes, and he wept, unwillingly and with great pain. How strange, he thought, that he should weep now for a living mother, when he had never grieved for a dead one!

Hugh turned his gaze back towards the matching portrait; the couple had posed wearing Court dress. The tall and elegant Fitzgerald might have been Hugh himself, so close was the resemblance. His father had been lied to, cheated, cuckolded, and humiliated. Was it any wonder that he had got drunk, and, in a fit of madness, hurled himself from an upper window? Hugh could hardly bear to dwell on his father's death. Since his aunt's revelations, he had looked into the whole sorry business. Newspaper reports of the time had described how his father's body had become impaled on the sharp spikes of the area railings. The story had gained drama in the telling. 'A broken heart, sent to its rest by an iron spike' was how the journalist had described it. Hugh had never since walked in Russell Square without remembering and experiencing a sense of horror.

He re-hung the portraits on the main staircase, and returned to his room. He opened his wallet and withdrew a tiny tattered sketch of a very young girl. Simeon Solomon had been the artist; the sitter was Blanche Greypaull. He had obtained the drawing in an assorted job-lot, at one of Christie's auctions. He had showed it to Blanche. She had glanced at it, briefly, and handed it back.

'Drawed in a bar-room, that was,' she said, 'the pub was called The Running Footman, it stands down in Charles Street, behind Berkeley Square. 'Twas the first time he ever drawed me. Poor liddle devil, he was short of paper, that's why 'tis such a scrappy item.' She paused. 'I never forgot that pub with the funny name, nor that meeting with Mr Solomon.'

Surprised at the tenderness in her voice, Hugh had asked, 'You're aw'fly fond of that old reprobate, aren't you?'

She had rounded upon him, then. 'Mr Solomon is a

victim of circumstances,' she had shouted. 'That means things happen what is not his fault. He can't help his nature, can he? He's the way God made him.' She had pounded her fist upon the table. 'So are we all,' she insisted, 'and who are you to sit in judgement of him? And I'll tell you something else while we is on this subject. Mr Solomon don't never try to paw and maul me! He've always respected me, and treated me like a lady.' She had looked meaningfully at Hugh. 'There's many a snotty nosed toff what 'ud do well to take lessons from Mr Solomon as to how a lady should be treated.'

Hugh smiled at the little sketch. What a curious mixture she was of primness and deliberate allurement; she was voluptuous and yet virginal, and both at the same time. He lusted for her like some village yokel in a hayloft, but there was so much more to Blanche than a tempting body. She had a mind, and actually used her ability to reason; her thoughts were original and provocative. In argument she could not be outwitted, and Hugh was unaccustomed to the company of clever females.

Hugh knew that women found him attractive, his dark-blue eyes and fair moustaches had ensured his presence at many dinner-tables and coming-out balls. Even as a small child he had been able to charm his Aunt Letitia to almost any folly. His failure to enslave Blanche, her continued avoidance of close physical contact with him, he attributed to the natural caution of a working girl who was, quite rightly, suspicious of any overt move made by a member of the upper classes. It was, he concluded, this very reluctance on her part which had both bewildered and enthralled him. He had sensed that even so much as a hand's touch could trigger a withdrawal in her; and yet, he persuaded himself, surely there had been the rare occasions when she had seemed to make the move towards him. They were, he thought, involved in some strange and silent dance, the steps of which were known only to her.

The city of Bath was a fine and romantic place for a young man to work out the scope and heat of his enslavement to a woman. Every morning he would stride downhill from the imposing terraces and crescents that formed the north side of the city, to stroll along frozen pathways in the Sydney Gardens, idle his way along Milsom Street, stand in the gracious square that faced the Abbey; and wander down the corridor, from a window of which he was able to view the King's Bath. He saw them riding together in Henrietta Park; walking in summer in the Sydney Gardens; taking tea and dancing among the elegant and cosmopolitan crowds who thronged the Pump Room.

His Aunt Porteous had already sensed the change in him, the shift from brooding unhappiness to purposeful optimism. 'You're looking much better, Hugh, since we came down to Bath.'

'I am able to walk here,' he explained, 'one rides about far too much in London, the streets being so dangerous there, don't you know?'

Mrs Porteous gazed deeply into her wine glass. 'Whatever,' she asked carefully, 'whatever became of that very strange young woman who said she was an artist's model?'

'Oh, Miss Greypaull?' He tried to cool the warmth in his voice, to sound off-hand, and failed. 'I've taken her to dinner once or twice.'

Aunt Porteous looked directly at him. 'She won't suit. But you know that, don't you, Hugh? She won't suit. Not at all!'

'But why not?' he demanded. 'What's the matter with her?'

'So it's already gone that far.' Mrs Porteous spoke quietly. 'How deeply involved are you with this person?'

Hugh looked wretched. 'Not half as much as I wish to

be, if you want the truth! She's not in the least like Claire. She won't let me buy her presents. She refuses two thirds of my invitations. Why, I asked her to spend Christmas here with us in Bath, but she preferred to go home to Taunton to see her mother.' His words seemed to sink without trace into a well of silence. 'That fracas last month, in Trafalgar Square. I told you that I had spent the night at my Club — well it wasn't true! Miss Greypaull and I were together when I got injured. She took me back to her lodgings. I was cared for and bandaged by a Mrs Gimball.' Hugh became desperate. 'I might have been killed but for Miss Greypaull. She attacked that ruffian with her hatpin. She saved my life, Aunt!'

Aunt Porteous looked thoughtful. 'When I was a young wife, without much experience of hiring servants, I engaged a kitchen-maid who had that exact shade of red hair. She also used her hatpin as a weapon. It is, so I am told, a favoured mode of defence among girls of the lower classes.' She sipped at her wine, smiled kindly on Hugh, and set her glass down. 'I had to dismiss her, of course, but not before she had, most regretfully, put the butler's eye out.' She shook her head. 'That young woman won't suit, Hugh. I shall say no more upon the subject, save this. Don't imagine, for one second, that you have deceived me in this matter. I was told, almost straightaway, the whole sorry tale of your involvement with this — this —'

'Who told you?' Hugh interrupted.

'Why Jones did, of course! It was my coachman who helped to carry you into that awful pawnshop. Oh Hugh! Whatever possessed you to become entangled with such low-class people?'

'I'm not entangled.'

'But you are. The change in you has been remarked upon by all our friends in the past few months.'

'Don't you want me to be happy?'

'You know that I do. You are as dear to me as though you were my own son.' She sighed. 'Oh, I can see this girl's very obvious attractions — one would have to be suffering from extremely impaired eyesight not to see them! But that is all she has, Hugh! Those sort of voluptuous looks in a young woman never last long. She'll have run to fat in a few more years. She's the kind of girl who very quickly becomes blowsy and common-looking. Heaven only knows what gutter she crawled out of! How can you bear that ungrammatical speech, those appalling table-manners? She shows not the slightest hint of any refinement; as to that tale of being an artist's model — if you want my opinion, that is just another name for her true profession!'

Hugh stood up. He had grown very white about the lips and nose. 'That will be enough,' he told his aunt, 'I don't have to listen to this and I will not. Miss Greypaull is a very chaste and moral young lady. I do not yet know the story of her background, but this much I do know. She has lived in London since she was sixteen, and in all that time she has supported herself, honestly and honourably! Which is more than can be said for the blue-blooded Claire, who is no better than a deceiving harpy!' He walked to the door, wrenched it open, and then slammed it behind him. He leaned, momentarily, against the oaken panels and tried to control the trembling in his limbs. It was, of course, her beauty, he told himself that had set Blanche apart. She could never be compared to ordinary people. He stared at Mr Nash's white marble staircase, at the dark portraits of the Porteous family, and felt overwhelmingly protective towards the absent girl. He paused, one foot upon the first tread of the staircase. He could, if he wished, be back in London by noon tomorrow. He and Blanche could see the New Year in, together.

❊

The enlistment of Mrs Gimball, thought Hugh, had been a good move. There was nothing quite as swift, he discovered, at establishing a rapport, than the relationship between a sympathetic nurse and her grateful patient. Since that Sunday when she had picked slivers of glass from his head and neck, Mrs Gimball had assumed proprietorial rights towards him. He had returned several times to St Martin's Lane, but never when Blanche Greypaull was present. He had even acquired a taste for faggotts and peas, hot cocoa and bread pudding. On his arrival at Paddington station, Hugh instructed the cabby to drive him straight to Mrs Gimball's pawnshop. He was taken at once into the back room.

'Oh, I'm that glad to see you, sir. I been praying that you'd come back again —'

'What is it?' he interrupted. 'She's not ill is she?'

'Nothing like that, sir. She's low in her spirits, hardly a word to say for 'erself, and that ain't like Blanche. She never went home this Christmas, and no letter 'ave come from her Ma.'

'But I asked her to come to Bath, to spend Christmas at my aunt's house.'

Mrs Gimball shook her head. 'She could never do that, sir.'

'But why not?'

'Now be honest, sir. Your aunty never took to 'er, did she? Now don't mistake my meaning, Blanche 'ave come from a very good family, she was brought up very nice, she's always saying wot a lady her Mama is. But she's lived 'ere with me for nearly seven years, and that's no apprenticeship for the ways of your lot up in Russell Square. She'd have been embarrassed — well, she ain't got enough clothes, for a start. Then there's jewellery — she ain't got none of that, neither.'

Hugh's chin almost touched his chest. 'I never thought,'

he murmured, 'it never occurred to me that she might feel awkward or unwelcome.'

'She puts on a hard front,' broke in Mrs Gimball, 'but she got a lot of tender feelings; a lot of very 'urt feelings, too. Seems to me, young man, there's a lot you got to learn about the fair sex.'

'This family of hers,' asked Hugh, 'what sort of relationship does she have with them?'

'That's something she'll 'ave to tell you herself, if you can ever persuade her.'

'What can I do, Mrs Gimball?'

'How truly fond of 'er is yer?'

'I love her,' he said simply. 'I've spent a pretty solitary Christmas. I did a lot of walking, and a lot of thinking. When I am away from her she fills my thoughts. When I'm with her then I am deliriously happy. She intrigues me, she fascinates me, I don't even begin to understand her — and I don't care! I want to marry her,' he paused, 'but I've got this frightful presentiment that she won't have me.'

'Well, there's no harm in trying, sir. But you'll have to court 'er. If I might give you a word of advice —'

'Anything — simply anything —'

Mrs Gimball considered. 'She's very keen on bein' respected is our Blanche. Now Simeon Solomon found that out when he first started to paint 'er. You treat 'er like a lady, and you'll be quids-in.'

'This Solomon —'

Mrs Gimball laughed. 'No call for you to worry about 'im, sir. I loves the little devil dearly, and always 'ave done, but,' she leaned forward to whisper, 'he's got some strange ways — well he can't help it, of course, but our Blanche is safer with 'im than she should be with many an archbishop.'

Hugh looked relieved. 'One hears such stories about him,' he said lamely.

'And probably all true, your lordship! But when he comes

'ere, he's on 'is best behaviour, that's understood. Oh, he's done some lovely pictures of 'er, but it never seemed to come to nothin'. I reckon Blanche thought them paintings was going to make 'er fortune. She never talks about it, but I can tell that she's disappointed.'

'I'll make it up to her,' cried Hugh, 'there's nothing I wouldn't do to make her happy.'

'Just you take it slow,' advised Mrs Gimball, 'she ain't one to be swep' off her feet. Start off with 'er birthday treat, and then see where that gets yer.'

'What shall I buy her? Is there anything she especially longs for?'

Mrs Gimball grinned. 'You really don't know 'er very well yet, does yer? Gawd help you, sir, there's not much in them shops up West wot our gel don't fancy.' She hesitated. 'There is something – but it might be too expensive for yer –'

'Tell me,' he pleaded. 'I'm in funds just at present.' He patted his pocket. 'I've just received my quarterly interest, and my aunt stumped-up with a handsome banknote for my Christmas stocking.'

'Well, she's working at Liberty's now, and a nearby jeweller 'as took delivery of these new-fangled timepieces. Wrist-watches, I think Blanche called 'em. They're all the rage, so she says. She just can't stop talking about 'em.'

❊

Liberty's of Regent Street was closer to Heaven than Blanche had ever been. To begin with, it was warm in winter; a major consideration for a girl who had modelled through all seasons in the chilly studios of Primrose Hill and Hampstead, and the Royal Academy's Life School. There was a wonderful odour compounded of eastern perfumes and massed fresh flowers; the store was a treasure house of tapestries and carpets, jewellery and china, silks and jade. There were shawls from Delhi and Cashmere, embroidered robes from China, Moorish slippers, furniture made of bamboo, with laquered inlays. From all parts of the Empire, people flocked to view its wonders; foreign Royalties came to shop there. The commissionaires and the cicerones – those elegant floorwalkers, who excelled their customers in courtesy and pride – treated Blanche with a respect which implied that she had conferred a great favour by consenting to work among them. Her duties were never quite clearly defined.

The Costume Department was her official location. It was there that the craft of dressmaking had been elevated to an artform. Gone were the stiff and ugly fashions of previous decades, and in their place came the draped and softened lines that were so beautifully expressed in the Liberty fabrics. 'A face and figure of her time' was how Arthur Lazenby Liberty had described Blanche. Her colouring alone, he said, had made her valuable to him. Blanche modelled gowns and jewellery before foreign Queens and Princesses, and wealthy courtesans and their admirers both at Liberty's and in private salons. That red hair, once seen as a curse by her Greypaull grandmother, was now, thanks to Mr Burne-Jones, and Mr D. G. Rossetti, the most fashionable shade to possess throughout America and Europe. She could never quite believe in her own good fortune.

Hugh had taken her to dine at Romano's on the eve of New Year.

'So you are happy at Liberty's, are you, Blanche?'

'Oh yes. I find myself mixing with an altogether better class of person.'

He noted her careful enunciation, the new and artificial tone of refinement in her voice, and felt touched and regretful at this sudden loss of her spontaneity and wit. She was wearing the revealing gown of black Spanish lace. Hugh admired the choker of jet at her slender neck, the matching earrings and the combs of jet which secured her hair. She put a hand to her throat and smiled. 'Mrs Gimball give – gave them to me, for a birthday present.'

'Twenty-three tomorrow,' he observed. He withdrew a small leather box from his pocket and handed it to her. 'You won't refuse a birthday gift from me, will you, Blanche?' He grinned. 'That would be not at all genteel!' A brief flash of anger swept across her features but she controlled it. She opened the jeweller's box and withdrew the tiny wrist-watch. Her gasp was one of pure delight, she held up the trinket and watched it glitter in the lamplight.

'Oh Hugh, 'tis the very piece what I been yearning over! Looksee, how it do sparkle.' She paused. 'But tidden proper diamonds, is it?' Excitement had restored her voice to its normal timbre; she had now abandoned all attempt at grammar.

'Diamonds set in gold,' he told her. He leaned across the narrow table. 'And I will give you other diamonds, and quite soon I hope. Here – allow me to fasten the clasp for you, I've wound it and set it to the correct time. You'll have no excuse now if you're late for one of our appointments.'

Blanche waved the arm that bore the wrist-watch. 'Oh I can't tell time, Hugh, but,' she hastened to reassure him, ''tis a lovely bracelet all the same. All they other models in the store'll be pea-green with envy when I flashes my arm about tomorrow lunchtime.'

Hugh looked bewildered. 'But how do you manage, Blanche? How can you go through the day never knowing the hours and minutes?'

She gazed pityingly at him. 'Time marches on,' she informed him, 'with clocks or without clocks. Didden you never hear the hour strike from church steeples? Why,

London is full of bells what count the hours! Anyway — there's always some obliging gent what is only too happy to whip out his pocket watch and give me the exact time.'

'But,' he said, curiously, 'wouldn't you like to learn how to tell the time. After all, you possess your own watch now, and I'd be delighted to teach you.'

Blanche looked mutinous. 'No,' she said, 'I never bothers to learn anything what won't put gold in my pocket. Knowing how late or early 'tis, won't never see me a farthing richer.'

Hugh gazed wonderingly at her. 'You really do love money, don't you?' he whispered. He studied the fine white skin revealed by the low cut gown, the perfection of her arms and shoulders. Her full red lips, pouting and slightly parted, aroused him to a pitch of desire that required some immediate outlet. He reached an impulsive hand across the table, and made to grab her hand. It was a mistake, and he straightaway knew it. He saw her recoil and cursed his own precipitate action. The withdrawal extended even into her voice.

'That don't mean that I idden particular how I earns my money,' she said coldly. 'Just you remember this Mr Hugh Fitzgerald — I bain't — I am not — for sale, and all the diamond watches in London won't never buy me.'

❀

Blanche knew that they had all been waiting to see her fall, especially Madelina. Each time she came back to Taunton the welcomes were laced with a faint hostility, a thinly veiled disappointment that she so clearly continued to prosper in London, unhampered by pregnancy or sickness, and displaying no infirmity of body or emotions. She arrived home at Easter, dressed in a gown of apricot silk with short peplummed jacket and parasol to match; a sailor-hat of natural straw perched above one eye.

'That's a new gown,' accused the visiting Madelina.

'And so I should hope, our Mina, seeing as how I paid four whole weeks wages for 'un.'

'So it's wages now, Blanche?' Her mother spoke quietly but with deep suspicion.

'Yes Mama — wages. Paid into my hand every Friday night by Liberty's of 399, Regent Street, London!'

'And what do you do there, maid?'

'Oh, I be still a model, but not for artists. I model gowns — shows 'em off to wealthy ladies what wants to see exactly how they look before buying.'

'But surely,' said Mina, 'they can see what a new frock looks like without having you stuffed inside it?'

Blanche looked down from her superior height. 'Oh you wudden never understand, my dear sister.' She smiled, deliberately patronising. ''Tis all a matter of high fashion. Some of they gowns do come from Paquins, and Monsieur Worth of the Rue de la Paix in Paris — that's in France; but I expect you knew that. Oh yes, Mina, frocks like that can't be properly judged from a coat hanger.' She ran her hands, very slowly, across her full high bosom, and down her narrow waist and rounded hips. 'Frocks like that needs a beautiful body inside 'em, to do justice to the dressmakers' art.' She took in the glance of pure hatred that came from Madelina, and then wheeled abruptly to where Annis stod, watching in the shadows. 'Now, Annis!' she cried, 'our Annis would make such a wonderful model. Her's filled out now in all the right places.'

'That'll be quite enough, Blanche.' Eliza's voice cut incisively across the conversation. 'Annis is doing very nicely where she is. She's not strong enough to stand the wild life you lead in London.'

Blanche addressed Annis. 'Are you still writing to that soldier-boy in India?'

'Yes, she is,' snapped Eliza, 'and I'll thank you not to

281

make any smart remarks about that, either.'

'I wasn't going to, Mama. I think 'tis quite sweet and touching.' Blanche sounded genuinely envious and almost regretful.

'What about you, then?' murmured Annis. 'Haven't you got a young man yet?'

Blanche grinned. 'I'll tell you that story some other time when we is on our own.' Her pause was significant, 'I expect our Mina have got to go home now. Husband will be stamping on the doorstep, baby'll be howling, eh Mina?'

'As a matter of fact,' said Mina, 'I brought my supper with me. Well – I never likes to impose myself on Mama. 'Tis David's Bible class night,' she explained, 'he've promised to call in for me on his way home.'

Blanche said, 'Where's your child, then?'

'My Laura i upstairs, asleep in Mama's bed.'

'Can I see her?'

'I would never have thought that you cared for children.'

'I'd like to see a child of yours, Mina!'

Mina looked gratified, but sounded defensive. 'All right then, if you're really sure. But you'll have to be quiet, she's a nervous sleeper.'

They tiptoed up the step-ladder, and Blanche entered the bedroom ahead of Madelina; she looked down on the sleeping child in the canopied bed.

Laura lay, tiny and defenceless, in a blue smocked nightgown, her freckled hands upon the white sheet, her hair a flaming aureole against the lace-edged pillow. She slept, as her mother had predicted, uneasily, and with barely closed eyes. As if sensing the presence of a stranger, a sudden tremor shook the little body; Laura moaned and turned her cheek into the pillow. Mina indicated that they should leave the room. Blanche followed reluctantly, with long backward glances. Downstairs, she said, 'That's a tender blossom you got there, Mina.'

Her tremulous voice amazed Madelina; she looked curiously into the damp and violet eyes. 'Those is strange words, coming from you.'

'You all decided,' Blanche said quietly, 'you all made your minds up long ago, that your Blanche cudden have no normal feelings. You was wrong. I'd exchange all my gowns to have a child like that, our Mina.'

'You'd soon alter your mind when she started screaming,' Mina's tone was indulgent. 'My Laura got the most explosive temper what was ever seen on mortal child! Them's David's words, not mine.'

'She'll be clever, though. She's got Mama's exact looks. Have you noticed the hands of her? They long and delicate fingers? You better start saving up for a piano, maid! You mark my words — a few more years and that'll need piano lessons.'

Mina nodded her satisfaction; she warmed towards Blanche, momentarily. 'Oh yes, us have already noticed all that. My Laura don't favour none of the Lamberts. Her is pure Greypaull, through and through, and clever like you say. But of course, all that braininess have made her terrible nervous. You'd never credit how high-strung that child is. I has to be so careful of her, Blanche. I never let her into the street to play with other children. I keeps her very tight-up beside me, all day long.'

'Oh, I bet you do, Mina,' murmured Blanche, 'I can just imagine how you dotes upon her. I bet you're the carefullest Mama in all of Taunton.'

'Well, I got to be mindful of her,' explained Madelina, 'she's all I got, Blanche. I can't never have no more children. Doctor told Dave that another birth 'ud be sure to kill me.'

Annis had spread a clean cloth upon the table, and Eliza had made supper. 'There's not much to eat, maid,' she told Blanche. 'Only bubble-and-squeak, and lucky to have that

283

much. 'Tis all I can make with the leavings what Simeon collects in the Friday vegetable market.'

Mina unwrapped a slice of bread and a wedge of hard cheese. She set the food ostentatiously, upon her own plate. She stared at Blanche. 'Well, I can't say as you looks half-starved, Blanche. Your bones seem very well-covered. It won't do you any harm at all to miss a few meals while you is down in Taunton.'

Blanche turned to Eliza. 'No call for worry, Mama. Us'll go out shopping in the morning. Like Mina just said, I eat very well in London. They serves me with fresh trout and crown roasts up at Romano's.'

Mina paused, the dry bread half-way to her mouth. 'And what,' she asked sharply, 'is Romano's, when it's at home?'

'Oh – 'tis only the favourite supper-room of the Prince of Wales. Not,' she added, 'not that dear Bertie do eat with the common herd in the main dining-room. No, no! His Royal Highness have got his own private suite at Romano's. 'Tis very convenient for Buck House, being situated in the Strand. He can be home in no time at all.'

Mina's mouth fell open; she set the bread down absentmindedly, almost missing the plate. 'I don't believe you,' she said flatly, 'you always was a liar. Why, they'd never let the likes of you get anywhere close to the Prince of Wales!'

'I never said I got close to him,' reproved Blanche, 'you really must wash your ears out, Mina. I said that I dined in the same place –'

'Who takes you to places like that, maid?' broke in Eliza. 'That must cost a lot of money.'

'My friend have got a lot of money.' She allowed the apricot silk of her sleeve to fall back and reaveal the wrist-warch. 'I got the time on my arm,' she announced, ''tis the very latest thing from Paris. My friend bought it for my birthday present.'

'But you can't tell time,' said Annis, 'we all tried to show you but you wudden learn.'

'Telling time is not the issue,' Blanche said grandly, ''tis having this liddle solid gold gadget what do matter.'

'Gold?' cried Eliza, 'why Blanche, whoever is this friend – ?'

Blanche leaned back in her chair, and waited. Once assured of their complete attention, she smiled. ''Tis the Honourable Hugh Deveraux Fitzgerald what do feed me on smoked salmon at Romano's.' She became confidential. 'They des the very best fish-dinners in the whole of London.'

David Lambert arrived at that moment of revelation to collect his wife and sleeping child. At the sight of Blanche his knuckles whitened around the black-bound Bible, and his eyes narrowed.

'This is my sister – the one from London,' stammered Madelina, 'her's called Blanche – I mentioned her to you –'

'Good evening, Miss Greypaull.' The dark young man inclined his head nervously towards Blanche, but did not look directly at her. He climbed the stepladder to the bedroom and reappeared with the sleepy Laura wrapped securely in a blanket. As they left the cottage, Blanche touched the little hand that lay upon her father's shoulder. 'Us'll meet again, my sweetheart,' she whispered to Laura, 'one day when you be wide-awake and merry.'

The departure of the Lambert family reduced Blanche to helpless laughter. She mopped her eyes and clung to Annis. 'Oh my,' she cried, 'did you ever see a man so bad embarrassed? Whatever have our Madelina been telling him about me? He run out of that door like I was a scarlet hussy liable to set upon him.' She sobered and looked thoughtful. 'He's a handsome looking fellah, all the same. I quite fancies men with black hair.'

'He's your sister's husband,' said Eliza, sharply.

'Don't fret, Mama. I bain't interested in jobbing decorators. Even so — what a waste to see a good-looking man like him chained for life to a liddle misery like our Madelina!'

They gathered around the fireside. Annis said, 'What kind of looks have your beau got, Blanche?'

'He's fair-haired — and he's not my beau — not in the way you mean.'

'What is he, then?' asked Eliza.

'Hugh's a friend — just a friend.'

'A man what gives you expensive presents and spends money on you will want more than friendship.'

'Then he'll be unlucky, Mama, won't he! Anyway, he can well afford it. He got this private income. His aunty got two big houses, one in London, and one in Bath. His cousin is the Govenor of some old islands.' Blanche noted their disbelieving faces. 'He likes to be seen with me,' she burst out, 'he enjoys the way people turn to watch us when we enter a restaurant or ride out in his carriage. 'Tis a matter of pride with gentlemen like him, to be seen in the company of a beautiful woman.'

'And what about you, maid?'

'I know what I want, Mama. I've always know'd it. I could never live like our Mina, chained-up to a Wesleyan Bible-thumper? She turned on Annis. 'Nor could I sit all day at a sewing-machine, waiting year after year for some soldier-boy to come home and wed me.' Blanche stood up, she placed her hands on her hips, raised her chin, and treated them to view of her exquisite profile. 'Now tell me,' she demanded, 'how many girls like me do you see trudging round the streets of Taunton?'

'Oh you certainly got the stamp of London on you,' said Eliza. 'Let us hope that this fine gentleman of yours will have the decency to wed you — if and when the need arises.'

✻

A racing owner who kept a string of horses at the Bishop's
Hull Stables, had ordered that Jack Greypaull should present
himself at Newmarket, in time to ride for him at the first
October meeting. Jack, who rode mainly in Somerset and
Devon, and adjoining counties, had been sent for in haste in
order to replace a more experienced jockey, who had at the
very last weigh-in, proved unable to make the weight. Jack
had packed a bag, said goodbye to his young wife and infant
son, and made his way, by train and waggon, across to the
flat land of East Anglia, and down to Newmarket.

Jack Greypaull had been apprenticed at the age of twelve
to serve his master for a full term of five years. A set of
Formal Indentures had been signed by his grandfather
Daniel, in which the child had undertaken not to commit
fornication or contract matrimony during the said term.
Neither would he play cards or dice, nor haunt taverns or
playhouses. He was also called upon to promise that he
would never absent himself from his master's service by day
or by night, without that master's express permission. It
had been a hard life for this boy who had been raised in the
expectation that he would, one day, inherit Larksleve. Jack,
at the age of twenty-five, now had the thin and anxious
features of a much older man; the marks of those early years
in Bishop's Hull were engraved in his face. He had been
bullied by older and stronger apprentices; hard-driven by his
employer; and separated from his beloved elder sister,
Madelina. His full name, discovered by an inquisitive
jockey, to be James John Daniel, had caused mockery and
scorn among his fellows, as did his rare ability to read and
write. Jack had cried himself to sleep every night in that first
year, away from home. It was only his love of horses, his
ability to communicate with, and understand them that

prevented him from climbing the high fence which surrounded the apprentice-quarters, and making his way back to Eliza and Madelina. Allowed home once in every twelve months, for a few days at the New Year, his loneliness and fear, never permitted expression, had gradually estranged him from all of his family, save Madelina. Jack was glad to be going to Newmarket, win or lose the races! He had known for a long time that he would never make a champion jockey. He was too reckless, he lacked the control and discipline that were essential in a first-class steeplechaser. It was said by certain owners that Jack Greypaull rode like a Mohawk Indian, his body moulded to his mount, scorning whenever possible the use of saddle and whip. But such daring also had its uses. It was to Jack they brought their unmanageable thoroughbreds, those potential winners which senior jockeys either would not or could not ride.

❀

It was one of those wine-red days that occasionally come in late October; a rime of hoar frost on the grass, and the sun low-slung and crimson in the western heavens. The stands were packed, the presence of Royalty was rumoured. Jack rode his race and came in second, which was better than he had expected. He was in the unsaddling enclosure (saddles being obligatory in races of such importance) when the uninhibited language and laughter of a woman caused him to look beyond the fencing.

The girl was dressed in a gown of russet velvet, of a shade that almost exactly matched her hair, over it she wore a cape of long-tailed sables; on her head was perched a tiny hat of peacock's feathers. Jack grabbed the saddle and walked towards the weighing-in room. He was a man who rarely noticed women: he could never, if asked, have told what style or colour of dress his wife was wearing, so why had this girl's appearance lodged in his eye? Something, he thought, about the tilt of her head, the coquettish arch of her body, that self-assured and unrestrained laughter. He attended to the business in hand and returned to the paddock, and this time he saw the girl full face, but still could not call her name to mind. Dressed in racing-silks and with only a short tweed jacket for warmth, Jack shivered and began to turn towards the changing-rooms. As he passed the girl her companion reached out a hand to detain him.

'Er – you there – jockey-fellah!' laughed the young man, 'what did you have to lose for, eh? I had money on you to win.'

Jack looked up into the smiling face framed by blond curls, and shrugged off the manicured hand that had detained him. Restraining an impulse to aim a swift kick in the fop's direction, Jack said, 'What you do with your money is no concern of mine; and I didden lose exactly – I came in second.' The girl had ceased to laugh, she was not even smiling. Jack looked into the violet eyes, saw the pout of her full lips and the way her hair glinted redly in the sunlight, and, all at once, he knew her.

'Blanche,' he said.

'Jack,' she answered.

The young man gazed from one face to the other. 'I say! Do you two know one another?'

Jack saw his sister's hesitation. 'My brother,' she said unwillingly, 'my brother Jack, from Taunton.' She attempted lightness. 'Meet the Honourable Hugh Fitzgerald,' she cried, 'what has got too much money in his pocket and no damned horse-sense!'

Jack grinned, briefly. 'You still living in London then, Duchess?' He eyed the sable cloak. 'Doing well too, by the looks of you!'

Hugh Fitzgerald laughed into the awkward silence.

'Come and have a drink and a bite to eat with us, old chap! We'll wait for you in the carriage.'

Jack tapped his midriff. 'Not possible, I'm afraid. Got to watch the waistline in this sort o' business. 'Tis easier not to eat, than have to lose weight in the Turkish baths, or by swallowing purges.' He nodded briefly and slipped out of view among the crowds.

'Well!' said Blanche, 'that was short and sweet I must say! But he was ever a funny liddle devil.' She spoke softly to herself. 'Jealousy – that's James John Daniel's trouble. Cudden keep his eyes off my sable cloak. Bin waiting all his rotten life to see me come a cropper.'

Hugh seemed embarrassed. 'You never mentioned a brother who was a jockey.'

'You never asked me. Anyway, I never expected to see him here. He was flying high today, and no mistake. He's as mad as a hatter. He do ride most times without a saddle. Wincanton and Bath is his usual meetings.' She shivered violently and pulled the cloak around her. 'Let's go back to the carriage. Take me back to London. I don't like this place.'

'But,' he whispered, 'everything is arranged. We're to take tea with the Duke of Clarence. Prince Eddy has asked most especially to meet you.'

She scowled. 'I had a quick look at him while I was placing my bets. I didden think much of what I saw, either.'

'What do you mean?'

'Don't pretend you don't know! Prince or no Prince – that feller's half-witted!' Enraged at Hugh's look of non-comprehension Blanche stamped her foot. 'I don't care if he is the son of the Prince of Wales – he's still only ninepence in the shilling!'

'How can you tell?'

'Because I got another brother at home. His name is Louis When you look in his eyes you know straightaway that nobody's at home. Poor liddle chap — he do sit in a corner and play with my old fur hat and a heap of straw. Your Prince Eddy is only a few degrees better. If he hadden been born a Royal he'd have been put in a safe place long ago. 'Tis scandalous, the way all they hangers-on do take advantage of him.'

'Blanche — do keep your voice down!' Hugh took her arm and hurried her towards the carriage. 'I'll take you back to town at once. We'll have dinner somewhere very quiet. Prince Eddy isn't very bright, I know, but it's something one doesn't refer to, at least, not in public.'

Out on the London Road Hugh put his arm around her. 'You're upset,' he said gently, 'it was seeing your brother like that. His coldness towards you.'

She turned towards him, and he held his breath at the wonder of it. He drew her closer.

'Oh Hugh,' she sobbed, 'why do everybody hate me so?'

'Nobody hates you,' he reassured her, 'look at me. I'm your devoted slave.'

'They all hated me when we was children. Even Mama. Only Loveday cared about me. They still hate me. I could see it in our Jack's eyes.'

Hugh placed a finger underneath her chin and raised her face to his. 'I love you, Blanche. Why don't you listen to me. I love you with all my heart and —'

'Oh,' she broke in, ''tis sometimes more than I can bear, Hugh.' She looked closely at him and then closed her eyes. 'Why did you have to look so exactly like my Papa,' she wailed, 'why ever did you?'

❋

This year of 1888 was almost over, and Jye Carew had never felt so lonely, so isolated. Stay away too long from any place, George Mitchell had once said, and you won't never find your way back. The time was approaching, Jye feared, when he would not truly feel settled in either Montacute or London. He exchanged letters with the Reverend Henry Hardin, in which the Baptist minister reassured him of Meridiana's continued good health and well-being. But Jye knew his mother; whatever there was of Rom blood in him could sense her deep deprivation, her strange needs. Too many weeks and months lived alone might well see a deterioration in her spirit, something irreversible, a depression that could never be halted.

St Paul's Cathedral was a fine and beautiful structure; all his life long, he would boast of having worked on the restoration of it. But the coldness of marble could never equate the warmth of Ham stone. There were days when the soul in his fingertips cried out for the rough touch of limestone; he even longed for the golden dust in his hair and clothing. He no longer haunted St Martin's Lane on fine Sunday mornings but made his way slowly and reverently towards Westminster, as a pilgrim who visits a shrine.

Jye came up to Westminster Bridge; he coughed and pulled the muffler close across his mouth. November in London, and the yellow fog rising from the Thames like some pestilential cloud that might well have been sent to torment Job. Was it not this same evil cloud that rotted the Abbey stones and the lungs of man alike? He remembered Ham Hill and the clean winds blowing, the far-off sheen of winter floods, and the thin cries of the shepherd boys as they turned their sheep across the Hill. What was he doing in this awful city? As he moved towards the north porch of the Abbey, he seemed to feel the weight of chains about his ankles. He came into the place he loved best: King Henry's Chapel. He never tired of studying its treasures, there was always some new discovery, some skilled carving not previously noticed. He knelt and bowed his head as if in prayer, but no prayer came. He recalled himself in this same chapel, in London for the first time and aged seventeen.

Now, here he was, almost seven years on, and no longer a nervous boy. It came to Jye then, with a rush of surprise, that he was at last, in fact, a man; and with all a man's desires and longings. What he needed was some quiet rooftree, his own hearthstone, a sweet woman waiting for him! The discovery came upon him with all the shock and power of a Divine Revelation. It struck him now like a blow between the shoulders that all he had needed to do in these long months of torment, was to return to this holy place, in order that he might see his own future, clearly. The thought excited him. He rose from his knees and began to prowl the chapel. In a recess, towards the east, he found the pulpit from which it was said that Cranmer had often preached. Made of oak, tall and deep, it was shaped like an old-fashioned wine-cup. The steps by which the pulpit must be entered, lay to one side. Jye bent to lift them, and found them exactly like the steps by which gypsy waggons were entered, sloping and needing to be attached to strong hooks. He thought about Meridiana, and smiled. How his mother would have enjoyed the joke! He could imagine her comment that parson and gypsy must climb the same kind of ladder to their separate heavens! He stood for a long time, studying the pulpit, running a hand across the fiddlestick-carvings, imagining the thundering voice of Cranmer as he preached at the coronation of King Edward VI. So engrossed was Jye, that the woman's sleeve brushed the back of his hand before he had time to recognise her presence, and her perfume.

It was Blanche Greypaull, looking sleek and glossy, and more beautiful than ever. He could never have told the precise nature of her transformation; she had always been lovely, but now something about her hair and dress, the whole style and aura of her, made Jye step back in awe and unwilling admiration. He gazed at her with resignation, as if he had known that this meeting was inevitable. Some power had again drawn them both to this place, in the same hour of the same day. He walked swiftly from the chapel, from the Abbey, and onto Westminster Bridge. The fog had begun to lift and he could see the faint sheen of the river. She had followed him as he had known she would. He turned to face her.

'What do you want with me?' he asked, although he already knew.

She made no pretence at modesty. She looked straight into his eyes. 'You,' she said. 'I want you, Jye Carew. Remember that Sunday, when you tore my gown off? I want you to finish now what you started then! That have stood between us like unfinished business. Come back to St Martin's Lane with me. We shall have the place to ourselves. Take pity on me, Jye! for God's sake!'

'Why me, Blanche?'

'I got to prove something to myself, and 'tis only you what can help me!' She began to weep. 'There's something the matter with me. I bain't like my sisters, I bain't like other girls. I don't seem to have no loving feelings.'

'How can I help that?'

'Because if I could ever feel love for any man 'twould be for you, Jye. I confessed that much when we first met. You fancy me, don't you? That wudden be no hardship for you.'

'I was a boy then,' he told her, 'I be growed to a man now. I learned a lot in the past seven years. The only one that you can ever love, Blanche Greypaull, looks back at you from every mirror what you ever stares in.' He hunched his shoulders, and began to move away. 'Let me take you to a cabby. Tidden safe for you to be wanderin' about by yourself.'

She grabbed his sleeve. 'What is it?' she cried, 'have somebody turned you against me? What you saw that day in Trafalgar Square didden signify nothing. He was just a friend. I was taking care of him because he had been injured.'

Jye halted and faced her. 'Listen,' he said, 'I'll say it slow and clear so that you can understand me. I don't want you! Not now — not never. There's something unholy in you, what puts the fear in me. My mother don't often foretell the future these days, but she knows all about you.'

'Tell me. Tell me what your mother said. I want to hear it!'

'You won't like it.'

'Tell me, Jye.'

'My mother said that death will come to the man you choose. That you and me would never come together.' He hesitated, placed a hand upon the parapet, and looked down towards the water. She hooked her arm into his and swung him back to face her.

'There's more! I know there is. You had better tell me, Jye. I shan't leave you alone until you do!'

He spoke the words in a voice made terrible by its tonelessness. 'No peace shall come to her,' quoted Jye, 'until she lies silent beneath the stone; until she rests with her face towards the sea, the sound of the ocean beating in her dead ears.'

'Sweet Jesus help me!' He watched Blanche Greypaull as her face and lips became white, even her eyes grew opaque and lost their brilliant colour. He was not sure if her cry had been a profanity or a prayer.

'I shudden never have told you that,' he muttered.

'Yes, you should,' she said, ''tis better to know your enemy, and now I know mine. Your mother is a witch. She put a spell upon me, on the Taunton road when I was just a child. Remember, Jye? You was there! You saw her do it!'

'My mother's no witch. Her goes reg'lar to chapel. 'Tis just something in her blood — handed down from her mother and grandmother. She can't help it. She told me about it once. 'Tis like pictures in front of her eyes what won't go away. She sees good for some people, and bad for others.'

'She see'd good for our Annis.' Blanche moved closer to Jye so that her sable cloak brushed against his clasped hands. 'Help me, Jye! You're the only true friend I ever had. You be like a rock — so strong and sure. That's all rubbish what your old Ma said. I wudden never do anything to harm you.'

His move away from her, swift and instinctive, brought him hard up against the parapet of Westminster Bridge. The fog had closed down again, making it difficult for him to follow the movement of her lips. Suddenly his mind was clear, and he knew what he must do.

'I got to go home,' he told her. 'I can't abide this city no longer. I never should have come yer!'

'When will you go?'

'As quick as I can. As soon as Mr Mitchell will release me.'

'So I won't never see you again?'

''Twill be better so, Blanche. Whatever do you want with a poor deaf bloke what got no money, nor ever will have?'

She was silent for some seconds, and then she said, 'Take me to the cab-rank will you?'

He placed her inside the hansom and closed the cab-door. Before he could speak or wave, the cabby had moved away into the fog. Jye tried to remember the sound of horses' hooves, the clip-clop of metal on stone, and found that he could no longer recall it. The silence of his world, the swirling mist, the appearance and disappearance of the beautiful woman, her demand upon him, had the quality of a dream from which he must now, for the sake of his immortal soul, awaken. He stood for a time, and tried to gauge direction. Jye became aware of his physical discomfort. The beaded moisture clung to his hair, his eyebrows, his clothing. The yellow vapour had seeped into his mouth and lungs, and threatened to choke him. He was seized with a paroxysm of coughing; he leaned against a shopfront and fought to regain his breath. He was convulsed with a sudden revulsion for this city. He began to walk, slowly and cautiously, his hands outstretched to fend off possible collisions. London, just after midday, was already as dark as any winter's night. As he made his uncertain way back towards St Paul's the lunacy of his position became very clear to Jye. He, who had always feared for his mother's wandering ways, had himself strayed too far, and for too long, from his native village. He thought about Blanche Greypaull. His last sight of her had been from the hansom window as it pulled away into the fog. Her face had seemed almost ghostlike in its pallor, the tendrils of dark red hair curling damply across her forehead, her huge eyes unfocused, and emptied of all expression. He lowered his hands, and began to stride out with more assurance, ignoring the hazards of the greasy pavements. His work in St Paul's was almost complete. He would go, straightaway, to George Mitchell's house and beg to be released. By Christmas Eve he would be back in Montacute; safe in his mother's stone cottage.

❋

The necklace turned up in St Martin's Lane in the middle of December. An Indian pedlar, wearing nothing but a cotton dhoti, had appeared in Mrs Gimball's shop with a box of assorted trinkets, which he begged to exchange for an overcoat and shoes. Blanche, sorting through the muddle of cheap gewgaws and gaudy brooches, drew out a heavy chain to which was attached a large silver oval. Her recognition of the object was immediate and fearful. It brought an image to her mind of Mama, all those years ago on Larksleve, desperate and white before the Taunton bailiffs, lifting a similar chain and pendant from her neck in order to settle Papa's debts. The image was swiftly replaced by another,

297

more terrifying memory. She saw Meridiana Loveridge, fierce-eyed and sinister beside a hawthorne hedge, demanding the return of a pendant which she swore was hers.

Reason told Blanche that this was not the same pendant. The silver leaves that lay upon her palm were more delicately fashioned, the coral petals of the flowers a deeper shade of pink; the whole piece was in fact much finer than the necklace she remembered. The pedlar had come direct from Bombay to the London docks; his box of trinkets had travelled with him among lengths of silk and bunches of ostrich plumes. Hadn't she examined the contents of his cardboard suitcase, and purchased a piece of turquoise silk that would make a Christmas present for Annis? But gypsies, she thought, had a look of Indians about them; it was likely, almost certain in fact, that both pendants had come from the same source. She paid Mrs Gimball the token sum required, wrapped the object carefully in swathes of tissue-paper, and laid it away among the hoard of gifts that would, at Christmas, be taken home to Taunton.

❊

The problem of Hugh Fitzgerald had assumed, without her notice, the dimensions of an avalanche which threatened to engulf Blanche. Arm's length, had been her firm intention towards him, and she had tried to hold to it, repulsing all his tentative advances, but still there was the arm that crept slyly about her waist whenever she rode with him in Aunt Portious' carriage; the kiss, aimed at her lips, which she had so far managed to deflect towards her cheek or eyebrow. Hugh was becoming more insistent in his touching and handling of her; ascending or descending from cabs and broughams, she would find his fingers placed too firmly and for too long a time about her waist. Even though she still insisted on meeting him in public places, he never wasted the opportunity to lay his hands, no matter how politely, upon her person. Removal and replacement of her cloak in restaurants and music-halls, had lately involved such swift hard pressures upon her shoulders, that she had complained to him that in view of her status as professional model, she could hardly appear on the Liberty's dais with her shoulders black and blue from bruising. He hovered and hung about her until she was bored and fatigued by the very presence of him. Blanche tried to be nonchalant about it; she joked uneasily with Mrs Gimball.

'He do get warmer, and stick faster than a Coleman's Mustard Plaster,' she giggled.

Mrs Gimball was not deceived. 'You ain't going to fob 'im off much longer,' she warned Blanche. 'The toffs is all hot-blooded. Well, they never works their oats off like working-class people! I bet your H'onourable ain't never done a 'and's turn in his life. There he is, bursting with passion and rearing to go, and the sight of you in that low-slung black lace ain't likely to cool his head down, neither.'

This year of 1888 had passed so swiftly that Blanche could hardly believe in the approach of Christmas. Liberty's store was bright with tinsel and coloured streamers. At least a thousand new ways had been devised by which the wealthy patrons might be separated from their money. The poor of London thronged the pavements, selling bootlaces and matches, and openly begging, while their children died from hunger and deprivation. Blanche looked into desperate faces and remembered Hunter's Court. All those plans she had once made for her Mama, and nothing yet accomplished. A move to a better house, in a clean street, a bay-windowed villa perhaps, with a kitchen and a bit of garden. She had not dreamed that it would all take so long and prove so complicated.

This year had been memorable with the voices and faces of

certain men. There had been David Lambert, that fervent
Wesleyan, who had taken one look at Blanche and fled. Her
brother Jack, the ploughlines of a typical Greypaull in his
face, had asked sneeringly, 'Still living in London then,
Duchess?' There had been Jye Carew, cruel and indifferent:
'I don't want you!' he had declared, 'not now – not
never.' No man had ever hurt her in that particular way.
The anguish of rejection turned her thoughts towards Hugh
Deveraux Fitzgerald, who had remained constant, who had
insisted that he loved her.

Going home to see Mama would no longer be a simple
matter; she would need to be devious, if not downright
deceptive. Blanche paused in her packing; she decided
against silken lingerie trimmed with lace, and fancy
stockings, and selected instead, gowns that had been worn
several times, and underwear of wool and cotton. The sable
cloak would be her greatest pitfall. Mama was not easily
deceived when it came to the valuation of a garment. She
could assess to the nearest week and penny, the amount of
wear a garment had received before that item had come into
the possession of Blanche, and how much it was likely to
have cost when new. The long-tailed sables could never be
explained away in terms of Mrs Gimball's pawnshop, but
Blanche was determined that she would wear them. Just to
see the envy on Madelina's face would be worth any lies she
might have to tell!

Her desire to upstage Madelina proved so strong that, on
the morning of her departure for Taunton, Blanche dressed
herself, after all, in the gown of russet velvet, the sable cloak
and hat of peacock feathers. She excused her frank
ostentation in terms of the bitter weather, and an urgent
need to reassure Mama that she was, indeed, doing well in
London.

She had encouraged Hugh Fitzgerald to disappoint the
Honourable Letitia, by refusing to accompany her to Bath

for Christmas. Blanche had then watched him arrange a whole week of dinners and entertainments in West-End restaurants and theatres, and still remained silent about her own plans. Since that meeting with Jye Carew on Westminster Bridge, a cruel and perverse wish to wound Hugh had ruled all her actions. She had sat, by candlelight, before her dressing-table mirror, and repeated aloud the terrible prediction of Meridiana Loveridge. She had examined it carefully, word for word, accepted the inevitability of it, and then sealed it away, with her longing for Jye, in some deep place of the soul. It was only at the very last hour, when he had already committed himself to a Christmas in London that Blanche confessed to Hugh that Mama had, this year, demanded the presence of Blanche in Taunton.

She had worked in the store until late into the afternoon of that Christmas Eve. Her early experience of sewing shirt collars, and the years spent in helping Mrs Gimball with her renovations, proved invaluable now. Of all the beautiful girls who modelled gowns, it was Blanche who was the most handy with the needle and thread. She it was who could assist in busy times with the last-minute letting out of seams, or putting-in of tucks; who had the precise knack of adding a silken flower or wisp of tulle to embellish a plain gown; and her employers were grateful. These long hours of dedication and interest had ensured that extra sovereigns nestled snugly inside the bodice of her dress. Blanche arrived that evening at Paddington Station, weighted down with gifts. She caught the West Country train with only seconds to spare, and slept soundly until it was time for her to change trains at Bristol.

❀

A note, written by Mrs Gimball, had been delivered to Hunter's Court in mid-December. Eliza had read of

Blanche's intention to spend Christmas at home with mixed emotions of dread and pleasure. The presence of Blanche always meant a time of plenty for her family; and such generosity was, without doubt, her finest quality. The price to be paid, however, was the constant bickering and envy, stirred up inevitably by her presence. Every visit had so far seen an elevation in the status of Blanche, a frightening enhancement of her already extraordinary good-looks. That she would antagonise Madelina, fight with Simeon, and incite to rebellion the normally docile Annis, was to be expected. But Blanche had always been deceitful, and the moral dilemma of Eliza was in accepting gold from what might well turn out to be dubious sources. Simeon, too, was not altogether honest, but her son's lies were always concerned with his own trivial affairs around the inns and markets. The deceptions of Blanche, thought Eliza, were more significant and frightening because of the crafty kernel of truth always contained at their heart.

Christmas Eve brought Blanche, pale and exhausted, and escorted by several urchins who had carried her bags from the railway station. She sank down into the rocking-chair, and Eliza took in the exotic image of sable cloak, peacock feathers, high-heeled boots and rouged lips. Once again, a stream of gold was poured across the table, and Simeon and Annis instructed to shop in the poultry and vegetable markets. It was all too reminiscent of the ways of Philip Greypaull, too poignant a reminder of the prosperity he had enjoyed before the loss of Larksleve. Eliza still could not bring herself to welcome or warm towards this daughter. She did what was necessary and hospitable: made a pot of tea, laid a stone hot-water bottle between clean sheets, and tucked-in the weary girl, to see her sleep once again upon the starched pillow-case.

Eliza gazed down on the translucent eyelids, the full soft lips, the auburn hair spread out in a shining fall across the bedclothes. She turned away to lift the cloak of long-tailed sables, and wondered what man, or men, had provided Blanche with the vast sum of money necessary to purchase such a garment. Questions, she told herself firmly, would have to be asked this time, and truthful answers demanded.

❀

There was a tenderness in Annis, a capacity for pity and love that made her vulnerable, and liable to be exploited. She could never say no to any plea of Simeon, never stand up against the reproving tone and piety of Madelina. Just to be Mama's good daughter, to work diligently at her sewing-machine, bring home good wages, and wait for Frank, was all, she persuaded herself, that a girl like her could reasonably ask for.

It was on Christmas Day, when the good meal had been eaten, the table cleared, and the fire mended, that Mama produced the post from Belgaum, which, she now confessed, had arrived in Taunton two weeks earlier.

'I saved it up for a nice surprise, maid,' said Eliza complacently. 'I read the letter, and found nothing in it what wouldn't keep until Christmas Day.'

Annis felt a rare stir of resentment at the thought of this concealment; a mutiny which turned to a silent anger as the photograph of Frank was passed from hand to hand around the table, before she herself had hardly glanced at it. The fact that a letter from Frank, read aloud in Mina's presence, might impress her elder sister, no longer seemed important. Annis sensed the curious and sympathetic gaze of Blanche, and guessed that Blanche alone had recognised her outraged feelings. Annis suddenly knew, without any doubt, that she did not wish to hear Frank's letter read aloud before her assembled family, but Mama was already on her feet and beginning to read.

'My dear Annis, Such a lot have come to pass since I last put pen to paper. In my health I am much better and shall soon take up a soldiers duties once more. In my spirits I am still very low. There is so much fever here, a lot of cholera and typhoid, what kills off men and officers alike. I don't like these hot places, Annis, nor ever shall do, but with six and more years of service life to go, yours truly have got to grin and bear it. I hope you like the photo, Annis. They pinned the medal on me a few months ago, they also give me that stripe on my arm for Good Conduct. It meant a bit of extra pay, what brings me to what I got in mind for you and me. It have been in my heart for a long time, but now I am twenty-one years old and got a stripe and a medal, and I feel that I can make a plan or two for the future. Before I left Taunton I asked you to wait for me, and you said you would. I think I am old enough now to ask your mother if we can be engaged. I am asking for your hand in marriage, Annis. Please let me know as quick as you can what you have decided. I shall be on thorns until I get an answer. I think about you all the time. It helps me to stand this awful place. The extra money I get now can be saved up towards a Happy Home –'

Blanche brought the flat of her hand down hard upon the table. 'No, Mama!' she cried, 'you mustn't read no further. Can't you see – 'tis such a private matter, he meant it for Annis alone, not for all her relatives!'

Eliza paused; she lowered the sheet of grainy paper. 'Annis,' she said coldly, 'is not secretive, like some girls I could mention. She don't have any matters in her life what is not open and above board.'

Blanche was not to be silenced. ''Tis a proposal of marriage,' she insisted, 'and what's more, you already knowed that, before you stood up to read. That poor liddle soldier-boy is over in India waiting for an answer from our Annis, and you have kept that letter hid for a whole two weeks.'

Eliza looked bewildered; she turned to Annis. 'I never meant no harm, maid. I thought it would be a special treat for Christmas. In any case, there can't be all that much hurry about it. Frank Nevill won't be back in Taunton for another six years.'

Annis began to cry. 'You don't understand about love, Mama. Our Blanche is quite right. 'Tis a very private sort of letter. You must have knowed that already when Frank started off by calling me his "dearest Annis". He never done that before,' she wailed. 'Just because I can't read the words for myself, that don't mean that 'tis all a public matter. You just don't understand about love, Mama! Frank's offer of marriage should have been told to me, alone. Then I could have stood up this day, and made my own announcement. Now,' she sobbed, 'now 'tis all ruined and spoiled, and I wish I was dead and buried!'

Annis gazed around the table, and saw the tight and angry faces, and felt despair. Louis, seated in his usual corner, close to the fire, sensed the tension in the room, and began to beat his head against the wall. Even Simeon, who was the acknowledged champion of Annis, pushed back his chair, stood up and shouted, 'I be sick of hearing about this Frank Nevill! I shall go round to the Turk's Head and you lot can fight it out amongst yourselves. Women!' He grabbed up his cap, slammed the door behind him, and ran across the courtyard-paving. Laura began to whimper, she buried her face in Mina's neck, and her small body trembled.

Eliza sighed. 'Funny, idden it,' she said to Blanche, 'how everything in this family do end in tears, the minute you sets your fancy boots across my doorstep. Take Annis — never a wrong word betwixt her and me until you comes home, interfering.'

'Oh how I wish my Dave was here,' cried Madelina, 'he'd soon put you in your place, our Blanche, and no mistake!'

'Ah yes,' Blanche asked, 'I meant to ask you, Mina. Wherever have your husband got to? That do seem funny for you two not to be together — and on Christmas Day of all times!'

'David Lambert,' said Eliza coldly, 'is a devoted and dutiful son, and good Christian. He got his chapel duties to attend to, and the rest of the day is spent with his own mother and father. That have always been understood between us since Laura was born. 'Tis only natural that I should want to see my only grandchild.'

Blanche shook her head. 'Well, I must say, you got some funny ways of going on, down in Taunton.'

'Not half so funny as your own ways up in London,' snapped Madelina. She indicated the sable cloak. 'Me and Mama got a few very private questions to ask you, miss, before you goes back to your pawnshop.'

'Ask away, dear sister,' laughed Blanche, 'we've already seen, this day, how nothing can ever be kept private in this family!'

Mina coloured, and glanced at Annis. ''Tis a matter what can only be touched on by married women,' she said primly.

Blanche guffawed indelicately. 'Oh my Lord! Our Annis is twenty-one years old. Her have worked in the factory for these past five years. If you want to know if I took my drawers off to get that cloak — then you can think what you bloody well like Madelina Lambert! Because I shan't tell you!'

❇

After so much high emotion, and the display of so many damaged feelings, the giving of gifts at teatime, could only have come as an anticlimax. Exhausted by tears and temper, they glanced uncertainly at one another. Pincushions and hair-tidies, embroidered samplers and hankies were given and accepted with careful hesitation. It was not until Blanche opened up her bag-full of delights, that animation appeared on any features. There was the length of turquoise silk for Annis; and a similar piece, but in mustard-yellow, for the sallow skinned Madelina. A moth-eaten tippet of fur had been begged from Mrs Gimball's stock for the amusement of her brother Louis; a cap and woollen muffler for Simeon had been purchased from the same source. The china doll, dressed elaborately in silks and ribbons, and selected with such care, had been offered to Laura, but instantly rejected by her. The child continued to hide from Blanche, as she had done since her arrival, burying her face in Mina's skirts and not uttering one word. Mina had accepted the gift with the sour comment that Laura was not, and never would be, a spoilt child, and since such a toy must have cost a great deal of money she could not, of course, allow Laura to play with it very often. The warm woollen shawl was accepted gratefully by Eliza, and Blanche, heartened by this sign of her mother's approval, drew from its box the silver pendant set with coral and placed it in Eliza's hands.

'There,' she cried, 'now I bet you never thought to see the likes of that again in all your life?'

Eliza stared at the necklace. She held it out towards the firelight, touched the silver leaves and coral petals. 'Where did you get this, Blanche?' she asked quietly.

'A pedlar brought it into Mrs Gimball's shop. He was an Indian, just off the boat.'

'An Indian,' mused Eliza, 'ah, that might well be the case. Meridiana always said that her people were 'gyptians. India and Egypt do lie close, one beside the other.' She looked up at Blanche. 'You knows that this is a different pendant?'

'I know it, Mama. Your pendant was heavier. The flowers was bigger —'

307

'My pendant had magic powers. I shudden never have parted with it.' All at once, Eliza recoiled. She let the necklace drop into her black-cotton lap, and looked at Louis. 'I can't take it,' she whispered, 'I don't know why that is, Blanche, but I just can't abide the feel nor the sight of it.'

Blanche bit her lower lip; she blinked away tears and made her voice deliberately cheerful. 'All right then, you maids!' she cried. 'Who will give me a bid for this fine and magical pendant?'

Madelina looked pensive. ''Tis a pretty object, but David don't approve of me waring fancy gewgaws.'

'Well, Annis?'

Annis reached out a hand and lifted the chain from her mother's lap. She fastened the pendant around her throat. 'Do it suit me, Blanche? Do you really mean that I can have it? Is it a magical piece — like the one of Mama's?'

Blanche laughed. 'Only if you believe it.' She paused and spoke seriously. 'Just think of it, maid. Fine and healthy babies for you and Frank. 'Tis worth an ounce of faith, now idden it?'

'But what about you?' Annis blushed. 'Shudden you keep the magic for yourself? Don't you want strong and healthy children?'

Blanche raised her chin and stared directly at Eliza. 'I shan't never need no help from a gypsy necklace, to get what I want in my life!' She indicated the sable cloak, extended her wrist so that they might admire her wrist-watch. 'These odds and ends is only the beginning,' she warned, 'there's no limit to the things that'll come my way.' She extended her fingers, and flexed them with a grasping motion. 'I just want and want,' she repeated. 'Oh you should just see the fine shops in London! Such jewellery and clothes, such furs and fashions!' Her gaze moved defiantly from one shocked face to another. 'You just watch how your Blanche goes about the business of becoming a proper lady.' Their continued silence pushed her to make the ultimate, extravagant claim. 'Two years,' she cried, 'two years, and I shall bring my rich husband home to meet you.' She lowered her tone and spoke gently to Annis. 'So you see, maid – 'tis better if you should wear the pendant. Your Blanche will always make her own luck!'

❊

The departure of Blanche had not altogether eased the tensions in Taunton. Eliza surveyed a belligerent Simeon, a peevish Madelina, and the still resentful and vapourish Annis. Unable to settle to any task, she untied the ribbon which bound her cousin Rhoda's letters, selected the topmost one, and was mortified to find that it was dated May 1887. Eliza at once fetched pen and ink, turned up the lampwick, and headed a sheet of writing paper.

2, Hunter's Court,
Taunton, January 4th, 1889.

Dear cousin Rhoda,

Am ashamed at my own tardiness in answering your last letter. I sent a short note of sympathy on the loss of your dear son, John, and no word have passed across the Atlantic ocean since that time. We *must not* lose touch, Dear Cousin. You are the only one in the World that I can confide in, and I am once again sorely troubled with my children.

Do you recall my own Mother? How *domineering* she was, Rhoda, how she ruled us with *rod of iron*. Well, I set out to be a different sort of mother. I wanted them to *love* me, Rhoda, not cringe away in fright. Everything what I do is done from *love* of them. I cant bear to think that they might turn out like Philip, their Father. I only try to *guide* them, but it seems that *I am wrong* in this. Was took to task by Annis over Christmas, what was *very hurtful*. Annis egged on by Blanche, *of course*.

309

Such tantrums and high words, Rhoda. It have all left me quite wore out, and full of doubts. Seems like I can do *no right* in their eyes. What is a mother to think? You are so fortunate to have Mr Black at your side, to back you up. I cannot let them *rule* me, can I? I got to be both Mother and Father, and I *will be*. Have read back over your last letters, and your trouble with Georgie. You were *quite right* to upbraid him, Rhoda. We both know what it is to have a thowtless husband, and Satie sounds like a sweet and gentle girl. Hope things have settled down between them after your *wise words*.

Still no word from my oldest daughter Candace. I cant tell you how that do grieve me, Rhoda. Why, I ask myself, should she cut herself off like that? If she is unhappy then she should *turn to me, at once*. Blanche still flourishing like the green Bay Tree. Such clothes and talk of London, no wonder her brothers and sisters do grow unsettled with their lot in Life. All do come so *easy* to Blanche. I cant make it out.

How is things on your farm? I always think about you, so busy in every season. What sort of house do you live in? Is it anything like Larksleve?

Give my love to Mr Black and all your dear ones.

Your loving cousin, Eliza.

❀

The appearance of Jye at his mother's fireside on that Christmas Eve had been so unexpected that Meridiana had cried out in shock. 'Oh, whatever have happened? Be you sick, boy?'

'No,' he said slowly, 'I was sick, but now I be all cured.' He sat down in his father's chair. 'That restlessness have left me, Mother. I shan't never be going back to London.'

She stared at him. 'But you was so set on learning the stone-carving. So devoted to they old London churches.'

'I've learned all I need to. There's nothing in London,' he told her, 'that I can't do as well, or better, here.' He smiled bleakly. 'This'll sound funny, I reckon, coming from a deaf chap, but I found out on this last trip, that peace and quiet is what I need the most.' He spoke like a man already old, and weary of life. Meridiana knelt down and began to unlace his heavy boots. 'See — 'tis like this, Mother,' he explained, 'they crowded places do faze a man like me. All they hansom-cabs and horse-buses. All they flys and broughams. Then there's the city people. Their ways bain't our ways. That was all interesting to begin with, but I have see'd things just lately what have sickened my soul. Things I can't bear to look upon no longer.'

'And what about the Greypaull hussy?' Meridiana's gaze was hard, her voice uncompromising.

'Finished,' he said, briefly. 'All finished and done with. I told her so, face to face. Her didden much like it.'

'No,' said Meridiana. 'They proud ones can't never take a straight no for an answer, but you done right to come home, boy.' She took his large hand in her own, turned it palm upwards, and touched the few deep lines engraved upon it. Her voice held the peace of a benediction. 'You was never cut out for the wandering way of life. That wicked maid of Eliza's was only trifling with you. There's decent maidens round about yer, what'd be only too eager —' She noted the mutiny in his face, and halted. 'All right,' she murmured, 'us won't go into that thorny subject.' She stood up and touched his face. 'I be so glad to have 'ee back, Jye.'

He grinned and pointed to the rabbit-stew, simmering upon the hob. 'I sees that you haven't lost your old trick of catching bunny-rabbits?'

She moved to a cupboard and returned with wooden bowls and spoons, bread and salt. 'There's many a law-abiding family what sits in chapel of a Sunday morning with bellies what rumble louder than their hymn-singing.' The black eyes glinted wickedly in the proud face. 'Be a bad day

311

for me, Jye Carew, when I can't roam over Parson's fields and catch myself a tasty dinner.'

The need to walk was urgent in him. Jye took clean air into his lungs, and felt that tingle in the blood, that cleansing of the mind which he had never known in London. The fields were empty, the trees leafless; hill-paths and lanes were bleached white and made iron-hard by the keen frost. Once again, he beat the boundaries of home with his feet, and found every aspect quite unchanged. Places, and the names of places, held a deep significance for him. Jye could not abide change. He came to Ham Hill last of all; he had feared that it would not be as he remembered. He stood upon a green knoll, and gazed down into the yellow stone-bed, counted the little tin-roofed lodges of the masons, saw the jackdaws wheel and dive in the still air, and knew in his heart that this was his special place in all the world.

He attended the Christmas morning service in the Baptist chapel. Heads turned to greet him, hands were outstretched in welcome: village maids who, five years ago, had been skinny schoolgirls, eyed him admiringly and with calculation. Suddenly, this tall and handsome mason, who had lived and worked for so long in London, had a certain piquant fascination for these girls, who had never strayed more than two miles in any direction from their own village Green. Deafness, it now seemed, was no longer a disadvantage when it came to romantic inclination.

Jye avoided all attempts to engage him in conversation, especially those of the Reverend Hardin. He was not yet ready for the inevitable questions. He would need to let fresh wounds heal over, to examine the scars of old hurts, to test his own tolerance for new rejections, and the possibilities of future pain. He had an overwhelming need to feel safe and sure within himself, to exorcise all his devils, and this would take time; but he had plenty of that, now.

The change in Simeon Greypaull had been dramatic; within a space of months he had grown in all directions. He now stood taller than Blanche or Annis, was wide in the shoulder, and had the slim waist and tapering hips which had once been the elegant marks of his father, Philip. He was no longer the wilful urchin who scavenged and begged around the markets, but a young man who cared, passionately, about his physical appearance, and the regard in which he was held by certain people. He had been made much of lately in the Turk's Head tavern, and treated with a new respect by stallholders and dealers in the cattle and vegetable markets. The word had gone out that Simeon Greypaull had caught the eye and ear of an impresario from London.

A flight of stone steps led up to a large room at the rear of the London Hotel. Here it was that the visiting theatre companies performed their plays, and the itinerant vaudeville turns displayed their varied talents. Towards the end of each show the company manager would invite those members of his audience who felt able to participate in the finale, and the aspiring comedians and singers of Taunton would climb up on stage, cheered by relatives and friends to perform their party-pieces. But what had proved a brief, gin-inspired adventure for the rest of Taunton's amateur talent, had been a sober and beautiful rendition on the part of Simeon Greypaull.

The company manager had been impressed. 'Not a dry eye in the place,' he informed his backers, 'he brought the bloody house down! A voice like I never heard in all my days — and he's got the sort of romantic looks that'll drive the women crazy.'

The letter was addressed to Mr Simeon Greypaull, and was headed, The Empire Theatre of Varieties, London. Eliza began to read, silently at first; but even when spoken aloud the words still failed to convey proper meaning to her.

'Dear Mr Greypaull, It has come to my notice that you are the owner of a singing voice which might benefit from training. I shall arrive at the London Hotel on April 2nd. I would deem it a favour if you would present yourself before me at 7.00 o'clock that evening so that I might judge for myself whether you are of sufficient talent to repay my interest in you. Signed. George Edwardes.' Eliza laid the letter down. 'What do it mean, Sim?'

'I went to the theatre a few weeks ago. I stood up on the stage – did a bit of singing – that was well-received, Ma.' He stammered and lowered his gaze before his mother's anger.

'You wudden sing in church,' she said fiercely, 'not even when Parson begged it of you. He offered to show you how to read music, how to read words. He said that you had got a lovely voice, that you might, in time, come to lead the choir –'

'But I don't want to lead the choir, Ma! I don't like they miserable old hymn tunes. I like a song what have got some life in it, or a sad piece what'll make people cry.'

Eliza nodded. 'Oh yes,' she said, 'well, I've seen all this before. You got to get yourself noticed, haven't you? All eyes must be fixed upon you. Hands clapping, eh boy? Voices cheering you to the rafters? You got to be the kingpin, looked up to, and admired.' Eliza's voice grew very quiet. 'Nobody claps you in church, boy. Nobody cheers you to the echo in that holy place, you'd be dressed in white wudden you, and looking just exactly like all the other choirmen? That's why you said no to Parson. I know'd what your trouble was then; now I sees it proved. You be like your father, like your sister, Blanche. You is only happy when you can perform and strut, and have people make much of you. Idden that the case, Sim?'

He looked wretched and uneasy. 'I don't know,' he cried, 'I never thought about it. I only know that singing do lift the heart inside me. For the space of my song I feels freed and warm. 'Tis as if I be somebody else, Ma! Can't you understand that?'

'No,' she said, 'I can't understand that. I never wanted to be anything other than what the dear Lord have seen fit to make me. Your poor father spent his whole life chasing after shadows, when all the time the substance of Larksleve was lying right close, underneath his hand.' Eliza rapped with her knuckles on the scrubbed-top table. 'Dreams,' she insisted, 'dangerous dreams, what do lead a man away from the path of true salvation.'

'I don't want salvation, Ma! I want to go to London. I want to be somebody important. I want fine clothes and money in my pocket,' He fell back, alarmed at the pallor of her face. 'I don't mean no harm. That wudden be sinful. Look at our Blanche, how she do thrive and shine in the city!'

The man from the Empire Theatre came to Taunton as promised; and Simeon, washed and combed and looking awkward in a borrowed suit, walked across to the London Hotel and was shown into the empty theatre. He climbed onto the small stage and looked outwards to where a bearded, silver-haired man sat alone in the front seat. The single word of greeting was 'Sing!', and he obeyed it. He sang without any affectation, the clear high notes of his tenor voice reaching back to the furthest corners of the theatre, and beyond into the hotel. People paused in the corridors to listen. When the song was ended the bearded man beckoned Simeon to come down and sit beside him.

'What made you choose that particular ballad?' he asked softly.

'Well, sir — 'tis like this — I don't know all that many songs. I picks up the words and tunes from the "turns" what I see here in this theatre.' He grinned. ' "Danny Boy" is my very favourite. That do bring a tear to my own eye.'

'I thought,' said the impresario, slyly, 'that you might have known that I was Irish?'

The allusion meant nothing to Simeon. 'I be Church of England myself, sir, but I don't sing in the choir.'

'Where do you sing then?'

'Round the pubs,' he grinned. 'They calls it singing for your bread and cheese in these parts, and I done plenty of that, sir.'

'What job do you do?'

'Got no proper job, sir.'

'If I offered you a part in my next production, would you come back to London with me?'

'Like a shot, sir!'

The man from London smiled and tapped his jacket. 'I've a contract here in my pocket. I shall need your signature on it. Meanwhile, I should like to hear you sing again. Do you know a song called "Thora"?'

Simeon looked uneasy. 'I know the tune, but not the words.'

'That's no problem. I brought the sheet-music with me.' He opened the small black case that rested on his knees and withdrew a sheaf of papers. 'Just step outside will you, boy. Ask them to give us some better light in this place. You'll never be able to read the words, else!'

Simeon stepped outside. He walked quickly along the corridor, down the stone steps and into the coaching-yard. He passed underneath the archway and came out into the gas-lit brilliance of Fore Street. He leaned against the hotel wall, and tried to control his trembling limbs. He could feel the anger rising in him, that uncontrollable urge to smash and destroy, to return equal hurt to hurt, measured pain for paint. He began to run downhill, towards East Reach. He came into Hunter's Court out of breath and sobbing. He threw open the door of his mother's cottage and then slammed it hard behind him.

Eliza and Annis were seated at the table, the oil lamp positioned squarely between them. Paper and envelopes littered the surface; Frank Nevill's photograph stood at Annis' elbow. Simeon leaned momentarily against the closed door to catch his breath. They were, he thought, about the business of accepting a proposal of marriage. When he moved towards Annis his breathing had quietened, but not his temper. He grabbed up the photo of Frank and dashed it to the floor.

'Never mind about writing to him,' he sobbed, 'you thinks about nothing else these days, save that bloody soldier! What about me, Annis? What about your brother?'

Eliza stood up. She pointed towards the door. 'You've been drinking,' she said coldly. 'Get out of my house and put your head underneath the pump, and don't dare set your foot across my threshold again until you be sober!'

Simeon advanced upon her, he towered above her. So great was his rage that flecks of foam lay upon his lips. 'Your fault,' he ground out, 'all your fault that I can't read and write.'

Eliza's hand sought the left side of her face. She began to rub at the scarred skin of her cheek and eyebrow. 'What is it, boy?' she asked quietly, 'whatever have happened to you?'

'I stood up there – on that stage – and I sung "Danny Boy" for him. He liked it – I know he did! I was good, better than I had ever been before. Why, I damn near brought tears to my own eyes! I sung so beautiful for him that he offered me a job in London, straight off. He had the bloody contract in his jacket pocket. Then he wanted another song. I told 'un that I knowed the tune but not the words. So what does he do? I'll tell you, Mother! He reaches into his liddle suitcase, and out he comes with this piece of paper, what have got the words and music writ on it?'

Annis gasped. 'Oh Simmy! That must of been awful for you! Whatever did you do?'

His features crumpled suddenly, like those of a small child. 'I run away,' he wept, 'I run away from him as fast as I could.' He looked at his mother, and there was hatred in his voice. 'Your fault,' he repeated, 'all your fault that I can't read and write. Now look what that have cost me! A job in London, in a fine theatre. My name wrote big on the posters, my picture in all the papers. I could of been famous! I could have been somebody! 'stead of living with you lot in this rotten hovel, I could of been like our Blanche!'

Eliza sat down, and he stumbled towards a chair and laid his head upon the table, all anger spent. She reached a hand out towards him, and then thought better of it. 'Not really so much my fault,' she murmured, 'there was no money left to send you to school, and no time to teach you myself.' She indicated Louis. 'Your brother have always been like a baby. He can't do nothing for himself. You knows all about that, Simeon. You knows well the work and the hours what I do spend on Louis.'

He lifted his head. 'You finds time for all the others, 'specially your daughters. You never did care much for me, did you? What is it, then? Do I look too much like Father? I heard tell once that he was a powerful singer; that he could have gone to London, but that he bided in Buckland to wed with you.'

'He blamed me too,' Eliza whispered. 'Always my fault, whatever happened.' She paused. 'Perhaps I should have made the time, tried harder with you and Blanche and Annis; showed you how to form your letters. That idden too late,' she said, hesitantly, 'us could still have a try at lessons – ?'

''Tis too late for me. That chance won't never come again. The one and only time in all my life that I was ever called upon to read words, and I cudden do it!'

Eliza watched him as he stood up and wiped his face with the back of his hand. He looked so young and vulnerable in his disappointment, and she felt that same unwilling ache at the heart that she had once known for Philip Greypaull. 'I be so sorry, boy, that things didden turn out the way you had hoped.'

But Simeon was unforgiving. He turned and walked towards the door. 'I be off to the pub now. I shall get stinking drunk, and I don't want to hear no complaints about it.' He squared his shoulders and pointed at the photo of Frank Nevill. 'That feller got the most sense. He took hisself down to Jellalabad and signed-on for a soldier. Petticoat government! That's my trouble. Too many women in this family, and all of 'em knowing best what should be done by the men. If you don't see me again, then you'll know what have come to pass. If they offer me the Queen's shilling – then I intends to grab it!'

They waited for him, lamp in the window, kettle on the hob, but he did not return. From an upper window of Cook's factory, Annis saw her brother, some days later, drilling with a squad of others on the parade ground.

'Oh Mama,' she wept, 'he never even said goodbye. I heard that the next company what moves out is bound for Ireland to fight the Fenians. How could he be so cruel, he know'd how much I care about him? He was ever my favourite.'

'Us shudden have favourites, Annis.'

'Don't you, Mama?'

Eliza frowned. 'I worries equally about each and everyone of you.'

'But there's a world of difference, Mama, between worrying and loving.'

Sons, Eliza was beginning to discover, could be every bit as enigmatic and worrying as daughters. There was Jack, who had stayed for less than an hour on New Year's Day.

She had never known him to be uneasy in her presence, but she could scarcely have missed the tension in his face, the secretive glances exchanged between him and Madelina, and the curious nervousness of Blanche, who had always affected to despise Jack. Control, thought Eliza, was slipping from her. Time had once been when she could read their slightest intentions, anticipate every likely folly. Now, they had moved away from her into places where she could not follow. They had always, she recalled, conspired together. Simeon with Annis, Jack with Madelina. Even Blanche and Candace had once set off quite amicably together, to work in London. Eliza could not believe that Blanche had lost all contact with her sister, Candace. Surely London could not be all that much bigger than Taunton? The two sisters must, in the nature of things, run across one another from time to time, when shopping down the High Street?

Eliza rocked in her chair beside the fire, and Louis crept up to kneel beside her. She stroked his fair hair and soft skin with an absent-minded gentleness, and was reminded at once of Philip Greypaull. She had only to close her eyes for the Blackdown Hills to rise, steep and green, all about her. Whenever she remembered Larksleve it was always summer. She recalled an evening when she and Loveday Hayes had gone gleaning with the children happy all around them. She thought about Samuel, whom she might, given the opportunity, once have loved. He must also be growing old, alone now, on Warren's Farm. Eliza tried to call up Sam's features, and was dismayed to discover that she could not.

The face that appeared before her closed eyes was always that of Philip Greypaull. A young face, unmarked and immature, the sunbleached curls tumbling on his forehead, the blue eyes fever-bright, the lips petulant and drooping. She accepted now, with resignation, that the ghost of Philip had moved in with her; waking and sleeping, he had become a positive presence, always pleading and persuading, speaking to her through all their children. She had thought him safe in Buckland churchyard, dreaming beside his doting mother, and it seemed like a kind of victory to Eliza, that he had not, after all that had happened between them, seen fit in the end, to desert his wife. With every year that passed, since his death, her memories of Philip had grown kinder, and surprisingly less judgemental.

❋

For a marriage to be successful, believed Hugh Fitzgerald, it was necessary that a husband should be able to view his wife as an extension of himself. His courtship of Blanche should have warned him from the beginning of the unlikeliness of such a prospect, but Hugh was in love. Even so, there were aspects of Blanche which caused him grave disquiet. He had noticed how easily bored she became when subjected to the exclusive company of one person. To keep her amused and in good humour, he was finding it necessary to introduce her to a variety of comedians and ballad singers, sword swallowers and fire eaters, jugglers and freaks, people who all drank champagne at Hugh's expense. At Romano's she insisted that he should introduce her to peers of the realm, criminals and racing tipsters. He tried to raise her standards, to guide her towards the theatre and the opera, and she had been persuaded lately that it was only in these temples of culture that her newest gowns, her sable cloak, and diamond wrist-watch, could be displayed to full advantage. He had taken her to Covent Garden; they had stepped from the hot and stifling London street, into the pleasant coolness of the Opera House, and climbed up the impressive stairway towards the red-and-gilt box which he had reserved. He had explained and instructed, pointed out the difference between violins and cellos, and contralto and soprano. He had given her a detailed and painstaking resumé of the story of Mozart's *Magic Flute*, but Blanche had found Grand Opera irresistibly funny. Always aware of her merest movement, he had noticed, once the overture was finished, the agitated use of handkerchief and fan, the quivering of her arms and shoulders. He held on until that moment when tears poured from her eyes, and the hanky was crammed hard against her teeth, then he led her, choking and incoherent, to relieve her mirth in the privacy of a rear exit.

Their one and only visit to the theatre had been to watch a performance of Henry Irving at the Lyceum. The acting of this great man, Hugh told Blanche, was an impressive, never-to-be forgotten experience. Blanche did not dispute this. Never, she afterwards declared, would she forget his mouthings and grimacings.

'I tried to titter all ladylike behind my hand,' she confessed, 'but that got me to such a pitch that I just had to laugh out loud.'

'Shakespeare,' he told her, 'is not meant to be laughed at.'

'Then that Irving shudden never have carried on so. Why, he'd bring the house down at the Empire.'

If she had shown any sign that she cared, if she had made some effort to impress him, then Hugh might have wearied of her. It was this very indifference to him, her lacklustre style of greeting, her air of total ennui, that lashed him to make ever greater efforts to enthral her. She no longer showed so much decorum when in the sole company of Hugh. She had told him, 'You must take me exactly as you finds me – like it or not! I can't always be talking proper and remembering what knife to use. Anyway! I just love to see your jaw drop when I get it wrong.' The more careless she grew in her attitudes towards him, the more jealous and possessive he became in his courtship of her; and yet he could not resist the urge to show her off.

The closing of Liberty's store at Easter meant that Blanche would have extra time to spend with Hugh.

Already, he had made plans. They would drive out to Kew, go to a few race-meetings. There were several auctions of contemporary art that he wished to attend. His interest in the works of Pre-Raphaelite painters had grown intense since meeting Blanche. He intended, so he said, to buy in every work of art for which she had modelled.

'Please yourself,' she told him, ''tis your money. If you wants to look at a wall full of old rubbish, that's your concern.' The very thought of wasting her leisure hours in the dusty rooms at Christie's was not to be endured. As she said to Mrs Gimball, 'He'll be wanting to drag me off to that Shakespeare, or to listen to they opera singers, clucking like a bunch of broody hens.' The memory of Covent Garden made her smile. 'Oh my, but that was funny!' She became serious. 'But once is more than enough for that sort of caper. I got to get away from him, Ma. Just for a few days. I try to keep him in his place, to always go where there's plenty of people about – you know what I mean!' She brightened. 'I know what I'll do. I'll go home to Taunton. Give my mother a nice surprise. There's always good sport to be had amongst my sisters.'

'But wot about Master Fitz, duckie? Wot'll you tell him?'

'Nothing. He don't have to know my every movement.'

'He'll be round 'ere, looking for you.'

'Let him. You're to keep quiet, Ma. Don't you dare tell him where I've gone.'

❋

Eliza possessed the frail looks of the truly red-haired, that pale skin, those thin bones, were familiar to all her children. They were not deceived by her air of delicacy, they knew her to be tough and resilient. But in the four months since Blanche had seen her mother, Eliza had grown suddenly old. The angry tint of her hair had begun to fade, there were

323

blue shadows underneath her eyes. She sat in her rocking chair and seemed disinclined to move.

'What ails her?' Blanche asked Annis, when Eliza had gone early to her bed.

''Tis our Sim. He've run away for to be a soldier. He's in Ireland so we've heard, fighting the Fenians. Mama is sure he'll be killed, he got such a dreadful hot temper.'

'But what made him go?'

Annis spoke in a voice that trembled. 'Oh Blanche, that was so awful! Poor Simmy, he was so sure that he would go to London.'

'London?'

'To be a singer. This man come down from the Empire Theatre to hear Sim perform. He sung "Danny Boy", and the man was all ready to sign the contract then he asked for another song, and Sim didden know the words. "That's all right," said the man, "I got 'em writ down for you on this sheet of paper." '

Blanche clapped a hand to her mouth. 'Oh my God!' she cried. 'I know only too well what that do feel like! Poor liddle devil. So what happened, Annis?'

'Sim run away. Well, what else could he do? He was too ashamed to say that he cudden read nor write. He come home and raved at Mama, said 'twas all her fault. Then he went off to Jellalabad and joined up. Signed-on for twenty-two years, so the Serjeant told Mama.'

Blanche sighed. 'No wonder her's looking sickly.'

'That's not all. Since Simmy went away, our Louis do seem dreadful restless. He don't sit quiet no more, but do want to pace up and down all the time.'

Annis pointed to the damaged chairs. 'He've started to pull the rushes out of the chair seats.'

'Well, you ought to stop him.'

'Look at him, Blanche. See how big he've growed just lately. I'm not sure, but I think he must be about fifteen years old. Mama is frightened. People in the Court is beginning to complain. They say that without Simeon at home, we two women won't never be able to control our Louis. He'll die if they take him to the Lunatic Asylum. They'll chain him to his bed and give him bread and water. He idden crazy, Blanche, he's only backward. He can't talk, or do much for himself, but he idden mad –'

'I knows all that,' Blanche interrupted. 'If Louis was a Royal Prince he'd be walking the streets like anybody else. There's one law for the rich and another for the poor.' She paused. 'There's only one answer to all this, maid. Mama must move to a bigger house, one with a long passage, so that Louis can walk up and down when he got a mind to. We must find a place where the neighbours keeps themselves to themselves. We don't want anybody looking at him and complaining. We got to find a place to hide him, Annis. For Mama's sake!'

'But that'll cost money. This house belongs to Uncle Samuel, we live here rent free.'

'Our Simeon have left home, so that makes one less to feed. I can put down a month's rent – how about you?'

'I got a few savings.' Annis sounded reluctant. 'But that's for my bottom drawer.'

'Never mind your bloody bottom drawer! Do you want to see your baby brother carted off to the Asylum? Just look at Mama. Much more of this worry is liable to kill her!'

'You be quite right, of course,' said Annis, meekly. 'I just wasn't thinking proper. There's our Mina too. Perhaps she could – ?'

'Leave her out of this,' snapped Blanche. 'You and me can handle it between us.'

The telegram arrived while Blanche and Annis were absent. Eliza, already familiar with its dramatic contents, read the words aloud on their return, in a tone of utter disbelief.

'Could not find you at Gimballs. Stop. Mrs G. gave me your address. Stop. Please come back at once. Stop. Am quite desolate and bereft without you. Stop. Shall probably drown myself in the Thames if you do not return. Stop. Signed. Hugh Fitzgerald.' A dull crimson flush burned on Eliza's cheekbones. 'I hope you realises, miss, that the Telegraph Office, and most of the postmen have read this — this disgusting message, and is now laughing their heads off at our expense?'

'Let 'em laugh, Mama. Poor souls, they don't get much excitement usually. Most telegrams do only announce a death in the family.'

'Who is this Fitzgerald? He must have a fortune to send long messages to you, what don't make any sense.'

Blanche sighed. 'I told you all about him. His money do come out of the South African gold-mines. He got hundreds of blackmen over there digging up the sovereigns for him. But we don't want to talk about him. Now listen careful, Mama. Me and Annis have found you a bigger house, one with a front-room and a passage. The rent is two shillings and sixpence a week, and I have already paid one month down in advance. Me and Annis is going to pay your rent between us. You won't need to worry any more. We've borrowed a handcart to move your bits and pieces. You shall be out of this hole by tomorrow evening.'

Blanche took her mother to view the house. It stood in a neat, bay-windowed terrace, where every doorstep was freshly whitened, and clean lace-curtains hung at all the windows. Blanche unlocked the door to reveal a long and spacious hallway.

'Oh maid,' Eliza whispered, ''tis worth two and sixpence just to have that space for him to walk up and down. You don't know how worried I've been since Simeon went away.'

'Worry no more, Mama. 'Twas about time you left that

326

rotten Court, anyway.'

'I don't know how I can ever thank you,' murmured Eliza.

'You don't need to. After all, 'tis you and our poor Annis what do bear the burden of Louis, day in, day out.'

It was on Easter Monday when they were loading Eliza's furniture, prior to moving, that the carriage drew up before the entry to Hunter's Court. Blanche, her skirts hitched up, her hair hanging down, and a smudge of dirt across one cheek, was about to lift a bundle of bedding onto the handcart.

'Look,' cried Annis, 'a brougham, and I reckon the feller's coming in here.'

'Oh my God! It'll be that bloody nuisance Fitzgerald come down from London to find me.' She ran into the house, and began to climb the stepladder. 'Don't dare to tell him I'm here,' she shouted to Eliza. 'Don't even admit that you know my name.'

'But what shall I say?' wailed Eliza.

Blanche paused upon the step of the ladder. She looked down into her mother's anxious face. 'Tell him,' she said coldly, 'tell that silly fool to go further.'

Hugh came into the Court. The coachman had warned him to be wary. He paused uncertainly and looked around him at the grimy little houses, the broken flagstones, at the slatterns who leaned up against the walls, arms folded. One of the women called out, 'You lookin' for me, is you, my 'andsome?'

'A family called Greypaull,' he said. 'Can you tell me if they live here?'

The woman spat upon the ground, and gestured towards the handcart. 'If it's they toffs you be lookin' for then you'm just in time.'

He walked to the cottage, knocked on the door and it was opened at once by a pretty, fair-haired girl. Just behind her stood a tiny red-haired woman whose face bore a terrible scar.

'My name is Hugh Fitzgerald. I sent you a telegram from London. I am looking for Blanche — she's a very dear friend of mine —' His voice trailed away and he could not continue. He knew that his bewilderment and shock at the sight of Hunter's Court showed plainly in his face.

'Come you inside, sir. You've had a long journey down from London.' Eliza waved a hand at the room's confusion. 'You picked a bad day to visit. We're about to move out to a bigger house.' She removed a heap of clothing from a chair and invited him to sit down.

'There's a cup of tea in the pot?'

He nodded impatiently. 'It's news of Blanche I'm really anxious to obtain. Is she here, Mrs Greypaull?'

Eliza poured tea and said nothing. It was left to Annis to tell the half-truth.

'Well,' she said, hesitantly, 'she was here, until a few minutes ago. She had to step out on some urgent business. We be moving house, you see. There's a lot to do.'

'Has Blanche told you anything about me?' He addressed his question to Eliza.

'My daughter said she had a wealthy friend. One what buys her expensive presents.' The implication in her tone was very clear.

'It's not what you think,' he said anxiously, 'I have only the most honourable of intentions towards her.' He looked towards the stepladder and raised his tone. 'I would ask you for her hand in marriage if I thought there was the remotest chance that she would accept.'

Eliza looked surprised. 'Marriage is it? — Well, that's another matter altogether. But you don't need my permission. Blanche is of age.'

He smiled. 'I need your approval,' he said simply. 'If I marry Blanche I shall want to be accepted by her mother, and her family.'

Eliza's smile reached into her eyes. The sharp aspect of her features softened, and, just for a moment, she glowed with an unusual beauty.

'I can see, Mrs Greypaull,' said Hugh, 'from whom Blanche obtained her good looks. It's most marked, when you smile. There's a very strong likeness between you.'

Eliza reached out a hand towards him. 'You're a good man. But I hope you know what you're about. I must speak the truth. My daughter is headstrong. I could never manage her, and if I'm any judge of character, then neither will you.'

'I know,' he grinned, 'but that's all part of her fascination for me.' He looked hard into Eliza's face, and then raised his gaze towards the ceiling. 'Can I assume,' he asked loudly, 'that you will give me your blessing on my courtship of Blanche?'

Eliza looked grim. 'You'll need more than a blessing from me, Hugh Fitzgerald, if you means to take on my daughter. I won't lie to you. 'Tis my dearest wish to see her settled down with a good man. But you be very careful, that's all I got to say.'

❀

Blanche returned to London to find a note from Hugh Fitzgerald waiting for her. Mrs Gimball read, 'My dear Blanche. It has become a matter of urgency that you and I have a serious discussion about certain recent events. I suggest a picnic lunch on Sunday. I await your decision as to time and venue. Ever yours, Hugh.'

'You've upset 'im, ducks.' Mrs Gimball threw the letter down upon the table. 'That's a cold little note, and no mistake. You shouldn't never 'ave gone off like that, he was fair off his 'ead with worrying about you.'

'And you told him where to find me, didden you? Oh, why did you have to do that?'

Mrs Gimball said, 'I'll tell you why, miss. Because he's a

329

damn nice fella, and he don't deserve the high-handed treatment wot he gets from you.'

'You don't understand,' cried Blanche, 'he's like bedbugs. He gets into every nook and cranny. I can't have nothing private from him.' She stamped her foot. ''Tis all going wrong! 'Twas me what was supposed to call the tune, and him what should pay the piper. I nearly died when he turned up at Hunter's Court. Me and our Annis was moving furniture on a handcart. I looked like a street drab. I had to run upstairs and hide.' She sat down and began to remove her fashionable boots. 'He sent a telegram first, you know.' There was pride in her tone. 'That caused a commotion, I can tell you!' She kicked the boots away into a corner, and began to massage her feet. 'I told my Mama to send the fool further. Pity was that she never done it!'

Mrs Gimball nodded towards the blistered feet resting on the fender. 'Spent all your money again, didn't you, on them down in Taunton? Had to walk all the way back from Paddington station in them silly high-heels? I tell you, Blanche, you can't afford to upset Master Fitz. You got too many big ideas, and no gold in your pocket.' She paused. 'I don't like the sound of that note, and that's the Gawd's truth. He's cooling-off Blanche! So you be careful.'

If Blanche felt piqued and a little alarmed at Hugh's sudden coolness, the single sentence of her reply showed nothing but her usual indifference. 'You may take me to the Zoological Gardens,' she dictated to Mrs Gimball, 'we can study the monkeys, what should make us both feel quite at home.'

❀

The Zoological Gardens were not open to the public on Sundays. The issue of tickets on the Sabbath was limited to Fellows of the Zoological Society and their relatives. Blanche was not surprised to discover that Hugh had a second cousin who conveniently was a member of this exclusive group.

Hugh's greeting lacked its normal warmth, they spoke, distantly, about the likelihood of rain. They walked in silence along the narrow sunlit pathways of the gardens in the company of bewhiskered old gentlemen dressed in black, who stared reprovingly at Blanche when she laughed at the more outrageous antics of the Barbary apes.

Hugh carried the rug and picnic basket to a secluded spot underneath a beech tree. He knelt down, spread the rug and a starched white cloth, and began to set out plates and glasses, food and wine. Blanche arranged her limbs and dress in an alluring pose; she was wearing her favourite shades of lavender and purple. She removed her hat, aware that the dappled sunlight would enhance the copper tint of her hair. She adjusted her skirts with an artful carelessness which revealed the coquettish arch of her foot, the slimness of silk-clad ankle. She exclaimed at the unusual warmth of early May, and loosened the neckline of her filmy blouse. The laughter came from deep within her throat. 'Well,' she said, huskily, 'here we are, then!'

Hugh sat down and began to speak in the clipped and level tones of suppressed emotion. 'I sent you a telegram, to which you made no reply. I came to Taunton and found your mother's house. You were there, you ran upstairs and hid. You needn't deny it, you were wearing the perfume I gave you. Why did you go away without informing me? Why would you not face me when I came to see you?'

'I don't care to be followed,' she muttered, and then suddenly her anger outstripped his. 'You take too much for granted,' she shouted. 'How dare you send telegrams. How dare you come chasing after me. You don't have the right. You don't own me.' She paused and went on in a quieter tone. 'I want you to know that what you found in Hunter's Court don't signify nothing. I wudden want you to think that I was born or growed up in that place. 'Tis an old story and I don't care to talk about it, but we Greypaulls have come from a high-born family.'

Hugh said in a gentler tone, 'Why didn't you tell me about your family's plight? It's quite obvious that your poor mother does not belong in that dreadful Court. I could have helped, long ago. In fact, I intend to —'

'Oh do you?' she interrupted. 'Well, you don't need to bother. I can look after my Mama. I already moved her to a better house. My mother is very grateful to me.'

Hugh lifted the tablecloth by its corners, and dumped the uneaten picnic into the basket. With one swift movement he had covered the distance between them to kneel beside her. 'Forgive me. I didn't understand.' He hesitated. 'Just one more question. You must have heard what I said to your mother, about wanting to get married?'

She laughed. 'Oh yes, that was real clever of you. You lit on the very subject what 'ud go down well with my Mama. I had to admire you for that, Hugh.' She gazed upwards into the beech boughs. 'Of course, you didden mean it.'

'Oh, I meant it, Blanche.'

'I don't believe you. Chaps like you don't wed with artists' models. I knowed that you was only amusing yourself, right from the beginning. Anyway — your old aunty 'ud see you six foot under before she would give you her blessing.' She glanced sideways at him. 'I don't know that I want you, after all. You idden no great catch, not with dear Aunty Porteous managing your purse-strings.'

'But I can persuade her. She'll come to love you as a daughter. I know she will. As for money — I draw the interest on a capital of ten thousand pounds. We shouldn't be paupers, Blanche. I also get a sum of two thousand on my marriage, and the jewellery left me by my maternal grandmother.' He drew out a box from his waistcoat pocket. He lifted the lid, and Blanche looked down upon a square-cut emerald, set in tiny diamonds.

'Oh,' she whispered, 'is it real?'

He lifted her left hand and kissed it. He slipped the ring across her third finger. 'I had meant to do this with wine and roses,' he grinned, 'not beneath a tree in the Zoological Gardens.'

Blanche dipped her hand into dappled sunshine. The jewel was so large that it measured from one knuckle to another. 'Our Mina'll just curl up and die with envy.' She lifted her face towards him. 'Do you mean that I can truly keep it?'

'Wear it as a token of our love,' he murmured, 'we'll be married in the autumn. We'll honeymoon in Paris. We'll buy a house in Bath, close to my Aunt. She'll be such a help to you, my darling.'

Hugh bent to kiss her lips with so much passion, that he quite failed to notice how passive and limp she stayed within his arms.

'Sometimes,' Mrs Gimball had once said, 'things 'appen what is not your fault,' and Blanche began to feel, for the first time in her life, the inevitable slide towards certain entrapment. She experienced a claustrophobic terror, as if she were some waxen funeral flower, imprisoned beneath a dome of glass. The square-cut emerald weighed heavily on her left hand; the responsibility of it was becoming more than she could bear.

'I'm a victim of circumstances,' she wailed. 'I never said the words. I never said I'd wed him!'

'But you will, won't yer, ducks?' Mrs Gimball grinned. 'The interest on ten thousand will keep you very nicely — not to mention the two thou' in cash what he gets on his wedding-day.'

In September Hugh insisted on travelling alone to Taunton. He booked rooms at the London Hotel, and visited Eliza daily. On his return he told Blanche, 'Your mother is a very fine woman. We had several long conversations. I told her about our plans to marry. She was quite delighted.'

Blanche twisted the emerald ring and asked shyly, 'Was my sisters there?'

'No,' he said, 'I called in the mornings, when your mother was alone – except for the boy, of course.' He paused, then said, 'I offered her money, but she refused to take it. For the boy's sake, I pleaded, to make his life a little easier. In the end she allowed me to buy her a ton of winter coal. Louis feels the cold more than normal children. I would have done more, Blanche –'

'She got her pride,' flared Blanche, 'and you and me is a long way yet from marching to the altar. 'Tis all very well, you making-up to my mother, but what about the Whalebone Queen, eh? I bet you've never dared to say a word to Aunty, have you?'

'She knows that I've given you my grandmother's ring.'

'Oh, I bet that stuck in her gizzard! Did you mention weddings to her?'

'Well, no,' he said awkwardly, 'these things have to be approached with delicacy, Blanche. I intend to break it gradually to her. Diplomacy is the thing, don't you know?'

She nodded. 'And you got the silver tongue for it, haven't you my fine boy!' They were dining in a quiet restaurant he had recently found down in Chelsea. Just lately, he had tended to seek out the secluded venues. She gazed at him across the table, and all pretence fell away. 'Don't you ask yourself, Hugh,' she said gently, 'what sort of mess you have landed up with? That Lady Claire Whatsit served you something rotten, now you got me! I'm not your sort. I don't like the opera, nor that Shakespeare. I get fed-up with viewing paintings and bits of china, and bidding at auctions. I like the music-halls, and a real good sing-song! I love to watch Marie Lloyd, and Dan Leno. There's that new girl down in Islington called Lottie Collins, the one what sings "Ta-ra-ra-boom-de-ay". You keep promising to take me −'

'And I will. I just need to be alone with you sometimes. Don't you know, Blanche, how much I love you? Don't you feel just a little affection for me?'

She moved uncomfortably in her chair. ''Tis different for a girl,' she said primly. She glanced at him from beneath lowered eyelids. 'My Mama always says that 'tis up to the girl to keep control of a relationship with a man. So you see, Hugh, 'tis my task to keep a tight rein on − well, on any warm feelings I might have towards you.' She paused, significantly. 'Of course, if you feels disappointed in certain regions − after all, you did give me the priceless ring and all they other presents? I wudden blame you for feeling cheated. A few kisses, and a squeeze or two in your aunty's carriage can't be much of a return for the ton of coal what you bought Mama − and the sable cloak what you bought to keep me warm last winter −' She watched his face grow white, saw lines of pain appear around his mouth, and felt triumphant. Oh, but he was so easy to manage, it was almost a shame to take advantage of him. She began to tug at the ring. 'Perhaps,' she murmured, 'it might be only fair if I was to give this back −'

'No, no!' His features crumpled like those of a small boy. 'Don't ever say such a thing,' he begged. 'I respect you, Blanche. You must never think that my gifts are in any way meant to make you feel obligated. You will come to love me in your own time. I can wait, my darling. Just to look at you, to be with you, is all I ask.'

As she told Mrs Gimball later on that evening, 'I quite likes him when he talks all sloppy. He gets so worked-up sometimes, and crushes my fingers until I have to shout for him to stop. Mention of my Mama do always cool him down though. He never had a mother of his own.' She looked thoughtful. 'He'll believe any mortal thing I tell him, just so long as I can convince him that 'tis the dearest wish of my Mama.'

Greenbrook Terrace,
Taunton. October 4th, 1889.

Dear cousin Rhoda,

This letter long overdue, but at last something *good* has come to pass. My girls have moved me out of Hunter's Court, to a nice clean house in Greenbrook Terrace. The rent is two and sixpence weekly, to be paid for by Blanche and Annis. You cannot *think*, dear Rhoda, what it means to live in the Daylight again, and with enough room to turn around in. It have taken some time to put all in order, kitchen range had not been blackleaded regular, nor doorstep whitened. Windows also *very dirty*, but these matters soon set right by me. I washed and ironed the curtains and fittings to my canopied bed, and it do stand looking very much at home in the big front bedroom. Annis and Louis both got rooms of their own, for the first time. Oh how my poor children have *suffered*, Rhoda, in their growing-up. I know that overcrowding is the lot of poor people, but they *was not born* in the circumstances where such Hardships is expected. Poor Blanche slept for years on the kitchen table. No wonder she was happy to leave Home. Now I must confess, dear Rhoda, that much of this good news is due to Blanche, what do give me a *pang at the heart* even as I write it. If I have been wrong in my judgement of her all these years, it will be a very wicked thing. I have not loved her as a Mother should, I know that.

Louis is *much* quieter now since this house have got a long passage what runs from front to back. Annis bought a piece of thick drugget to deaden the sound of his boots on the tiled floor. He do have spells what last a *whole week* when all he can do is pace up and down, *night and day* until he is wore out. My greatest fear is that the new neighbours will get to know about him and start complaining. His fondness for straw have got much worse lately. With Simeon enlisted and gone for a soldier we forgot to fetch Louis any straw from the Market, and he have pulled apart every rush-seated chair in the house. My getting *burned* in that strawrick on the night he was born do explain, of course, this *terrible longing* that he got to handle straw.

It is nice to walk up and down a proper *staircase* once again, and not balance on a stepladder. I got plans for the bit of back garden, if only I can afford seed. That do seem like another lifetime, when I growed the name of Larksleve Farm in flowers.

My other good news have been saved for the last part of this letter. Blanche have got a *rich admirer*, what come down from London to ask me for *my blessing* on their marriage. It was such a shock, Rhoda. He come on the very morning we was moving out from Hunter's Court, and I was quite mortified to have him see us in such shameful conditions. He is a *true gentleman*, Rhoda, more than what I could ever have hoped for Blanche, never mind all her lovely looks and smart clothes. I got a nasty feeling that she is *playing him up*. What is very foolish of her, and I shall *say so*.

I hope this letter finds you all well. You must now be well over your Haysel and Harvest and not so busy. Shall not expect to hear from you again much before the New Year, Rhoda.

My kind regards to Mr James Black, and love to you and your children.

Your devoted cousin, Eliza.

❀

The year of 1890 came in bright and frosty. The glass roof and many windows of Cook's shirt factory, designed to provide the maximum of daylight for sewing machinists, were also prime sources of cold and draughts. Annis almost wept from the fire and pain in her chilblained fingers; she hardly knew which season was the worst. In summer, the machinists drooped and sweated under sunshine and the heat made intolerable by so much glass; whenever it rained they were dripped upon. It was only the spirit and camaraderie among the girls that made life tolerable for most of them. They borrowed hats and bits of finery from one another, sang the latest songs learned in the theatre, and gossiped wickedly about the mean and sanctimonious foreman, a well-set man who bore the nickname 'Lady Clarence'.

The Taunton races were held in Ashmeadows, on ground which lay at the rear of Vivary Park. When the wind was in a certain quarter, on a still day, it was possible for the machinists to hear the cheers and groans of the race-course crowds. Annis had returned to Greenbrook Terrace on that Thursday lunchtime; Louise was entering another period of endless pacing, and she was always fearful, and anxious for Eliza at such times. Reassured that her mother was safe, and the neighbours unaware, Annis returned to the sewing-room, and another five hours of steady labour. She had passed the throngs of race-goers on their way out to Ashmeadows, and wondered, as she always did at such times, if her brother Jack was riding. If only, she thought, if only Mama was not tied, hand and foot, with Louis, she too could have witnessed the triumphs of Jack.

Annis came into the cloakroom where several girls had gathered around a strip of mirror to indulge in their favourite occupation of trying on each other's hats. Finding an almost new hat of black tulle lying unclaimed, Annis perched it on her fair hair. One by one her workmates turned towards her; their chattering and giggling fell away into an unnerving silence. Annis put a hand up to the brim of the hat.

'Why, whatever's wrong, maids?' she cried out, 'I don't look all that hideous do I?'

The owner of the hat took a step towards her. 'I purposely laid it away, on one side,' she said slowly, 'so that nobody 'ud touch it. My mother died two weeks ago; that's my mourning hat what you be wearing.' She paused, significantly, 'And you knows very well what that do mean, Annis!'

Annis knew. She removed the hat and restored it to its owner, and all the time her mind was frantic with the awful thing that she had done. Who would it be? Who in her family had she condemned to an early death, by her careless trying-on of the black hat? She sat down at her machine but could not concentrate upon her stitching. She waited, crouched in an attitude of supplication. 'Dear God, forgive me,' she prayed, 'don't let anything terrible happen because of me.' But she was not at all surprised when, later on that afternoon, a man's voice called up from the stairwell, 'Is somebody working up there what goes by the name of Greypaull?'

'Yes,' she called out, ''tis me you want. My name is Greypaull.'

He was a small man, dressed in racing silks, and out of breath. He had run from the racecourse, through Vivary Park, and into Mount Street. 'They said you worked here,' he told her, ''tis bad news, I'm afraid. Your brother Jack is dead.'

She had threatened so often to faint in times of anguish. Now, Annis felt the blood leave her head, a coldness grip her body; she swayed and would have fallen, but for her workmates' outstretched arms. When she opened her eyes it was to find her clothing loosened, and a glass of water at her lips. She pushed the glass away and sat up. 'Have you told my mother?' she asked the jockey.

'Well – no. Somebody said that Jack's sister worked at Cook's. I thought the news 'ud come better from you, you being fam'ly, see!'

Annis stared into the anxious faces. 'How can I go and tell her,' she cried, 'when 'tis all my fault? If I hadden tried on Milly's funeral bonnet then none of this would have happened.'

The girls tried to reassure her. It was no more than a daft story, they insisted. A superstitious tale told by the old wives. Her trying-on of the black hat could not possibly have caused Jack's death. They looked to the jockey for confirmation.

'That's right,' he said, 'you must know, miss, how reckless your Jack was. Us have always said that he'd come undone, sooner or later. There was this roan, see! Ugly great bugger, and nasty-tempered. Why, no jockey with any sense would have tackled him, not even for the extra money. So up steps Jacko! Keen as mustard, like usual. "I'll take him on", says he, and up he gets, no saddle, no nothing!' The man hesitated. 'You might as well hear it all from me. He come off at the very last fence, straight onto his head; the ground is rock hard with frost, as you know. His neck was broke. He was dead before we reached him.'

❁

Eliza had pegged out her washing, not really expecting it to dry in the freezing air. She went back into the kitchen, to find Annis seated and silent before the fire. She looked at the clock, and knew at once that something terrible had happened. 'Why, whatever brings you home at this time?' she demanded. 'You haven't lost your job, have you?'

Annis stiffened and clasped her hands together. 'I shan't cry,' she said dully, 'because I know that'll only upset you. We got to be brave, Mama. Some very bad news was broke to me, this day, in the factory, and Mr Clarence have give me permission to come home and tell you.'

The words, rehearsed many times as Annis had walked from Mount Street, sounded unnecessarily theatrical to Eliza. 'Oh for goodness sake,' she complained, 'get it out, girl. Whatever have you left your work for?'

'Our Jack is killed. He fell at a high fence at Ashmeadows. His neck was broke. One of the other jockeys come to tell me.'

Eliza's hand sought her old scar; she rubbed at her cheek and eye and said quietly, 'When did all this come to pass?'

'Must have been about half-past one, I think.'

''Tis nearly four, maid. Where have you been, till now?'

'I walked about. I cudden come home. I didden know how best to tell it.'

A sound at the kitchen door made them look towards it; Madelina stood, in the open doorway, white-faced and wooden. 'You've heard?' she asked.

They nodded.

'I shan't cry, Mama,' she said, 'because I know that'll upset you.' Mina's voice broke upon the last insistent word. She moved to stand closer to Annis, and Eliza was conscious of a mounting horror at the dry-eyed and unemotional aspect of her two daughters. Suddenly, she remembered that old selfish cry of her own mother. 'Now don' 'ee cry, maid. That'll only upset me.' She recalled, how in times of sorrow she had longed to let go and weep in her mother's arms. Eliza made a tentative move towards Mina and Annis, but was halted before the coldness of their eyes. It came to her that she, by her own lifelong attitudes of withdrawal, had destroyed all that was ever to be spontaneous and tender in them. Here they stood, three grieving women, brought suddenly face to face by the death of a beloved son and brother. So great was their isolation, one from the other, so strong their inhibitions, that not a single tear could be shed for James John Daniel. The Greypaulls, thought Eliza, had become the saddest of all company; they were a family who did not know how to weep together.

❀

Madelina collapsed and was taken to her bed on that same night. Nothing, it now seemed, could console her for the loss of Jack, not even Laura, who, at the age of five, was confused and frightened by her mother's strange prostration. Annis was obliged to share her time equally between Mama and Madelina.

'The funeral's to be on Monday afternoon,' she told her sister. 'No doubt you'll be feeling a bit stronger by then. Mama had a note from the stables in Bishop's Hull. The owner of the horse is to pay all Jack's funeral expenses.' She paused in her tidying of the bedclothes and looked down at the drawn and sallow face upon the pillows. 'So he won't need to have a pauper's funeral,' she assured Mina. 'Everything will be done proper, you'll see!'

But Mina did not see. Her grief, when the day came, was so severe that she could not leave her bed. It was not until Wednesday evening that she revived sufficiently to demand of Annis a description of the sad event. David Lambert had volunteered to watch over Louis for those few hours of Jack's burial and, as Annis said, it had been a sad little cortège, with only herself and Mama to follow. Annis wondered if she should confess to the trying-on of Milly's funeral bonnet, but decided that Mina had enough to bear. Mina however continued to ask questions.

'Was it only you and Mama at the graveside?' she persisted.

Annis considered. 'Can you keep a secret? Mama said you was not to be told, but I think you should be.' She hesitated. 'There was another party at the graveside. A young woman, with a child in her arms. She stood a little way off, like as if she was frightened. Oh, Mina it was awful! As we began to move off down the path, the girl barred our way. "Don't you know who I am?" she asked Mama. Well Mama said no, of course. "I'm Jack's wife," the girl said, "and this is his son. Didden he never tell you about us?'' ''No,'' said Mama, ''and I don't believe you! My Jack would never have kept this from me.'' ''Oh,'' said the girl, ''you needn't worry, Mrs Greypaull. Nicholas and me won't be asking nothing from you. My brother is about to emigrate to the place called Canada. Me and Nicky is to travel with him. Take a good look at your grandson, for you'll never clap eyes on him again.'' '

The effect of this confidence upon Madelina was not at all what Annis had expected; she had foreseen shock, amazement even, but not the slow burn of guilty red that reached to Mina's hairline. Annis said, 'You knowed, didden you? You was already privy to it.'

Mina nodded. 'Jack told me he was married more than a year ago. I kept promising him that I'd break it to Mama, but I never seemed to manage it.'

'But why did he keep it so secret?' demanded Annis, and then she saw the hooded lids close down upon the green eyes, and understood. 'Oh – so 'twas like that was it? You was ever the secretive one, our Mina. You always did keep Jackie all to yourself.'

'I kept meaning to tell it, truly I did.'

'You should have told Mama,' Annis whispered.

'I know that now. Why do you think I feel so bad? I wudden have harmed our Jackie, not for all the world! Why, I loved him more than any living soul, save my Laura!'

'And now that baby is took away to Canada, and Mama won't never see Jack's son grow up.' Annis looked at the stricken face of Madelina, and felt an easement of her own guilt. Compared to the crime committed by her sister, the trying-on of a funeral bonnet was neither here, nor there!

❉

Up in London, Blanche, who had hardly known, and most certainly had never loved her older brother, now wore black with all the strictness and devotion of the most dedicated Victorian mourner. She could hardly be unaware that unrelieved mourning served to emphasise the whiteness of her skin, the glory of her auburn hair. Jet necklaces, and earrings, dramatic sidecombs, ostrich-feather fans of deepest black, all combined to convince Hugh Fitzgerald of her grief for Jack. Spring slipped into summer, and summer into autumn, and to every suggestion of wedding plans she turned a shocked and disapproving face.

'You knows very well that my family is in mourning. Why, whatever would my Mama say if we was to announce a wedding before the year's up?'

Down in Taunton, the letters arrived regularly from India, and were answered by Eliza. Madelina Lambert left her bed, and emerged once again to live her life. People who had not seen her since the death of Jack, were shocked to observe that in the intervening months Mina's black hair had turned to a snowy white.

❋

It was not until the month of August that Eliza felt sufficiently composed to write a letter to Suamico.

Greenbrook Terrace,
Taunton. August 10th, 1890.

Dear cousin Rhoda,

Have tried to pick up the pen many times in the past months, but could not. Have sad news to tell you. My oldest son, James John Daniel, known to me as Jackie, was killed in a riding accident at Ashmeadows last January. Even now, seeing it wrote down, I cant hardly believe it. It was such a shock to us all, Rhoda. Madelina's hair have turned *snow-white*, they was always so devoted to one another.

My other shock was that Jack *was married*, in *secret*. He had a baby boy, what he had *never showed me*. The wife and child

344

turned up at the graveside, all unbeknownst to us. Why, Rhoda? That's what I ask myself, over and over. Why should he have been so *secretive*, and never told me? I know that I sent him away from Home, but I had no CHOYSE. There was no more room for him at Home. Why – our Blanche had to sleep atop the kitchen table, we was so overcrowded. Jack always come back once a year to see me, and now he's gone for ever, and things cant be put right between us. This is the *greatest* sorrow I have ever lived thru, Rhoda. That have made an old woman of me.

I mentioned that Simeon had gone away when I last wrote to you, but I never told you the whys and wherefores. He lost the chance of a good job in London because he cant read nor write. He *blamed* me for it, and went off and joined the Army. Now he's mixed up with wars and fighting, and cant let us know where he is. Of all my children, only Annis do bide close me, but *why*, Rhoda? I have tried to be a good Mother. All I have *ever* done was done from love of them.

Feel too bad to write any more at present. Please send a line or two if you can spare the time. My state is parlous, and nobody to weep with. I never *allowed* my girls to *cry*, and now they dont seem able to.

Love to Mr Black and all your family.

Your loving cousin, Eliza.

❀

Rhoda's reply was prompt and sympathetic. In October she wrote:

Suamico. October 4th 1890.

Dear cousin Eliza,

Your letter received today with great sorrow by me and Mr Black. To learn about the death of Jack was a great shock to us. A death from illness is bad enough, Eliza, but *accidents* is awful hard to bear. But the Lord works in a mysterius way, and we shall have to wait until Judgement Day to know the whys and wherefores of such sorrows. I hope you are feeling a bit better in yourself. What a *blessing* that you still got your Annis at Home. Is there no young man in her life yet? Mr Black puts a speshul prayer for you in our family prayers. Do not think yourself *alone*, Dear Cousin. There is them in Suamico who think about you every day, and will *never forget* you. Praps Jack was only waiting for the *right time* to tell you about his wife and baby?

I will tell you some of our news, what will take your mind away from your troubles for a spell. I cant call to mind if I told you about *all* my grandchildren. Dont think I did, so will tell you now.

I wrote you about Alma, she was George and Satie's first born. Well, since then have come little Rosalind and baby George, and another child expected in December. So you can see, dear cousin, the *Salter line* is going strong in De Pere, Brown County. My son George turning out to be a *family man* and *good father*, after all. Satie makes such a lovely Mother and good Wife. Already she got a book of recipes wrote out, all in her own hand, what puts my plain home cooking *in the shade*.

Life seems to be all cooking, and laying down of provishuns, Eliza. We have Winters here like I *never saw* in Old England. I make my own sausage and render a year's lard at one go. I seem to be pickling and preserving for three parts of every year. Letter writing, as you will have noticed, gets done mostly in the Winter, also sewing. We eat a whole lot of hog meat. Father Black bilt us a smokehouse last year what is a *great help* in keeping meat. I never did get used to the v. hot summers in Wisconsin. We Greypaulls always did have skin what burned awful bad, and I always have to wear a big broad bonnet, outdoors.

You once asked me about our farmhouse, Eliza. Well, wood is v. cheap here, and plenty of it, so most building done with wood. Church, schoolhouse, houses and barns all bilt of wood drawed from the Wisconsin forests. That takes a deal of paint, of course, to keep our house and barns spruced-up, and Fire is a *big risk* with so many kerosene lamps about the place. When we want another room we just build-on. I got a nice front room, Eliza, and a piano, but never *time* to play it. It is a hard life, but the prarie land v. fertile, and farming in my blood, as you well know. Father Black have made up his mind that we need a new barn, and is all set to raise us a *round one*, that is the new fashun hereabouts. Will let you know how this goes on. Father Black busy in the fields at this time of year, plowing and discing. Can never let up, not for a single day. *Prices falling* all the time.

Hope this letter finds you in better spirits, Dear Cousin. I know how it is to lose a son. But God is good. He will send you consolations.

Please write soon. We all worry about you.

Much love to you all.

Your loving cousin, Rhoda.

✤

There would always be those perimeters beyond which she was incapable of straying. With the exception of Mrs Gimball, who stood as both surrogate mother and mentor, Blanche considered friendship to be an unnecessary and dangerous indulgence. The only relationships she would ever trust were those bound by blood, and sealed with a lifetime of association. The little house in Greenbrook Terrace, and that uneasy and explosive gathering of the sisters around their mother, was the cabal that was always to draw her back, inevitably, to Taunton.

Blanche had only to open her mother's door to feel doubts and indecision seize her. In London she was cosseted by Mrs Gimball, treated with respect by her Liberty employers, and loved to distraction by Hugh Fitzgerald. She stepped high in London, but in Taunton she had remained the interloper, and was the target for hostility and envy; yet she came back, hopeful that perhaps this time her Mama would come to love her.

Mama had been gratified to see Blanche in deepest mourning. 'You'll have a shock,' warned her mother, 'when you first see Madelina. Since poor Jack's death, her hair have turned snow-white. So just mind your tongue, miss, and don't remark upon it.'

'But her can't be more than thirty.'

'Shock,' said Eliza. 'Shock and grief, and disappointment.'

'Disappointment?'

Eliza sighed. 'You might as well know, I suppose. Jack had a wife and child in Bishop's Hull. I've tried to understand why he never saw fit to tell me. I know he was sent away from home when he was only twelve, but that was never my fault. We was still his family! Poor Mina. She felt it worse than anybody. They was always so close and loving as children.'

When Mina appeared at Greenbrook Terrace, Blanche was overcareful not to look in her direction.

'Well, you might as well say what you're thinking, Blanche!'

'Say what?'

'That I look older than Mama with this white hair.'

'No,' said Blanche, 'I finds it quite becoming on you.' She bit her lower lip, and stammered her way across a bridge of unfamiliar words. 'You – you must have loved him quite a lot? I mean – for your hair to change colour – that must have been a great shock. I never felt like that, about anybody. I can't even imagine how that could feel. I was sorry to hear about Jack, but that seems to have done something terrible to you.' She spoke gently but with meaning. 'After all, he was but a brother, Mina. 'Tis surely your husband what should come first in your affections.'

'Husbands is different,' said Madelina. 'David Lambert is not a blood relation. Jackie was my baby brother. He was give to me to care for when he was in the cradle. He was ever wild and reckless. 'Twas always my task to put salve on his bruises, and bandage his cut knees. Nobody knows what I suffered when he was sent away from home. I think I always knowed that something dreadful would befall him.' She looked up at Blanche. 'I got no tears left. But you wudden understand that. I only ever saw you cry from rage or disappointment. You didden care about Jack, never mind all your fancy mourning outfits.' Mina sighed. 'I know that you don't like me. You made that very plain when we was children. But you only get back what you give to other people — and I don't mean money!'

'What do you mean, then?'

Mina sighed. 'You shows no proper thought for others. Mama thinks a lot of that Fitzgerald fella. She wants you married, Blanche, settled down and safe. Two years, you said. Two years and I'll bring my rich husband home to show you.'

'And so I will! I always keep my word.'

'Better watch out, our Blanche! Long engagements can lead to disappointment.'

Blanche laughed. 'Don't you worry about Hugh. I got him dangling from my little finger. Anyway,' her features took on an expression of martyrdom and self-denial, 'we cudden get wed while I was still in mourning.'

'Come January,' said Mina, 'your year of wearing black will be finished. Better watch out, Blanche! You might lose him yet. You can't be the only fetching piece what treads the London pavements!'

❊

Blanche sat alone in the chilly compartment of the West Country train. Solitude had always made her feel uneasy.

She stood up and moved restlessly about the carriage. She gazed into the oval mirror, and remembered that first journey up to London. Then, as now, she had been dressed in black, but filled with hope and anticipation. In almost ten years she had achieved so little. A certain gloss had been set upon her beauty, she wore Hugh Fitzgerald's emerald ring. She recalled Madelina's words. 'You only get back what you give, and I don't mean money . . . you can't be the only fetching piece what treads the London pavements.'

The absence of Jack, and the desertion by Simeon, had cast a gloom across this visit. Blanche grimaced at her reflected image; suddenly she hated the unrelieved black and resolved that she would never wear it again. Her thoughts began to wander. There had been a tea-gown of summer-blue that she had admired in Swan and Edgar's window. She began to study her upper lip, fearful of finding an incipient cold-sore. Perhaps Hugh might be persuaded to take her to dinner at Romano's? She began to think about Edward Albert, Prince of Wales. She had recently bought a photograph of him, and positioned it on her dressing-table, where she might see it straight away on waking. She loved to dwell on those sturdy Royal legs, that stocky body, the neatly pointed beard, and those slumberous, heavy-lidded eyes. He was said to speak with a thick and gutteral accent. He was rumoured to be the brutal and inconsiderate lover of at least a thousand women. It was also said that Bertie, heir to the throne of England, was careful only to indulge himself in the company of married ladies. Blanche thought about Liberty's store and her own position in it. She had no real skills, only a fashionable face and figure; and tastes in women, she suspected, were apt to change.

❀

The snow began to fall in late afternoon, light powdery

stuff that blew about the city pavements but did not settle. Hugh sat on a bench in Paddington Station and waited for Blanche. It was, he thought, rather like sitting in some vast and echoing cathedral, with gaslights instead of candles, and a shifting congregation. He had met every West Country train since midday, had watched the great engines roar in and out, belching steam and fire. He had waited, first at the barrier and now upon the platform. He had heard from Mrs Gimball how Blanche, money all spent on her family in Taunton, would often have to make her way on foot all the way from Paddington to St Martin's Lane.

The station was crowded with people of all classes. He had watched their arrivals and departures, their farewells and greetings. He had witnessed that day the laughter and tears of a hundred people. He wondered how she would greet him this time. He could not bear it when she went away; he required her always to be within his hands' reach, needed to know her every movement. He was jealous of her relatives; those people in Taunton to whom she seemed drawn back like a moth to flame. These visits, according to Mrs Gimball, were never happy occasions. Hugh confessed that he did not understand about families, could not imagine the ways of a mother with her children. He had never known his mother; his brother was a stranger. Aunt Porteous, indulgent but undemonstrative, had given him banknotes in lieu of kisses. He suffered a small death each time Blanche went away. Would his emerald ring still be on her finger? He stood up, drew the Inverness cape close about him, and began to pace up and down the platform.

A train drew in, topped with snow and looking like an iced cake. She was standing at the lowered window of the first compartment. His relief at the sight of her was so great that at first he could not move. She stepped down from the train, assisted by a porter, and he saw the familiar tilt of her head, the arch of her outstretched foot, the exquisite face,

351

framed by the collar of her sable cloak. He took a step towards her, barred her path, and waited.

She smiled at him, and lowered her travelling bag onto the platform. She reached both hands out towards him. 'I thought you might be here,' she murmured. She lifted her face up to his, and he kissed her.

'Your lips are cold,' he whispered.

'I know,' she said, 'it's got something to do with the weather.'

They laughed, and it was, he thought, the first time they had ever truly laughed together. He could sense the change in her, and knew that something important must have happened to her down in Taunton.

'Blanche', he said, 'I –'

She closed his lips with one gloved finger. 'Hush,' she said, 'I want to ask you something.'

He became very still. So this was how she would betray him, with a smile, a kiss, a finger to his lips. He ceased to breathe. He felt his heartbeat quicken. He failed to hear her words, and she was obliged to repeat them.

'Hugh,' she said, 'how soon can we get married?'

❇

Mrs Porteous was neither surprised nor condemnatory. She was not delighted, but Hugh had not expected miracles. Her comment, on hearing his exciting news, was sharp and to the point.

'I've had the young woman thoroughly investigated.'

'You've done what?'

'Only my duty, Hugh. The Lord God in his wisdom saw fit to entrust you to me. How will I ever face my poor brother when we meet in Heaven, if I have not done all in my power to ensure the safety of his motherless son?'

'So what have you found out about Blanche?'

Mrs Porteous smiled. 'The news is satisfactory in some ways, dear boy! These Greypaulls it would seem, are quite a high-born family. My investigator discovered a line that goes back to King Henry the Eighth.' She paused. 'Not that a blood tie with him is anything to boast of! However, it would appear that there were Greypaulls at the Court of Elizabeth. They have counted architects and barristers among their number. They have their share of black sheep – but then, so does the Royal House of Hanover. It seems that the young woman's father was a man of doubtful character, a weak and gullible creature who pledged his entire estate to cover a gambling debt incurred by a friend. The mother is a very different proposition. A woman of strong and definite character, who had accepted her altered position in life with Christian fortitude and great courage. As for the young woman herself, my investigator reports that he was unable to discover any scandal or scurrilous talk about her, even in that Life School!'

'You had no right to have questions asked about her. Why could you not taken my word? Have you ever known me to be a liar?'

'No,' she said, 'I have not. But an infatuated man will believe only what he wants to.'

'It's not an infatuation. I love her with all my heart and soul.'

'I hope you haven't told her that!'

'Repeatedly. Why should I not do so?'

'Oh, my poor Hugh! How little you know of the ways of women.' She looked enquiringly at him. 'You are absolutely set upon this marriage with her? You wouldn't consider some less binding arrangement? Of good lineage she may be – but her speech is quite atrocious. Her manners appear to ape those of that pawnshop-keeper. How we shall ever introduce her to our friends I simply do not know!'

'Marriage!' he said firmly. 'And if Blanche offends your ideas of what is fitting then I shall take her far away. Paris might be an interesting place in which to live –'

'Oh no!' she interrupted. 'Oh no, dear boy. You must

never think of leaving me in England.' She smiled, with difficulty. 'Dearest Blanche! I'll do all within my power to help her. We'll go shopping together. You shall continue to have your own private apartments here with me, in this house. The wedding will be in Bath Abbey. All the Fitzgeralds have married there! We must start to make plans, right away. Bring the dear girl round to dinner this evening. There's so much we shall have to decide and talk over!'

❀

The nightmare had troubled Blanche since childhood. Months would pass, sometimes whole years, and she would not dream at all; and then, at times of excitement and anticipation, she would rise up in her bed, screaming and fearful and quite unable to explain the precise nature of her haunting. In this latest and most spectacular episode she had shrieked loudly enough to bring Mrs Gimball running.

'Why, whatever is it, ducks? I thought that you was being murdered!' Mrs Gimball, homely in bright pink flannel, her grey hair loose across her shoulders, brought in cups of cocoa, and sat beside Blanche while her trembling lessened. 'Over-excited, that's your trouble. High-strung girls like you needs to live very quiet. Since Master Fitz put your wedding date in *The Times* you've 'ad screaming fits every night.'

Blanche sipped her cocoa. ''Tis too soon, Ma. I can't never be ready by March the 9th.'

'Why not, gel? That gives you all of three months, and from wot you says the Whalebone Queen 'ave already took over most of the arrangements.'

'That's the trouble. She wants us to live with her in Russell Square. She says that we got to get married in Bath Abbey. She've even picked out my wedding gown, and what she calls my trousseau.' Blanche giggled. 'If 'tis left up to her I'll be going-away in fleecy-bodices and red-flannel drawers.'

Mrs Gimball looked troubled. 'Wot says Master Fitz to all this?'

Blanche frowned, and forgot to smooth away the crease. 'He don't stand up to her enough. Like I told him, 'tis our lives and our wedding. He says that we must make her happy.' Blanche bit her lower lip, and looked thoughtful. 'I get the feeling that he do rely on her for gifts of money.'

'He's certainly spent a fortune on you, ducks! Perhaps he's in debt, and depending on aunty to save his bacon!'

'Well, if that's the case, he can whistle for his bloody wedding! I won't be wed in Bath Abbey. I'll get hitched here in London, or not at all.'

'Don't suppose the likes o' me will get invited?'

'Of course you will, Ma! Mr Solomon, too, if we can find him.'

Mrs Gimball looked thoughtful. 'Come to think about it, Blanche, we ain't seen hide nor hair of 'im for ever such a long time. I wonder what he's up to, where he's living.'

'Oh, he'll be all right, Ma. Mr Solomon got other friends besides us. Perhaps he won't never come back no more,' her tone was regretful. 'I shan't forget him though, not in all my life long. He's the only man I ever know'd who didden want something from me. He could pay a compliment and make me feel so important! He compared me once to some woman in the Bible. "Who is she that looketh forth as the morning, fair as the moon, clear as the sun, and terrible as an army with banners?" I think on they words very often when I feel low. Poor Mr Solomon. We is two of a kind. He is always looking for his true love. "I sought him but I found him not", that's what he told me. "The watchmen that go about the city found me: to whom I said, Saw ye him whom my soul loveth?" ' She turned to Mrs

Gimball. 'That's what he'll be doing, looking for his true love.' She sighed. 'Trouble is,' she murmured, 'Mr Solomon's like me, he do more often find the liddle foxes. They foxes what do spoil the vine.'

The arguments dragged on over Christmas and into New Year. Mrs Porteous informed Blanche that a loving wife should submit, with a good grace, to each and all of her husband's wishes.

'But I bain't his wife yet,' Blanche cried, 'nor never shall be at this rate!' She plucked the name of a London church from the air, 'St George's in Hanover Square,' she declared, 'I wudden dream of getting wedded anywhere else but there!'

Mrs Porteous described Blanche to Hugh as being aggressive, headstrong and hot-headed. 'You should,' she advised him, 'begin as you mean to continue. Why, she owes everything to you. If you hadn't taken her up, as you did, she might, at this moment be – ' She halted at the fury in his face. 'Oh well, you are obviously resolved upon this marriage, but I must speak my mind. Blanche, I feel sure, is a dear and sweetly-good girl; she is, after all, your own choice. But there are certain provoking habits – a tendency to flaunt – a lack of self control – a pertness in her manner towards me. Her evening gowns, I have noticed, are a little too low-cut. Her day gowns are never quite long enough to conceal her ankles.'

Hugh grinned.

'You won't find it so amusing,' snapped his aunt, 'when, as your wife, she provokes unsavoury gossip.'

Blanche could not, Mrs Porteous insisted, be married from a St Martin's Lane pawnshop, and so Hugh was moved out of Russell Square, six weeks before the wedding, to live at his Club, while Blanche was installed in a vast and gloomy guest-room. Aunt Letitia, seized with wedding fever, overrode the bride's objection that she had only wanted a quiet ceremony.

'We have a duty, my dear, to make this a social occasion.
I've attended so many functions over the years, this will be
my opportunity to return some favours. Your choice of St
George's was, it appears, very sound.' Mrs Porteous seemed
surprised. 'It's become quite the place for a fashionable
wedding, so they tell me.'

The decision by Blanche that her dress should be made of
Liberty's wild-silk, and in sweet-pea colours, was firmly
overruled.

'My dear girl, we cannot have you walking up the aisle
looking like a rainbow! Virginal,' said Mrs Porteous, 'that
is the effect for which we shall try to aim.' She looked
doubtfully at Blanche. 'Honiton lace, I think, over ivory
satin, with a hood of thick lace which will help to cover up
that – that noticeable hair. White shoes and stockings.
White gloves and flowers.' She paused. 'No; perhaps a
prayer-book, bound in white leather, might help to give a
better –'

'Just a mo',' Blanche interrupted, 'is you planning a
wedding-gown or my bloody shroud?'

'Don't say "just a mo'"', dear girl, it's such bad form.
As for your rather colourful language; it might have been
acceptable in the pawnshop, but it simply won't do for
Russell Square.'

Blanche escaped from her gaoler on only one occasion.
Finding the Honourable Letitia laid low with a sick
headache, and confined to her room, Blanche ordered the
brougham to be brought round, and instructed Jones to
drive her to St Martin's Lane.

'He'll split on me, of course,' she told Mrs Gimball, 'he's
a proper liddle spy. But I just had to get out of that house
for an hour.' She kicked her boots into a corner, pulled the
wicker chair up to the fire, and spread her stockinged toes
before the blaze. 'Oh,' she sighed, 'that do feel lovely.'

Mrs Gimball grinned. 'Cup o' cocoa, and a good lump of bread-pudding?' she enquired.

'Oh, please!' said Blanche. 'I could eat a horse; I gets that hungry.'

'Don't they feed you proper then, ducks?'

Blanche shook her head. 'That old bitch is so mean with food, Ma. You wudden never believe the carry-on what we had at that first breakfast together. There's always kidneys and bacon, but like I told her, I don't fancy offal, not first thing in the morning. Then they eats some sort of rice stuff. Well, I never did go much on rice-pudden, especially for breakfast. No,' said Blanche, 'what I really fancied was the toast. Give the old girl her due, she only buys the very best butter; and as for the jam, preserves she calls it, well that was really lovely!'

'At least you got something to eat, then?'

'But I didden, Ma. I took this slice of toast, see, and spread it ever so thick with butter. Then I topped it up with apricot preserve stuff.' She giggled. 'By the time I was finished I could hardly get it in my mouth.' Blanche sighed. 'I could see she was watching me. She tries to make me nervous at the table, but I knows my way around a bit better these days. All of a sudden madam purses up her lips. "Now, Blanche," she says, "don't you think that's rather greedy? There's really no need to take quite such large helpings of butter and preserves — especially on only the one slice of toast." '

'Whatever did you say, ducks.'

'I cudden say a word at first, my mouth was so crammed full of toast. Not that I didden try, mind you! I had butter running down my chin, and crumbs spitting-out all over the table. In the end, I took a swig of coffee — oh, and then I told her!' She grinned. 'I can talk as posh as her, when I really needs to. "Aiy am not," I said, "in the habit of being told what I can or cannot eat. In my previous lodgings I was asked what I preferred. If bread and jam is the only decent thing what you can offer me at breakfast, then don't complain when I make a bit of a pig of myself. I get hungry, and if you can't afford to feed me, then I'll ask Mr Liberty if I can have my job back!'' ' Blanche nodded her satisfaction. 'That shut her up, I can tell you. I eats exactly what I like, since then, and no complaints!'

'So you gave your job up permanent, Blanche?'

'Well, I had to, Ma. They didden want to lose me, and I didden want to go. But with Hugh being one of the leisured class, it wudden have looked proper for him to have a wife what works.'

'You'll miss it.'

'I already do, Ma. That's not all I miss either.' She looked around her. 'This have been my home for the past ten years. The only real home I ever had.'

'You'll 'ave your own place now, Blanche. All fine and elegant, exactly as you always dreamed about.' Mrs Gimball closed her eyes. 'Just like a fairy tale, this is! You marrying Master Fitz, and living 'appy ever after.'

Blanche looked anxious. 'You'll be at the church, won't you, Ma? You'll be the only one to sit on my side.'

'I'll be there, ducks. Wouldn't miss it for the world.'

Wedding invitations had not been sent to Taunton. Blanche had told several lies in order to ensure that Mama and the family were not asked to come to London. She could not have explained this determination to keep secret her plans. Perhaps even now, she was not totally committed to Hugh Fitzgerald. If, at the very last moment, she could not bear the prospect of marriage to him, how much easier escape would be without the critical and condemnatory presence of Mama and Madelina.

The suite of rooms used by Hugh when resident in London was on the second floor of the house in Russell Square. His insistence that she should view these rooms, only one month before the wedding, seemed ominous to Blanche. Whenever she asked questions he became evasive; he would talk about the honeymoon to be spent in Paris, followed by a trip to Scotland in the springtime. He talked about South Africa; recent unrest in the gold and diamond mines had made a visit from the English owners a matter of some urgency, and Blanche, so he said, would love Johannesburg in May. No mention was made of a separate residence. The rich it seemed were concerned only with the immediate future. Blanche had envisaged her married life in some tree-enshrouded house in St John's Wood, or an apartment in some Regent's Park mansion. The thought of herself in close and inescapable proximity to Hugh had been made bearable only by his vague assurance that she would, one day, have her own home, to furnish and staff as she pleased. His manner as they climbed the stairs to his apartment was defiant and ingratiating.

'It's a typical bachelor establishment,' he said, nervously, 'probably needs the woman's touch. It's arranged pretty much to suit my own tastes.'

Her recent exposure to the new style of furnishings and fabrics as sold by Mr Arthur Liberty, had given Blanche a distinct and revolutionary notion of how she would arrange her own home. She dreamed of light and airy rooms, furniture of hand-carved Chinese blackwood, and Japanese bamboo. Her walls would be papered in the new 'Damasque' hangings; she would choose gentle blues and lemons, discreet shades of ivory and eau-de-nil. Her rooms would be divided by fretwork and Moorish arches. Her shelves would hold blue-and-white Porcelain, and ornaments of cloisonné enamel.

Hugh opened a heavy oaken door and Blanche breathed in the smell of stale cigar smoke; a fire bured in every room, even in his absence. This place was dim and stuffy, shrouded in tasselled curtains and furnished with items so hideous that she thought it a kindness to keep them in permanent gloom. The walls, papered in red flock, bore a rash of amateurish sketches and water-colours. There were mahogany overmantels above every fireplace, bulging jardinières which held aspidistras, a hearthrug that had once been a tiger, an umbrella-stand made out of an elephant's foot.

Blanche marched to a window, dragged aside the layers of lace and velvet, and threw up the sash. She looked down upon the Square, bright and cold under winter sunshine. Hugh stood on the recumbent tiger, his back towards the fire.

'Well,' he said hesitantly, 'what do you think?'

She closed the window and turned back to face him. She spoke bluntly. 'It's bloody awful! The view is the only decent thing about it. I should suffocate in this place.' She grinned. 'I can guess what you're thinking. A girl what's lived for ten years in a pawnshop shudden have ideas above her station.' She crossed the room to stand before him. 'I got my own plans, Hugh. I don't want to start off our lives together underneath your aunty's roof.' She lowered her eyelids. 'I know that I got a lot to learn, and I hope that I can change my ways, be the sort of wife what you expect and deserve.' She gazed up into his face. 'Oh, Hugh! I'd set my heart on us having our own place. You and me, going shopping together, choosing furniture and carpets. Liberty's got such lovely things. Let's go up to Regent Street, let's pick out –'

'I can't, Blanche,' he interrupted, 'I don't have any money.'

She reached for the nearest chair and subsided into it. 'No money? Whatever do you mean?'

'Oh it's only a temporary embarrassment,' he reassured her. 'I receive a lump sum of two thousand pounds on my marriage. But these things take time, Blanche. Solicitors move slowly, don't you know!'

'No,' she muttered, 'I don't know; and who, might I ask, is forking-out for this posh wedding, and the honeymoon in Paris?'

'My Aunt Porteous. She wants to do it. It gives her great pleasure.'

'It also makes me and you beholden to her, and that's exactly what she wants.'

'That's most unfair, Blanche!'

'Is it? Is it really?' She began to prowl; she opened cupboards and peered into corners. There were glass-fronted cabinets crammed with china figures, drawers filled with birds' eggs packed carefully in cotton wool. She found cases of pinned butterflies and moths, lumps of rock and strange coins.

'I'm a bit of a collector,' he explained, but she did not answer. He followed her into the study; she knew that it must be his study because of the books stacked on every surface, and shelved from floor to ceiling.

'Have you read all this lot?' she enquired.

'Most of them. I do a lot of reading.'

She halted before the music-stand, and twanged a string of the violin which lay beside it. 'You never told me that you played the fiddle.'

'I'm not very good. I merely scrape a little.'

She moved to a stack of unframed canvasses, and began to flip through them.

'Yours?'

He nodded. 'Land and seascapes, painted in South Devon. A little place called Dawlish. I go there every summer, or at least I used to before – '

'Before you met me?' She turned to face him. 'So this is how you spend your time? You do a bit of drawing, have a scrape on the fiddle, count up your birds' eggs, and they dirty old pennies. You never done an honest day's work in your life, have you?' She gestured towards the bookshelves.

362

'I bet you think yourself very clever. Well I think all that reading is a waste of time – I think –'

He took her arm and led her from the study. 'Don't be upset, Blanche. I know that you don't want to live here, and I promise that you shall not. As soon as my money comes through we will buy our own place.'

She shrugged his hand away and pointed to a closed door. 'What's in there?'

'Go and see,' he smiled. 'I think you'll be surprised.'

Blanche opened the door and stepped across the threshold. She saw a bed, canopied in blue, and mounted on a dais. There were huge mahogany wardrobes, a wash-hand-stand, and a sofa upholstered in dark blue velvet. She stood beside the bed and remembered Larksleve, and her eyes filled with tears. She stared at the facing wall with wet unfocused eyes, and then realised, slowly, that in this room all the paintings were of herself. What lunacy, she wondered, could have possessed him? He saw her almost daily, surely he had no need of these daubs and sketches to bring her to mind? Her face and person must be the last image in his eyes when he lay down to sleep, and the first to meet his gaze when he awoke each morning. The very notion made Blanche feel uneasy. So much intensity of feeling, so strong an obsession, seemed at first thought to be almost indecent. Until she remembered her own bedevilment with Jye. Now there was a case of true possession; of a woman so pixilated, so deranged by love that she had used a dangerous magic on the only man who could ever arouse such a passion in her. Blanche became aware, fleetingly, that when it came to a matter of unwise attachment, the dividing line between herself and Hugh was indeed thin! She thrust away the uncomfortable insight, and turned back to the paintings.

The portraits covered one whole wall. There was Blanche as Simeon Solomon had seen her, sixteen years old: a pagan and supplicant figure, praying beneath bare branches. There was Blanche as she had posed in Chelsea, soulful in flowing robes, one perfect breast artfully exposed. Another Blanche gazed endlessly into several mirrors, her nudity repeated in ever diminishing views. Then came the respectable Blanche, as seen by The Primrose Hill School. Simpering and sweetly-pretty, in pink and white frills, holding a parasol and spaniel puppy.

Hugh came up behind her. He placed his hands upon her waist, and swung her around. 'I've been collecting them,' he muttered, 'since the day I first met you.'

She stared at him, uncertainly at first, and then with growing anger. 'My God!' she shouted, 'it's small wonder you got no money left! New wallpaper 'ud have come cheaper!' She waved a hand at the wall. 'If I'd a-knowed you wanted my pictures that bad, I could have had photographs taken for you.'

'But — I thought you would be flattered. I've tracked you down through every studio and saleroom.' He sighed. 'I'm afraid you just don't understand about Art, do you Blanche? In years to come these works will be worth a great deal of money.'

'Oh — so I don't understand about Art.' She flounced out of the bedroom, shouting as she went. He followed, and sat down beside her on the sitting-room sofa. He tried to take her hand but she pushed him away. Her teeth ground together; she almost spat at him, so great was her anger. 'I know more about bloody Art than you ever will, Hugh Fitzgerald! I've seen it from the inside — if you'll pardon my grammar. Take that picture of me looking in the mirrors — freezing hard it was, when that was painted. I was so strapped for money that winter, I had chilblains on my arse I might tell you, long before that daub was finished.'

He gave her his half-smile, the one that showed he found her speech outrageous, but irresistibly amusing. He sat down beside her. 'I know that your life has not been easy, although you so rarely talk about it. I will make it up to you, Blanche. There's nothing in this world that I could refuse you! If you only knew how much I love you!' He stood up, took both her hands, and raised her gently. He pulled her towards him and she did not resist. He drew her head down onto his shoulder and began to stroke the exposed nape of her neck. She could hear the pumping of his heart, his rapid breathing. Suddenly, his free hand fumbled at her skirts, and his knee was thrust between her legs. Blanche began to struggle. All at once she was fifteen again, trapped in Hunter's Court, held by the Bidgood brothers, and without Mama to save her. She screamed, and he released her. They stood facing one another, out of breath and panting. His eyes were wide, his colour heightened.

'Blanche! I'm sorry! It was being alone with you, up here, in our own rooms – I've tried so hard not to alarm you – but I'm only human, after all, and –'

'And the winning-post is almost in sight now, eh Hugh? You thought you could see the finishing-line, was that it?'

Blanche gave him a mighty push, and he fell back into an armchair. She leaned over him, and poked an index finger hard into his midriff. 'Let me tell you something else, my frisky little gent. The race betwixt you and me is a long way from being over. Artist's model I may be. Whore I am not? Maidenheads is fetching a high price in London these days, and I'm not sure yet that you can afford mine!'

❁

A great frost had come down early in December. People died of the cold in Whitechapel; children froze to death in their beds, and on the streets of London's East End. Blanche had worried about her mother down in Taunton. Thanks to Hugh, she would, at least, have sufficient coal. If you were rich enough, Blanche now discovered, it was quite possible to enjoy cold weather. In Russell Square, a fire burned constantly in the guest room, the blankets were fleecy and plentiful, and food was served five times a day, even if you were not hungry. The frost had held throughout Christmas and into January. In view of the inclement weather, Mrs Porteous had declared that her usual pilgrimage to Bath would not be made this winter. There was, in any case, so much to be done, and so little time in which to do it. The refusal by Blanche to interest herself in the many wedding lists and the sending out of invitations did not seem to surprise her.

February had been warm and springlike, there were primroses on sale in Covent Garden, and the prospect of a honeymoon in Paris had not, after all, seemed quite so alarming. A trousseau was assembled, a bridal gown fitted. Blanche grew weary of the endless discussions; she was amused by the feats of organisation required by the wealthy to achieve a state so simple as marriage.

March came in wet. Blanche watched the downpour from her bedroom window, saw the winds toss and bend the plane trees in Russell Square, and dreaded the prospect of a Channel crossing. She had never seen the sea, she informed Hugh, but she had heard about it. Why could not the honeymoon be spent in England? Monday, March 9th, dawned wet and cold in London. By two o'clock of that afternoon the first signs of the impending blizzard would be noted in the English Channel.

❀

Hugh looked doubtfully at his best man, an unprincipled rake called Gervase, and resolved not to leave him alone with the bride for a single moment. He was aware of his Aunt Letitia, seated just behind him, and formidable in peacock blue. He glanced across the aisle to where Mrs

Gimball sat, conspicuous in an outfit of Royal Stuart tartan. She had entrenched herself in a front pew, and refused to be moved. Hugh drooped an eyelid, and received her broad grin in return.

The church was full of flowers and people. Many of the wedding guests were friends of his aunt, invited to repay old hospitality and favours: dowager ladies, who, according to Mrs Porteous, would be of use later on, when Blanche was ready to be launched on Society gatherings, and in Royal drawing-rooms. Hugh's thoughts were chaotic. Blanche was quite capable of changing her mind at the very last minute. She had never understood that the role of a woman was to be submissive, to accept love. Her tempers alarmed him to a point where he would do almost anything to placate and calm her. Even now, on this wedding-day, he could not be sure that he had won her.

The organ, which had been playing softly, broke out into the Wedding March, and every head turned towards the west door. Blanche came in on the arm of an elderly stranger, a distant cousin of his Aunt Letitia. Hugh could hardly believe that this was Blanche. Her face, beneath the veil, was very white, her rich hair hidden beneath the lace hood. In a gown of Honiton lace over ivory satin, she looked both virginal and statuesque. Her composure amazed him; her responses were firm and clear, while his own were husky and uncertain. He slipped the ring across her finger, lifted the veil and bent towards her. As he kissed her lips he could smell the brandy on her breath.

The vestry was small, and the entire wedding party, so it seemed to Hugh, was determined to crowd in around them. People laughed and slapped him on the shoulder. The old men eyed Blanche lasciviously; the dowagers looked down their noses. The younger men whispered ribald comments, while their wives glanced elsewhere. Somebody cried, 'Come on, old boy! Let's see you sign-up! Let's have it all made legal!' The Register lay open upon a table, beside it lay a silver pen and inkwell. The laughter was silenced. Everyone pressed forward. Hugh took up the pen, dipped it in the inkwell, and signed himself Hugh Deveraux Fitzgerald. He straightened up, dipped the pen again, and handed it to Blanche.

Blanche took the pen clumsily; for a moment, he thought that she might drop it. He pointed to the correct space on the paper. 'Just there,' he whispered, 'write your name beneath mine.'

'Come along, dear!' boomed Mrs Porteous, 'please do not keep everybody waiting. Do write your name, Blanche! There's a good child!'

Blanche stared at Hugh's aunt. 'All right,' she said, 'I'll make my mark if you insist.' In the silence that followed, Hugh heard the drag of the silver pen across the Register of Marriage, as Blanche Fitzgerald made her cross.

✵

The wedding reception was an awkward affair of forced laughter and veiled glances. The older guests openly ignored Hugh, while the younger ones were curiously excited by Blanche. The best man trapped Hugh in a quiet corner.

'Where the hell did you find her, old boy?' Gervase asked. 'I'd spotted you sometimes dining with her at Romano's. I often saw the two of you together at the races.' Gervase winked and raised his champagne glass. 'What a girl, eh! Made her mark in more ways than one, I shouldn't wonder. Her looks are familiar. What is she? Gaiety Girl, actress? Don't blame you for keeping her all to yourself, old man. You're a sly dog and no mistake.' He swayed and then recovered his balance. 'Bit extreme though, don't you think, letting her trap you into marriage? She's an absolute corker of course, but hardly in the same class as Claire.' Gervase laughed. 'What the hell do

368

you two talk about? Gels like her don't have a single thought that rises higher than their navel, and you're quite a brainy fellah!' He glanced across his shoulder at the group of laughing men who had clustered around Blanche. 'By God, though! She's a gorgeous filly! Take a word of advice from a friend, dear boy. Whatever you do, don't let Bertie see her.' He began to move away. 'Lady W. is getting frightfully plump these days, so I hear. H.R.H. will soon be looking around for a replacement.'

Their drive to Charing Cross had the aspect of a Royal procession. The excited young men insisted on accompanying the bridal pair through the cold and gloomy London streets. Coachmen were exhorted to whip up their horses; there was a lot of good-natured banter; the kind of joking for which Hugh was in no mood. In spite of his efforts to dissuade them, the wedding guests formed an escort around Blanche, and Hugh, jealous and resentful, stood a little apart and watched his wife. Dressed in a coat of emerald velvet, banded with sable, with a matching pill-box hat, the ribbons of which were tied in a green bow underneath her chin, Hugh had never seen Blanche look so animated, or so lovely. As they claimed their seats aboard the Paris Club train, Hugh realised that since the moment in the vestry, when Blanche Fitzgerald had made her cross, bride and groom had not exchanged a single word together.

Blanche settled herself into their reserved compartment. She tossed her sable muff and snakeskin handbag into a corner seat, removed her hat, and sat down to face Hugh. She was still flushed and glowing from her recent triumph. She had never shown such exhilaration in all of their two years' acquaintanceship, and that, of course, was all it had ever really been. Blanche touched the green brocade of the window curtains, fingered the little rose-shaded lamps, and looked approvingly at the engraved glass and mahogany of the Paris Club train. She was like a child. 'What the hell do you talk about?' Gervase had asked him. 'Gels like her don't have a single thought . . . and you're quite a brainy fellah!' It was obvious that all his friends had believed this to be a shot-gun wedding. How surprised they would have been to know his true situation!

Blanche said suddenly, 'This is nice. I like this train, don't you, Hugh?' He thought she sounded placatory. Her slow and careful enunciation would always warn him when she wished to please him.

He nodded. 'I've travelled on it several times.'

'You must know your way around Paris.'

'I know it quite well.' He could not keep the cool note from his voice. She looked away towards the window.

'It's beginning to snow,' she said softly. 'I hope the Channel crossing will not be a rough one.'

The steward brought them tea, and Hugh felt a pang of shame at his own brusque behaviour; he saw how careful Blanche was to hold her saucer just beneath the cup, and crook her little finger at the angle demanded by his Aunt Letitia. She put down her cup, touched her hair, and twisted the band of gold around her wedding finger.

'I know you are angry with me,' she murmured politely, 'and it is not surprising. What I done – did – in the vestry was a terrible thing. But I never meant to spite you. I done – did –' All at once Blanche began to giggle. 'Oh, bugger it,' she cried, 'I wanted to swipe your aunty's eye. You can't think what that old bitch have been putting me through in the last three months! I cudden have stood another minute of it.'

He wanted to laugh, but only smiled his half-smile. 'I wish you had warned me, Blanche. It never occured to me that you couldn't –'

'Write my own name?' She grinned. 'Well, now you knows my guilty secret, don't you? I can't read nor write. Never could, and never want to.'

'It was embarrassing for me, Blanche. Heaven knows how my poor aunt has explained it away to her friends. She was too mortified to even speak to me before we left.'

'She'll have forgot all about it by the time we get back.' Blanche paused. 'That didden seem to worry your mates, did it? They all seemed to be quite – taken – with me.' She yawned, suddenly. 'I'm whacked,' she declared, 'your Aunty had me soaking in a hip-bath of scalding water at five o'clock this morning.' She turned her cheek towards the plush upholstery and closed her eyes. She began to breathe evenly between slightly parted lips, and Hugh knew that she slept. He remembered her as she had looked that morning, virginal in lace, and carrying lilies. He recalled her flushed face and brilliant eyes as she had flirted with his friends, and the way she had always pushed him away whenever he had attempted an intimate embrace. His desire for her had lately assumed a strength and ferocity that alarmed him. The affection that he had once felt for Claire bore no comparison to the passion aroused in him by Blanche. Hugh had always considered himself to be a controlled man. He was wary of excess in any department. Aunt Letitia's recent revelation of his heritage of suicidal father and profligate mother had forced him to adopt a careful, very rigid code of morals; particularly towards women.

Women, he had always believed, fell into two quite separate categories. There was the sweetheart, later to become the wife, who must, at all costs, remain unsullied. Then there were those others, the 'light' and convenient girls, who catered to all tastes and fancies. He saw no sin in their profession. The girls in Foley Street were well-cared for, and highly paid. But for men like himself, such girls would have led quite a miserable existence. It might even be said that gentlemen like Hugh were actually improving the social system. This philosophy had served him through his university years, and a few wild months spent in Paris, and he might have remained safe, but for that flaw in his nature: that inherited tendency which had led him into fatal and irreversible folly. He had never doubted the inevitability of their meeting. Blanche Greypaull was unique. She fell into no convenient category. Her speech, although slipshod and ungrammatical was witty and wickedly amusing. Her inability to write her name had been embarrassing, but not surprising. Nothing about her ever amazed him. He had known, from the very beginning, that she would settle for nothing less than marriage. He knew that his passion was not returned. Her very coolness had served only to inflame him. Hugh had not at first understood why his cuckolded father had made that fatal jump from an upper window, but he was wiser now. There were certain women who could put a spell upon a man, and Blanche was such a woman. He picked up the scattered hat and muff, and set them tidily beside her. He lifted the snakeskin handbag, and found it unaccountably heavy. He opened it and peered inside; the half-pint bottle of Martell's four-star brandy was already three parts empty.

❀

The Paris Club train had left Charing Cross in weather that was cold and blustery but not exceptional for early March. They had been travelling for less than an hour and yet it was almost dark. Hugh noticed the blue-black clouds massed on the horizon, and the force of the winds that buffeted the train. He questioned a passing steward about the weather which might lie ahead.

'Nothing to worry about, sir. We've heard there's a bit of a squall blown up, out in the Channel. Come on a bit sudden-like, so it seems. Never mind, sir. You'll be walking down the Champs Elysées, this time tomorrow.'

It began to snow, lightly at first, but as they came nearer to the coast, it seemed to Hugh that the speed of the express engine had slackened perceptibly. The flurries of snow were heavier and more frequent. The noise of the wind as it hit the train broadside-on, was loud enough to make normal converation inaudible, sometimes impossible. He awakened Blanche as they approached Dover. 'Stay aboard the train,' he shouted, 'I intend to find the station-master and ask a few questions about the weather prospects. We seem to have run in to some kind of blizzard.'

Hugh stepped out onto a station platform that was blocked by the debris washed up by massive seas. Within seconds he was drenched in spray and cold to the bone. The Admiralty Pier was a fearsome sight; he looked around at the devastation and at once climbed back onto the train. The guard had called all the passengers together. Ships, they were told, were foundering all along the coast, parts of Dover already lay in ruins, and a return to Charing Cross was quite out of the question since the blizzard had moved so rapidly inland that most railway lines were now blocked.

There were several distinguished travellers aboard the Paris Club Express. Hugh recognised Prince Tel Akbar, the racing-owner; Sir Alec Lindsey was speaking urgently with Lady Rothschild. The advice of the guard had been that they should all seek accommodation in the local inns and hotels. 'It's either that,' he told them bluntly, 'or freeze to death aboard my train.'

Dover, Hugh soon discovered, was filled that night with angry and frightened travellers. It required a couple of sovereigns to persuade two reluctant porters to carry their trunk to a nearby inn. 'We are on our honeymoon,' Hugh told the landlord, 'we were married this morning.' This information, and a proffered banknote, ensured the newly-wed Fitzgeralds the last available bedroom in the Jolly Sailor.

They had arrived at the inn shivering and wet through, their smart London clothes quite ruined by spray and snow.

The trunk was wrestled upstairs by a potman, followed closely by the landlord's wife who carried a tray with two glasses, a jug of hot water, and a whisky bottle. The bedroom was small and cosy; chintz curtains were drawn across the window and a bright fire burned in the grate.

'Dinner, sir?' enquired the landlady.

Hugh shook his head. 'We ate on the train,' he explained.

The woman smiled her understanding. 'Best get out of your wet things right away,' she advised, 'you don't want the pneumonia on your honeymoon, now do you?' She indicated the jug and bottle. 'A good hot toddy is what you both want.' She put a finger to her lips and whispered, 'I'll see to it you're not disturbed, sir and madam.' The woman closed the door very softly, as if to emphasize their unique situation. Blanche fiddled uneasily with the catch on her handbag. Hugh removed his cape, and threw it, nervously, across a chair. He poured whisky into a tumbler and added hot water.

'None for me,' Blanche said swiftly, 'I can't abide that stuff.'

'Don't drink it much myself,' he admitted, 'wine is my usual tipple – wine or champers.' Suddenly he shivered. 'I've heard about bashful bridegrooms, but never one whose teeth were chattering!' Blanche did not smile, if banter was meant to ease the tension, then he was not succeeding. She removed her hat and coat, hung them on a hook behind the door, and then went to stand beside the window. She lifted the curtain, to find snow piled high against the lattice; she stood there for a long time.

'We shall be snowed-in before the morning,' she said quietly. He did not reply. She dropped the curtain and turned towards her husband. Hugh stood, stripped and white in the firelight, a heap of wet clothes around his feet. He refilled the whisky glass and drank deeply from it. His face grew flushed and his blue eyes glittered.

'Come on,' he urged her, 'for heaven's sake take off that soaked gown.'

She opened the lid of her trunk, wasting time in a search for his silk pyjamas, her chiffon nightgown.

'Don't bother with those things,' he cried, 'we'll never need them!'

Blanche had never found nudity embarrassing and, in fact, the sight of unclad male models in the Academy's Life School had become so familiar as to be thoroughly boring. In the case of Hugh Fitzgerald she felt very different. It was not that he was unattractive; Simeon Solomon, she thought, would have sacrificed one leg and his left arm to have painted such a body. It was the thought of his particular body in proximity to her own that was so distasteful; and the unaccustomed whisky was having a peculiar effect on him.

'For God's sake take off that wet gown!' he repeated, 'or are you waiting perhaps for me to do it for you?'

Blanche took a few steps forwards towards the fire, in the hope that this move might pacify him. He continued to drink the almost-neat whisky. The heat of the fire was intense, and steam began to rise in a great cloud all about her.

'Oh, this is ridiculous!' he shouted. He sat the whisky glass upon the mantelshelf, and came towards her. She twisted away from his outstretched hands. 'I'm quite capable of taking off my own clothes,' she said primly, 'and don't you dare drink any more of that whisky.'

'You're a fine one to preach at me. Anyway, it's damned good stuff! Bloody marvellous for overcoming one's inhibitions.' He lifted an eyebrow. 'Or maybe you don't need it, eh Blanche? Old Gervase had you summed-up pretty well, this morning.'

'What did Gervase say about me?'

'Gorgeous filly, that's what he said, absolute corker! Don't let Bertie see her, that's all!'

Blanche became very still. 'Bertie being the Prince of Wales, I suppose?'

'The very same, old darling! Devil for the women, you know; and you're just his type. Cold on the outside – passionate as all Hell on the inside. That's you, Blanche, eh what? Played me like a fish for two bloody years, haven't you, my beauty? But now we shall see just what you're made of!' His tone changed. 'Get your bloody clothes off, woman. I've told you for the last time!'

Blanche began to feel frightened. She glanced towards the fire-irons but thought better of it. Enraged as he was, with desire and whisky, he could easily outmatch her. She had never imagined that he could treat her so; he had never spoken coarsely, or treated her other than with deep respect. She bit her lip in chagrin, and tried to pretend that this was the Life School, and she about to pose for Mr Burne-Jones or Mr Millais. After all, the nude pose had been the one most frequently demanded of her. She began to rip at the tiny velvet buttons with fingers made clumsy by fear. The heavy gown fell around her ankles, followed by stockings, petticoats, chemise, camisole and drawers. She straightened up, proud in the knowledge of her certain beauty. To be shy in the presence of a fool like Hugh Fitzgerald was not only stupid but laughable! Her courage returned. She pointed a derisive finger.

'Come on then, aunty's boy,' she sneered, 'let's see just what you're capable of, if anything at all!' She became reckless, 'Have another glass of whisky, why don't you? I bet the Prince of Wales don't never need no Dutch courage! One more drink, my lover and you'll be flat on your face – I've seen your sort before. All mouth and trousers. Go on! Drink the bottleful, you appear to need it!'

Her words were choked by his hand, slapped hard and fast

across her mouth. He pushed her towards the bed. 'Shut up, you bitch! We shall start as we mean to continue. Not another word, you hear me!' The blizzard howled and moaned around the inn. Such weather had not been seen in England for a hundred years. Blanche Fitzgerald screamed and raged but such was the noise of the storm, that nobody heard her.

❀

Blanche opened her eyes, remembering the night and all that had taken place. The light from the window was diffused and white. The blazing fire of the previous evening had burned down to a mere glow, but the room was still warm. She tried to hold her mind back from a too-sudden recollection; preferring to dwell on the brass rails of the bedstead, the oil-lamp guttering weakly on the dressing-table, and Hugh's slippers set tidily beside the fireplace.

She turned her head and saw him lying at the far side of the bed. His hair had been trimmed just before the wedding; it lay short and smooth in his neck and above his ears; thick and blond across his head and brow. Except for that bright flush of colour on his cheekbones, his skin was very pale, like that of a child who rarely saw the sun. His lips were a thin line beneath silky and luxuriant moustaches. Other women found him handsome; she found his looks to be girlish, and faintly repellent.

Blanche thought about Jye: the strong column of his neck, the grave, unsmiling features, the dark sheen of his walnut-coloured skin. She remembered a Sunday morning when she had lured him into Mrs Gimball's back room. She had abased herself, knelt before him, begged his kiss and then grown frightened at the passion she had aroused. How different her wedding night would have been, if only the man at her side had been Jye Carew. But then she recalled an incident long ago, when the Bidgood brothers had waited for her in the darkness of Hunter's Court. She had found that episode exciting. Jye had also, when inflamed, ripped her gown and used violence on her. With a rare perception, Blanche began to question her goading of Hugh. Was she, in fact, no better than the street drabs who needed the kicks and blows of lovers in order to obtain fulfilment? She tried to turn away from the man who lay beside her, but found that the slightest movement of her legs sent waves of pain shafting through her body. She moaned, and he came awake at once.

'What is it?' he muttered.

The blizzard still screamed and howled around the house. Blanche lay very still and pretended not to hear. He came fully awake, supported himself upon an elbow, and spoke louder, 'What's wrong? Are you still in pain?'

She did not answer, but closed her eyes. Tears seeped from beneath her eyelids and ran slowly down her pale cheeks. Blanche knew that her cheeks must be interestingly pale, they always were in the early morning. She glanced at him, but then her sense of outrage returned, and with it a slow and grinding anger. She was not at all like her Mama. Forgiveness and forbearance were not in her nature. Any man who inflicted physical hurt on Blanche Greypaull must pay the price. She recalled the Bidgood brothers whom she had once cursed, all long dead, and buried in the Burmese jungle. She turned to Hugh.

'Of course I'm in pain,' she cried. 'Why, the whole town of Dover must have heard me screaming.'

'No,' he said, dully, 'nobody could possibly have heard you, not above the sounds of the blizzard.'

'So that do make it all right, do it? You be quite content, since nobody do know how bad you hurt me?' She spoke softly, but with such venom that he flinched and looked away.

'It was the whisky,' he muttered, 'it went to my head.

I'm not really a drinking man, Blanche.'

'Then you shudden have drunk it, should you?'

'You had been drinking brandy, Blanche!'

'How did you know that?'

'I could smell it on your breath.'

She pulled herself up into a sitting position; she pushed the long red hair back from her shoulders, and allowed the concealing sheet to slip an inch or two. Aware of the charming picture she presented, Blanche said demurely, 'I drank it for your sake, more than my own. I'd heard that a maiden's wedding-night was never easy, and brandy do have a powerful numbing effect – trouble was, it never worked in my case, did it?'

'The whisky went to my head,' he repeated.

'That's right! Blame it all on something else! That's what my Papa did.'

Suddenly, she began to cry genuine tears. 'You have turned out to be an animal just like him. I often heard my Mama cry out in the night, when I was a little girl, living on Larksleve. I already knowed then what a man's talk of love truly meant.'

Hugh lay back on his pillows. 'I didn't want it to be so awful for you,' he moaned, 'it never was with the –'

'With the whores in Foley Street?' she interrupted. 'But Kate Hamilton's girls is well broke-in, eh Hugh? They wudden have been hard to master, I told you many times that I had never give away my final favour. Didden you believe me?'

'I believed you,' he muttered. 'Of course I believed you. Do you think I would have even considered marriage to you if I hadn't been sure that you were still a –' he paused. 'How did you find out about Foley Street?'

Blanche laughed. 'Every model in the Life School knowed about it. 'Twas the next step downwards for some of them what had been careless enough to lose their best looks.'

'You were never that careless, Blanche,' he murmured.

'No,' she said, 'I was saving myself for the likes of you, wasn't I? But that don't mean that I was stupid. I saw you one day going into Kate Hamilton's House.'

'You didn't mind?'

'Why should I? I asked Mr Solomon about it. He said that 'twas a clean place, that a doctor came in regular to examine the tarts.'

'Oh my God!' cried Hugh, 'I shall never understand you! How can you be so wordly-wise and yet so ignorant; and both at the same time?'

She moaned again, much louder this time. 'I got such a thick head, Hugh, and the pain is getting worse every time I move!'

At once, he was all concern. 'Lie still,' he commanded, 'I'll go in search of some hot coffee. Perhaps a hot-water bottle?' He stroked her forehead, and gazed into her eyes. 'I don't know what I can ever do to make amends, Blanche?'

She smiled, but without warmth. 'Don't worry,' she told him, 'I expect that I shall be able to think of something, But not till this terrible pain have gone away, of course.'

❋

The thick walls and tight thatch of the Jolly Sailor had, so far, withstood the hurricane force of the storm. Great gusts of snow and wind tore the slates and tiles from adjacent buildings; timber crashed and masonry tumbled, but Blanche felt safe in the little chintz room beneath the eaves. She had almost forgotten about Paris. She had never wanted to go there anyway. To be penned with her new husband in an hotel bedroom was the situation Blanche had most feared; and yet, handled with skill, this very isolation might be turned to her advantage. Long after the shock and pain of humiliation had receded, her pose of bravery, in the cause of duty, still remained.

There was nothing like guilt, Blanche discovered, to bring a man to heel, to make him gentle and considerate. She permitted Hugh to bathe and tend her, to put on her nightgown, ease her into a frilled robe, and support her to the armchair beside the fire. Blanche relaxed, toyed with toast and coffee on a tray, and declared herself quite content to remain with him in Dover. She had managed to convince Hugh that he had done her irreparable internal damage, and he, visibly moved by her forgiveness, would not yet dare to make further asaults upon her person. Blanche smiled. Her present indisposition, properly handled, could be made to last for quite a long time.

The coming of daylight had brought no change in the terrible weather. Hugh stood at the casement, and pointed out the blue distress flares which glowed briefly far out in the bay, but the foundering vessel was always shrouded in a white mist. Many luggers and coasters were running for shelter; alongside the Dover jetty, paddle-boats and ketches crashed together and sank. A lull in the storm would throw up the voices of men, shouting from the harbour, and the flames from flaring beacons, but almost at once the blizzard would close in upon them, and the world be lost.

The storm raged for six days. Blanche fretted about the state of her trousseau, and insisted that Hugh should unpack the trunk and hang the creased gowns around the bedroom walls. He read to her; they played cards and draughts together. He taught her the mysteries of Mah Jong and bezique. On Sunday a thaw set in, bringing thick fog into the Channel. A crossing to Paris, Blanche declared, was quite out of the question. Moving stiffly, but bravely, she allowed Hugh to brush her hair, and hand her the necessary combs and hairpins. Leaning heavily on her husband's arm, the new bride left the Jolly Sailor, and returned, gallant but thankful, to Russell Square.

❋

It had been the hardest winter that anyone could remember in the South-West. In the days of thaw that followed this time of blizzard and great frost, Eliza wrote a letter to her cousin Rhoda.

Greenbrook Terrace,
Taunton. April 1891.

My dear cousin Rhoda,

Your last letter thankfully received, and glad to know that all is well with you and yours. Have just lived thru the kind of Winter that you have in Wisconsin, and I hope *never to see* such blizzards again in my lifetime. It was *very hard* on the old and poor. Many souls perished from cold and hunger. Noticed many gaps in our Sunday Congregation.

That all began on a Monday morning. I had just finished my big wash. I was late with it that day, Louis being in one of his *pacing moods*, what is always worrying, dear Rhoda, in case the neighbours should hear him. I was about to hang out the wash when a great wind sprung up, and then the snow started. By evening, poor Annis had trouble finding her way from Mount Street to Greenbrook Terrace. The blizzard lasted for a week, and only my habits of thrift, in keeping some food and candles put by, saw us safe in those bitter days. Must also mention *one ton of coal*, paid for by *Blanche's Affianced*. Without this coal Louis would have surely died. He gets more delicate every Winter, especially his chest.

Now for my big news. The above mentioned Affianced, is now, I am pleased to tell you, at last my Blanche's *Husband*. They both come down to Taunton as soon as weather permitted to tell us about the Marriage. Put up at the London Hotel. Money no object so it seems. They was married at St George's Church, Hanover Square, London. A big do, with *two hundred* guests. We was not told, nor was we invited. Madelina was very upset about this. Her Laura have always wanted to be a bridesmaid. But I think it all for the best that we knowed nothing about it. One of us must always stay at Home with Louis, and in any case we never had suitable outfits for such a party as that.

Like I have said in other letters, Rhoda, *he* is very nice and friendly. A perfect Gentleman, and no *side*. He do call me Mama, what is very pleasing to us both, him having never seen his own mother. Blanche have *not* married beneath her. These Fitzgeralds is an old *Bath family*. The Honeymoon was to have been in *Paris*, but they was caught in the blizzard at Dover, and spent the whole week in an *Inn*. Blanche, it seems, would not set foot on a steamship after the storm, but *would* come down to Taunton as soon as she could, to see that we was alright, and still counted among the living. Had no chance at all to speak to Blanche on her own, *he* being always close at her elbow. *He* treats her like a bit of fine china, Rhoda. What is funny for us to watch, us knowing our Blanche as we do. I can only pray that she will be happy. There is certainly no *lack of money*. They rides First-Class on the railway, and puts up at the best hotels. I hopes his pocket is *deep enough* to stand it. *Her* clothes was like nothing ever seen here in Taunton, and jewels what *he* said had been his grandmother's. Such gowns and furs, Rhoda, and all to match with boots and parasols and handbags. They hired a brougham while they was here in Taunton. They *never walk* anywhere. *He* wanted to take me up to Buckland St Mary, but I said no. Better not to wake up old memories, I told him. What is past is done with. Samuel Greypaull must be looking like an old man, these days. He would never recognise me, either.

Our Mina is very upset since she is so *short*, and only Annis do fit perfect into Blanche's cast-offs. A great trunk of clothes and boots brought by Blanche from London, for the use of Annis. But most of them of course, not *decent* or *respectable* enough to be worn by an *unwed girl* on the streets of Taunton.

My other news is that Blanche and husband have bought furniture for me. *He* said that I was not to feel beholden in any way. To see *me* happy would make *Blanche* happy, what is all he truly wants. I said nothing on *that subject*, Rhoda. Making Blanche happy is going to be a life's labour lost for that poor young man, I fear. However, my front room is now elegant, with drugget on the floor, armchairs and a what-not, an overmantel with looking-glass in it, and a *mahogany round table* what is a joy to polish. Up till now, this room *only* held my piano. Did invite the ladies of my Bible Class and the Reverend Elias Jones to come and take tea with us, last Sunday afternoon.

No word from Candace or Simeon. I can only pray for their safety, Rhoda. Did allow myself one short ride in Blanche's hired brougham. Went with Hugh and Blanche to the Cemetery, and planted a white rose on Jack's grave. Felt *much eased* in my heart at having done this. He is buried in a quiet spot, away from the main Staplegrove road, and in a corner underneath a yew tree. He had that streak of Recklessness what I have lived to see in all my children, save Madelina. Even Annis do lately grow *moody*. But Jack had a brave soul. He never complained about the cruel trick what led to him losing Larksleve. I do not need to touch on the special sorrow a mother must feel at the loss of a child, for you, dear Rhoda, have lost Eddy and poor little John, and both of them so young.

My regards to Mr James Black, and a kiss for the children.
I remain your loving cousin, Eliza.

❁

The letters from Frank, tied up in neat bundles with bits of blue ribbon, were all the proof that Annis had that she was, in fact, betrothed. There was the bottom drawer filled with embroidered pillowslips and assorted household linens; in the six years of Frank Nevill's absence these items had multiplied and overflowed into every available cupboard and drawer. At those times when Annis felt particularly low, she would take a tally, and Eliza would write to Frank informing him of the number of sheets, the quantities of table-linen, antimacassars and string dishcloths, all sewed or knitted by the waiting Annis. Since the visit by Blanche and her new husband, this occupation had lost all of its pleasure. Annis would finger her handiwork, and the bundled letters, only to turn away to the handsome brass-bound trunk that now stood beside her bed.

Mama had insisted that the gowns left by Blanche should remain, folded and concealed, inside the trunk. But on Sundays, with Mama safe at evening service, Annis would open the lid and allow herself to dream. She would feel a stab of anticipatory pleasure at the creaking of the leather hinges. She would sigh and clasp her hand together, as the heady perfumes used by Blanche were released into the room. She would lift out each carefully folded garment and drape it across the bed. Then she would line up the matching boots and handbags, the tiny feathered hats, the frilled parasols, fringed evening shawls, and sequined purses.

Louis, who could tell no tales, was her audience of one. She would dress in each successive outfit, and then take note of the strength of his approval. He tended to smile and nod at the brightest and most extravagent outfits. The deep pinks and yellows made him laugh; the scarlet and black would move him to clap his hands with pleasure. The evening gowns and fringed silk shawls were his special favourites; at the sight of these he would utter little cooing noises. Mama would return from church to find Louis unusually docile, and Annis would be complimented on her wise and sympathetic handling of him. But her desire to wear the clothes grew stronger with every week that passed. Surely, she pleaded, at least some of the outfits could be made over, so that they were more serviceable for use in Taunton? But Mama would not relent. How, she demanded, could Annis turn up for work in Cook's shirt factory, dressed in pink silk trimmed with roses, or in sequined satin and embroidered shawls. The scarlet-and-black striped grosgrain would cause spiteful gossip, and as for what passed as evening wear in London! Where in the world did Annis propose to go dressed in such a manner?

Summer gave way to winter, and even Mama was forced to admit to the folly of leaving good clothes unused. There was a costume of grey velvet, demure and hardly worn. Annis lengthened the skirt so that it barely cleared the ground, and repositioned certain buttons so that the jacket no longer fitted quite so snugly. With Mama's approval she wore it to church on a Sunday in December, together with its matching muff, feathered hat, and soft grey boots. She remembered a Christmas long ago, when Blanche had said, 'Clothes is important! Don't you never forget that, Annis!'

It was true. She walked slowly along North Street, watching her reflected image in plate-glass windows. She straightened her shoulders, lifted her chin, and moved from the hips in a gliding motion, in imitation of her sister Blanche. Her presence in church was noted on that Sunday morning; people looked curiously at her, as if she had, overnight, become a stranger. In order to prolong the pleasure, Annis took the long route home.

The day was cold and overcast. She walked briskly past Jellalabad Barracks, out of Mount Street and into Vivary Park. She practised her gliding walk down deserted pathways, among empty flowerbeds; the narrow boots began to pinch a little, but that, she supposed, was the price of pride. She thought about Frank in India; he wrote to her every Sunday morning, she imagined he was writing at this very minute, seated on his bed among the heat and flies. He sent her a photograph of himself every Christmas, wearing his best uniform with the medal pinned on it, his face stern, his hair parted in the middle. Frank no longer seemed to be a person she had ever known. She could not recall his voice, or anything about him. He talked about marriage in every letter; it was only the thought of Annis, he said, and their plans for the future, that kept him soldiering-on, year after year.

The footsteps had been audible for some minutes, but Annis had not dared to look around. She felt frightened, her heartbeat quickened. How foolish she had been to come alone into the deserted Park! Afraid to run, she made for the bandstand, and began to walk, very swiftly, around it. A danger faced, she told herself, is a danger halved! She trod softly, and heard the smart crunch of leather on gravel as the follower approached in the opposite direction. They came face to face beside the bandstand steps; he clicked his booted heels together, touched his cap in a mock salute, and smiled. He was holding out an expensive lace-trimmed hanky, 'I believe you dropped this,' he said. 'You were walking so fast, I thought I'd never catch you.'

Annis looked bewildered, took the hanky, although she had never possessed so fine an item. 'Thank you,' she murmured, 'it was good of you to bother.'

He began to walk beside her, towards the Park gates. He chatted about the weather, recalled the horrors of last year's blizzard, and said that a posting to India at such times would suit him very well. As they walked, Annis gazed covertly at him; she studied the insignia on his scarlet tunic. A second lieutenant, she guessed, or perhaps a full lieutenant? Oh, but how smart he was! How very tall and handsome. They halted beside the Park gates. He was quite the most dashing young man she had ever stood close to; in fact, he tended to stand rather too close. Annis took a step backwards, and dared to look up into his face.

'I must be going now,' she stammered, 'I should have

been home from church this long since. My Mama'll be getting worried.'

'Do you walk here every Sunday morning, Miss – I'm afraid I don't know your name?'

'Greypaull,' she murmured. 'Annis Greypaull.'

He held out his hand. 'Jeremy Castlemain, Captain! At your service, pretty lady!'

No one had ever told her that she was pretty, except for her brother Simeon, and he hardly counted. Annis blushed, and looked down at the pointed toes of the tight boots. Blanche would have known what to do in such a situation. Annis took the proffered hand, and shook it. His skin was warm, his grip firm and prolonged. Annis almost swooned from the unexpected pleasure of his touch. Could there, she wondered, be anything sinful about a simple handshake? She released her hand, and concluded that there might be when the other hand belonged to Jeremy Castlemain, Captain.

'Do you walk here every Sunday?' he repeated.

'I never did before today.' She touched the velvet of her jacket.

'I had some new clothes, see –'

'And you wanted to show them off?' He glanced around him. 'What a damn shame! Here you are, the most charming sight in the whole of Somerset, and not a soul about to appreciate the fact, but me!' He smiled. 'Tell you something, Annis Greypaull. You're as lovely as your name.' He glanced at her left hand. 'Not married yet?'

'Promised,' she said, 'promised this past six years.'

'Six years?' he cried. 'By the Lord Harry, but that's a lifetime!'

'He's away – in India. He got another four years to serve yet.'

'Has he, by Jove! Well, that's a damn shame.' He began to move away towards Mount Street and the barracks.

388

'I might see you here next Sunday,' he called across his shoulder, 'if it isn't snowing.' She watched him stride away, tall and broad-shouldered, the little cane tapping at his boot. She stood, rooted beside the Park gates until he had turned the corner. He did not look back.

Annis had no appetite for the midday meal; she felt curiously disinclined for the task of the Sunday letter. 'That poor Frank will be disappointed,' scolded Eliza, 'I had better make-up some words of my own. We shall have to send him some sort of message.' She gazed sharply at Annis. 'Fine clothes don't appear to have improved your disposition, miss! You've hardly spoke a word since you came in from church. Is there something that I should know about, Annis?'

She had never really lied to Mama, had never needed to, but this Jeremy Castlemain, Captain, was her first important secret. Annis turned a pale, bland face towards her mother. 'I got one of my sick headaches coming on. I think I shall have to lie down for a bit.'

The sick headaches of Annis were feared by all her family. Eliza at once took remedial action. A hot-water jar at her feet, a cold compress on her forehead, and Annis was left to sleep for the rest of that Sunday. She did not sleep; behind closed eyelids she relived every second of that amazing meeting. How lucky that she had been wearing the grey velvet costume! How strange that he should have thought the dropped hanky to be hers? She repeated his name: Jeremy Castlemain! Oh, but it had a fine ring about it. His speech had reminded her of Hugh Fitzgerald. He had that same way of saying certain words. He said things like 'By the Lord Harry,' and, 'By Jove!' which proved that he must be a gentleman, and, like Hugh, one who could be trusted. She would have to be careful when entering and leaving Cook's factory. The factory gates stood facing an entrance to Jellalabad Barracks, but he would never recognise her in her old black working skirt, the shawl around her head and shoulders. She smiled beneath the icy compress. There was a gown of russet velvet in the trunk, and a tiny hat made of peacock feathers. Now, if Mama could only be persuaded that the indispositions of Annis were due to a lack of sufficient warm clothing?

Her attendance at the Sunday evening church service had now become Eliza's only time of freedom. She would sing every word of every hymn, listen attentively to the Reverend Jones' sermon, and kneel to pray with the same devotion that she had shown lifelong. Just to be quiet within herself, to escape for an hour or two from the demands of Louis, had become so important to her that she feared it might be seen as a sinful indulgence. Dressed in shabby black, and carrying her prayer-book, she would walk home very slowly through the streets of Taunton, gathering up the sights and sounds that would have to see her through the coming week. She would gaze into shop windows, observe the strolling crowds, and study the broadsheets pinned to the door of the *Gazette*. There was always some item of news that could be told to Annis over supper. The inability to read, feared Eliza, had left her daughter woefully ill-informed. The news was dull on this particular Sunday; only one paragraph merited attention. 'The Duke of Clarence,' said the Bulletin, 'better known as Prince Eddy, oldest son of the Prince and Princess of Wales, is suffering from a severe chill, and influenza with complications. The Queen's doctors are in attendance upon him. Further bulletins will be issued.'

Blanche had often talked about Prince Eddy. A wild young man, so she had said, drunken and dissolute, well-known on the racecourse and at the gaming-tables for his spendthrift habits of disposing of his father's money. Blanche had also said that the Prince was not very bright. Eliza sighed. Well, it happened in the best of families. The

Lord was very just in His distribution of Crosses to be borne. He shared them out among rich and poor alike. The influenza epidemic had now spread, country-wide. Several people had coughed and sneezed most alarmingly in church that evening.

It was the Reverend Jones, snuffling and red-nosed, but still determined to do his Christian duty, who came to Greenbrook Terrace on that January day and brought death into the house.

Louis, polite and attentive, as taught by Eliza, had taken the Vicar's cloak, pulled up a chair for him close to the fire, and handed him a cup of tea. Of them all, it was only Louis who had contracted the influenza.

For Eliza there was no solace to be found but in writing. Rhoda alone would understand her feelings. She sat alone at the kitchen table, faced-away from the empty fireside corner, and drew pen, ink and paper towards her, and began to write.

❋

The plight of the respectable poor had shocked Hugh Fitzgerald. He had done all that Eliza would permit towards making the house in Greenbrook Terrace a little more comfortable and warm, but still it did not seem sufficient. In December he sent instructions to a poulterer in Taunton, that a goose be delivered to Eliza; he wrote her a letter in which was enfolded a banknote for £10.

'But that's not enough!' Blanche argued. 'Why, you could afford to send her fifty!'

'Not just at this moment; you might as well know the truth, Blanche. My account is badly overdrawn. I've had a pretty stiff letter from the bank.'

'But it can't be! You had £2,000 last April, and then there's your quarterly interest — you didden — haven't — spent all that, have you?'

'I didn't receive the whole two thousand.'

'Why not?'

'Aunt Porteous persuaded me to invest a thousand pounds.'

'I might have knowed – known – it! That woman interferes in everything you do!'

'But investments pay dividends, Blanche. They bring in a regular income.'

'I like to see the cash in my hand. Bits of paper don't mean noth – anything to me.'

'You lost a hundred at Newmarket in October,' he reminded her, 'and you would insist on going to Worth for that new ballgown. Two hundred pounds will have to be found for that single item!'

Blanche looked complacant. 'Your Aunty agreed that I must go to Worth for that particular gown. After all, an invitation to a Royal Wedding ball is very special. We shall be introduced to the Prince and Princess of Wales. I would not like to shame you.'

Hugh was finding her recent attempts at grammatical speech both alarming and endearing. Having once declared that she would always speak exactly as she chose, Blanche now wrinkled her brow over tenses and pronunciations. Words like 'maid' and 'bain't' had vanished from her vocabulary. Since the arrival of an engraved card from Buckingham Palace, the refined accents of Russell Square had crept rapidly into her speech. The summons to attend the wedding ball of the Duke of Clarence had surprised Hugh. His acquaintanceship with Prince Eddy had been a strictly bachelor contact of the racecourse and gaming-table. It required vast quantities of money to keep up with that elevated set, and, since his marriage to Blanche, Hugh had forsworn all extravagance on his own account. His friend Gervase, on the other hand, was a close friend of Prince Eddy, and Gervase was a mischief maker.

'Whatever you do, old boy,' Gervase had said, 'don't let Bertie see her!' Hugh frowned. The Prince of Wales would play host at this wedding ball of his eldest son, and Blanche, dressed in a Worth gown of ivory satin, low-cut, tightly-fitting, and embroidered all over with tiny seed-pearls, would stand before him, take his hand and curtsy deeply. That Gervase was in some way responsible for the wedding invitation, Hugh had no doubt.

For the sake of economy, and to placate his Aunt Porteous, the Fitzgeralds were obliged to spend that Christmas at Freshwater House, in Bath.

❀

The black-edged letter was waiting for Blanche on her return to Russell Square. Hugh opened it and read it to her.

'Poor Louis,' she said, 'it was never much of a life from the very beginning. But at least he'll have had a decent send-off. Your measly £10 will have managed that!'

The real tragedy, said Hugh, had been the imprisonment of Eliza for the past eighteen years, and the recruitment of Annis as a minder of her brother, and the full-time supporter of her widowed mother.

'We did what we could,' Blanche insisted, 'I never once visited Taunton without leaving money and clothes, and a cupboard full of food!'

'I know,' said Hugh, 'and I admire you for that, Blanche. But don't you see, you all went away; you all escaped. It was Annis who had to stay; Annis who felt obliged to remain with her mother.' He paused. 'Haven't you ever,' he asked quietly, 'taken a good look at your younger sister? She's twenty-four years old, Blanche, and yet your mother still treats her like a child. Annis is too quiet; she rarely dares to voice an opinion on the smallest matter. All she has in life is that sweated-labour in the shirt factory, and a promise of marriage from an absent soldier!'

'She's happy enough. She was never robust. The rheumatic fever weakened her when she was a child. It was better for Annis to stay at home with Mother. She's more suited to it than the rest of us.' Blanche frowned, and smoothed away the crease. 'Anyway, if she'd had any spirit she'd have gone in service. I did and so did Candace. Even our Mina caught herself a husband!'

Hugh looked keenly at her. 'You never mentioned that you'd been in service?'

'It was only for a few months.' She raised her chin, turned her head sideways, and allowed him to observe her perfect profile. 'You must confess,' she laughed, 'I was never cut out to be anybody's skivvy!'

Hugh leaned back in his armchair, he laid down his copy of *The Times* and looked thoughtful. 'Prince Eddy is ill,' he told Blanche, 'the paper says that this influenza epidemic has spread to the Royal Family. Several of the Princesses have succumbed to it, but in Eddy's case it appears to be a more serious matter. It would seem that several bulletins have already been issued. I hardly glanced at the newspapers when we were down in Bath.'

'Too busy squiring dear Aunty about,' muttered Blanche. Hugh ignored her.

'He must have been ill for quite some time.' He picked up the paper. 'It states here that Eddy was unwell over Christmas.'

'Don't worry,' Blanche laughed, 'the likes of him won't die from influenza. He's probably got a dozen doctors lined up at his bedside.' She pouted her top lip. 'He'd better not die! We've spent £200 on a gown for his wedding ball, and I've quite set my heart on meeting the Prince of Wales.' She grew bitter. 'He'll be getting very different treatment than my poor little brother. The Princess of Wales won't have called out the parish doctor. It must be a pleasure to be ill in Windsor Castle.'

'It doesn't sound much like it. It says here that the Prince has been wrapped in the fleece of a newly-slaughtered sheep.'

Blanche nodded. 'That'll make him sweat. He must be very ill for the doctors to use an old trick of that sort. But our Louis only lived two days, and that Eddy is a weedy-looking fellah! Oh Hugh, I so wanted to meet the Prince of Wales — and the Princess, of course. I've scarcely thought of anything else since the card came. If he ups and dies six weeks before the wedding, I'll — I'll near forgive him, so there!'

The bulletins, each one more gloomy than its predecessor, announced a rapid worsening of Prince Eddy's condition. A telegram was sent to Queen Victoria at Osborne. Blanche insisted on driving to the gates of Buckingham Palace, so that Hugh might read the reports first-hand. 'Inflammation of the lungs, and other complications', was the news of January 12th. On the morning of the 13th, a milkman brought the news to Russell Square that the Prince was dead.

Hugh at once called round the brougham. Black-edged notices were being nailed to bill-boards in all the streets of London. They drove quickly down the Mall, and slowly past the Palace; the blinds were drawn at all the windows, and flags were lowered. People who had never known Prince Eddy wept openly at the sadness of it all. Aunt Porteous sniffled into a fine lawn hanky.

'Only twenty-eight,' she moaned, 'and all his life before him.'

'If all they say of him is true,' muttered Blanche, 'then he'd lived quite a lively slice of it already. Proper chip off the old block, he was!' Blanche looked mutinous. Up in their own apartment she said to Hugh, 'Your aunty never said not one word of sorrow when I told her about our Louis, and he was only sixteen.' The rules of grammer still tended to elude her at times of high emotion. 'It seems to me,' Blanche said bitterly, 'that the poor people only slip away. 'Tis only the filthy-rich what is allowed to die proper!'

The funeral of the Duke of Clarence took place at Windsor; at the same time, a service was said for his soul in Westminster Abbey. Blanche felt piqued. New mourning clothes had been obligatory, and these purchases, charged to the account of Aunt Letitia, had seemed quite an unnecessary extravagance, since Blanche had already spent £200 on a gown which was meant to be worn at this same man's wedding. She had offered, in the name of economy, to remain at home, and was sharply rebuked by Mrs Porteous for her lack of proper feeling.

They drove slowly through the mourning city on that dreadful Wednesday. All the streets were very quiet, shops had closed, their windows hung dismally with black crêpe. They drove up to Westminster Abbey and entered by the north door. Blanche paused at the spot in the porch where Jye Carew had once knelt at their first meeting. Forced forward into the Abbey by the great press of mourners, Blanche could only think of Jye. She looked towards King Henry's Chapel, and the sadness of the anthem seemed to be for herself and her lost love. Tears welled in her eyes and rolled down her cheeks, and Hugh, thinking that she wept for the dead Prince, gently pressed her fingers. Strange, thought Blanche, how a place could call up so many memories of a person. The congregation sang 'Oh God our help in ages past', and Blanche closed her eyes against the images of Jye. She saw him, tall and dark in his mason's apron, his features grave, his eyes intent upon her moving lips. She saw his hands, the nails worn short, the palms and fingers very clean from contact with the limestone. If she could ever have loved any man, then that man would have been Jye. She saw him striding away from her, decent in his Baptist black; kneeling in prayer in King Henry's Chapel.

As the service for Prince Eddy ended, Blanche stumbled from the pew into the aisle. Hugh slipped a hand beneath her elbow to support her.

'You're upset, my darling,' he said gently.

Blanche nodded. 'It took me by surprise,' she confessed, 'I never expected to feel so sad — and all for a chap I hardly knowed.'

❀

Jye's habit of speech, seldom practised, was now in danger of deserting him altogether. The silence of the deaf, so readily accepted by those around them, aroused no anxiety or comment in the case of Jye. He had never been loquacious, and even his mother had at first attributed his silence to a broken romance.

'That wicked maid of Eliza's was only trifling with you,' Meridiana had said, and Jye knew in his heart that this was the truth. Blanche Greypaull had used him, much as a mason might wield his tools, but carelessly. She had chipped at his pride, hammered at his senses with her beauty. He had seen his return to Montacute as a simple cure for all that ailed him, but London still sat upon his shoulder. George Mitchell had once warned him of the insidious power of that city. 'Stay away too long from home,' he had said, 'and you won't never find your way back.'

Jye had searched, half-heartedly, for the plump brown-eyed Dorcas, and found her married, with a child at her skirts and a baby in her arms. He had gone back to the Baptist chapel, only to be embarrassed by the frank admiration of the young girls in the congregation. The handicap of deafness, he now acknowledged, would always set him apart, and, in any case, these girls were not of his own generation. After the first year at home, Jye no longer attended the Baptist chapel. He questioned his mother on the subject of bewitchment. What, he asked her, would happen to a man who had stepped, unknowingly, across six iron nails, hammered into a threshold by a scheming woman? Meridiana paused before giving him an answer. Where, she demanded, had he come across that particular magic?

Oh, he said, he'd heard tell of it in London. Jye's mother looked doubtfully at him. That sounded, she said, like some sorcery she once saw practised in the Blackdown Hills, in a village called Buckland St Mary. The people who lived in those hills were a queer lot, in league with the Devil. That particular spell was a very bad one; any man so tricked would remain for ever in the thrall of that scheming woman; and Blanche Greypaull, she said slowly, had been born and had grown up in the village of Buckland.

Jye expected further questions, but Meridiana remained silent. She bent that piercing gaze upon him, and then walked from the house. He watched her from the kitchen window as she took the hillpath up towards Jack o'Beards.

❂

'I could understand 'un brooding for a few weeks, Reverend. But months have run into years, and Jye don't get no better.' The distress of Meridiana, voiced to the Reverend Powys, was pitiful and unusual. They sat, in the soft May evening, on a knoll of the Hill, beneath a furze-bush, preacher and village woman together. 'There's times when I think he'll go out of his mind. He don't hardly talk no more, just a nod or a headshake is all he gives me.' She paused and looked away towards the Levels, to the finger of Glastonbury Tor on the far horizon. 'I never did hold much with Parsons, sir, if you'll 'scuse I saying so. But I always did believe in Jesus.' Her gruff voice shook a little. 'My Jye always was a chapel goer, like Luke his father. But he don't never set foot no more inside the chapel.' She glanced sideways at the black-garbed Vicar, 'I knows as how you won't believe me, but my Jye have been bewitched! I never thought to see the day when he turned off religion! 'Tis my belief that a spell was put on my son when he was up in London. Nothing else could account for the way he've been behaving lately!'

'It may simply be a temporary aberration.' The Reverend Charles Francis Powys, Vicar of Montacute, gentleman and scholar, spoke absently but with conviction. He looked at the woman, saw her lack of comprehension, and said swiftly, 'I'm sure he'll get over it. Young men like Jye, raised quietly in devout and simple households, are bound to have troubled minds when they got out into the wide world. Take the case of my oldest son, John Cowper. It is university which has – but that's my own problem. Our concern must be for Jye, for his spiritual well-being. Would you like me to have a few words with him?'

'Wudden do no good, sir! He can go total-deaf when he's a mind to.' Meri sought for the right words. 'He've gone away – somewhere inside hisself – 'tis a wicked maiden's magic what have done the damage, and that'll take a Christian maid to put right the mischief.'

The Parson rose stiffly, and pulled his robes around him. He stood like a great black crow on the rim of the incline. 'Perhaps,' he said, 'the company of some devout young woman?'

'Jye's turned twenty-seven,' said Meridiana, 'them of his own age is already married and got childer.'

Charles Francis Powys had the gift of inspiring trust in the most unlikely people. He was also a dedicated walker. He knew every field and hillock, every farm and hovel, every shepherd's shelter. Among his most valued friends he counted the poacher Naboth Rugg, Nancy Cooper the witch, and the many itinerants who passed regularly through the village. His contacts with Meridiana Carew were strange and intermittent. For much of the time she

399

tended to ignore his presence upon the Hill or about the village. Meri only ever spoke to any person when she was of a will to do so. A conversation with her was something to be dwelt on, to be turned over in the mind in quiet moments. Her ways of thinking were original and often outrageous, but from such people many lessons could be learned. The Reverend Charles Powys halted for a moment on the brow of the Hill. He looked down on the golden village, and the tall, proud figure of Meridiana, walking slowly downhill. The woman was troubled, and in a way that was all too familiar to him. The unhappiness of his own son was an ever present problem, but in the case of Jye Carew a solution might be found. The Reverend Powys began to walk, purposefully, to the south side of the Hill, to the shelter where he would find David Honeybone, the shepherd.

❃

In a community of ponderous but dignified stone-carvers, and slow-moving agricultural labourers, the Honeybone family moved about the village with a quicksilver brightness. The Reverend Powys had often wondered at the origins of these people: from whom had they inherited their red-gold hair, that freshness of complexion, the blue and knowing gaze, that singular and intriguing surname? Just to watch them go about their business gave him pleasure. Nimble-fingered, sharp of wit and tongue, quick to laughter, he had made an especial study of them. The fact that they were of the Particular Baptist persuasion concerned him not at all. He thought about them as he trod the Hill paths: four sons and one late-arrival, a precious daughter, whom they called Damaris. The boys were all clever. Already the two oldest were passing through the Seminary in Bristol and would become ordained Ministers of the Baptist faith. Two younger sons had moved away, to work in Yeovil. The daughter, he believed, stayed at home, and sat at the gloving with her mother.

He found David Honeybone on the south slope of the Hill. The shepherd, wrapped in a dun-coloured blanket pinned crossways upon his left shoulder, looked like some Biblical figure, lost in the contemplation of his flock. Reluctant to disturb the man's concentration, Charles Powys called softly to him.

'David Honeybone — may we speak together?'

Their conversation was brief; Honeybone was always quick to grasp a point and take it further. An idea, once planted, would mature in his mind; if it was approved, then he would act upon it. Shepherd and Parson sat down together on the cropped turf.

'Jye Carew,' observed the Reverend Powys, 'twenty-seven years old, trained as a stone-carver in London. Lives at home with his widowed mother.'

David Honeybone nodded.

'A member of your chapel, I believe?'

'Lapsed,' said the shepherd.

'A great shame.'

'Aye, sir, 'tis that!'

'A good fellow,' said Charles Powys, 'clean-living, dependable. Of course his deafness is a great drawback. They tell me his state of mind is very low since he returned from London. I've seen him out walking in the evenings and on Sundays. A very sad and lonely young man, if I'm any judge of these matters. It seems a great pity that chapel members have seen fit to abandon a soul that is so sorely afflicted.'

'Abandoned, Vicar? US don't never abandon nobody! Jye made up his own mind to leave us. Nuthin' we could do to stop 'un.'

'The Lord,' murmured Charles Powys, 'works in mysterious ways, His wonders to perform.' He paused, significantly. 'I see your daughter going about the village. A

401

very good girl, so they tell me. Let us pray, Honeybone, that contact with the gloving wenches will not defile her.'

'My Maris is a Sunday-school teacher,' said the shepherd, 'and a devout maiden, I might tell 'ee! Mind you,' he said thoughtfully, 'Mother do keep her very close to home, and maids do get sort of restless sometimes round about her age.'

'How old is she, Honeybone?'

'Sixteen, sir.'

'Of course,' observed the Vicar, 'the influence of a pure young woman has been known to work miracles upon the soul of a young man who has strayed from the right path. Take the case of Jye Carew, now. A thoroughly good fellow, a fine craftsman who has never caught that abominable cider-habit. He goes away to London, to follow his trade, and what happens? He comes back a changed man, dare I say it, a broken man?' He glanced sideways at the shepherd. 'We have a duty in these matters, Honeybone. Jye is not a member of my congregation, but I am deeply concerned about him. The young people of the village are my particular worry.'

The shepherd nodded. 'Well, you should know all about it, Vicar. You've brought up eleven children of your own.'

'Daughters,' Charles Powys said quietly, 'are much safer married at a young age.'

'Aye, sir! 'Tis a notion what have come into my own head quite a lot just lately.'

The Reverend gentleman stood up. He dusted down his cassock and began to move away, beyond the grazing flock. 'I'd be obliged if you would give some thoughts to the subject of our conversation, Mr Honeybone.'

'Aye, sir. You've give I a lot to think about, and no mistake.'

David Honeybone's shelter was a simple construction. It comprised three walls built of loose-laid stone, and was open fronted with a roof of turves laid across beech rails. A judicious thrust of the shepherd's shoulder sent the topmost stones tumbling easily from the rear wall. David Honeybone surveyed the damage with a grin of satisfaction. 'Well now,' he muttered, 'idden that a pity! That'll take a London-trained mason to build my wall up.'

❋

Jye Carew repaired the wall of the shepherd's shelter on a warm June evening. It was hardly the job for a skilled banker-mason, but Honeybone had approached him, and to refuse would have involved too much unwelcome effort. Jye's lethargy was almost total: it now extended into his garden; even his roses remained unpruned and untended.

Honeybone surveyed the newly-built wall. 'Stand for a hundred years, that will, boy! Now, what say you come along home wi' I? Mother got a nice bit o' rabbit in the stewpot, and bread fresh-baked.'

Jye made excuses. 'Mother'll be expecting me, Mr Honeybone.'

'No she won't boy. I see'd her a half-hour since. She was setting out for Odcombe.' He paused. 'I mentioned to her after chapel that you might be taking supper with us.'

Jye walked slowly downhill, adjusting his stride to the shorter steps of the little shepherd, the black and white sheepdog close at their heels. They passed through the village and into the lane where the Honeybones' cottage stood among apple and pear trees. A woman's voice called from the kitchen window.

'Supper in ten minutes, Father!'

The older man grinned. 'Just nice time to show 'ee my bit o' garden, eh Jye?'

David Honeybone spoke carefully, making quite sure that the mason could understand him, and Jye, accustomed as he was to the isolation of his deafness, found it hard to respond

403

to the warmth of the little shepherd. They stood together on the narrow path and Jye nodded his approval of the rows of vegetables, the gooseberry and blackcurrant bushes. But all the time his eyes were drawn to the bench beneath the pear tree at the bottom of the garden.

The girl was seated with her back towards them. Her hair was loose and damp, she was pulling a comb very slowly through it, lifting each separate strand to the warmth of the evening sunshine. The girl was very tiny, the bench high, and yet that extraordinary hair hung down to touch the rough grass beneath the tree. As Jye and the shepherd moved along the path, the drying locks were already changing colour. By the time they had walked up to the pear tree, the hair was quite dry; it lay, straight and shining to the ground like a sheet of gold.

David Honeybone, acutely conscious of Jye's inattention, but still gratified by it, followed his gaze to where the girl sat, seemingly unaware. The shepherd faced Jye.

'Thass my only daughter,' he warned the mason. 'Thass my liddle Damaris. Her's but sixteen-year-old, and mighty precious to me.'

Jye's dark skin reddened. 'I didden mean no harm,' he muttered, ''twas just that hair. I never did see such a length and colour!'

David Honeybone nodded. 'Never been cut in all her life. When her stands up that do reach to below her knees.' He smiled. 'I once done some work for old Squire Phelips. He paid I wi' a mint-new sovereign. I laid that bit of gold up against my maid's hair, and that hair was the self-same colour.'

❊

Her name was Damaris, but they called her Maris. Jye looked at her, secretly, across her father's table, and felt the weight of his twenty-seven years: all that bitter time of loneliness and disappointment. Reckoned feature by feature she was no great beauty, not even pretty. The forehead was too broad and high, the nose too pronounced for the small face. But there was a kind of delicacy about her, and oh, but her eyes were blue and merry! He liked the way her lips turned up for instant laughter, the freshness of her skin, the crown of gold braids now wound high upon her head.

Jye ate absent-mindedly, surprised by this Honeybone family; the quick and animated movement of their lips, the constant exchange of conversation, their swift and expressive gestures. He felt like a clumsy giant at their supper table. They were all so tiny, so neat and compact. But most of all he watched the girl, surreptitiously from beneath his eyelids.

Jye could not remember the tones of laughter, especially his own. His parents had been sober people, not given much to humour. The sounds of merriment had rarely been heard in his home, even before the silence had claimed him. This Maris had a wry, three-cornered trick of smiling. When she laughed her lips came all the way open to reveal her small white teeth and pink tongue. He was fascinated by the physical movements of that laughter, the way her head swayed back upon her slender neck; he thought he could almost hear those ecstatic chuckles. He could feel his own stiff lips curving up into an answering smile, even though he had quite failed to follow the Honeybones' lightheated conversation.

He walked back to his mother's house through the stillness of a late June evening, and knew that not for a long time had he been so achingly aware of the summer scented fields, the dark lanes, the hidden presence of youthful lovers. She had walked with him to her father's gate. The light from an uncurtained window had fallen across her, and she had indicated by a swift movement of her fingers the extraordinary difference in their respective heights.

'Look,' her lips had said, 'why, I only reaches up to the middle button on your jacket!' He had smiled for the second time that evening, but had not found any answer for her.

'You don't come no more to chapel,' she accused him.

He had shuffled his feet then, and looked away. 'No,' he said, 'I been a bit busy jus' lately. I got to mind my mother's garden, and then there's wood to be chopped –'

'You shudden bide away from chapel,' she had reproved him, 'the Lord have got need of you, Jye Carew.' She had made a beckoning movement then with her index finger. 'Now, you promise I that you'll come to meeting next Sunday morning.'

The message of her lips and fingers, used together, had quite overwhelmed him. 'I'll be there,' he had vowed, 'I'll come next Sunday.'

When the Sabbath day came, Jye took out his suit of Baptist black and brushed it; his chapel shirt lay white and ready in the dresser drawer, alongside his father's Bible. He surveyed himself in the scrap of mirror, and not without pride; his hair, still damp from immersion beneath the pump, lay curling and black upon his fine head. He touched his upper lip, and thought that perhaps a moustache might be an improvement. He had noticed just lately that the young bloods of the village all wore large moustaches.

He put on the white shirt and the black suit, and just to touch these garments was to remember Blanche Greypaull, and other Sundays. He recalled that back room in St Martin's Lane, and Blanche down on her knees before him. He remembered that November day, the yellow fog, standing with her on Westminster Bridge, and then the final parting. Jye reached out a hand to lift his father's Bible; he held its grainy leather close to his chest, and he at once grew calm. It had been on that same dreadful Sunday that he had also prayed in King Henry's Chapel, had known that he was at last a man, with all a man's desires and longings. A quiet rooftree, he had thought then. His own hearthstone. A sweet woman waiting for him. How could he have forgotten about all that?

He left his mother's cottage and walked through Bishopston, down Middle Street, and into South Street; and there was the little Baptist chapel, dependable and foursquare. Jye trod the marble step that had once led up to the high altar of St Paul's Cathedral and, in some strange way that he could not comprehend, yet another link between past and present seemed to forge in his mind. The battle, he now saw, had always been, must always be, between good and evil. His recent months and years spent in the wilderness had not been wasted, after all.

He came into the whitewashed chapel, and found Maris Honybone, kneeling with her parents in prayer in a foremost pew. Jye hesitated before making his declaration, but only for a moment. With a brief nod to the assembled congregation, he moved forward to kneel beside Maris in the Honeybone pew.

❋

Meridiana sat underneath the furze bush, her knees drawn up to her chin, her black skirts wound tightly about her ankles. The Reverend Powys came over the rim of the Hill, to sit down beside her on the cropped turf. They exchanged no greeting, but sat silent and brooding, looking outwards towards misty Athelney and the autumnal shrouds that hid the Levels. It was the preacher who first broke the quiet. 'Damaris Honeybone,' he observed. 'A bright girl, industrious and worthy.'

Meri's dark brows drew together. 'A funny liddle mommet,' she said gruffly. 'Her 'ud never have been my choice.' She glanced meaningfully at Charles Francis Powys. 'But, like usual, nobody ever thought to ask I what I wanted.'

'Choice becomes somewhat limited,' murmured Reverend Powys, 'when a man is approaching his thirtieth year.'

'My Jye is coming twenty-eight next New Year,' snapped Meridiana, 'but 'un don't look his age.'

'The girl is very young of course.' The Vicar's tone was deliberately doubtful. 'The parents are most particular — a devout chapel family — two sons are already ordained Ministers in their religion — the girl might be said to be something of a pearl — ?'

Meridiana stiffened. 'Age don't count between my people. I've see'd maids of fourteen and fifteen wedded in the tan. 'Tis safer all round. What's more, a young wife'll settle easier into her man's ways. As to this Maris being a pearl, let me tell 'ee, Reverend, that my son is pure gold! If he takes her to wife, and that is something far from settled, then all the fortune'll be on her side.'

'I see them walking out together after chapel,' said the Vicar.

'Her mother walks ten paces behind 'em.' Meri grinned. 'Poor old 'ooman! Her needn't have no fears about my Jye. I knows my own son, Reverend. He'm slower than a dratted drayhorse.'

Charles Powys rubbed his hands together. 'The Lord moves in a mysterious way?' he suggested.

Meri grunted. ''Un needs a good push and shove from time to time,' she said wryly, 'but thass your job, idden it, Parson?'

❈

Greenbrook Terrace
Taunton. November 2nd, 1892.

My dear cousin Rhoda,

Am trusting to hear word from you any day now, but

time heavy on my hands, just lately, so thowt I would pen you a few lines. Cant seem to settle myself to do anything at all since losing Louis. *Fist time* in my whole Life that I have been free to do *exactly* as I please, and find now that there is nothing for me to do. All these years lived down in Taunton, and found that I only knowed my way to Church or out to Bishop's Hull for a Sunday stroll with Annis. I walks many miles *on my own* these days, dear cousin. Have looked at every corner of this great town, even strayed so far as Rowbarton. I go to the Cemetery twice a week. Flowers growed in my bit of garden for that speshul purpose. Sweet-peas done well this Summer, I took a nice bunch on every visit while they lasted. The white rose planted on Jack's grave was full of blooms.

I cant get used to the thowt that *nobody needs* me, Rhoda. I sit in my chair and look at my hands lying idle in my lap, and I gets to wonder what the dear Lord have *got in mind for me*. There is days when I cant see no reason in *soldjering on*. Dont never see enough of my grandchild, Laura. Laura is v. clever, she have already passed her first exams in *music*. That puts me in mind of *myself* and *you*, Rhoda, when we took our first Prinsipuls of Music with the Rector's wife in Buckland St Mary. Do you still play your piano, Dear Cousin?

Madelina do keep Laura very *close-up*. Child is always dressed like she was *going* to a *wedding*. Mina busy sewing *all hours* to make new outfits for her. Poor child is never allowed to get dirty or play with other children. That dont seem right, Dear Cousin. But more than my life is worth to *say so*, Mina having growed v. *sharp-tongued* of late.

Simeon still away, and never a single word of Candace. Blanche and husband not been here for some time. Should think they have probably *run out of money*. What brings me to my *biggest worry*, Rhoda. My Annis have *changed in her ways* towards me. It is v. hurtful after all these years. Annis dont ask for *my permisshun* no more, but goes about the town *at all hours*. She have took to wearing Blanche's clothes, in *full disobedianse* of my stern wishes. She have curled her hair in the front, *like Blanche*, and have took to walking with *such a strut and pride* that I hardly *recognises* her, Rhoda.

What that poor little soldjer-boy will *think of her* when he comes back from India, I just dont know. She is *not* the maiden he said goodbye to. She have growed v. secretive, Rhoda. I followed her last Sunday morning, after Church Service. As you know, my sight is not too good, but I am sure that I saw Annis *talking to a soldier* by the gates of Jellalabad Barracks. I have give her plenty of *openings* to confide in me about it, but young madam do keep her *own counsel* these days. I had set my heart on Annis marrying Frank Nevill, and all of us *living happy together*. He only got about another two years of Army Service, and then he will come home. She *dont care* no more about his letters, Rhoda. Dont hardly listen when I reads them to her. As for writing back to him, I makes-up they letters *on my own*, Dear Cousin, and have done so for *several months* now. But for *me*, our Annis would have *lost* poor Frank, altogether.

I can see now how you must have felt when your Rosa went away to Oshkosh. The *last* daughter to *bide at home* is v. speshul to a Mother, and my Annis should have *knowed that*. My own Mother used to come and visit me *every day* when I first got married. However it will all *end-up*, I dont know, Rhoda.

Hope that your Haysel and Harvest went well this year, and the Wisconsin Summer not too hot for you. Hope to hear from you when you got some time. Regards to Mr Black and all your family.

Your loving cousin, Eliza.

✻

410

The ivory satin ballgown, embroidered all over with tiny seed-pearls, had been laid away, swathed in tissue paper, for more than a year. Blanche had never forgiven Prince Eddy for dying so inconsiderately only six weeks before his wedding to Princess May of Teck. She had refused to wear the dress to any other function, and Hugh suspected that it had been designed especially for the delectation of Bertie, Prince of Wales. The childlike and growing attachment of Blanche for the Royal Family, her passionate interest in the merest of their doings, was a trait which Hugh found touching, endearing even.

There had been rumours in the past months of a romance between George, second son of the Prince of Wales, and the bereaved Princess May of Teck. An engagement had been announced, and Blanche had visited the unworn ballgown, still waiting shrouded in a closet; Hugh had spied her, stroking the expensive garment, and whispering to it. On hearing of the Royal engagement, Blanche had sounded doubtful.

'I suppose it's quite a handy arrangement, really. They've just passed the poor maid – girl – on, from the dead brother to the live one. They do say,' her tone became confidential, 'they do say that the Princess of Wales have – has – passed on all the wedding presents that were given to Prince Eddy. That poor George! Everything'll be second-hand. He'll get a hand-me-down bride, not to mention fifty silver cruets, and twenty china dinner-services what was never intended for him!'

Hugh raised an eyebrow. 'Really Blanche! I can't imagine where you hear such gossip.'

'I can!' Aunt Porteous stared imperiously from her place at the head of the breakfast table. 'How many times must I tell you, Blanche. You simply must not indulge in so much idle chit-chat with the servants.'

Blanche pouted and raised her chin, but said nothing.

'And while we are discussing this subject,' added Hugh, 'I must ask you to refrain, Blanche, from this recent habit of coming downstairs to examine the post, while it still lays upon the hall table. It is the servants' duty to bring in the letters to the breakfast table.'

'In view of the fact,' put in Mrs Porteous, 'that you cannot recognise your own name when you see it written, there seems very little point in your diligent search for a letter, every morning.'

'Well, that's where you be both wrong! Martha do tell me when I got a letter, and then she do read it to me.'

Mrs Porteous grew rigid. 'Do you mean to tell me,' she whispered, 'that my scullery-maid reads your letters to you?'

Blanche's voice although tremulous was still defiant. 'And why not?' she demanded.

'I'll tell you why not, my dear girl. If the scullery-maid is reading your letters for you then it must by this time be common knowledge in every drawing-room and kitchen throughout the City of London, that Mrs Hugh Fitzgerald is totally illiterate.'

Blanche threw down her table napkin. She stood up, pushed back her chair, and pounded the table until the dishes rattled. Hugh also stood up. 'That will be enough, Blanche. There have been far too many of these scenes, just lately.'

Blanche pointed a finger at Mrs Porteous. ''Tis that old bitch what always starts it. I'm off, I tell you! I'm going back to Mrs Gimball. I was happy in St Martin's Lane.' She rushed from the room. The sounds of her running footsteps, and the slamming of heavy doors marked her progress as Blanche made her way back up to her husband's apartment.

Mrs Porteous sighed. 'What ever are we going to do, Hugh? I tried to warn you.' She paused. 'You're not happy, dear boy.' She coloured slightly. 'I have heard her screaming at you, late at night. This marriage would appear to be a

412

complete disaster in every department.'

'Please, Aunt,' pleaded Hugh, 'just try to be patient with her. She has improved most enormously in the past year. She's – well, she's very highly-strung. She gets nervous in your company, and when Blanche is nervous she reacts with anger.' He bit at his lower lip. 'I understand her you see. Every day that passes, reveals some new facet of her nature. She's frightfully complex and fascinating –'

'She's a cheap little baggage who has thoroughly bewitched you!' Aunt Letitia looked concerned. 'Sometimes, Hugh, I fear for your very sanity – your life even! There's something about your wife that frightens me; and I am not the woman to be easily alarmed.'

Hugh stared at his aunt. He had never heard her admit to fear of anything or anybody. He recalled the photographer, Kraus, who had once confessed to experiencing a similar anxiety. 'There's something about Miss Greypaull,' Kraus had said. 'She's a strange one, and no mistake. When you take a picture, sir, you naturally spend some considerable time looking at the face . . . something about this Miss Greypaull that chills the blood . . . I'm not an imaginative man . . . but be warned, sir!'

Hugh climbed the stairs very slowly. Experience had taught him that he would need to be collected and strong before confronting Blanche. He entered the bedroom to find her tossing garments haphazardly into a small bag. At sight of him she grew hysterical. 'I 'ont bide yer,' she screamed, 'your bloody old aunt is dead set on knocking me down, every chance she gets!' Blanche threw herself lengthways upon the unmade bed; she bit at the tapestry bedspread, and began to thrash with her arms and legs. Her hair came loose, pins and combs flew in all directions. When she lifted her face, Hugh saw, dismayed, that her lips were foam-flecked. He sat down on the dark-blue sofa. To touch her at that moment would be to invite further paroxysms of violent temper.

'Blanche,' he said, 'this behaviour is not worthy of you. It only confirms my aunt's worst opinions, and, what is more important, it is very harmful to your health. You complain incessantly of headaches, and feelings of ennui. These bouts of rage are quite exhausting for you, and achieve absolutely nothing.' He nodded towards the small, half-filled bag. 'We go through this same charade every time.' He risked a hesitant smile, 'now why don't we talk, quietly and reasonably together, about all these matters that you seem to find so very distressing.'

Blanche raised her head; she gazed assessingly at him. She sat up and pushed the heavy hair back from her shoulders. She held out a hand towards him, and he went to her. She leaned against his shoulder, sniffled delicately, and wiped her eyes and lips on his proffered hankerchief. She glanced sideways at him, but he maintained his cool expression. She sobbed deep in her throat, and then hiccoughed sadly.

'Why,' he enquired, 'do you find it so imperative to search through the post every morning?'

'You know how disappointed I was to be done out of that Prince Eddy's wedding?'

'Yes,' he said, 'you've complained incessantly upon the subject.'

'Well – there's all this talk now about Prince George taking on with the Princess May where his dead brother Eddy left off! Can't you understand, Hugh? I can't wait to see if we get another invitation!'

Hugh looked, disbelieving at her. 'Do you mean to tell me that all this – this unseemly upheaval is to do with a silly invitation?'

'Yes,' she said. 'Certain matters are important to me. Your mind and my mind runs on separate trainlines. I don't say noth – anything against your fiddle-playing, or all the hours you waste reading books and painting pictures.' She plucked at the bedspread, and glanced doubtfully at him.

'You was — were — a lot more fun before we got married. We hardly ever go out anymore. You just sit by the fire, counting up your birds' eggs, and your scruffy old pennies.' She paused. 'I thought we'd have good times together.'

'And so did I, Blanche?' Hugh's voice was bitter. Suddenly he gripped her shoulders and twisted her body around to face him. 'How,' he pleaded, 'can you possibly look so desirable and inviting, and yet be so cold towards me?' He watched the conflicting emotions twist her lovely features as she sought for the words that would explain her indifference towards him.

'I don't know what it is,' she murmured. 'I have thought about it, Hugh, truly I have. I don't seem to get no — any — loving feelings for you. Trouble is, you're such a gentle sort of fellah. Perhaps if you was to,' she hesitated, 'if you was to knock me about a bit — you know — treat me rough — it might —' Her words trailed away before his scandalised features.

'Perhaps,' he said sourly, 'you'd like me to get drunk as I did in Dover. Remember Blanche? You said then, that if I ever —'

'I know,' she broke in, 'but that was different.' She continued to flounder in this rare attempt to put words to her emotions. 'I think I like masterful men after all,' she confessed, 'and since whisky is what it takes in your case, then you'd better buy a bottle.'

He released her and she fell back upon the pillows.

'My God,' he whispered, 'I shall never understand you. You told me once that you "didn't hold with drink". Now you're demanding that I drink whisky.'

'Not demanding,' she said, 'only if you want to.' She grinned, 'I take a small nip of brandy, just now and again. There's no harm in it. I find it a great comfort. I never needed Dutch courage,' she said bitterly, 'until I was forced to live in this damned house.'

Hugh nodded. 'You're quite right, of course. We need the responsibility and interest of our own establishment. We still tend to behave like children while living under my aunt's roof.' He grew thoughtful. 'It's all a question of finance, Blanche. I can't afford to maintain a London address, and a home in the country.'

Blanche sat swiftly upright. 'Who said anything about the country?' she cried, 'I was born on a farm. I hated it! I only want to bide – stay – in London, Hugh! I told you before we got married. A little house in St John's Wood, or a suite of rooms in Regent's Park.' She reached for his hands and gazed imploringly at him. 'Don't ever take me out of London. If you do – then you'll live to regret it! I can put up with the Whalebone Queen, just so long as we go out and about more.' She released her hold upon him, and he watched with a growing sense of revulsion the way her fingers opened and closed with a grasping motion.

'I want life, Hugh,' she said urgently, 'I want music and dancing, lovely clothes and elegant company. You gave me a taste of all that before we were married. Since then, I've been shut up like a nun, hid away in this awful house.' She sent him a look of total understanding. 'You needn't fear for my behaviour,' she assured him, 'I won't be unfaithful to you. There was only two men in this city that I ever fancied. One was too poor to tie my shoelace – and the other is so important that I doubt if I'll ever get anywhere near him. Just promise that we'll stay in London and I'll do anything you ask. I'll be nice to Aunty, I won't lose my temper.' She began to stroke his cheek, and her voice grew husky. 'I'll be a loving wife in future. You'll see such a difference in me.'

Hugh sighed. 'I can't promise to live in London, always.' He hesitated. 'I think, when we first met, you probably gained a wrong impression of me. You saw me as the idle

416

dandy, the wild young blood – '

'And so you was – were,' she interrupted, 'you were well-known in Romano's and my friend in the Life School said you were always going round to the girls in Foley Street. When you took me racing all the bookies recognised you. Why – you were a pal of that Gervase and Prince Eddy! Everybody in London knew what they got up to!'

Hugh looked like a guilty child. 'I can't deny it, Blanche, I – I was more upset over Clair's deception of me than I cared to admit. I became a little crazy for a few months.' Even as he spoke, the corners of her full red lips turned downwards, and he was afraid.

Blanche grew very still. 'I never knew that she meant that much to you. You've always kept very quiet on that subject.' She peered suspiciously at him. 'You don't still harbour no – any – warm feelings towards her, do you?'

Hugh said, 'Would it matter so very much to you, if I did?'

Her reaction amazed him. The grasping fingers clutched at his arms, she shook him violently. 'You're mine, you hear me, Hugh Fitzgerald! Just let me catch you even eyeing up another woman, and I'll put your sight out! I'm not like my Mama. I don't go in for forgiveness and all that rot. An eye for an eye, that's what I believe! Debts paid in full, and God help the poor sinner what ever gets across Blanche!'

A tiny thrill of fear contracted Hugh's stomach muscles. There were times, he thought, when the statements of Blanche sounded more like predictions.

❈

The wedding of Prince George Frederick Ernest Albert, and Princess May of Teck, was to be celebrated in the Chapel Royal in St James's Palace on July 6th, 1893. Blanche and Hugh Fitzgerald were not invited to attend the ceremony, or the celebration ball which followed.

'I simply don't understand,' Hugh said innocently. 'Some confusion in the sending out of fresh invitations, I should imagine. One can hardly,' he murmured, 'approach the Palace and demand an explanation. I am sorry for your disappointment, my darling. I know how much you had set your heart on a glimpse of the Prince and Princess of Wales.' He smiled. 'We will watch the procession from Romano's upper window.'

Blanche watched Hugh carefully through slitted eyelids. What a fool she had been to let slip that remark about a man so important that she might never meet him! That Hugh had somehow contrived to destroy their invitation to Prince George's wedding ball, she was quite convinced. Never mind! The Prince of Wales still went about a very great deal, and paths often crossed in the most unlikely situations. She thought, with regret, of the ivory satin gown all covered with seed-pearls. If she didn't wear it soon, it would be out of fashion!

❃

Alfonso Nicolino Romano had given orders that his window-boxes were to be packed with flowers and hung with garlands; great clusters of flags and banners bedecked the first floor balconies of Number 399, The Strand; the old Roman restaurateur and wise man of business, was careful to impress his most aristocratic and valued patron with a display of patriotic fervour on the wedding of that gentleman's oldest son.

Hugh had secured front seats on a first-floor balcony at Romano's. As Aunt Porteous remarked, they were perfectly placed to see the whole procession. Blanche, wearing cream-coloured silk, with a corsage of freshly picked roses of an apricot colour, took her seat in the morning sunshine; she gazed down on the surrounding streets made strange and

418

silent by the absence of traffic. Every viewpoint was already occupied by excited people; the pavements and gutters crammed with spectators. The younger citizens of London were seated precariously on the spikes of railings, and in overhanging branches of trees. Blanche recalled Queen Victoria's Jubilee Procession, observed long ago from Mary Higgins' attic window. That happy day had been spent in the company of Mr Solomon and Mrs Gimball. They had eaten eel pie and drunk fizzy ginger-beer; and oh, how they had laughed together! It was on that same morning that she had watched Hugh Fitzgerald arm his Aunt Letitia up the steps of Westminster Abbey. 'There you are,' Mrs Gimball had said, 'now what 'ave I bin telling yer? Could 'ave bin you trotting in beside him if you had only played your cards right.'

Blanche turned to the man who sat beside her, but Hugh, intent upon seeing the first approach of the procession, was unaware of her sly scrutiny of him. Well, here they sat, she thought, bound together in holy wedlock! Her wavering cross stood beneath his written names in a register of marriage. She had made her mark that day and no mistake. Blanche smiled. What a satisfying action that had been! But it had not, she concluded, achieved the intended result. Today she would drink champagne and eat smoked salmon; she would ride back to Russell Square in the Porteous carriage. Her closets were packed with exquisite gowns; her jewel-cases filled with the Fitzgerald heirlooms, oh but she was so weary of Hugh! He was always there: solicitous hand beneath her elbow, gentle whisper in her ear. 'Hit me,' she would shout. 'Kick me if you want to, take your belt and leather me to ribbons — but for God's sake don't be so bloody understanding!' Whatever, she wondered, was this man doing to her? Even now, on this brilliant morning, Blanche could feel the anger rising in her. All those years of self-denial and waiting, and all she had landed in the end was a poor fish like Hugh Fitzgerald.

The procession had arrived. She looked down on the state carriages, on the Dukes and Princes, the King and Queen of Denmark. If she had only waited a bit longer. This thought had come into her head at the wedding reception, when every titled male guest had been drawn so effortlessly towards her. Hugh's concealment of her from his friends had been deliberate and unfair! He was, she now realised, a very dull young man. He was kind and gentle, but lacking utterly that dash of cruelty which she found necessary for fulfilment. She was tired of violin sonatas, and lectures on the habits of the goshawk. He talked endlessly of Dawlish, and the estuary of Starcross. Life in St Martin's Lane had never been monotonous; with Mrs Gimball there had always been laughter and the spice of danger. Blanche recalled with glee the witty conversations of Mr Solomon, and the outraged faces of the cheeky men who had felt the cold steel of her extra-long hat-pin in their rumps. Small wonder that she now suffered from ennui and headaches! It was said that even cats could die of kindness.

Blanche turned her gaze upon the Honourable Letitia, stiff and ugly in her dark brocade and ostrich feathers. The temptation to put a spell upon her tormentor had recently led Blanche to visit a deserted church in search of candle-ends, but even in the very act of filching, a terrible lassitude had overcome her, and she had walked away empty-handed. A great shout went up from the crowd.

'It's the Prince and Princess of Wales,' announced Aunt Letitia. Blanche leaned forward. She looked briefly at the Princess. The reputation of great beauty, thought Blanche, was probably deserved, although it was said that the front hair was an expensive transformation and the beautiful complexion owed its texture to an enamel, which would crack if the Princess should attempt to smile. But who cared about her anyway! It was the Prince who commanded the crowd's atttention!

'Good old Bertie,' they yelled. 'What's going to win the two-thirty?'

Blanche half-rose in her seat, she leaned across the balustrade to see the Prince of Wales gazing upwards at Romano's restaurant. In the background she could hear the old 'Roman' shouting an Italian greeting. Impulsively Blanche ripped a rosebud from her corsage, and tossed it down towards the Royal carriage. The answering nod and wave, she was sure, had been meant for her and no one else. Hugh turned a disapproving face towards her. He drew her attention to the approaching state coach, drawn by four cream-coloured ponies in purple reins and ribbons.

'Do pay some attention, Blanche,' he whispered, 'this carriage holds the Queen of England.'

On their return to Russell Square, Hugh locked himself into his study; Blanche heard the moan of his violin, and supposed that this time he intended to sulk in private. She had begged that they might go out that evening to look at the illuminations, but he had refused. No carriages would be allowed in the streets he said, and it would be dangerous for them to walk among the vast crowds. Blanche had offered to protect him, she still possessed, she told him, that extra-long hat-pin which had served her so well before her marriage. When the servants returned to the house later in the evening, Blanche went down to the kitchens. She found Martha, the scullery-maid, happy and exultant.

'Oh, madam,' she cried, 'you should just 'ave seen it! Like a fairy-tale it was. All them great palaces lit up, and Hyde Park cho-a-bloc wiv' people. You couldn't move in Piccadilly and they had put on a special show up Park Lane.' She paused. 'There wasn't no danger, madam. Everybody was so nice and cheerful, you could have gone out to see the fun, after all.'

Blanche presented the girl with an empty decanter. 'Get it

filled for me, Martha,' she said dully, 'it's going to be one of those nights when I can't sleep.'

❊

After years of piety and self-denial, after evenings and Sundays spent in helping Mama to care for Louis, Annis Greypaull had finally succumbed to the Temptations of the Devil. She had learned to waltz in a corner of the factory workroom, to the music of the tea-boy's mouth organ, in moments stolen from her break-time. She suspected that dancing must be very sinful. Any act which aroused such an intensity of physical pleasure was bound to be wicked, and carry a penalty of some sort.

'But you're so good at it!' the seamstresses had told her. 'A natural dancer if ever I see'd one!' All at once those girls who had, for years, ignored and despised her had become her bosom friends. 'You got to get out and about,' they had urged. 'With both of your brothers dying so sudden, and your feller miles away across the ocean, why – 'tis enough to turn your brain off! How old are you, now? Twenty-five? However can your Ma be so blooming selfish! If you don't look sharp, Annis Greypaull, you'll be going to your grave without no fun at all!'

Annis knew that they were right. They certainly had fun; she had heard them whispering about it. They went into pubs and the Variety Theatre. Sometimes they danced in the ballroom of the London Hotel; and the high-jinks that went on in Vivary Park after dark were nobody's business! Annis always smiled when she heard these revelations, just to be obliging, but, secretly, the thought of such abandoned behaviour still terrified her. You were reckoned lucky, the button-holers giggled, if you got out of Vivary Park on a Sunday night still wearing your best bloomers. Only to think about such matters wasn't really sinful; even so, there were moments when sitting at home with Mama, that the cheeks

422

of Annis would turn bright pink for no obvious reason.

A constraint had grown up between Annis and her mother. Mama now veered very much towards Madelina; Annis knew that they talked about her, and her changed behaviour. She did not, she told herself, really care at all! When church-bells rang out from St Mary's in Hammett Street, Annis stopped her ears against the sound. She would hum a few bars of the latest waltz, and practice the steps before her dressing-table mirror. So far, her sins had been very small ones. She had once gone into the Four Alls, and bought a port and lemon in the company of her workmates. She had, just to see what it would feel like, allowed Captain Jeremy Castlemain to kiss her, on a quiet Sunday morning behind the bandstand. She rarely, if ever, thought about Frank Nevill.

Annis wondered why Captain Castlemain remained so long in Taunton when other soldiers were always on the move. He had never been to India or Ireland. She asked careful questions of her workmates.

'A family called Castlemain,' she said, 'do any of you maids know anything about them?'

'Don't you never read the papers?' Sally laughed. 'Why the Castlemains is the very top nobs in all the County. They got a big estate somewhere out towards Quantock. The old lady Castlemain rides her carriage through Fore Street as if she was Queen Victoria herself.' The speaker was smart and knowledgeable; she sent a keen glance in the direction of Annis. 'What for you want to know about they Castlemains, eh maid?'

Annis bent her head above her sewing-machine; she manoeuvred the shirt beneath the moving spindle, snipped cotton from the completed buttonhole, and laid the finished garment upon a pile of others. She looked up to find the attention of the whole workroom concentrated upon her. 'Oh,' she said calmly, ''twas just a name I heard somewhere.'

Sally came across to stand above her. 'I've seen you in Vivary Park on a Sunday evening,' she said softly, 'talking to an officer behind some bushes. I never recognised you at first, all dressed up in they outfits what your Blanche brings down from London.' Sally looked uneasy. 'I know we brought you the curling-tongs and the brown paper, and showed you how to curl your hair. We teached you to waltz, and took you to drink in the Four Alls, but that was only for your own good. We never meant you should get into any trouble.' She paused. 'See, 'tis like this, maid! You idden exactly very smart where fellers is concerned. Your Ma kept you on a short rope all your life. You don't know what's what. You listens to Millie when she reads us bits from they novelettes in our break-time. I've see'd your face, Annis, when Millie tells about all they toffs, and how they weds wi' simple country maidens.' Sally laughed, 'Well you be a simple country wench, all right! Don't reckon they comes much simpler than you from that Buckland St Mary. But 'tis only in books that the nobs makes an honest woman of the kitchen-maid. In real life they haves their wicked way, and then they hops-it!' She sighed, 'I don't reckon you believe me, do you?'

Annis looked up, cheeks scarlet. 'Our Blanche got married to a' Honourable,' she said, 'and she started off as a scullery-maid in London.'

'But you idden your Blanche,' pointed out the tormentor. 'Your Blanche was ever high and mighty. Why, I minds her at the age of fourteen, flaunting her bosoms and her ankles up and down the length of North Street; and didden she just catch a walloping when your Ma catched her at it! But your Blanche had her head screwed on the right way. She never dropped her drawers until the wedding band was on her finger. Now you, Annis Greypaull — you'd be an easy mark for any bloke what had a fancy-handle to his name. What is he? she asked slyly. 'A lieutenant or a

424

captain. I cudden get close enough up to see what pips was on his shoulder.'

Annis picked up a shirt from the heap which lay beside her. She thrust the raw edge of the buttonhole beneath the threaded needle, and touched her foot to the treadle. 'I got work to do,' she said coldly. 'Who I talk to in Vivary Park is my own business.'

Sally began to move away. Across her shoulder she said, 'Well, just you be careful, that's all. You get yourself into any trouble, and your Ma'll skin and gut you!'

Annis had tried so hard to be Mama's good girl, had willed herself to remain her mother's liddle maiden, to be Frank Nevill's waiting sweetheart, and the sister of whom David and Madelina Lambert could be proud. But lately she had often thought about her Papa, and his wild and reckless nature. She had felt the flaring of her senses when Jeremy Castlemain kissed and touched her, a longing for something more in her life than work and church. Was this how Papa had felt on those summer mornings, when he strode out from Larksleve? She could just remember herself, standing by the front porch, watching him saddle and mount the bay mare: that same horse which would later find its own way home from Taunton, with her father, insensible and drunk, across the saddle. She recalled her mother's bitter face, her voice tight and hard with anger. 'Now don't come late back – there's work to be done here Philip – must I always sit alone every evening?' Those same words were now directed by Mama towards Annis; she was painfully aware of her mother's and Madelina's anxious disapproval. The autumn ball was to be held in the London Hotel on the 5th October. Captain Castlemain had said that he would be there, waiting for her.

❋

Jye had grown moustaches; they curled, black and luxuriant above his top lip, and Meridiana grinned at the latent vanity of him.

'Took your time, didden you,' she said, 'to get yourself up a bit fancy for the sake of a maid? Not,' she added, 'that thik skinny liddle mommet is worth growing extra hair for. She'm no bigger than a half-sized rabbit. When I think of all the fine-bodied women of my people – there was Petronell Locke, only too keen to –'

'That'll do, mother.' Jye spoke with quiet authority these days. He walked in the autumn lanes with Maris Honeybone; they took the path that led out towards Odcombe, and the air was heavy with the scent of cider-pummy. Apples lay, crimson and gold, among the long grass of the orchards and Jye had looked upon the world that summer and found it sweet. Suddenly, his roses had been fed and tended; his plot of ground dug over and planted with late seedlings. His black suit and white shirt were on show in chapel every Sunday morning. This Maris, who reached up only to the middle button of his waistcoat, this slip of a girl with the sharp tongue and that yard-long golden hair, had wrought such a miracle in him that even Meridiana had grown quiet on the matter.

Mrs Honeybone always followed ten paces behind them whenever they walked out together. It annoyed her mother that Maris and Jye spoke so softly to one another. 'Speak up, there!' she would call out to her daughter. 'I can't hear a blessed word what you two be saying.'

Maris only smiled. 'You be just as bad-off as Jye, then, idden you?' she answered tartly. 'He can't hear a blessed word I say, neither!'

Jye admired the ability of Maris to think even as she spoke. He had always needed several moments before he could set the most simple answer into words. Everything Maris did was done swiftly and with great skill. Jye sat in

426

the Honeybones' living-room on a Thursday evening when the stacks of completed leather gloves were about to be checked and counted, ready for collection by the gloving-master on the following morning. The pungent smell of newly-cured leather was strong in his nostrils; 'that stench' was how his mother had always described it. Jye did not find it an unpleasant odour, it reminded him of his grandmother, Charity Carew, and the dark little cottage in Wash Lane. He watched Maris sew three rows of fine feather-stitching into the amber-coloured backs of a pair of doe-skin gloves that were a special order for some lady up in London. He admired the concentration which she always brought to the very simplest task, the intensity of her smallest actions. He watched with a sense of awe at so much dedication packed into so frail a frame. There were times when it seemed to Jye that Maris must burn-up or shatter with the force of the energy which powered her. Her mother and brothers were the same. The Honeybone cottage was bright and clean: white muslin fluttered at the open casements, the earthen floor was brushed and made comfortable with many pegged-rugs. There was always a pleasant odour of simmering and baking from the range, a pot of flowers on the window-sill, a spotless cloth upon the table. Jye did not wish to be disloyal, but he could not help but compare the home of Maris with the larger stone-house in Bishopston. The housekeeping habits of Meridiana had grown even more haphazard since his absences in London. Solitude was anathema to a woman who had been born and grown-up in a tan full of companionable females; more and more had his mother given way to her old wandering habits. A sickle moon over Glastonbury Tor, an evening breeze from the south, a glimpse of painted waggons across on Windwhistle Hill, and on would go her old plaid wrap, and he would see that long stride take her out and away, far beyond the clustered houses.

There were many books in the Honeybone household, whole shelves of pious and shabby volumes. Jye read the titles, held the books in his hands, and was impressed to see the names of the student brothers inscribed on every flyleaf.

'They be away to College,' Mrs Honeybone told Jye, 'a-studying for to be Baptist ministers.'

'They must be mighty clever!'

Mrs Honeybone nodded. 'Sharp as needles,' she hesitated, 'our Maris got a long head on her too, for a maiden, that is. Pity she'm a girl! All they brains do make her very forward and unsettled. Us have tried to keep her down, but tidden no use. She've read all they books on the shelves, many times over, and any other printed word what she can lay her hands on. To my mind that idden natural in a female. 'Tis like this, see Jye! There's such a thing in this world as a maid what is too clever for her own good, and that can lead her, all unintentional, into all sorts of mischief.' Mrs Honeybone moved to the open window and looked at Maris who was picking beans for the Sunday dinner. 'I got to tell this quick. Her'll be coming back in, any minute now.' She stood close to Jye and moved her lips carefully so that he should understand. 'Her got a fancy to talk with they Powys brothers, over to the Rectory. I copped her last week, arguing the Bible with that tall one, the one they calls John Cowper. No make no mistake, Jye, that talking all took place outside, in the open graveyard, for all the village to witness. Vicar's sons is all gentlemen, and well-behaved, but, like I've warned her, any secret meetings with him and her'll feel the flat of my hand!' She paused. 'That have give I a lot of worry, Jye. Why! I yeard my young Maris beat that clever Powys right into the ground, just wi' the power of her tongue. He never had no answer for her; he sat perched on a headstone, all disrespectful, and looked like a stunned ox! "Shame on you, sir!" my Maris told 'un, "for not believing on the Lord what made you!" ' Mrs Honeybone sighed. 'I was proper 'shamed of her, I don't mind telling. 'Shamed and proud all at the same time. After all, he is Parson's oldest son. They do hob-nob with Squire Phelips up at Montacute House. 'Tis hardly for our Maris to tell such as him what he should believe on.'

'What did he say?'

Mrs Honeybone grinned. 'I yeard 'un laugh to first. "Why, Miss Honeybone," 'un said, all posh-like in that voice of his. "Why Miss Honeybone, your peror — peroration carries infinitely more conviction than the sermons of my revered father." I tell 'ee, Jye, I was scandalised at how he spoke. No respect at all for his Pa, and him just home from that Cambridge. I wudden take that sort of back-answering from my own boys.'

Jye was silent for some moments. At last he said, 'That Powys is a very good-looking feller. My Ma always reckoned that she never saw such a beautiful head and face on a "gorgie" man.'

Mrs Honeybone bridled. 'No he idden then, Jye Carew! You does yourself poor justice. Why, since you growed they fine black moustaches, you be the handsomest chap for miles around.' She looked coy. ''Tis the opinion of our Maris that you be a proper beauty. I mention it,' she said swiftly, 'because you ought to be told how her feels about 'ee.'

'I bain't clever,' Jye said. 'Sometimes I think your Maris must find I to be dull sort of company. 'Tis only the likes of young John Cowper Powys what she can sharpen her claws on.'

'Aye, boy. Her got a sharp tongue too, what don't always do her credit.' Mrs Honeybone hesitated, and then came to a decision. 'Why don't 'ee offer for her, Jye? Get the matter settled before winter. Her'll be coming eighteen in November.'

Jye's dark face broadened into a smile that curved his lips

429

and reached up to crease the skin around his eyes. 'I was hoping you'd say that,' he murmured, ''tis my dearest wish that Maris and me should get married.'

When dinner was eaten and the table cleared, Mrs Honeybone nodded, significantly, in Jye's direction. 'I 'spect you two young 'uns is wanting your Sunday walk together? Well, you'll have to manage wi'out I, this week.' She glared defiantly at her husband. 'I got a sore foot what do need resting!'

The shepherd looked up from his seat beside the fire. He was feeding his precious ferret with scraps from the dinner table. The creature lived inside David Honeybone's flannel shirt, and only emerged to be fed, or to answer calls of nature. 'That bad foot come on a bit sudden didden it, Mother?' The shepherd looked genuinely concerned.

His wife sighed. 'Don't be a bigger fool than the good Lord have already made 'ee, David. There's times when the young folks can do wi'out us old 'uns.'

Damaris Honeybone, neat and prim in her dark Baptist frock and bonnet, tried to keep up with the long stride of Jye Carew as they walked the Yeovil road. She reached up to grab his elbow, and pointed to her lips to indicate speech.

'Slow down!' she begged, 'I got the stitch something dreadful! Your long legs do cover the ground at a terrible rate. I'll just have to sit down for a minute.'

They sat down by the hedgeside, but remained in full view of the open road for propriety's sake. The absence of Mrs Honeybone, thought Maris, was more of a hindrance than had been her presence; it could of course mean only one thing. Jye Carew was about to offer for her. She had known what was in the wind from that very first evening, when her father had brought Jye home to share their rabbit supper. That tale of a broken wall had been so much moonshine, but the mason was a shy man who needed to be handled with great care. The machinations of her parents had been a source of secret amusement to her; she would have taken the mason straight away, if only they had thought to ask her.

She watched him now as he prepared to speak. There was nothing impulsive or spontaneous about him; she could almost hear the wheels of his mind as they creaked into action. His eyes came wide open and he cleared his throat.

'What,' he said sternly, 'is that Powys feller to you?'

Maris blinked from surprise, her lips twitched into laughter.

He frowned. 'I know that you finds most things funny, Maris, but in this case I wants a proper answer.'

Maris looked into his face and thought how much she loved him. He was like a great and needy child, hungry for affection. She reached out and touched his hand.

'John Cowper Powys,' she said carefully, 'is a very clever feller. He do write poems and books. One of these days he is going to be a great man. He said so. But,' she paused and curled her own thin fingers around his thick ones, 'but that don't have to mean that I like him. He'm an unbeliever and a mocker, for all that his Pa's a Rector! He do speak to I ofttimes when I do go to churchyard to put flowers on my Granfer's grave. Oh Jye! That silly feller do only rant and chat, and most of it rubbish. How could you ever think that he was anything to me?'

Damaris, accustomed to the mobile and revealing features of the Honeybone family, found the face of Jye a difficult page to read. It was only the eyes, deep-set and dark-brown, that gave any hint of what went on in his mind. He gazed at her for a long time. At last he said, 'I believe you, Maris. But I had to be sure.' His tongue stumbled more than was usual across the next words. 'See, 'tis like this. I been made mock-of once before by a maiden. A clever baggage what thought to trap me. You can see, can't you, how I had to be sure.'

'Yes,' she said, 'I can see it. Was it up in London, then,'

she asked offhandedly, 'that you met this clever baggage?'

'Aye.' A shutter seemed to close down across his face. There were times, thought Maris, when the mason looked very much like his old mother. She did not dare to question him further, instead she said, 'Did you mean to ask I something?'

He smiled his rare smile. 'You be the quick one, I must say.' He looked at the little fingers still curled around his hand. He gripped them so tightly that she cried aloud, knowing that he could not hear her.

'Will you wed wi'I, Maris?'

She looked directly into his eyes, and nodded. 'Yes,' she said, 'I'll wed wi' you, Jye.'

They walked back, hand-in-hand along the Yeovil road, towards the village. There were a dozen things she wished to ask him, but his temperament and deafness made any rapid exchange of words quite impossible between them. She would need to learn patience, to find ways to communicate easily with him. They had never, until now, been alone together. Already, she had begun to watch his eyes, to seek for the message in those graven features. Today she had seen an angry pulse beat in his throat, recognised the way his eyes would crease up just before he laughed. He did not, she admitted, laugh very easily or often. An air of melancholy always hung about him. Jye was, thought Maris, like the final notes of a sad hymn. But she, of course, would soon set about the changing of all that! In the house of Maris there would be many smiles, babies who laughed and grabbed at those thick black curls of his, those fine moustaches. Jye would become a merry fellow, quick and bright, like her father and her brothers. He had lived too long alone, without the comfort of a loving wife and his own rooftree.

Maris had heard certain rumours in the village. These Carews were a strange aloof kind of people, proud of the

432

ownership of their stone cottage, and the skills of the stone-carver Jye, who was said to be the finest mason ever bred in Montacute. But still people talked. It was said that his mother was a peculiar and silent woman who roamed on Ham Hill in all winds and weathers. There was a brother, deformed in spine and shoulder, who allowed no woman ever to cross his threshold. Then there was Jye, handsome and shy, virtually without words, and already twenty-eight years old. There had been speculation among the gloving maidens of some sad disappointment up in London; some fine lady who had trifled with his affections and then finally spurned him. Maris had read about the high-handed methods of the landed gentry, and Jye's mention of a clever baggage who had deceived him, seemed to bear this out. She glanced up at him as they walked; she squeezed his fingers gently and was rewarded by a slow smile. She would have liked to halt, there on the Yeovil road, and ask him about the girl, but he looked so unusually content that it seemed a shame to drag up painful matters.

Jye adjusted his stride to match her shorter footsteps. They strolled on, between the brown ploughed fields and blackberry hedges of late October. They came up to a lane where the blue smoke of evening curled up into the elm trees, and Maris gasped with pain as the hand which held hers, bunched suddenly and convulsively, into a fist. A caravan had been set crosswise in the lane's entrance; she could not help but admire the bright green and yellow of its paintwork, the brass knocker on its door, the pretty lace curtains, looped-up and tied back with ribbons at the tiny windows. She glanced up at Jye with every intention of indicating that she wished to speak to him, but found his head averted from the lane and its gypsy occupants. She stood still, forcing him to halt with her. He pulled at her hand. 'Come on,' he muttered, 'there's no cause for me to bide yer.' At the sound of Jye's voice a man looked up from his seat on the shaft of the waggon.

'A good-evening to 'ee, brother,' he said gravely, 'how goes it with our cousin, Meridiana?'

Jye relinquished his hold on the hand of Maris. He cupped his fingers to both ears to indicate his deafness. He shook his head, touched two fingers to his Sunday cap, and began to walk away, very quickly, leaving Maris to run along behind him. She caught up with him on a bend in the road, she grabbed at his sleeve, forcing him to stop. 'What was that all about?' she cried angrily, 'the man was only being civil to you!' Once again Jye cupped his hands around his ears. 'No!' she shouted, 'no you needn't come they tricks with me. You understand every word what's said, as long as you can watch the lips what is speaking to you. Whyfor was you so stupid with the man? He knowed very well that you understood him.'

Maris could not comprehend her own embarrassment at Jye's action; after all, the chap had only been a gypsy. But there was something else that tugged at her mind. 'Who,' she demanded, 'is their cousin, Meridiana?'

The colour burned red beneath his dark skin. 'Didden you never see my mother about the village? Didden you never see her carrying that bloody hawking basket?'

Maris clapped a hand across her mouth at his use of the profane word. The meaning of what he had said came only slowly to her. Her blue eyes widened, her fingers came down from her lips. 'You mean,' she asked slowly, 'you mean that your Ma is a –'

'A full-blooded Romany,' he interrupted and, as he spoke, she saw his head tilt up with a kind of pride.

'Then you bain't ashamed of her?' she asked him.

'No,' he growled, ''course I bain't ashamed. She'm a very fine woman!'

'Then why,' demanded Maris, 'did you run away from the waggon in the lane?'

Jye's head hung down, so that she could hardly make out the mumbled words. "'Cause they be always trying to marry I off to one of their daughters! I been on the run these past ten years. 'Tis my greatest fear that one of these days some gypsy maid 'ull manage to trap me!'

Maris stared at him, at his stern and humourless expression, the genuine fear in his eyes. Her lips twitched, her face began to crumple, she opened her mouth, and her head tilted back as she exploded into helpless laughter. She leaned against him, and the middle button of his waistcoat pressed into her forehead. She looked up into his puzzled face. 'Don't 'ee worry, my handsome,' she cried, 'you got me to stick-up for 'ee now. I bain't very big, I know, but I'll save 'ee from they wicked Romany maidens.'

She saw the skin crinkle up around his eyes, he began to smile and very gradually, that smile broadened out until it became a great and triumphant shout of laughter. Roughly, he pulled her to him, there in the darkening lane. His shoulders bowed, his head bent low to find her lips, and Damaris Honeybone was kissed, for the very first time in her eighteen years.

❊

The encounter had come about accidentally, just as Hugh had always feared it might. The chance had come, in spite of all his subterfuge and efforts at avoidance, and the whole cataclysmic meeting over in a space of seconds.

They had been invited to a party at Romano's. Hugh had never known what it was that they were supposed to be celebrating. Somebody's coming-of-age, or a big win on the racecourse? The engagement of a Gaiety Girl to a belted Earl? It had hardly seemed to matter. Long before the hour of midnight, people were swinging from chandeliers, and pouring claret over one another. Blanche had become very drunk. She had sung a song, the first words of which were,

'Be oi Zummerset? Be oi buggery? I be up from Wareham!' The rest of the lines were equally disgusting, but the clients of Romano's had demanded several encores. Hugh had sat, determinedly sober in a corner of the restaurant. It was during a bout of uninhibited horseplay that he had heard a ripping noise; he had gone to investigate the screams of Blanche, and discovered that her pale-blue gown had been torn open from shoulder-strap to ankle. Her voice could be heard down the length and breadth of the Strand.

'You bloody oaf,' she was shouting, 'this frock cost a hundred quid! Don't you know that clothes is the most important damn thing in the whole world!'

Hugh had seen the Prince of Wales, halted and curious at the swing doors of the restaurant, his equerry standing at his elbow. At a gesture from their host, the Prince's party had continued on their way upstairs to the Japanese Suite. His Highness had crossed the room to where Blanche stood, endeavouring, without success, to hold the torn edges of her gown together.

'My commiserations, Madam!' he had said. 'A most serious matter!' Hugh had seen lust in those slumberous, heavy-lidded eyes. 'As you say, my dear, clothes are the most important matter in all the world.' The Prince smiled. 'Perhaps we can discuss the subject further one day, in more suitable surroundings?' He had inclined his head in an ironic bow. 'I would like to have your opinion on certain sartorial matters.' Drunk as she was, Blanche had deliberately allowed the torn edges of the blue silk to fall apart. She had tilted her chin, thrust her bosom forward and arched one foot in her most coquettish fashion. She had curtsied far lower than was necessary.

'Why, of course, sir,' she had murmured, 'I should be willing and honoured to serve you in any way I can.'

✳

436

They were seated at breakfast on that November morning, when a letter arrived delivered by a footman. The envelope, embossed with a coat-of-arms, and sealed with wax, was addressed to Mrs Hugh Fitzgerald. Quite suddenly, Blanche, who had until now, been wholly dependent upon Hugh and his aunt for company and conversation, appeared to have acquired a friend; and such a friend! Hugh read aloud the few scrawled words, and knew at once what they must signify.

'It would seem,' he said coldly, 'that you are invited to take tea with a Duchess.'

'What Duchess?' Aunt Porteous demanded.

'The one who acts as procuress for the Prince of Wales!'

Mrs Porteous glanced swiftly about her to confirm the absence of listening servants. 'Quietly, dear boy!' she urged. 'This is a very private and delicate matter.' She reached out and took the letter from him; examined minutely the crest and sealing-wax. Finally, she adjusted her lorgnette and studied the contents. Hugh observed the changing emotions that moulded her features. Disbelief and chagrin had been followed by shock, and then, calculation. The face she now turned upon Blanche was smiling and bland, but the hands that gripped the sheet of heavy vellum were tense with terrible excitement.

'Well, my dear,' she cried, 'it would seem that we are to be singularly honoured.'

'It is Blanche,' interrupted Hugh, 'who is to be singularly honoured. The Royal "we" can hardly be extended to you and I, Aunt!' He scowled. 'For myself, I do not feel in the very least favoured by such a summons.' He banged his fist unexpectedly among the toast and silver serving-dishes. 'You know damn well what such a letter means, Aunt!'

Aunt Letitia smiled. 'A Royal command!'

'Precisely, and one which I have no intention of obeying. He's already deeply involved with his "darling Daisy", the name of a certain dancer is on everybody's lips, not to mention that actress –'

'The Prince,' broke in his Aunt, 'has a penchant for novelty and variety. It is a well-known fact that he suffers greatly from ennui, and a deep dislike of the ladies of his mother's court. He likes to look around him – to seek fresh faces – to be entertained and diverted by –' Mrs Porteous began to flounder. 'Well you must admit Hugh, that your wife has built up quite a reputation of somewhat outrageous behaviour. I was told that only last week she sang a most indecent song in Romano's, and that she was seen in a shocking state of undress by the Prince himself. Oh yes, Hugh! I keep myself very well informed. I was also told that a certain Major of the Dragoon Guards had shot himself quite deliberately through the foot, so that he might remain in London, to be near Blanche.'

Hugh began to speak, but Aunt Porteous raised her hand. 'There was also that singular episode in the vestry of St George's, when Blanche signed her name with a cross in the Register of Marriage. That story has gone the rounds of every drawing-room in London; guests who were present at your wedding are still dining out on the strength of having witnessed such a marriage! I've been told that certain people turn up at functions to which you and Blanche have been invited, simply to be present when Blanche opens her mouth to utter! Her looks, and her, well, her piquant sayings and behaviour have made her something of a cult just lately, among a particular set.' She paused and looked significantly at Blanche. 'It is common knowledge that the Prince becomes easily wearied these days by his own family circle. Diversions have to be found for him, otherwise his temper –'

'I will not have my wife used as a diversion for that repulsive old lecher!'

'You will find it extremely difficult, if not downright

438

impossible, to refuse him, Hugh. These affairs are arranged with the utmost secrecy and caution.' The colour rose in painful streaks across Mrs Porteous' yellow cheeks. 'Think carefully: the man is fifty-two years old. He is grossly overweight, suffers from chronic shortness of breath, and is altogether in a parlous physical condition. His abilities as a seducer must have been sadly curtailed. He simply likes to have pretty and unusual women around him. He needs to be entertained and diverted –'

Hugh pounded the table. 'But not with my wife!' He turned to Blanche. 'Well?' he demanded. 'You've got the invitation you've been angling for, what precisely do you intend to do about it?'

Blanche had listened to the long exchange between her husband and his aunt, while making a substantial breakfast. She heaped apricot preserves onto a tiny square of buttered toast, and turned a face of innocent perplexity towards Hugh.

'Would you pair mind very much,' she asked meekly, 'telling me what you're getting so hot-tempered about?' She indicated the letter. 'Seems to me you're making an awful lot of fuss about an invite to some old dowager's tea-party.'

'It is not some old dowager's tea-party,' cried Mrs Porteous. She snatched up the sheet of vellum and waved it at Blanche. 'This is by way of being a Royal Summons,' she said grandly, 'an invitation from this particular lady can mean one thing, and one thing only!' Her tone was lowered dramatically. 'Edward Albert, Prince of Wales, had expressed a desire to become acquainted with you. I do not think you are properly cognizant of the honour he does you!'

A perplexed line appeared on Blanche's forehead, her violet eyes came all the way open. 'Ah,' she said softly, 'I didn't understand you to begin with. I thought you didn't hold with such goings-on, dear Aunty.' Blanche appeared to become absorbed in her own thoughts. 'So that's the way it works among the gentry,' she mused, 'if your wife elopes with your business partner – then she's a scarlet woman, and her name not fit ever to be mentioned.' She paused and looked wonderingly at the square of toast in her hand. 'But if the Prince of Wales takes a fancy to you, then 'tis called by a different name.' She turned to Hugh's aunt. 'Don't worry,' she said, 'I'll keep the appointment.' She thrust her face very close to that of the older woman. 'But not to please you, you bloody old hypocrite. I shall go because I want to. I've been dying to meet that man all my life!'

❋

Annis had submitted to the agonising process of having her ears pierced. A pair of drop-earrings, in what Annis assumed to be blue glass, had been included in a recent parcel from Blanche. She had shown them to her workmates in the factory.

'Well, there's no help for it now,' they had giggled, 'you'll have to bear the pain of Mabel's red-hot needle.' The operation had been performed in haste, in the brief absence of the forewoman. A candle had been lit, and the darning needle made sterile in its flame. Sally had held Annis firm in her chair, while Mabel had run hot metal through each earlobe, and then immediately inserted the blue drop-earrings. Annis had wept from the anguish, but as Sally said, vanity always pinched a poor maid, somewhere! Eliza's disapproval had been short and sharp. 'If the good Lord intended us to have holes in our earlobes, then He would have put them there Himself.' How much further did Annis intend to go, Eliza enquired, in her intention to be just like her sister Blanche?

The autumn ball was held in the London Hotel on the 5th October. Captain Castlemain waited for her at the hotel entrance, paid for her ticket, and then promptly disappeared.

Annis felt upset and worried by this cavalier treatment, but he came to her, later on, as she stood watching the dancers. He took her hand, and without a word of explanation, drew her into the ballroom floor. It could not be, thought Annis, that he was ashamed to be seen entering with her. Annis looked around at the other girls and was satisfied, not to say elated, at the superiority of her own appearance. Her gown was of silk, summer-blue and trimmed with bands of indigo-velvet. Blanche had included the silken stockings, the velvet evening-bag and shoes, the fan and matching cape. The outfit, thought Annis, bore the stamp of London on every inch! With her fair hair washed and gleaming and dressed high with combs, she did not need the smiles of Captain Castlemain to confirm her beauty. There had been the usual trouble with Mama of course. Frank Nevill's name had been mentioned many times among the rest of her mother's arguments and recriminations. Annis had gone to the mantelshelf and lifted down Frank's photo. She had studied his earnest expression, the stripe on his sleeve awarded for good-conduct, the medal for valour pinned upon his tunic. She no longer recognised him, had never really known him. If Frank walked in at her mother's door at that very minute, she would be bound to greet him as a total stranger. Eight years, she told Eliza, was a very long time to wait. 'I'm nearly twenty-six,' she had cried, 'already I'm an old maid! Up on the shelf with Frank, Mama, that's where you've put me!' Her degree of desperation had lately grown more intense with every week that passed. With a trunk full of beautiful clothes standing in her bedroom and Jeremy Castlemain murmuring endearments and issuing invitations, what was she supposed to do? She had surely done her bounden duty, reasoned Annis. When all the others had deserted Mama, it was she who had stayed at home. She had helped with the care of her brother, Louis, had minded him, so that her mother might visit Jack's grave, and attend St

Mary's church. It was the hard-earned money of Annis that paid the rent of the house in Greenbrook Terrace. Contributions from Blanche had tended to be generous but not regular; and Annis was weary of being Eliza's prop and stay.

She remembered the warnings of her workmates. 'A simple country wench,' they called her. 'You'd be an easy mark for any bloke what had a fancy-handle to his name.' Well they had all been wrong! Captain Castlemain treated her like a lady. He did, thought Annis, if anything, carry chivalry too far. He danced, holding her from him at a more than proper distance. He did not ply her with wine, or try to maul her. He walked her back to the end of Greenbrook Terrace, and kissed her once, very briefly, on the forehead. So cool was he, so correct and respectful, that Annis began to worry about it. She was sure that he intended marriage; why else would he wait for her in the Park? Why had he invited her to the autumn ball? His intentions had been seen to be more than honourable. Perhaps he was waiting for some sign of her affection?

There was to be another grand ball held at Christmas, in the Officers' Quarters at Jellalabad Barracks. Jeremy had asked her to be his special guest, and she had already accepted his invitation. A parcel had arrived from Blanche: among the many gifts for Mama, had lain a separate package for Annis. The gown, hardly worn, was of coral pink chiffon over satin. With it had come pink satin slippers and a fluffy feather boa! Oh, how fortunate that she and Blanche were of an identical size and shape! The similarities, thought Annis, between herself and her older sister, had become even more marked and numerous just lately. She spoke aloud the names that were always on her mind. 'The Honourable Hugh, and Mrs Blanche Fitzgerald,' she murmured; and then in a stronger voice, 'Captain and Mrs Annis Castlemain.'

Eliza had used every argument, had pleaded and threatened, now she had admitted failure. 'Well, don't ever say you wasn't warned,' she told Annis. 'Even I have heard about the wild goings-on at that Jellalabad Christmas ball! Tidden as if you got a proper escort to look after you. I don't know how you ever found yourself invited up there, in the first place?'

'Oh – 'twas through a friend of Sally's – you know – that girl what works alongside me in the factory.'

Eliza was sure that Annis lied – she recalled that same averted glance, that faint heightening of colour, in Philip Greypaull. 'What time will you be home?'

'I can't say, can I? Don't try to tie me down, Mama. I be twenty-six years old. When you was my age, you was married and had two children!'

The reproach uttered frequently by Annis, was so near the truth that Eliza could find no telling answer. The old nightmare had returned, that dream which had haunted the early years of her marriage to Philip. Once again, she was up behind a bolting horse, the reins loose in her grasp, and the waggon out of control, running downhill all the way. Her sense of foreboding was very strong on that Christmas Eve. She looked at Annis in the coral gown, the fair hair piled and curling on her forehead, the feather boa around her throat. She put out a hand, like a blind woman seeking reassurance in an altered room. 'Don't go, maid,' she whispered, 'not tonight, please Annis!'

Annis bent to fasten the buttons on her satin shoes, and with her movement the feather boa slipped aside.

'What's that around your neck?' demanded Eliza.

Annis touched the necklace. ''Tis the silver and coral pendant what Blanche brought for you, and you wouldn't take! See how nice it looks, Mama! It do match the colour of my gown, exactly!'

Eliza dozed in her rocking-chair beside the fire; she dreamed of other Christmas Eves long ago, up in Buckland St Mary. Of herself as a child on Castle Farm, warm and secure in the company of her four brothers. Later on, there had been the life on Larksleve, with her cousin, Philip. A marriage made bitter-sweet by her husband's indifference towards her, and only made tolerable by the compensating love of her many children.

She came awake, briefly, and looked at the corner where Louis had once sat. Then she glanced downwards at the idle hands lying in her lap. A tear squeezed between her eyelids and trickled down her cheeks. She was old, that was the truth of it, old and useless, and unheeded. Suddenly, she thought of Annis, and with the memory came the sound of footsteps in the street. Eliza looked at the clock. Half-past two! She ran to the front door and pulled it open, and there was Annis, unescorted in the dark street.

Eliza threw wood on the kitchen fire, stirred the coals to make a blaze, and set the kettle on the trivet. She pointed at the clock. 'So what time do you call this, miss? No decent maid 'ud walk the streets of Taunton at such an hour! After all that I went through with your father, how could you tread in his same footsteps, Annis? 'Tis all the fault of that Blanche! Bringing her fancy clothes down here, for to tempt you into danger!' Eliza made tea in the big brown teapot, and filled two stone hot-water bottles 'Probably caught your death of cold in that disgusting frock,' she muttered, 'not to mention they flimsy underclothes what our Blanche sent you.' She poured the tea and took a cup to where Annis sat, close beside the fire. In the light from the leaping flames Eliza observed, for the first time, the stained satin of her daughter's skirts, the torn chiffon. She picked up the lamp from the kitchen table, and brought it closer. Now she could see the rigidity of Annis, her white face, the fists clenched tightly in her lap.

'Oh maid,' Eliza whispered, 'whatever is it? Whatever happened to 'ee?'

'Nothing what need concern you, Mama.' Eliza hardly recognised the cold and distant voice of her favourite daughter. Annis looked up, and her eyes were blue and fixed, and curiously empty of all expression. 'Don't worry,' she reassured her mother. 'I won't never cry — that 'ud only upset you, Mama, wudden it!'

❊

Mina came round on Christmas Day, bringing Laura with her. The little girl performed her party-piece on the front-room piano, and was praised for her cleverness by Eliza. Annis appeared briefly, and then returned to her bed.

'What's the matter with milady?' enquired Mina.

'A late night,' snapped Eliza, 'or to be truthful, an early morning! Half-past two she come trailing home, and in such a state as you never did see. She'd been drinking, Mina! I could smell it on her. Since then — not a single word have she uttered to me. No explanation, no nothing!' Eliza sighed. 'I should have burned they clothes, trunk and all, as soon as our Blanche brought 'em down here. 'Tis they indecent frocks what is causing all the trouble. My Annis never give me a minute's worry in all her life, until just lately.'

Mina said, 'Sounds as if she've got herself mixed-up with some feller. Where was she until half-past two this morning?'

Eliza hesitated. 'The Christmas Eve ball for officers, at Jellalabad Barracks.'

'Oh Mama!' Mina turned a scandalised face upon her mother. 'You never let her go to that! Why, you must have heard what goes on there?'

'What could I do?' wailed Eliza. 'Her's twenty-six years old, and very wilful since poor Louis died. I can't do nothing with her, Mina. She do put me in mind of Philip Greypaull, just lately.'

'And we all know, Mama, how he ended up.' Mina's lips stretched into a thin line. 'You mark my words! There's a feller behind all this. If she went to the officers' ball then 'twas only by special invitation.'

'But where would our Annis meet an officer from the Barracks?'

'The factory gates do stand close up against the Barracks,' hinted Madelina.

'Oh, maid, you don't think — ?'

Mina looked suspiciously at her mother. 'I think you already guessed, a long time ago, Mama, what our Annis was up to. Like you said, her had always been such a good girl.' Mina hesitated. 'I've tried to warn her, sometimes. You know, in a general kind of way.' Mina blushed at so indelicate a subject. 'But Annis is — well she's sort of innocent and simple. She do believe just about anything what other people tell her.'

Eliza nodded. 'I know,' she whispered, 'I've always knowed that about my Annis. She've always been so biddable and easy to manage —'

'Exactly, Mama!' Mina frowned. 'And a maiden what bends so easy to her mother's will is just as likely to give-way before the wills of other people.'

❋

Annis soaked her head with cold water, took up a comb and scraped the hair back from her face until all the curls had disappeared. Then she snatched the curling-tongs and the brown paper, and dropped them into the ash-bin. She went up to her room and folded the many-coloured gowns, the silken stockings and delicate under-garments. She packed them carefully into the trunk; on the very top she placed the handbags, and boots, the dancing shoes, the muffs and feather boa; she closed the lid, quietly but with finality. Annis put on her old, navy-blue skirt and plain white blouse; she pulled on the ugly black woollen stockings, and placed the crocheted shawl around her shoulders. Last of all, she unhooked the pretty, dangling earrings. For a moment they lay in the palm of her hand. The earrings held a special significance for her; they seemed to represent all the romance and high adventure that had transformed her life in the past months. She left the house, and walked down to where the river Tone flowed high and brown between its banks. She stood for a long time, staring down into the depths; at last, she held out her hand and allowed the pretty blue glass to fall into the water.

Annis had been violently sick for several weeks now; she had set out for work much earlier than usual, in order to conceal her condition from Eliza. She had staggered and retched her way through the dark and deserted streets of early morning, to arrive at the factory gates in a state of near collapse.

'You'll just have to tell somebody!' her workmates told her.

'No,' she cried, 'I'll kill myself before Mama or Mina finds out about me!'

The sickness had stopped, to be replaced by other aches and pains. Annis recalled her sister Madelina, and how she had almost died in giving birth to Laura. She touched the coral pendant, the only item of adornment which she permitted herself these days. She remembered the story of its magical powers, but was not consoled.

It was in March that the letter arrived from Frank Nevill. Eliza read it aloud in a voice that was hushed, and tight with anguish.

'Dearest Annis,

'At last I can write you the news what you have been waiting for these nine years. We left Fort St George on January 12th. Went from Madras to Poona by train, and from Poona to Bombay. Have just reached Bombay on the 20th and embarked on H.M.S. *Euphrates* bound for Folkstone. We was much praised for loyal and devoted Service by the Brigadeer-General, in spite of the terrible sickness and fevers what we have all suffered. Some of us is being sent home early due to poor health.

'So now, we is coming home at last my dear one, after all these long and sad years of parting. I cant hardly wait to see you, Annis. We will put up the Banns right away. We got no cause to wait now. We shall be married as soon as possible, too much time have already been lost between us. There is not many girls what would have waited for me, the way you have, Annis. Many of my mates have had bad news from their sweethearts back in England. Most girls is very fickle, Annis, and wont wait for a soldier. But not you, my dearest girl. You are the truest and sweetest maid in all this wide and wicked world.'

Eliza paused, and looked into the blank face of her daughter. It was only with difficulty that she continued reading. 'Please go round to Silver Street and take the good news to my father and mother, and then have a word with the Minister of my Chapel – ' Eliza looked up again to find the kitchen empty; overhead she could hear the sounds of a drawer being opened and then banged shut. Swiftly, she mounted the stairs, and pushed at the half-closed bedroom door. Annis stood beside her dressing-table, all around her lay the hundreds of letters which had come from Belgaum and Burma. Pressed tightly up against her heart, was the open blade of Frank Nevill's clasp-knife, the souvenir he had left behind, all those years ago.

Eliza spoke very quietly. 'No, maid,' she said. 'that's not

the way for you to act, and I think you already knows it. Put the knife down, Annis, very slow and careful, and then come downstairs, and we'll drink a cup of tea, together.' She paused and then said gently, 'You don't have to tell me what your trouble is. I had seven children of my own, maid. I've see'd the signs in you, these many weeks past. Put the knife down, Annis. Frank wudden want to have your death on his conscience. Enough harm have been done already, let we see how it can be soonest mended.'

Annis lowered the knife very slowly. Eliza saw the muscles relax in her daughter's neck and jaw, the sudden bowing of her shoulders. She had expected to see tears, to hear the voice of Annis roused in the familiar tones of high drama; but there was nothing, no sign of hysteria or histrionics; only a terrible and silent resignation.

❋

'So who is he?' Eliza asked.

'A Captain up to Jellalabad.'

'How long have you known him?'

'A long time. We met in Vivary Park one Sunday morning. I used to run into him, accidental-like after that. He asked me to meet him at the autumn ball at the London Hotel. He invited me to the Barracks last Christmas.'

'Have you told him, yet?'

Annis shook her head. 'I've looked out for him everywhere, but I can't seem to find him.'

'His name?' Eliza demanded.

'Castlemain.'

Eliza's hand went up to her scarred cheek, she began to rub at her sightless left eye. 'Castlemain?' she whispered. 'Be you absolutely sure, maid?'

''Tis what all his men do call him.'

'Do you know anything about him?'

Annis shook her head.

'That young man's family,' said Eliza, 'is the wealthiest in all this County. Why! they owns land right across to Dorset, and reaching down into Devon. What's his first name?'

'Jeremy.'

Eliza nodded. 'Well, well! I thought it might be. I've been reading about that young buck just lately, in the *Courier*. He got himself engaged on New Year's Day. His father made a big occasion of it. You won't never see hide nor hair of him again, maid!'

'I think I already knowed that,' murmured Annis. She stared into the heart of the fire and would not meet her mother's gaze. 'I've been such a fool, Mama. Such a vain and silly maiden. I believed every word he told me,' her voice broke, 'oh, and what will our Mina say when she finds out? What will David Lambert think about me?'

'You leave the Lamberts to me,' said Eliza. ''Tis what Frank Nevill thinks about it all what is truly important.'

'He'll never marry me now. I wudden expect him to. You'll have to write to him, Mama. Tell him all what have come to pass —'

'Too late!' Eliza interrupted. 'Frank have already sailed from India. He'll be half-way home by this time.'

'I can't go round to see his father,' Annis whispered.

'There's no need. I'll write a note and put Frank's message in it. You shan't do nothing at all what you don't want to. Us'll keep this business as quiet as we can. You can go on working for a few months more, then you shall bide at home with me.' Eliza smiled. ''Twill be just like old times, eh maid? You and me, nice and cosy together. We'll see if we can get some outwork, gloving perhaps, or collars?' Eliza held out her hands. 'These fingers of mine have been idle for too long. A baby,' she mused, 'after all these years, a cradle for me to rock. We must get out

450

our knitting needles. Six of everything, mind Annis! I feel sure that 'twill be a girl. We shall dress her in white for the first twelve months, after that, a pretty shade of pink, perhaps —' The voice of Eliza was warm with plans, but Annis hardly heard her. Once again she could feel the bonds of her mother's love growing tight around her, and this time there was nothing she could do about it. Without the care and protection of Mama, which Annis neither merited or deserved, her only alternatives would be the gutter or the river.

✳

It was Madelina Lambert who proved to be the practical one, their rock and stay in time of trouble. She it was who took positive action, who despatched a telegram to Blanche Fitzgerald in Russell Square which read 'Come at once. Trouble in the family.' Mina demanded an interview with a high-ranking officer at Jellalabad Barracks.

'My brother is Simeon Greypaull,' she stated. 'He run-off and joined the Army a long time ago. We've never heard a single word from him in all that time. Now we've got serious trouble in the family, and he ought to be informed about it.'

'What kind of trouble, Mrs Lambert?' the officer enquired.

''Tis my aged mother,' Madelina hinted darkly. 'It might yet prove fatal.'

'I see. It might be difficult to trace him! Have you never received any letters from him?'

'He can't read nor write,' snapped Madelina. 'I heard that he'd been in some fighting in Ireland. That he'd been given some medals for it.'

'Ah,' said the major, 'that might help to facilitate matters.'

Within a week, Madelina had covered every aspect of the

fall of Annis, both temporal and spiritual. She had summoned those members of the family whom she had decided should shoulder their fair share of the burden. She had discussed with Eliza, and then concluded, that an appeal to Captain Castlemain to accept paternity of the child, would be a waste of time, and her mother would never permit a request for help to her family in Buckland St Mary.

'But never you fear,' she had reassured her mother, 'I write a very telling letter when I be of mind to do so. Just wait until this baby's born, and I'll make certain that the Castlemain family knows all about it!'

Her unexpected championship of the cause of Annis did not extend as far as David Lambert. 'Now listen to me, Annis! I want no word of this to get to David. You knows very well what high opinion he have always had of you. 'Twould be the death of him if he should find out what have happened to you!'

'But,' said Eliza, 'somebody is sure to tell him. All they maids in the factory knows about it – '

'My David don't never talk to factory-hands; and Taunton people know better than to go to him with tittle-tattling gossip. No,' Mina said, confidently, 'Dave won't never get to hear about it, at least not for a long time. After all Mama, he don't never call on you very often, and if he did, 'tis but the work of a second for you to hide our Annis. There's only one other matter. I don't want this talked about in front of Laura. She's a knowing little maid, and all ears just lately.' Mina's sallow cheeks were flushed, her green eyes shone. The first shock, and condemnation of her sister's plight had been quite driven out by her crusading zeal. Not since the birth of the singular Laura had she been granted such a mission; and who in the Greypaull family was more qualified than Mina to advise and warn about the hazards of childbirth. To hold such a secret, to hug it close, even for a short time, would compensate Mina for the many lonely hours when David Lambert was absent from his home.

Blanche and Hugh came down to Taunton in great haste. They stayed overnight in the London Hotel. Blanche, suspecting some shameful disaster, in view of Mina's cryptic message, would not allow Hugh to accompany her to Greenbrook Terrace. She walked into her mother's kitchen, to find Madelina seated by the fire and knitting furiously with white wool, and Annis out at work.

Blanche kissed Eliza's pale cheek, and then began to laugh. 'Don't tell me,' she cried, 'that this is why you've dragged me down here? So it's to be the patter of tiny feet again, is it Mina? You've decided to chance death, after all?'

Mina aimed a look at Blanche which at once quelled her laughter. Mama's face was equally fierce. 'I baint knitting for myself,' Madelina said grimly.

'Who then?'

'You ought to know, if anybody does,' cried Eliza. 'You always done your utmost to encourage her in disobedience and shame. What sort of example in life have you ever showed to your liddle sister?'

The hooded gaze of Mina fastened onto Blanche. 'Yes,' she said, 'that do really seem unfair, when 'tis our Blanche what have always flouted the Lord's Will, and 'tis poor liddle Annis what must now pay the wages of sin.'

Blanche sat down abruptly. She laid her bag and gloves on the kitchen table, removed her hat and patted her hair. She waited for them to say the actual words, but they were not about to help her. At last she said, 'You mean — our Annis is — ?'

The two heads nodded.

'Who is he?' cried Blanche. 'Tell me his name, and I'll go round to his house and wring the bastard's neck with my bare hands!'

453

Mina flinched. 'I don't think,' she said softly, 'that we should be using that particular profanity in this house. Poor Annis got no hope at all of getting married. The father is from a class of society what takes no responsibility for any of its actions.'

'What about that soldier-boy, that Frank?'

'Expected home at any minute,' said Eliza, 'and thinking to find all the preparations made for a marriage to poor Annis.'

Blanche stared. 'You mean he don't know what have come to pass?'

'Of course not,' snapped Eliza, 'and who ever is going to tell him the dreadful news? Poor liddle chap, he've waited nine years for his Annis!'

Blanche snorted inelegantly. ''Tis more like our Annis what have waited nine years for Frank! Didden I warn you both, at the very beginning? Not natural, that's what I said, for a maid to bide single and shut-up in house, for all of her best years! 'Tis a wonder to me that Annis stayed quiet for so long.' Blanche sighed. 'Well! It seems like she have fallen at the very last fence!' She looked enquiringly at her mother and older sister. 'You never fetched me down here to pass the time of day,' she said bitterly, 'so what am I here for?'

'Money,' said Madelina bluntly. 'You got plenty of it, and our poor Annis will soon be in dire straits.'

Blanche opened her handbag. She took out five sovereigns and placed them on the table. 'I would have give it, anyway,' she told Mina, 'you didden have to be so sharp about it.'

Eliza said in an embarrassed tone, ''Tis very good of 'ee, Blanche. Poor Annis will be very grateful to you.'

'For God's sake stop calling her poor Annis,' Blanche cried, 'there's many a woman who would give all she's got to be in a similar condition!'

'No sign of a family yet, our Blanche?' Mina asked slyly.

454

'But there,' she said, 'you was ever the smart one. A baby 'ud spoil that figure of yours, wudden it? Not to mention the inconvenience and pain.'

Blanche crossed the room in three swift paces. She put her hands around Mina's neck, pressed hard and shook her sister's head back and forth. 'One of these days, Mina Lambert, somebody'll do for you! Just you button your lip, that's all!! I want a child of my own more than any of you! I'd give the world to stand in Annis' shoes.' Her shoulders bowed, and she threw Mina backwards into the chair. 'It don't never seem to happen to me. I can't understand it.'

Eliza said, 'Perhaps 'tis the life you lead, maid? All that dancing and going-about. That don't seem natural somehow. I 'spect you is up till all hours, late to bed, and late to rise.'

Madelina stroked her neck to encourage the appearance of possible bruises. 'Not to mention,' she whispered hoarsely, 'the imbibing of strong drink!'

Blanche smiled. 'Oh yes,' she cried, 'I got all the sinful habits, Mina.'

She reached for her handbag and withdrew a box of matches, a fancy packet and a long jade tube. Deliberately and slowly, Blanche pulled a cigarette from the case, fitted it into the holder, and struck a match. She applied the flame to the tobacco, breathed deeply, and blew out clouds of scented smoke. Eliza and Mina began to cough. Blanche laughed, and tried to wave the smoke away. 'Whoever taught you such a filthy habit?' gasped Eliza.

'Only the Prince of Wales.' Blanche lifted the highly-coloured packet and pushed it towards her mother. 'Bertie do always smoke this brand,' she said lightly, 'they be called Dembergi's Egyptian. Try one, why don't you?' she advised Madelina. 'All the best people is smoking, these days.'

Annis showed little enthusiasm for sewing baby garments, even less for knitting. It was only the relentless broadening of her waistline, the snug fit of her blouses, that confirmed the blow which had fallen. The unalterable progression of motherhood took longer to establish itself in her mind. Many girls miscarried; she had often seen it happen, right there, on the factory floor. But Annis had worn the silver and coral pendant on that Christmas Eve. The child was as safe and inevitable as the sunrise in the morning.

The bad news was brought to the factory by the tea-boy, who could read a little. His habit was to study the *Courier* broadsheets in his break-hour, and retail the worst bits of news on his return to work. He could hardly wait to declaim to the buttonholers on that afternoon in March.

'Sad news,' he cried, and one by one the treadles slowed and each machine grew silent. 'The S.S. *Euphrates* have sunk on its way back from India. Four hundred men of Prince Albert's Own have gone down without trace! A great storm struck. 'Tis said that the troopship keeled over. She run along on her side for a full four minutes, and then she turned turtle and sank.'

The shocked silence was broken by the sobs of several women. 'Both my brothers was on that boat,' cried one girl. 'Oh my poor husband,' wailed several others.

Annis stared at the earnest little tea-boy in his tweed cap, and she seemed to be seeing Frank as he had looked on her first day in Gliddon's collar factory. Frank had defended her then; he had walked her home to Hunter's Court. Now he was dead, drowned with all his comrades in the Bay of Biscay, that stretch of ocean which he had once described in a letter to her as being the place where all the seven seas of the world crashed together. She closed her eyes and saw Frank's image, and it was no longer the face of a young and eager boy, but the photographed likeness of a calm and serious man. The picture stood on her mother's mantelshelf. She had seen it every day, but never appreciated it. Now she remembered the kind eyes, the firm but gentle mouth, the Burma Medal pinned on his tunic, the stripe for Good Conduct sewn on his sleeve. For the first time since she had discovered her condition, Annis wept.

It was left to Eliza to rein-in the wild hysteria of Annis. She spoke sharply to the incoherent girl. 'Nobody in Taunton have been notified yet of such a mishap. Why, that shoemaker Nevill would have come round with the news right away if his Frank was dead!'

Eliza was not prepared to accept the tea-boy's version of events in the Bay of Biscay She pulled on her bonnet and shawl. 'Come on now,' she told Annis, 'we'll go to the *Courier* window and see for ourselves what this is all about. If only you had learned to read, maid! Can't you see? Such ignorance do leave you to the mercy of every scandalmonger in the town.'

'I'll never learn now,' sobbed Annis. ''Tis only the bad news what they men prints in the broadsheets, and I don't never want to see it!'

She stood at the *Courier* window, tormented by visions of a drowned Frank, while Eliza peered, by gaslight, at the black type of the broadsheet.

'Just as I thought,' she muttered. Eliza turned to Annis and shook her gently. 'Brace-up maid! That silly boy didden read it proper. He must have only understood the first few sentences, and then made-up the rest of it.' She turned back to the window. 'It says here that there was a near-disaster. The *Euphrates* run on her side for a full four minutes, before her Captain managed to right her. The men was all shook-up and bruised, but nobody lost.' She paused. 'They all come safe through the Bay of Biscay. Frank must be almost home by this time.'

'But 'twas all my fault,' persisted Annis. 'Like when Jack was killed, and I had just tried-on Millie's funeral bonnet! I've been wishing that Frank would never come home, that something would happen to him so that he never got to know what – what have happened to me! I never meant that he should die –'

'And no more he didden!' Eliza said. 'Oh, maid! You be always so easily swayed by every wind what blows. Why don't you put your trust in the Lord God! You mustn't believe every word you hear. Half of the people in this world is liars. That was your poor father's trouble. He was never a truly bad man. His biggest fault was that he trusted people.'

'Like I trusted Captain Castlemain?'

'Yes, Annis.'

❀

As if to confirm the fact that he still lived, a letter arrived from Frank Nevill. The postmark was that of Folkstone, the date indecipherable; but the message it contained held a promise of reprieve for Annis.

My dearest Girl,

We docked last night, and my serjeant have promised to post this for me. I hardly know how to tell you this, Annis. It grieves me very much to disappoint you, but it cant be helped. I am sick and they say I must have an operashun. They are taking me to Netley Military Hospital, and they say I shall be there for quite a long time. You remember when I was ill in Belgaum, when my neck swelled up, and they said I had infected glands from drinking dirty water in Burma? Well, that old trouble come back again while I was aboard ship. I got a terribul fever, and am very weak. They takes me everywhere on a stretcher. Got no strength at all in my legs. The ships surgeon says that my infected gland must be took out. I shed tears when they told me, Annis. Not for the pain, but because I shant see you yet, my dearest girl. Perhaps you could come to the Hospital to see me. I have plenty of money saved up. I could send you the train fare. Please come, Annis. We had a rough passage thru the Bay of Biscay. Ship run on its side for about 4 minits. We thought it was all up with us at one stage. Seems to me like something wickid is standing in the way of us two meeting, and getting wed. Better say a few prayers for us, Annis. I reckon we needs them just lately.

I will write to you again when I get to Netley. Thank you for all they lovely letters, what have kept me going in the past nine years. I love you with all my heart and soul, Annis.

Yours ever, Frank Nevill.

Annis took the letter from her mother's fingers, and gazed at the marks on the cheap grey paper; those black signs which only seemed to bring her bad news.

'He expects to be at Netley a long time,' mused Eliza. She glanced at Annis. 'That won't come as quite such a shock to Frank, if the little one is already here and lying in the cradle.'

'He won't marry me, Mama. I wudden expect it of him. You know the names what people are calling me, already.'

Eliza sighed. 'I expect you be right, maid.' She straightened her shoulders and lifted her chin. 'Never mind! Us'll soldier-on somehow. As long as 'tis a healthy child, and you safely delivered –'

Annis touched the coral pendant at her throat. 'Oh, it'll be a healthy child, Mama, and I shall be safe-delivered of it. I got no doubts at all on that score.'

❁

The sewing-room, walled and roofed with glass for maximum daylight, was so hot and airless in the summer weather, that Annis fainted at least once every day. Long hours of work, the close concentration required of a buttonholer, an inadequate diet, and most of all, her own shame at her condition, combined now to weaken Annis. Each morning she climbed the steep outer staircase which led up to the top of the building. She stumbled down those same steps every night in a state of near collapse. Sometimes she would pause in her descent to watch the comings and goings at Jellalabad Barracks. Officers, their cap badges gleaming in the evening sunlight, short canes tapping at their high boots would march in and out of the gates; but Captain Castlemain was never among their number. His people were rich and influential. The plight of Annis, even if revealed, would be of no consequence to them. She looked down at her swollen body, and could scarcely believe that so brief an acquaintanceship could have resulted in so positive an outcome. The unreality of her condition became more pronounced with the progression of months. There were times, in the warm June nights when she could not sleep, that she would almost persuade herself that the child was Frank Nevill's. The fact that he had played no part in the shame of its conception, hardly seemed to matter. It was Frank whom she loved. That truth had been made clear on the day she believed him drowned, and to think of the child as belonging to Frank somehow made it seem more acceptable to her.

The problem of Frank himself was so vast that she did not even attempt to face it. Eliza wrote short, sympathetic notes to Netley Military Hospital. The replies, written on Frank's behalf by a fellow patient, told of the dangerous operation: the removal of the infected neck gland, and the subsequent delirium and fever. Annis remembered the day when Frank had marched away: a boy of seventeen years, brave and tall in his scarlet tunic and shiny helmet. She had followed the column of men as they marched to the railway station. Her feet had kept time to the military music as they had swung out into North Street. She fingered the embroidered pillow slips, touched the letter N, sewed with such effort into the sheets and towels. The cambric and twill had grown yellow and dusty from waiting for Frank. Mama had said they could no longer afford to save the valuable linen. Each item was boiled and hung out to dry in the summer sunshine. It would be needed in September, when Annis was brought to bed of her fatherless child.

❀

Greenbrook Terrace was respectable. Lace curtains hung at every window; behind most of them a flourishing aspidistra was perched on a what-not. Doorknockers shone, front steps were whitened, children wore starched white pinafores, and many of them attended school. Husbands now crossed the road at the approach of Annis Greypaull; wives dipped their bonnet brims, and affected not to see her.

Annis no longer worked in the shirt factory, and Eliza, fearful of her daughter's frail appearance, had walked many miles that summer in search of outwork. The message had been the same in every factory office.

'Didden you never hear about unemployment, missus? There's no work for the men of this town, never mind the women!' Eliza measured her resources; counted up the sheets and towels of Annis' bottom-drawer, reserved the wicked gowns of Blanche as a very last means of obtaining material for infant dresses. If they were careful and dispensed with the extravagance of an experienced midwife, they might just manage the accouchement without incurring debt. Rising prices had lessened the value of the Greypaull annuity; that single pound, paid weekly, must now be

461

stretched to cover all their needs, including rent. Money, sent by Blanche from London, was hoarded against sudden emergencies, and used to buy the occasional delicacy to tempt the poor appetite of Annis. A sum was set aside, never to be touched, in case the services of a doctor should be needed.

Eliza had cultivated her small back-garden; she went out on that Sunday morning to cut a cabbage, to find her next-door neighbour beckoning across the hedge.

'Mrs Greypaull,' the young man whispered, 'I'd like a word, if you don't mind.'

Eliza grew wary. 'If 'tis to ask questions about my daughter –'

'No, no! Well, not in the way you mean.' The young man grew confidential. He leaned across the hedge. ''Tis like this, see! My missus is expecting. Baby is due at the end of September.' He blushed. 'Reckon your maid is due to be confined at about the same time?'

Eliza nodded.

'Well, see – we already got four boys, and the chances is that this one'll make a fifth. Now, my poor missus got such a longing for a daughter – the thought of another boy in the house is driving her out of her mind!' He hesitated. 'Now, we was thinking – well, we was talking it over, and we reckon there's a good chance that your Annis might have a liddle daughter. We was wondering – if my wife should have a boy – if you'd be willing to exchange 'em. I'd make it worth your while.' He hastened to reassure Eliza. 'I'd register both babies as being mine. Doing it that way would give your grandchild a name, and you'd still be able to see her, us living just next-door.' He paused for breath, and Eliza shook her head.

'Oh no,' she said, 'sorry as I be to hear about your problem, I cudden never give away my daughter's baby. That wudden be the same,' she tried to explain, 'I'm sure your child will be a very nice one, but it wouldn't be our flesh and blood, now, would it?'

The young man looked disappointed, but only for a moment. 'There's another young woman down in Silver Street,' he told Eliza, 'and her's in a similar fix to your Annis. I reckon I'll go and have a word with her. She might not be as blooming fussy as you lot!'

❦

Eliza fetched drinking water from the Silver Street standpipe; she waited, just lately, for the fall of dusk, so that Annis might walk with her unobserved, in the cool of the evening. Annis moved only very slowly, these days; it was September, and her time was near. They came into the alley which housed the standpipe; a bucket clanged and they could hear the sound of running water. The figure of a man was just visible in the fading light. As they approached, he turned his face towards them. 'Oh my God!' Annis moaned, ''tis Frank Nevill! Whatever shall I do, Mama?'

'You got to face him sometimes, Annis. Better do it now. Get it over and done with. I'll go back home. I'll come and fetch you later on.'

Annis drew the edges of her cape together, and folded her arms across her body, as if she might still conceal its secret. She moved, inevitably, towards the standpipe, where Frank stood waiting for her. She looked into his brown and bitter face, saw the sad eyes, and knew that she could not face him. She turned to walk away, but he touched her arm. 'Annis,' he said, ''tis Frank. Don't you recognise me?'

She continued to move away, but still he followed. At last, he barred her path, stood squarely before her, and would not let her pass. He held out his hand, and she saw the gleam of her blue glass beads, linked between his fingers. She turned her face towards the alley-wall; she leaned her head against the stone and began to weep. He laid a hand upon her shoulder. 'Look,' he said, 'I still got your glass beads safe — have you got my clasp-knife?' Gently, he turned her around until they were facing one another.

''Tis all right, maid,' he murmured, 'I knows all about your trouble. My sister, Jane, come down to the hospital and told me.' He swallowed hard. 'That don't make no difference to me, Annis. I still love you. We'll get married when — when you is feeling better.'

The lamp-lighter came shuffling into the alley. They drew apart and fell silent while he reached up to ignite the gas mantel.

Annis stood with her head bowed; when the old man had gone away she saw Frank, very clearly, in the gaslight's bloom. How thin he was! How pale his face beneath the tanned skin! She could hardly bear to look upon the broad and livid scar which seared his neck from throat to earlobe.

'I never asked if you was feeling better, Frank. You was in the hospital for a long time.'

'Never mind me.' He reached out and grasped her restless fingers. 'I said we'll get married — later on —'

'No Frank! You mustn't say such a thing! You don't know how wicked I've been. You don't now what people are saying about me. I've lost my good name, Frank.'

'Then you shall have my name, and God help the man or woman what says one word against you.'

'But 'tis another man's child,' she moaned.

'That don't matter,' he said, fiercely. 'If you marries me, then 'twill be my child, bearing my name.'

'I cudden bring shame on you. Whatever would your Ma and Pa say?'

Frank sighed. 'The feller won't marry you, will he, Annis?'

'No,' she said, 'he won't never marry me.' She withdrew her fingers from his grasp, and turned her head away. 'I'll speak of him just the once, and then never again, Frank. You understand me?'

He nodded.

'He's an officer, a Captain. I met him, accidental, in the Park one Sunday morning. He was nice to me, told me I was pretty – I was so lonely, Frank, and all the other girls was courting.' She paused. 'Then our Louis died, and I was free. I could go out any time the fancy took me. The maids in the sewing-room showed me how to dance; they curled my hair, and pierced my ears for earrings. Blanche brought me a trunk full of gowns down from London, and there I was, twenty-six years old, and it seemed like you was never coming home to wed me –'

She began to weep, and Frank said, ''Tis all right, maid. You don't need to say no more about it.'

'But I got to, Frank.' Her voice was urgent. 'I never told anybody else, not even Mama.' Her tone became hushed with the surprise of her own words. ''Twas the music, Frank, and the waltzing, and being free after all they long years spent in house.' She turned back to look at Frank's face. ''Twas never him what I wanted – I swear it to you! I was like somebody what is bewitched.' She was silent for a moment, when she spoke again her words were bitter.

'Well, the spell is broke now. He was careful not to ply me with drink at the Autumn Ball. I trusted him. I was flattered that he even noticed me. But I got no head for drink, Frank, and he took advantage of it. He waited until Christmas time, and then he invited me up to Jellalabad Barracks. I'd been told what went on at they officers' dances, but I didden believe it. Didden want to believe it, if I speaks the truth!' She sighed. 'He said I cudden refuse to drink a toast, not at Christmas time.' She gazed earnestly at Frank. 'They officers do drink an awful lot of toasts, Frank, and 'twould have looked churlish not to join in. They started off by drinking to the old Queen, then to the Prince

465

of Wales and all his children. By the time we had reached Queen Victoria's youngest daughter, I was so swoony I could hardly stand up. He said some fresh air was what I needed –'

Frank shook his head. 'I don't want to hear no more,' he interrupted.

But Annis said, 'I got to tell you – just this once – and we'll never speak of it again. I knowed that something terrible was happening to me, but there was nothing I could do to stop him. I'll never take another drink, not in all my life-long!' She laid both hands across her stomach, and drew breath in sharply. 'I looked everywhere for him Frank in the next weeks, but he was nowhere to be found. He went missing all through spring and summer, and then, just last week, I spied him in North Street. I was coming to the standpipe with Mama, and there he was, stood in a shop doorway. I think he'd been watching me for a long time. According to Mama, he's engaged to be married. He comes from a powerful family, Frank. It 'ud never do for me to try and name him. They Castlemains could have me put away in prison just for saying such a wicked thing about him.'

Frank looked grim. 'The army is finished with me. They don't want sick men. I got a job to go to. I was took-on for work this very day, at French's Tannery in Tancred Street. We'll get married next Easter.'

Nine years of Army life in India and Burma had not brutalised Frank Nevill. That fierce, protective note was still in his voice. Annis was reminded of that day, long ago, when she had first gone to work in the Poolwall collar factory. He had championed her then, he would protect her now.

'I don't deserve you, Frank,' she whispered.

'You don't have to,' he said swiftly. He picked up his pail of water and began to move away. 'Here's your Ma, coming

466

back to fetch you. I'll be round to see you both tomorrow evening.'

✳

Annis Greypaull's daughter was born two days later. In spite of the silver and coral pendant, a doctor needed to be called, and Frank Nevill, careless of gossiping neighbours, paced Eliza's kitchen, when the first thin wail sounded through the house. It was, declared Mina, a very frail and tiny creature, but possessed of the Greypaull's fighting spirit. Eliza registered the birth. She stood for a moment in an outer office and studied the square of official paper. It was, she thought, perhaps as well that Annis would never comprehend the words. The entry in the Register of Births for Taunton said simply: 'A female child. Name, Abigail Greypaull. Father unknown.'

✳

Greenbrook Terrace,
Taunton. October 25th, 1894.

Dear cousin Rhoda,

I hardly know how to begin this letter, but wrote it must be, for I have never kept anything from you, good or bad. The news is all about Annis, she was delivered safe of a baby daughter on September 26th. The father is a Captain at Jellalabad Barracks. There was no hope that he would every marry her, his family being *very rich* and *Influenshul.* This have been a bad year, Rhoda, in some ways. But my Faith in the Good Lord *proved right,* many times over. The baby is v. frail and tiny, but thrives well. Annis weak, but improving. The house is full again, Rhoda, and that is my *great joy.* I cant tell you how wonderful it is to have a Baby to rock and care for. Her name is *Abigail.* So much news to tell you, Rhoda. It do all read like a Fairy Story.

Frank Nevill come home from India this year. He turned up in Taunton two days before our Annis was confined. I knowed that Frank would never be unkind to Annis. I could tell the stamp of him from reading his letters. What I never expected was that he would turn out to be *pure gold*. He still wants to *wed* with her, Rhoda, in spite of *all* what have come to pass. He talks about an Easter Wedding. He do already love little Abigail just like she was his own child. I never saw such a *good man* in all my born days. O, my girls have been luckier than ever I was, Rhoda. They have all found fine and decent husbands, and I am thankful for that. *Even Blanche.*

You must be finished with Harvest, Rhoda, and your weather turning cooler. Shall be anxshus to know your thoughts about Annis. She was not a *bad girl*, Rhoda. Only mis-led by a *wicked* man, and v. foolish.

Hope to hear from you v. soon.

Love to Mr Black and all your family.

Yr. loving cousin, Eliza.

❊

Meridiana sat on her low stool beside the fire and whittled, absent-mindedly, at the piece of elder wood, until a chrysanthemum head grew between her fingers. A heap of privet sprays lay close at hand, and a pot of onion skins simmered on the hob. She leaned forward, laid the completed flower head among a row of others, removed the pot from the fire and set it aside to cool. She looked to a corner of the room, where the hawking basket, half-filled with sprays of red and yellow blossoms, stood ready for the next day's journey. The money belt, heavy with gold and silver, fitted snugly at her lean waist. She rested both her hands upon it and felt the bitterness of regret. Jye was not to be turned from his intention. The first banns had been called for his wedding to the shepherd's daughter, and they were to be married on the eve of Christmas, in the Baptist chapel.

Meridiana cursed the weakness of spirit that had led her to confide her fears for Jye to the Reverend Powys. She rocked her body back and forth in an agony of indecision. There seemed to be no way in which Jye could be made aware of his mother's deep displeasure. Words had never held much significance between them. He had denied her the satisfaction of withdrawing her gift of his own, freehold stone cottage, by refusing the offer as soon as it was made. 'No Mother,' he had said, 'us'll start as we means to go on. Us don't want to be beholden to nobody. I got enough put by for furniture and pots and pans. Maris'll have her gloving-money, and I got my steady job. There's a liddle house lying empty in Middle Street. 'Tis a bit damp and dark, but the rent is low.'

'Rent?' she had cried, 'why, no man in my family have ever lowered himself to pay rent! We have always owned our own tents and waggons. Rent-paying puts money in the landlord's pocket. No, Jye, I 'ont let you do that!'

''Tis already settled,' he said calmly. 'Maris fetched the key last Sunday.'

Meridiana strained the onion skins from the pot of liquor, and began with great care to dip each wooden flower head. She waited until the pale, curling blossom had turned a deep shade of saffron before setting it on one side to drain and dry. The work of her hands gave her satisfaction; the disturbance in her mind ebbed away and she became reflective.

Damaris Honeybone had entered Meri's house on only one occasion. Jye had brought the girl home to meet his mother after chapel on a Sunday evening. The keen blue gaze had widened at the room's strange aspect, had moved from the stool placed before the fire, to the strings that stretched above it. Maris had studied the suspended leaves and tree bark, the scraps of animal skin and bone, all hung up to dry. She had noted and frowned her disapproval of the little clay pipe, and the packet of thick twist tobacco which lay on the mantelshelf, the jars of parsnip and elderberry wine, the keg of cider. Jye Carew was neither a drinker nor a smoker.

Meridiana had stood straight and tall that evening; she had fixed the chit with a penetrating gaze, but blue eyes never faltered before the power of black ones. The girl's face had wrinkled with distaste, the thin nose had quivered at the room's disorder and its pungent odours. A small possessive hand had reached up to Jye's forearm. 'Nice to have met 'ee, Mrs Carew,' said the light voice, and Meridiana had known herself to be, once and for always, dismissed.

❋

The marriage ceremony of Jye Carew to Damaris Honeybone was performed on the eve of Christmas in the Baptist chapel. The Honeybone brothers took leave from their theological studies to attend the wedding of their only sister. There was no feasting or drinking, no dancing or celebration. The words were said, the gold ring given, civil nods were exchanged between Meridiana and the Honeybone family. The bride and groom, clad in their Sunday-best, stepped sedately from the chapel, and went, arms linked, down the frost-rimed street.

The shepherd and his family returned to their house. Meridiana lingered in the street, keeping Jye in view. She watched him open up the door of the little rented cottage, saw him stand aside to allow his wife to enter, take the one step that carried him across his threshold, and then close that door, firmly and finally behind him. She looked up towards Jye's rooftree, and almost at once saw smoke rising from the chimney, thin and blue in the frosty air. She felt the heart grow small within her, a physical contraction that squeezed breath from her lungs. She stood rooted for several moments, quite unable to move, and then she began to run, taking long strides towards her own house.

It took time and strength to manhandle her heavy wooden bed down the narrow staircase. She hauled it into the living-room, and set it, in traditional fashion, underneath the rear window. Cupboards were dragged, from all parts of the house and placed, close together, around the living-room walls. Meri busied herself, transferring and rearranging until all her most valued possessions stood comfortingly within one small space. She searched for, and found, her bits of faded ribbon; with them she looped-up and tied back her respectable lace curtains. She opened a locked drawer and lifted out treasures never exhibited in the time of Jye. Her bed was spread with a clean white cover, across it she draped a shawl of scarlet silk, and positioned two cushions of faded yellow velvet. From a cupboard she withdrew several plates and dishes of thin, bone-china; with a single gesture she swept the thick brown crocks from the dresser shelves, and began to replace them with fine Crown Derby. Already, the room had a safer, more contained aspect; she remembered the housewifely pride of her mother and grandmother; brass lamps must now be polished, the fire-grate blackleaded, the floor swept.

Meri worked long into the night. When the transformation was complete she surveyed her vardo with mixed feelings of defiance and satisfaction. What would Jye say? How would he view the coloured china, the yellow cushions, the scarlet shawl? Like his father, Luke, her son had little tolerance for what was bright and fancy. But why should she concern herself with Jye's approval? The house was hers now to do with as she pleased.

Meri sat down upon her low stool and faced-to before the fire. She reached up to the shelf for her little clay pipe and

471

packet of tobacco, rubbed the thick twist between her fingers, tamped it into the bowl and lit it. She drew smoke deep into her lungs and smiled. Jye did not like to see her smoke, neither did he approve of drinking. She went to the dresser and fetched a china cup, into it she drew a measure of her own, potent elderberry wine. This day had seen a wedding in her family, a contract at which not a single soul had been joyful. Meridiana looked down at her own dark skirt, plain blouse, and sober shawl. From a cupboard she withdrew a dress of red and yellow plaids, a pinna' of embroidered silk, a brooch made from a single crown piece, and a pair of hooped gold earrings. She put on the plaid dress, grabbed the scarlet shawl from the bed and fastened it at her throat with the single crown brooch. She hooked the hoops of gold into her ears, tied the pinna' at her waist, and danced a few stiff steps of her old Tarantella. She drained the cup of elderberry wine and then refilled it. A handful of brushwood thrown onto the fire filled the room with leaping shadows. She sat down on her stool and gazed into the flames, touched the gold in her ears, smoothed the bright plaid of her dress, and was young again, with Luke at her side, and all the long white roads of life winding out before her.

The fire grew low, the charred fronds of the brushwood trembled in the heat, fell apart and re-formed to make intricate patterns. Meri hunched, elbows on knees, head supported in spread fingers, and gazed into the glow. Her grandmother had possessed the gift of 'seeing'. To a lesser extent that old power had also troubled her mother. Certain times of evening, an early-morning mood of heightened awareness, could trigger the same visions in Meridiana. The lifting of the veil did not often reveal happy portents. She had known, long before their birth, that her twins would be deformed. She had sensed that Luke was about to die. For many days before the fall of rock which killed him, the whisper of that dread word 'widow' had been loud in her mind. Now, on this wedding-night of Jye, she found herself to be sensitive as a stretched fiddle-string; her mind so receptive and without defences, that she could not withstand the images that filled it. Almost against her will she began to recall that meeting on the Taunton road, and Eliza Greypaull, just evicted that morning from Larksleve Farm, her few belongings loaded on a farm cart, her children perched aloft on the piled feather-beds. Oh, but Meridiana had been far-seeing on that day! Back and forth her soul had shuttled, into the past, and forward again, to see the years that were still to come.

How strange, that such knowledge should have come to her there, on the dusty road, beneath the blackthorn's shadow! She had gazed on the seven faces of Eliza's children, but it had been only those two, the redhaired beauty and the timid fair one, about whom the nimbus of light had streaked and quivered! She remembered her own hand, placed upon Jye's shoulder, and the certainty of her voice as she had gazed upon the face of Blanche. 'You!' she had cried, 'you with the proud looks! The day shall come when you will try to get close to me and mine!' Well, that prophecy had come to pass, and no mistake! But there had been that other, that quiet maiden, with the soft uncertain features, and the light hair. 'You, maid,' Meri had asked gently, 'whass your name, then?'

''Tis Annis, ma'am.'

'So, Annis Greypaull! Remember this day when you met up wi' a gypsy, for 'tis you what'll put this matter right betwixt me an' your mother.'

The fire burned down into a pale ash, the room grew cold and Meri shivered. She had known, out there in the village street, at the moment when Jye closed his own front door, that this day would see an end to her long subservience both to him and to the gorgie. For the sake of Jye she had

473

accepted makeshift, worn black instead of scarlet at her husband's funeral, and remained beneath the thatch of this stone house, when her every instinct cried out to set foot once more upon the white road. Meri stirred and sighed; she took up a few thin applewood logs from the hearthstone and set them carefully among the embers. Almost at once the dry wood caught, and her thoughts, set free by the blaze, began to roam hungrily among the blue flames. She had never wished to know her own future; the cry that she would never make old bones had been made as a plea to any listening gods who might wish to claim her before her allotted time. It was only now, on this special night, when she had narrowed her life to the compass of a single room, that she might dare to lift a corner of the veil. She placed thicker logs upon the fire, watched them catch and flare until all the spaces of her mind filled up with their blue and gold. Meridiana waited; she willed the images to return to troop before her; all those faces and voices that would come to her so slyly and surely when unbidden.

She saw nothing. She gazed deeper into the flames; body all tensed and fists clenched she commanded the coming years to reveal their secrets. Gradually, her hands uncurled, the tension left her body, and she was weak and empty. The room was very quiet now, not even a moan of wind sighed inside the chimney. Perhaps, she thought, her very failure to see had been a sign; perhaps there was to be no more future for her?

All at once, the logs fell apart with a sudden flurry of white ash, Meri raised her head, alerted by the soft sound and unexpected movement, and then, from the heart of the fire she heard the whisper of an old name, once used among her people, but long neglected. She heard it clearly, spoken in her father's voice, and that word, that name, was Silvanus.

❋

The baby Abigail was turning out to be a fighter. There had

been many times in that winter and early spring, when Eliza
had doubted the ability of so tiny a child to survive. There
had been sleepless nights and anxious days when it seemed
that the battle might be lost. But now, at the age of six
months, Abigail sat erect and unaided in the rocking-cradle.
In her looks it was already clear that she was no Greypaull:
the down of hair had grown to a straight and pretty cap of
nut-brown, her eyes were a clear and observant grey. Frank
Nevill had been enslaved from the moment he first held her.
The goodness of Frank was a source of comfort to Eliza; his
acceptance of Annis and her child was a matter for comment
by all who saw it. Eliza counted up her blessings and knew
that she was happy. Even the spring had come early this
year. She visited the graves of Jack and Louis, touched the
tight green buds already showing on the white rose bush,
and found herself able, at last, to give thanks to God for the
blessings of their short lives. For the very first time she was
able to remember Philip without rancour or resentment. He
lay at peace in Buckland St Mary; violets and primroses
covered his grave; above him the sweet bells rang out from
the belltower. She, of course, would lie here in Taunton,
side by side with her two sons. But not yet! There was a
new soul to care for, a child to rear, a lady to be made out of
Abigail Greypaull!

❈

Chapel marriages in Taunton, Frank Nevill discovered,
came cheaper by the dozen. He and Annis stood in line
before the altar with eleven other couples. Their vows lost
in a chorus of faltering responses; twelve rings were slid
simultaneously onto twelve waiting fingers. Twelve brides
raised their veils and were kissed, and the business was all
over.

Annis wore a jacket and skirt of some thin beige stuff,
stitched hurriedly together by her sister, Mina. He wore a
suit of blue serge, a communal outfit, used by all his family

for funerals, baptisms, and weddings. In the case of Frank the trousers were too short, the sleeves too long, but it hadn't seemed to matter. Funny, he thought, how life itself had a knack of turning out to be too short in one place, too long in another. 'Coming to terms' was a phrase he had heard first in the Army. 'Come to terms with it, soldier!' Serjeant Bath had shouted, and Frank had done so. At the age of seventeen in Burma, he had adjusted to the deaths of comrades, suddenly cut-down by gunshot or machete, or suffering the lingering horrors of typhoid and undiagnosed fevers. India had called for other shifts and tacks. At first he had almost swallowed whole that heathen and unhappy land. He had detested the heat, the flies, the insolent natives, who believed the English soldiers to be criminals, deported to their country. 'You can get used to anything,' Sergeant Bath had told them. 'When you get home, your own mothers won't recognise you! You may think now that you hate this place, but I'll tell you fellers something – you'll never be able to forget it, not if you live to be a hundred.' It was true. He had seen sights, heard sounds, experienced feelings that he could never share, not even with Annis. She had asked him about it, but he had been evasive; he lacked the words that would describe for her such a mystery as India, such a secret.

They talked a lot about the old cottage that was up for rent; it stood by itself in a little lane just off North Street. The house, so people said, had been overlooked by an absentminded landlord when some unsafe properties had been recently demolished. Frank could not believe this. One of these days, he told Annis, just as we get nicely settled in, the men will come back with their hammers to knock the place down. Annis had laughed. At a rent of one shilling a week, the cottage was a proper bargain; and what with his wage of only twelve shillings a week, and work being short in the shirt factory, they could not, she said, afford to turn it down.

They had been married at midday on Sunday; by tea-time they were a settled little family, with the kettle boiling on the hob, a cake made by Madelina standing on the table, and the baby Abigail sleeping in her crib beside the fire. It was not the marriage he had dreamed about in New Delhi and Belgaum, not the wedding night he had anticipated when he had embarked for Folkstone in Bombay. His sisters had visited him when he lay sick in the military hospital at Netley.

'That Annis,' his sister, Jane, had told him, 'is no better than she should be, never mind all her fancy airs and graces. Carrying-on, she was, behind your back, with some officer up the Barracks. Dressed up in their Blanche's London outfits, with earrings dangling from her earlobes, and her hair frizzled up in curls. Oh, our Frank, you should just have seen her!'

His sister had blushed and looked away. 'I don't want to tell 'ee this, Frank, but somebody got to. Her's in the family way, and no wonder! You had best forget all about her. We don't speak to her, and no more should you.'

Frank had sat on a bench in the hospital gardens; he avoided the company of all other patients, sought secluded places in shadows and beneath trees. His thoughts were all of Annis, of how little he really knew about her, how the scrappy, unromantic notes that had arrived in India from England might well have been written by his own mother. He had looked at her photograph, remembered her as she had been on that first day in the collar factory, and known that he still loved her. He would always love her.

'Come to terms with it, soldier!' Sergeant Bath had roared, and Frank had made his adjustment right there at Netley, underneath a beech tree on a morning in late June. It had been the hardest blow he would ever suffer; no use pretending otherwise, he had wept bitter tears. His whole future depended on this girl. What else would he do if he didn't marry Annis? There was no room for him in his father's house, and, in view of his poor state of health, the Army was unwilling to re-engage him. He thought about the other man, the officer who had betrayed her. In the years that were to come, Frank Nevill was never to be sure at what point acceptance had become resignation. Without Frank there would be nothing but hardship and shame for Annis Greypaull and her base-born child. He had faced other trials, other setbacks. He could, he was sure, come to terms with this lot.

Telling his family had been the worst part. His sisters had declared themselves to be insulted, and what was more, he must be out of his mind! Nice-looking Annis might be, but handsome was as handsome does – and just look at what she had gone and done! His mother and father had said little on the matter, knowing full well that his only alternative to marriage was a lonely existence in some cheap lodging house in Taunton. The final insult to the Nevill family had been aimed by the village carter, who came down from Buckland St Mary every Friday morning, bearing boots to be repaired.

'I hears as how your Frank is getting wed next Sunday.'

'Yes,' said Mr Nevill, 'he's marrying a girl from your part of the country.'

'Who's that then?'

'Maid by the name of Greypaull.'

The carter had paused, a pair of newly-soled boots in each hand. 'Did I hear you say Greypaull?'

'The very same. Her father had a farm in Buckland many years ago.'

'Well, I never! There's a thing now!' The carter looked consideringly at the shoemaker. 'Do 'ee know much about they Greypaulls?'

'Not a lot.'

The old man grinned. 'I'll tell 'ee something then, shoemaker! That maid must be lowering herself a very long way if her's ready and willing to get hitched-up wi' your

478

son! They Greypaulls was ever a proud lot!'

✳

Simeon Greypaull came home to Taunton early in September, looking brown and fit and handsomer than ever. He marched into Eliza's kitchen, kissed his mother, appeared not to see his sister Madelina, and whirled an excited Laura high above his head. His predictable first words were, 'Where's our Annis?'

Mina glanced nervously at Eliza. 'You'd better sit down, boy,' said his mother, 'I'll make you some tea. You can tell us all your news, family matters can wait. You be looking well, Sim. Seems like a soldier's life do suit 'ee?' Eliza spoke swiftly, wishing to distract him, but already his gaze was upon the empty chimney-corner.

'Where's our Louis?' he whispered.

Madelina turned away to busy herself with kettle and teapot. Laura grew silent and watched the grown-ups with wide and fearful eyes. Eliza sat down at the kitchen table, and motioned Simeon to sit beside her. She touched his hand. 'I didden want to tell 'ee straight away, boy, but a lot have come to pass since you left Taunton.' She paused. 'How did you find us?'

'Went to Hunter's Court,' he said tersely, 'found strangers living in the house. They told me you had moved to this place.'

'They never told you nothing else?'

'Nothing.'

Madelina poured tea and handed teacups, she sat down in Eliza's rocking-chair, keeping Laura close beside her. Eliza smoothed the tablecloth and could not begin.

'What's happened, Mama? Is our Annis — hurt? Is that what you be feared o' telling?'

Eliza looked up, almost relieved to be able to reassure him. 'No Sim. Not hurt — not Annis. Her's fit and well, and married to Frank Nevill.'

'What is it, then?'

''Tis my Jack,' burst out Madelina. ''Tis my dearest brother what lies dead.'

Simeon looked, for the first time, at Mina. 'My God,' he muttered, 'whatever have happened to 'ee Mina? Your hair have turned snow white.'

'It changed colour when Jack died,' said Eliza. 'Mina was ill for a long time. They two was ever devoted to one another.'

'What killed our Jack?'

'Can't you guess? 'Twas they bloody horses!' Mina swore for the first and only time in her life. 'He was riding bareback, just like usual. 'Twas January, and the going was rock-hard wi' frost. He fell on his head. His neck was broke. He was dead before they reached him.'

All colour had drained from Simeon's face. He took a deep breath and then repeated his earlier question. He gestured towards the empty corner. 'Where's our Louis?'

'He've been gone these three years,' said Eliza.

'Not the Asylum?'

'No boy. The dear Lord took him Home to rest! There was a 'flu epidemic. Lots of people died here in Taunton.'

'Not the both of 'em?' Simeon's voice was hoarse with pain.

''Twas the Lord's will,' said Eliza.

Simeon turned to Madelina. 'Do you believe that?'

Mina raised a defensive hand to her white hair, the green, hooded eyes came all the way open. 'No,' she said, and her voice was hard and uncompromising. 'I don't believe it. In the case of Louis you could say it was a happy release. But that was no merciful God what took away my Jackie! Jack had me, and a wife and child. He had everything to live for!' She turned upon Eliza. 'I loved him more than you ever did! 'Tis easy for you to call his death the Lord's Will. 'Twas ever Annis with you, eh Mama? Mother's liddle maiden!' Her voice was full of scorn, her features bitter. 'Well, Sim

– you got another shock to face this day. Whyn't you ask Mama about her dearest, most beloved daughter?'

Eliza's hand crept up to her scarred face; her gaze went involuntarily to the line of baby garments airing on a line above the fireplace. Simeon looked from one closed face to the other. 'Well,' he shouted, 'what is it with our Annis? You said that she had wed wi' Nevill. When did that happen?'

'At Easter,' said Eliza.

'Tell him the rest of it, Mama. He got to know about it, sometime.'

Simeon brought his clenched fist down hard upon the table. 'No, Mina,' he ground out, 'you shall be the story-teller. I can see you is dying to get your word in about my sister. You was ever jealous of her.'

Eliza sighed. 'I'll tell him myself, boy. When Annis married Frank her fatherless baby was already seven months old. Frank come back from Netley Hospital two days before Abigail was born. 'Tis all sorted out,' she hastened to reassure him, 'Frank got a job straightaway, and they rented a little house just off North Street. I mind the baby for her in the daytime.' Simeon looked grim, the set of his jaw alarmed Eliza.

'The name,' he said quietly. 'I want the bastard's name what wronged her. Nothing else. Then I'll wring his bloody neck and gut him!'

'No,' said Eliza, 'we've had trouble enough since you went away. You got no call to worry about Annis.'

Simeon stood up. He pushed his chair back from the table, and raised one hand in a dramatic gesture. 'All right!' he cried, 'I won't kill him! But I'll call a curse down on his head. Let him never prosper! Let everything what is terrible in this world happen to him. Let it happen to all his heirs, even unto the fourth and fifth generations!'

Madelina clapped a shocked hand across her mouth, Laura whimpered in fear, and Eliza looked troubled. 'You didden ought to have done that,' she said, 'to call down a curse is the worst kind of sin you can commit.'

481

'And what about the sin done against my sister? If I had been home at the time, I'd have done more to him than curse him.'

Madelina said in her coolest tone, 'But you wasn't at home Sim, was you? Me and Mama have had to deal with two deaths in the family, as well as Annis' downfall.'

'And I'll bet you enjoyed every minute of it!'

Eliza said, 'That's not fair, Simeon. Mina fair broke her heart when Jack died.'

Simeon looked mutinous. 'Nothing have changed much in this family, have it, Mother? All us wants to complete the picture is for our Blanche to walk in here now, acting like a duchess.'

Madelina's laughter grated across the kitchen table. 'Just bide here long enough,' she warned him, 'and your wish'll be granted. Her ladyship have also got married — to an Honourable, no less! Her is hob-nobbing now with the Prince of Wales, if half of what she says is true! 'Tis carriages and tiaras these days. Not to mention cigarette smoking!'

Simeon smiled suddenly, all anger spent. Eliza looked up at him. How handsome he looked in his scarlet tunic! Sim's likeness to his dead father caught at her heart with a peculiar anguish. The Army had changed him: the petulant droop had gone from his mouth, he stood tall and proud, the fair hair cropped short, the blue eyes steady.

She said, 'You be the man in the family, now Sim. My only surviving son. How much longer will you have to serve?'

'I signed on for a full twenty-two years.' His hard voice wavered briefly. 'The Army have showed me how to read and write. Never had no choice about it. I can write letters now, Mama. You'll be hearing from me in the future.' He touched the moisture away from the corners of his eyes. 'Now come on, you two! Where's our Annis living? I got to go and see this new baby, right away!'

Madelina went home, the silent Laura close behind her. She entered her neat little house and visited her many treasures: there was the sewing-machine, on which she made clothes for all the family, the baking tin, bought especially to make a wedding cake for Annis. There was the cabinet, filled with bandages and home-made remedies. It was always to Mina they came in times of sickness. She bit her lips so as not to cry. She went into the small front room, elegant with blue walls and brocaded sofa; she stroked the cabinet, filled with wedding china, examined the state of the aspidistra on the what-not. She twitched aside her spotless curtains, and looked out into the street to see if Dave was coming. The road was empty; he had probably gone straight to his Bible Class that evening without bothering to tell her. She sighed. Since her deception of him in the case of Annis, David had scarcely spoken to her. It had been Laura, who, in spite of her mother's threats and warnings, had blurted the exciting news of Annis. Hardly had David Lambert stepped across his doorstep, before Laura had run to him, crying, 'Daddy, daddy! There's such a lovely little baby come to live with Granny Greypaull. I want one, too, Father! I want a baby sister!'

Mina knew she would never forget the stricken eyes of David; the strange almost indecent collapse of his normally stern features. She could only guess at the deprivation he suffered by sleeping alone in the little back bedroom. She knew that he longed for another child, although the subject was not discussed between them. They both knew that another pregnancy would cost Madelina her life. Mina saw him turn away from Laura's bright face, to look at her own stiff features. Dave's expression turned gradually from grief to anger as if all his private agony had changed to public fury.

'You should have told me,' he shouted. 'I heard a rumour

about your Annis, but I was so sure it was a lie, that I never even repeated it to you!' He sat down abruptly, and rested his head in his hands. 'I had a great respect for your Annis. I shall never be able to speak to her again.'

'That's all right, Dave,' Madelina had soothed him. 'Annis wudden expect it from you, you being so high up in chapel business. That wudden be right for you to be seen to condone sin.' She had waited for him to speak, but he had stayed silent. In a different, more determined voice, Madelina had continued. 'Of course,' she had said, 'Annis is still my baby sister, and Laura's aunty. The child – the little baby – is my niece and Laura's cousin. I shan't turn my back on them, David. After all, family is family, and blood far thicker than water!'

The downfall of Annis had caused a rift between Madelina and David Lambert. It would heal over, thought Mina; most things did, given time. Meanwhile, she was lonely and uneasy, and feelings of distress always made her sharp of tongue and inclined to be malicious. She knelt down in her chill little room, and remembered the Larksleve parlour. She touched the blue pegged hearthrug she and Dave had woven together. Mina called Laura to her; she smoothed the fierce red curls back from the freckled forehead.

'Do you love your Mama, Laura?' she asked gently.

Laura wound her arms about Mina's neck. 'Oh yes, Mama. Best of all the world.' The child hesitated. 'Do you think we could go to see Abigail tomorrow? Could we see Uncle Simeon, too?'

'Of course we could, if you truly want to.' Mina held the thin little frame very close. It was only, she thought, her own blood relatives who really counted, when all was said and done.

That night Madelina wrote a letter; she addressed the envelope to Lady Castlemain, and marked it PRIVATE in the top left-hand corner. Mina described the wrong done by that lady's son to her sister Annis; the wicked abandonment by Captain Castlemain of a girl cruelly wronged. Her sister, wrote Madelina, had been fortunate enough to have recently married a *good man*. There was, however, a matter of money to be considered. Babies come expensive, especially to a family in reduced circumstances. Lady Castlemain's Christian conscience would no doubt be giving her trouble from this day onwards. Madelina spelled out Eliza's address in large, black capitals, and signed herself 'A Well-Wisher'.

✸

On the day that Lady Castlemain received her letter from Madelina Lambert, two envelopes were delivered to Eliza Greypaull in Greenbrook Terrace. One bore the postmark of Suamico, Wisconsin. The other was in the small cramped hand of her daughter Candace.

Dear Mother,

This will no doubt come as a surprise after so long, but I have had troubles what I could not put on you, you having plenty enough of your own. My husband died very soon after we was married, leaving me with child, a boy called William. Times have been hard, Mother, but we have pulled thru' somehow. Billy is twelve now and keeps asking about you and all his aunts and uncles. I have saved up the train fare and we will be coming down to see you before too long. Hope you are all well. Money not worth much here in London, food being dearer than in the country. It is pouring with rain as I pen this letter.

Yr loving daughter,
Candace

Eliza held the scrap of paper for a long time; reading and re-reading the words which told her everything, and yet explained nothing. She tested every item of new information, but treading gingerly, afraid that it might notbear her weight. The letter, so characteristic of Candace, mentioned widowhood and poverty in the same undramatic voice as her comments on the price of food, and the London weather. The seam of gold, hidden in one sentence, was contained in the words 'Billy is twelve now, and keeps asking about you'.

The letter from Suamico, Brown County, was Rhoda's sympathetic reply to the sad news about Annis.

❀

The news from Taunton was brought to Blanche, surreptitiously, by Martha, in a corner of the Porteous kitchen quarters. For the price of a cast-off hat or blouse, the servant, now promoted to housemaid, still risked dismissal by extracting letters addressed to Mrs Fitzgerald from the hall table, and reading them to her in the pantry which held dry-goods and preserves. This interception of mail had lately become even more important. There were other notes, delivered by hand: sentimental missives couched in oblique language, always unsigned, and burned on the kitchen fire immediately after reading. In the case of these notes, the vigilance of Martha was rewarded by a half-crown piece. Blanche regretted this deliberate destruction; but for her promise to the sender she could have tossed the scraps of innocent nonsense casually, across the breakfast table, and watched the embarrassment of Aunt Letitia, at her own connivance in the strange affair.

Her need to protect Eliza's words was instinctive; Blanche could not bear to have the simple feelings and thoughts of Mama read aloud in the cultured and mocking voice of Mrs Porteous. The ear of Blanche had finally become attuned to the finer points of grammar, and Eliza, lady though she was, would make the occasional slip into the Somerset idiom. Letters from Taunton were mostly about Frank and Annis: their fortuitous marriage, the little house just off North Street, the precious baby. Even Martha, who read with the whine of Cockney in her voice, could never make the infant Abigail sound other than totally entrancing. Blanche would lean against the closed pantry door and gaze absently at the rows of jars which held chutneys and pickles, jams and conserves. She would breathe in the mingled odours of dried apricots and prunes, spices and pepper, cinnamon and curry-powder, while Martha told in Eliza's words of the little girl's first smile, first tooth, first attempts at sitting upright.

The relationship between Blanche and Hugh, never stable or particularly tranquil, had deteriorated alarmingly during the past year. Blanche did not hold with the fashionable view that an inability to conceive must be due, entirely, to some lack on the part of the female partner. She blamed Hugh; if she had known words like effete and emasculated she would have used them to describe him. She was brutally frank about his continuing failure; even her Papa she said, with his soppy fair curls and his drinking habit, had managed to give her Mama seven living babies. Hugh should, she said, consider himself lucky that she remained faithful to him; many a lady in her position would have gone, long ago, to fish in more productive waters.

Hugh was jealous. His questions about her twice-weekly visits to the house in Park Lane were probing and anxious. Blanche enjoyed the sight of his dilemma. Blanche, once seen by the Prince to be in an 'interesting condition', would have no further appeal for the heir apparent, but it did not happen.

'What do you do? What does he do?' Hugh demanded.

'Oh! Bertie and I have so much in common,' she would say in her new Mayfair voice. 'We talk a lot about clothes. He's very fastidious, don't you know! He changes his outfits at least six or seven times every day. He'll talk for hours about the colour of his shirts and waistcoats. He asks my advice about buttons and cravats. He says I've got a true eye for style and colour.'

Hugh said, 'It all sounds incredibly boring. I had no idea

that he was such a dull man.'

'Dull?' Blanche grinned. 'No man with eyes like his could ever be called that! Oh, he was Jack the Lad in his young days, that I do believe. He's getting old now. A bit of a romp across the sofa is as much as he can manage. What with his stomach and his breathing –'

Hugh winced and would not look at her. 'Spare me the revolting details,' he said. 'Just the thought of you in his company appalls me.'

'He's promised me a present,' she said softly, 'he asked me what I would like as a memento of our afternoons together.'

'And what did you decide on?'

'Oh, I was ready with my answer. "Anything that pawns well, Your Highness." That's what I told him. You should just have heard him laugh, Hugh. I thought he'd have a fit! "And so you shall, my little dear. I'll give you a present that will keep you in brandy for the rest of your life. My horse is entered for the 1896 Derby. If he wins, you shall have his name in diamonds!" '

Hugh said, 'I don't believe you. It's a well-known fact that he never makes gifts. If you have to tell me lies, Blanche, you might at least make them believable untruths.'

'Please yourself,' she said. 'It's also a well-known fact that Bertie keeps his word. He promised me his horse's name in diamonds.' She crossed the room to where Hugh sat, surrounded by his butterfly collection. She dropped a casual kiss on the top of his head. 'Considering the state of our finances,' she whispered, 'you'd better get down on your knees every night for a week before the start of next year's Derby and pray to God that the bloody horse wins!'

❊

Jye's first child was born in late October of 1895. Meridiana, who had never been invited into the rented cottage, did not visit now. She waited for the baby to be brought to her and, sure enough, Jye came after chapel on a Sunday morning bearing the swaddled infant in his arms. He and Meri exchanged one long and significant look above the sleeping bundle, but no words.

Jye marched into his mother's house, took one swift glance at her bed still positioned underneath the rear window, the sinful scarlet shawl, the ostentatious and richly coloured china. He opened his mouth to speak as he had on several previous occasions; he intended to upbraid her again for this flagrant return to her old gypsy ways. But Meri held up a warning index finger. 'Bide quiet,' she said in her gruff voice. ''Tis none o' thy business no more what goes on yer!'

She took the child from him and sat down on her low stool before the fire. She began to unwrap the many coverings, until Jye grew nervous. 'Maris 'ont like that,' he warned his mother. 'Her'll know straight away what you been doing.'

'Thy Maris can bide quiet as well,' snapped Meridiana. To the baby she crooned, 'Now you just lie still my pretty liddle dear, and us'll see what the shepherd's skinny maiden have managed to give us!' She unwound the final flannel binder, and the infant lay revealed upon the plaid lap.

'How old?' she asked Jye.

'Two months,' he said, briefly.

Meri nodded her pleasure at the plump limbs, the head of black curls, the brown eyes. 'Her's all Carew. Not a sign of Honeybone in her.'

She clapped her hands together, close beside the infant's ear and smiled at the resultant start and frightened whimper. Slowly and thoroughly Meri flexed each tiny arm and leg. She raised the baby to a sitting position, laid her down again, this time upon her stomach, and ran probing fingers along the spine and shoulder blades.

'Straight,' she muttered, 'and nothing lacking in the hearing department.'

Meri began to replace the flannel bindings, the muslin

layers, the many petticoats and long gown. She wound the crocheted shawl exactly as Damaris had wound it, she examined the handiwork of it.

'Maris made that,' Jye said proudly.

'Her have also made a fine child.' Meri's voice was grudging. 'But tidden the one I be waiting for.'

Jye, accustomed to his mother's strange announcements, ignored this one. He said, 'We be thinking of calling her Matilda, after Maris' mother.'

''Tis your Silvanus I be waiting on,' said Meridiana.

'My Silvanus?'

'Your boy, your son! You'll only have but the one male child. His given name shall be Silvanus, no mind what your Maris got to say about it!'

Jye took the sleeping Matilda and laid her across his shoulder. 'I thought,' he said, 'that you wudden never "tell" for family?'

'I cudden help it this time, boy. It come to me on a whisper from in there.' She pointed towards the fire-grate. 'I heard the name, plain as daylight. Your son,' she said firmly, 'Silvanus Carew, and that chavvie shall be all mine!'

Jye went away, so troubled and uneasy that he was bound to tell Maris all about it. 'She were always a bit – well, diff'rent,' he confessed, 'but now I be worried about her. She've dragged all her belongings into one room. There's no need for that Maris! Her have got a whole house to live in! She's smoking that clay pipe too and drinking wine and cider.'

'And what else, Jye?'

He stayed quiet for several minutes, and then he burst out, 'She can see things! She knowed when my Pa was about to die. She don't usually talk about it.'

'They used to burn witches,' Maris said softly.

'She bain't no witch! She sees pictures, that's all. Sometimes she hears voices.'

'And what have your mother heard what has got you in this state?'

490

'A son! that's what she said. Only ever the one boy, and his name must be Silvanus.'

'Must be?'

'Oh yes,' Jye said. 'Prophecy do have to be fulfilled, you knows that as well as I do.'

'I knows nothing of the sort, Jye Carew! As for your mother choosing my son's name — well, that'll never happen! If I should have a boy he'll be called David, after my father. There'll be no heathen names amongst my children!'

Jye appeared not to read the word that was on his wife's lips. 'Silvanus,' he repeated. 'My Ma have said so, and in this particular case, us two dursent go against her.'

❊

Hugh had started to drink, steadily and with such dedication that even Blanche showed concern. His addiction had become severe soon after their visit to Taunton in early December. It had been a week of painful experience for Blanche. She had watched Hugh grow more involved with and attached to her sisters and their children. How strange, she thought, that he, with all his sophistication and grand airs, should be drawn so inevitably and deeply into the dramas and heartaches of the Greypaull family with each successive visit.

They had called on Madelina and David Lambert, and Blanche has gazed around the little blue parlour, at Mina's brave attempt to recreate the charm of Larksleve. She recalled the dark brown claustrophobic rooms in Russell Square, and envied Mina's freedom to live and furnish as she pleased. In a corner cabinet, locked safely away behind glass doors, sat the doll which Blanche had once given to tiny Laura. Laura had grown tall, and was careful of her possessions, but the doll was never handled. It had not once been played with: the pretty porcelain face remained

491

unmarked, the elaborate dress still stiff with newness. Like Laura herself, the doll had a frightened, withdrawn air about her. Hugh had declared himself impressed by Laura's musical talent. He listened attentively to her renditions of Chopin and Brahms. His observation, made, Blanche was sure, out of politeness, that Laura might, one day, become a teacher of music, had been seized upon by Madelina with an intensity that Blanche found terrifying. Even as she and Hugh left the little terraced house, Mina was planning the move to a more prestigious part of Taunton.

'We must rent a house that stands by itself,' she told David Lambert. 'It must have a porch, and a place to put up a brass-plate. Oh, Dave! I can just see it! Miss Laura Lambert, L.R.A.M. Qualified Teacher of the Pianoforte.'

Blanche had dreaded the visit to her sister Annis. She had borne, without too much anguish, the sight of Madelina, arms entwined about the precious Laura. But to actually see, and be expected to hold, the baby she had already come to know and love through Eliza's letters, was punishment of another order. Blanche and Hugh had walked from the London Hotel to the pretty cottage just off North Street. It was evening, with the lamp lit, curtains drawn, and a bright fire burning in the small room. Blanche hardly noticed the lack of carpet, the rickety furniture, the thick, cheap cups and saucers, the absence of upholstered comfort. The one cramped room served as kitchen, parlour and bathroom; it was entered immediately from the garden, without benefit of porch or hallway. The tableau of the little Nevill family might, thought Blanche, have been posed deliberately to torment her. There was Frank, in his hard, uncushioned chair beside the fire, and Annis, standing flushed and proud, beside him, the freshly-bathed Abigail in her arms.

Blanche shook hands with Frank and embraced her sister. She introduced Hugh to her new brother-in-law, but all the time her mind was busy with the child. Brown hair, grey eyes, and a delicate complexion! Most definitely no Greypaull,

Blanche decided. Abigail Nevill was the daughter of her natural father, the defaulting Captain Castlemain. Thoughts racing, heart pounding, Blanche had eyes for no one but her sister's baby. How sweetly pretty she was, so much like the china doll in Mina's corner cupboard that Blanche hesitated to touch her. Her experience long ago with the infant Laura had made Blanche nervous in her approach to babies. She stood at a respectful distance, but almost at once the little arms reached out towards her, the warm face was laid against her cold cheek. This little girl laughed and chuckled her delight at the touch of Blanche's sable collar, and the brilliance of her diamond and emerald earrings. Blanche shrugged away her restricting cape, and held the child close against her body; her gaze met that of Hugh, and she knew that he read her mind. How often had she reached out her hands for other treasures? How many times had she flexed grasping fingers, crying, 'I want and want! 'Tis like a pain inside me!' Oh, but Blanche was in pain now: the ache was fierce, both physical and heartfelt. She wrapped her arms about the little body, until Abigail gasped and grew pink from the excessive pressure.

'Not so tightly, Blanche,' pleaded Hugh, 'you'll alarm her, and make her cry.'

'No, I won't! She likes it, don't you, my sweetheart? She already loves me, Hugh. Can't you see that?'

Blanche turned to Annis for confirmation, but the look on her sister's face was a warning to be cautious. There was jealousy and bitter envy in the eyes of Annis, but mixed with contempt and a grudging kind of pity. The dangerous moment was covered with a spate of words. Annis pulled up two rush-seated chairs, and placed them closer to the fire. She filled the kettle and set it on the hob to boil for tea. Blanche sat down beside Hugh, the baby still happy in her arms. She was acutely aware of the unlikely picture she presented; she began to speak rapidly to Frank to cover her own dismay at the yearning expression on Hugh's face.

'So you're in work then, Frank?'

'I was lucky. I got a brother what works at French's. He put in a good word for me.'

Hugh asked, 'What sort of job is it?'

Frank held out his hands to show the raw state of his knuckles. 'I be what they calls a "flesher",' he explained. 'I use a big, broad-bladed knife. I scrap clean the skins and pelts before they goes for tanning.'

'A hard job,' Hugh murmured.

''Tis a terrible job,' cried Annis. 'Just look at his poor hands, and all for a measly twelve bob a week!'

Blanche said, 'I hear that you've gone back to work at Cook's.'

'Well, I had to didden I? Us can't never manage on Frank's money. Mama was more than willing to take care of baby, and Mr Cook offered me my job back.'

'You were always their best buttonholer, Annis. I'm sure there will always be work for you at Cook's.' Blanche sensed the hostility of Annis, and made further efforts to placate her. 'I've never see Mama look so happy in all her life. This baby has made all the difference to her.'

Frank said, ''Tis a shame that Annis got to leave her for so many hours. They be only little for such a short time.' The adoration in his face when he spoke of Abigail was something Blanche had not expected.

'You love her, don't you?' she said softly.

'He's besotted with her,' said Annis. 'I sometimes think he only married me, for to be a father to my Abi.' She paused, in her pouring of tea to consider her husband. 'He gets a pension,' she told Hugh, 'disability money from the Army. It gets paid over every quarter-day. Do you know what he does with it? He takes that child to Moggridge's toy-shop down by the Tone Bridge. He buys her whatever takes her fancy, and her not yet two years old!' She laughed. ''Tis a good thing that we didden exchange Abi for next-door's baby. He's the ugliest child I ever did see. Even that poor maid in Silver Street refused to have him when the time come. Frank idden hard to please, but he might not have been so taken with that boy.'

Frank grinned. 'Petticoat government reigns in this house,' he told Hugh. 'I be properly under the thumb, and no mistake.'

They drank their tea, and prepared to leave. Blanche stood up and relinquished the sleepy Abigail into her sister's arms. The two women stood close together in the open doorway, while Hugh took his leave of Frank. Annis indicated the jewels on Blanche's throat and wrist, the sable-trimmed velvet cloak, the amazing hat. 'You landed yourself a soft billet,' she muttered sourly, 'but then, you was always good at looking out for number one, eh Blanche?'

Blanche became aware, for the first time, of the poverty and bareness of her sister's cottage. She relapsed, momentarily, into her old speech. 'I be sorry 'tis such a struggle for 'ee, Annis. But Frank's a good man –'

'And I be lucky that he took me on! Go on then, you might as well say it as only think it. I be sick of hearing about my good luck. They still refers to me as "poor Annis", even though I got a wedding-band on my finger. People got long memories in Taunton town. They won't never let me forget what have happened –' She spoke on a sob, 'and I can't forget it neither,' she whispered. 'If that Castlemain had only married me I'd be living now in a fine house, I could be dressed like you, and riding in my carriage. My Abigail would have a nursemaid – she'd be called by her rightful name –'

Blanche moved even closer to her sister. 'You stupid little bitch', the words were forced from between clenched teeth. 'You don't deserve that good man in there. He's one in ten million, to have married you in your situation. You treat him proper, you hear me, Annis!' The lips of Annis began to turn down. 'Don't do that!' cried Blanche. 'It makes you look exactly like Papa!'

'There's some,' muttered Annis, 'what acts exactly like

Papa. I'd like to know what tricks you been up to lately, my dear sister? That poor husband of yours looks the picture of misery. Who is it this time, our Blanche? You was boasting about the Prince of Wales – ?'

The shaft went home. Blanche could feel her colour rising; she put up both hands to hide her flaming cheeks, and Annis smiled. 'Don't ever come telling me how to treat Frank Nevill. I only ever sinned but the once, and I've paid for it in shame and tears.' Annis leaned back against the door jamb. 'Now you, our Blanche, is what could quite properly, be called a whore. No wonder,' she said spitefully, 'no wonder that you got no children of your own. You don't deserve none!'

Blanche could just make out the shape of the silver-and-coral pendant beneath her sister's high-necked blouse. Her had went up to display the diamond and emerald ring on her third finger. 'Exchange with me, Annis,' she pleaded, 'you need the money more than I do. My ring will pawn for many hundreds – you'll have to go down to Exeter to hock it – no Taunton pawnshop could afford to take it –'

'No Blanche!' The satisfaction of her refusal far outweighed the dragging reluctance in Annis' voice. 'Oh we needs the money, don't you ever doubt it. But I got a debt to repay Frank Nevill. I had a bad confinement – just like Madelina – that do seem to be a fault in all Mama's daughters. No more children, the doctor have told me. Well, you have seen Frank, noticed how devoted he is to Castlemain's child! That good man deserves a child of his own, Blanche, and 'tis only the pendant what'll make it comes to pass. No – you shall never have it! Not for the Crown Jewels!'

❁

It was on their final day in Taunton, when they were bound for the railway station, with Hugh waiting in the hired brougham, and Blanche saying her last farewells in Eliza's kitchen, that Candace turned up, holding Billy by the hand.

'My God,' Blanche cried out, 'it must be all of thirteen years. Whatever happened to you? Nobody knew where you had gone – not even Ellen Gimball –' Her words trailed away as Eliza came forward to embrace her oldest child. The boy stood apart. He assessed his surroundings with cynical, world-weary eyes. He studied the terrace of bay-windowed houses, the hired brougham with Hugh Fitzgerald seated in it. He turned his attention to Blanche, who still stood, uncertainly, in the open doorway, and at once his eyes flickered wide with calculating interest. She could almost guess at the exact valuation he was placing on her jewellery and clothes. Children like Billy were common-place in London. He spoke with the whine of the East-End Cockney.

'Whatchyer,' he grinned, 'you'll be me Aunty Blanche, wontcher? You're the fancy-piece what goes racing wiv' the Prince o' Wales. Me and Ma have seen you wiv' 'im many-a-time on the racecourse at Epsom.' He poked at the region of Blanche's ribcage with his grimy forefinger, and drooped an eyelid. 'You must know a thing or two,' he whispered. 'Bet you get some bloody good tips, eh? How abaht giving your nevvy a hint then, Aunty dear?' He laid the finger alongside his nose. 'What abaht some inside info on 'Is 'Ighnesses runners? Bet you already know what the fancy is for next year's Derby?'

Blanche recoiled from the clairvoyant child, but he was not easily discouraged. She turned back into the house to say goodbye to her mother, but Eliza, deep in conversation with the apologetic Candace, was quite unaware of the existence of Blanche. The appalling boy remained close at her side.

'They ain't bovered abaht you an' me,' Billy observed drily. 'My Ma talks a lot abaht you. She reckons they only wants yer for yer money.' Blanche edged towards the hallway, towards Hugh and the safety of the brougham. She looked down at the pale, Greypaull face and green eyes; the boy's thin frame and lack of height must come from Candace, but the fair waving hair was a direct inheritance from Philip Greypaull. She tried, desperately, to push past him, but he stood foursquare in her path.

'How old are you, Billy?'

'Twelve, going on thirteen.' His knowing face twisted with contempt for Blanche. 'You proper fancies yourself, dontcher? Ma said you was once a artist's model. Well, let me tell you somefink sweetheart! My name is Billy Stone. I bin on the stage since I was eight years old. I treads the boards dahn in Camberwell and Peckham! I dances and sings – I means to be an actor. I'll be famous one day. You remember my name, eh Aunt? Billy Stone from Peckham!'

✳

They arrived back in Russell Square to be met by the housemaid, Martha, who just happened to be passing through the hall. Hugh saw the significant glances that were being exchanged between his wife, and his Aunt Letitia's servant. He looked at the girl's capacious apron pocket, and there were the many letters, written on blue, familiar paper, sealed with wax, and certainly unsigned. Hugh began to mount the stairs to their own apartment, but Blanche lingered in the hall. He could hear the false note in her voice as she made conversation with the maid. He pushed open the heavy oak door and made straight for the side-table that held glasses and decanters. Hugh poured a large measure of brandy, drank it quickly and then poured another. Blanche did not come upstairs. She would, by this time, be closeted with Martha, while the housemaid read to her the Royal love-notes. His own post was propped up on the sofa-table. Pleas for an early settlement of outstanding accounts had come in from couturiers, milliners, jewellers, shoemakers, hairdressers, and wine-merchants. He drained the brandy goblet and refilled it; he sat down on the sofa, and began to think about the week spent in Taunton, about the man, Frank Nevill.

Frank had spent nine years of his life in the service of his country. He had returned to England, broken in health, requiring surgery upon an infected neck gland. The poor young fellow looked too frail and sick for work of any kind, but there he sat in his bare little cottage, nursing blood-raw knuckles; a 'flesher' who earned only twelve shillings for a labouring week of eighty hours. Hugh remembered Annis; her nervous, apologetic manner as she had handed him the thick chipped teacup and its unmatched saucer, the resentment of her gaze as she had watched the ways of Blanche with the baby, Abigail.

Blanche had once been listed among the ten most beautiful women resident in London. Down there, in Taunton, she was treated with scant respect by a family so tight and inward-looking that the one who did not conform tended to be ignored. Even Eliza, good mother that she was, still had her reservations about Blanche. 'Why?' he had once asked, 'do you constantly go back there? It never makes you happy. Each visit to Taunton ends in quarrelling and tears.'

Blanche looked thoughtful. 'I don't know,' she said, 'I don't know really why I go there. Something always seems to draw me.'

This latest visit, thought Hugh, had been the most disastrous Blanche had ever faced. There was Candace, a tiny indomitable woman in her simple black, whom he had glimpsed briefly from the brougham as she had entered her mother's house. Candace had courage: widowed early, she had brought up her son, alone in the city, without once turning back to ask for help from her hard-pressed mother.

There was Mina, so self-righteous and proper, but woefully misunderstood by the rest of her family. Hugh liked Madelina; he felt strangely reassured and calmed when in her presence. If I am ever sick, he thought – really sick – it would be Madelina Lambert whom I should call upon to nurse me.

Annis was the pitiful one; the sister who looked most like Blanche, and yet was so unlike her. He had sensed those same cravings for excitement and luxury in Annis, even her plain, dark dress had been worn with a certain, unconscious style! Poor Nevill! The frail ex-soldier was obviously no match for the envious and disillusioned girl, of whom he had made an honest woman.

It was Blanche, of course, who was the saddest. The thought surprised Hugh into sudden soberness. She wanted and wanted, but only those things that she could not have. He had watched her with her sisters' children. Her tentative friendliness towards the nervous Laura, her frank adoration of the baby Abigail. Even the street-wise Billy Stone had been spoken of by Blanche with unwilling admiration. Poor girl! Poor darling! What strange trick of breeding had given her an inheritance of remarkable beauty, and yet withheld the ability to conceive a child exhibited by all her sisters. Hugh saw her clearly, for the first time: her little vanities, her superstitions, the tricks she worked, the games she played. Even her latest trophy, the Royal Prince whom she was forbidden to exhibit, had kept her amused and amenable for the past year. But that infatuation was coming to an end. Hugh wondered if Blanche realised that when the giving of a gift was mentioned by Prince Edward Albert, it invariably meant farewell.

❋

The horse Persimmon had been bred from St Simon out of a mare named Perdita II. He was said to be an unpredictable mount, prone to trouble in the mouth, and disliked by his jockeys and trainers.

'I can't understand why the Prince has entered that horse for the Derby,' Blanche told Hugh. 'The odds against him are being given at five-to-one. My chances of a diamond brooch are riding on his nose —'

'Persimmon is a long name,' Hugh interrupted drily. 'Nine letters, set in diamonds, could prove pretty expensive. The man is less of a fool that I had thought him. To enter the race with a doubtful performer is a safe and certain way of reneging on a promise.'

Blanche was angry. 'Bertie's no welsher! What is more, he stands to win thousands if the nag wins.' She waggled her left hand. 'I've shown my good faith. I've pawned my engagement ring, and slapped the whole lot down on Persimmon's nose.'

'Even though you believe the horse can't win? Oh, Blanche! That was my grandmother's ring. How could you? We owe over £2,000. The bills are pouring in.'

'All the more reason for me to take a chance then. I've got odds five to one against, so that will mean –' Blanche began to do arithmetic using all her ten fingers. 'Anyway,' she added, 'the wine-merchants' bill is all yours, and don't you forget it. Mind you tell that to dear Aunty the next time you borrow money from her.'

'I can't go to her again, Blanche. As it is, we live here at her expense.'

'Not my idea, was it?' Blanche asked tartly. 'Aunty wouldn't loosen her apron strings, and you were too frightened to fly the coop!'

Hugh, enraged by her insight of him, waved the sheaf of bills above his head. He plucked a random envelope among the many. 'Look at this! A landau, priced at one hundred guineas!'

Blanche laughed. 'It was you who said that if I kept riding in the Duchess' carriage, the whole of London would know where I was going. You said that you were already a laughing stock at your Club. You said –'

'All right! All right! But why so many gowns and hats, so many shoes. So much of everything, and all so damned expensive. You can't have been brought up to be extravagant. I've seen your mother's and your sister's

501

situations. Don't you ever give a thought to them when you're running up bills all over London?'

Blanche grew very still. 'How dare you?' she said quietly. 'How dare you criticise me? I take the blame for all your heavy spending. Oh yes, Hugh! I also have my spies among your Aunty's servants. I am supposed to be the one who is soaking up brandy like a sponge. That's what you tell her, don't you? Well, just you be careful, that's all. There are plenty of men in London wealthier than you. I could, at this very moment, take my pick of lovers.' She put up a hand and twisted a tendril of auburn hair around her finger. She smiled her satisfaction in a gilt-framed mirror. 'After all,' she said, 'I've started at the very top, haven't I? After the Prince of Wales, a girl can only work her way downwards!'

Hugh half-raised a hand to strike her. 'But I've given you all you ever asked for,' he shouted. 'Remember your own words – I want and want – that's what you said.'

Her top lip quivered, and her tears spilled over. 'But you can't give me what I really want, can you?' Her whole body swayed with the violence of her emotion. 'Take another look among your bills. You'll find a demand from a Harley Street doctor. He's passed me as perfectly fit and healthy. No reason at all why I shouldn't conceive a child and bear it. So it's got to be your fault!'

Hugh sighed. He made no move towards her, did not attempt to comfort her or dry her tears. 'Just be patient,' he told her, 'these things often happen when you least expect them.'

❀

It often rained in early June, everybody said so. Blanche had gazed doubtfully at the cream-and-black striped silk gown, the long black gloves, and enormous hat of frilled cream tulle. Hugh had not yet seen the outfit, made by M'sieu Paquin, and sent from Paris. The exquisite gown, held

502

against her body, had given her a shiver of pure pleasure. Bertie was so right. Clothes were frightfully important!

The day dawned, hot and cloudless. Blanche was so excited that she could hardly bear it. From her place high up in the stand she looked out across a shimmer of grey toppers and elaborate Ascot bonnets. Hugh said, 'They're under starter's orders,' and she closed her eyes. She heard the shouts and the hand-clapping; people were stamping their feet and yelling, 'Good old Teddy!' Blanche opened her eyes to the sight of the Prince of Wales leading his horse, Persimmon, into the Winner's Enclosure. She saw Jack Watts, the Prince's jockey, smile briefly up towards the stand. Blanche gripped Hugh's arm. 'I've won,' she whispered, 'I may not be in the same class as Lady Warwick or Mrs Lily Langtry; but by God, I've won, Hugh!'

❀

The house, said Hugh, was in South Devon, in a little fishing village called Dawlish. It stood on an isolated clifftop, overlooking the Bay. It would need a certain amount of repair and renovation. The price of the house was £400; with another £400 for the alterations he had in mind, they could just about afford it.

'It will be a different life,' he told her. 'Clean air, peace and quiet, long country walks, picnics on the beach at midnight.' He took her in his arms and kissed her eyelids. 'Who knows?' he said. 'It might even work the miracle for you, my darling.'

Hugh held Blanche closer, until a sharp pain in his breastbone forced him to release her. He looked down upon the wide brooch pinned to her lapel. It was the name of the horse Persimmon, spelled out in diamonds and set in gold, that had come between them.

❀

Eliza dreamed and dozed, and held the sleeping baby close.

She touched the long-fingered hands, the slender feet, the small, well-shaped head. Abigail Victoria! A name of quality and distinction. She counted the names of her own children. Candace and Madelina; Jackie and Blanche; Simeon and Annis; and the tragic, final name of Louis.

Eliza looked down all the sad years of her own life, and saw them turned to sudden glory. She sensed future generations; a gifted procession of singers and musicians, teachers and men of letters. How rarely, she thought, in this mortal life, did a woman's dream become flesh and blood!

❀

Meridiana Carew sat upon her low stool, and faced-to before a fire of applewood and beech logs. She dreamed of the boy-child that would, one day, be born to Jye and Maris; a chavvie who would be to her all that Jye, her son, had never been.

Silvanus! The name had a wild and risky sound about it. She crooned the word as she took the hill-path in the early morning, and as she roamed back every evening between the blackberry hedges. It was a name that brought her in mind of the white road, winding. Of green-and-red painted waggons, and the music of the gypsy fiddles, played by her father and her brother, Ephraim. Meri had been granted visions; but always until now she had seen the shadows, the dark side. Silvanus was bright gold! She could not see him, she knew him only by her instinct, and never mind his Particular Baptist mother, and silent father, Meridiana was certain that this chavvie would be pure Rom, and without taint.

The old patteran, ignored and despised by Jye, would be passed on to Jye's son and observed by him. It was to be Silvanus Carew, after all, who would tell all the old stories to the generations that were still to come.

ACKNOWLEDGEMENTS

My grateful thanks to my mother, my brother Edward Sharpe, my uncle and aunt Mr and Mrs Ernest Sharp, Mrs Maureen Chantry and Miss Brenda Barnard, for all their help and enthusiasm during my research for this book.

I am particularly indebted to Mr Lionel Lambourne of the Victoria and Albert Museum for his invaluable advice and kind interest in the story of *Blanche*. Also to Mr Fleetwood of the Taunton Military Museum for his help with the history of the Somerset Light Infantry.

My sincere thanks to Mr Arthur Stewart-Liberty and Mrs Sonia Wykes of Liberty Retail Ltd., Regent Street, London, for their interest and assistance.

Once again, I would like to thank my American cousins Mrs Esther Salter Watson, and Donald and Patricia Salter of Wisconsin, U.S.A., for their continued enthusiasm and great help with family history.

I have met many interesting and generous people during the extensive research for this book. I am especially grateful to the stonemasons at St Paul's Cathedral who allowed me to interrupt their lunch-hour with my questions, also the masons and carvers at Westminster Abbey who allowed me to talk to and question them at great length.

The completion of a book is dependent on many factors, one of the most important being the interest and encouragement of friends. My deepest gratitude is owed to Mrs Isa Fenner and Miss Andrea Quirk for their unfailing patience and support.